CRITICS ARE RAVING ABOUT *PETE*, LEIGH GREENWOOD'S LATEST ROMANCE IN *THE COWBOYS* SERIES!

"*Pete* is another stroke on Leigh Greenwood's colorful canvas of the Old West. The plotting is brilliant and the conflict strong. Reading *Pete* is like a bronco ride—you can't stop reading until the end."

—*Rendezvous*

"Leigh Greenwood's efforts have reached the pinnacle few have obtained consistently as a premier author of the western arm of the romance genre."

—*Heartland Critiques*

"Leigh Greenwood is back with another heartwarming book in *The Cowboys* series. Like his cowboy brothers, Pete is a wonderful hero. Anne is a refreshing delight as Pete's innocent young bride. The author has crafted a real winner with *Pete* and readers will be happy to add this cowboy to their collection."

—*Literary Times*

"Every one of *The Cowboys* leaves readers breathless for more great heroes and unforgettable stories."

—*Romantic Times*

A PROPER BATH

"We're married," Pete said. "It wouldn't be improper. If you don't like it, I'll stop."

He couldn't imagine why he was doing this. He'd never washed a woman's back before. Well, not a *nice* woman's back. He had no intention of letting any kind of feeling warmer than friendship develop between them. She was married to someone else. He was crazy to be standing in the bathroom, staring at her. He was insane even to think about washing her back, much less offer to do it.

What did he think he was going to do, wash her back, get himself completely stirred up, then go quietly to bed *with her lying only inches from him?* That bullet must have addled his brain. He would back out of here as fast as he could. Forget how adorable she looked, her big black eyes wide with shock, wonder, and . . . he was certain of it now, expectation.

"Okay."

Too late! One word, and he was lost.

The Cowboys

PETE

LEIGH GREENWOOD

LEISURE BOOKS   NEW YORK CITY

For Anne, who always wanted to be a heroine,
this one is for you.

A LEISURE BOOK®

August 1999

Published by

Dorchester Publishing Co., Inc.
276 Fifth Avenue
New York, NY 10001

Cover Art by John Ennis

ISBN 0-8439-4562-1

The name "Leisure Books" and the stylized "L" with design are trademarks of Dorchester Publishing Co., Inc.

Printed in the United States of America.

Chapter One

Pete Jernigan became aware of something wet and soft against his cheek. A puff of warm, moist air directly in his face aggravated him. Then a pain somewhere in his head crashed down on him like rocks in a landslide. If his eyes hadn't already been closed, the pain would have blinded him. He tried to move but couldn't. Despite the wall of pain, he was keenly aware of the ground. He felt its roughness in piercing detail—the prick of stubby grass against the tender inside of his thigh, the bite of a sharp-cornered rock against his shinbone, the abrasiveness of dried seedpods against his chest, the smart of coarse gravel against his—

Good God, he was naked!

The pain made it nearly impossible to think, but he rummaged through his memory for a reason he should be lying on the ground without a stitch of clothes on. He couldn't find one.

His horse nuzzled him. Again. That was what had awakened him. At least he hoped it was his horse. The Big Horn Mountains were only a few miles to the west. If it was a grizzly or a cougar, there was nothing Pete could do to stop it from making a meal of him.

He managed to open one eye. The fuzzy image of a horse's hoof a few inches from his nose reassured him. He tried to lift his head, but the pain grew worse. He pulled his arms up on either side of him and tried to lift himself, but failed. He waited a few moments. He tried and failed again. Accepting temporary defeat, he rolled onto his back. The pain nearly caused him to black out.

His horse threw up his head and snorted. Pete feared something had spooked him, that he would run away, but he soon lowered his muzzle to graze. While Pete lay there gathering his strength for another attempt at sitting up, he tried to remember where he was, what he'd been doing. He'd been in the Montana goldfields, but the wanderlust had struck again, so he'd packed up and headed south. The last thing he could remember was making his first camp in the Wyoming Territory.

Then he noticed blood on the ground. He knew immediately it was his. He put his hand to his head, felt the raw wound that went from front to back of his scalp. He'd been shot in the head. Fortunately, it was only a deep graze. But who had shot him? Except for the two men who had ridden up to his camp last night, he hadn't seen anyone for days. They'd asked if they could join him. He'd said yes and they'd started to dismount. That was the last he remembered. They must have shot him. Left him for dead. But why?

His money!

They couldn't have known he had more than seventy thousand dollars sewn into the linings of his saddlebags.

Despite the pain, Pete forced himself to sit up. He had to know. It took a few minutes for his vision to clear, for the pain to subside enough for him to open his eyes to the bright sunshine of a chilly autumn day. It took only another minute to know robbery had been the motive. The camp had been picked clean. Everything was gone—saddle, saddlebags, bedroll, clothes. They'd even taken his coffeepot.

Pete couldn't understand why they hadn't taken his horse, then realized they probably had. Sawbones, named in honor of the doctor who'd fixed Pete's broken limbs during childhood, had come from Texas with him ten years earlier. He'd probably broken his picket, for which Pete was now profoundly grateful. He'd been left naked with no food and water and Sawbones was his only chance for survival.

He had to get on his horse. And stay on. Without a saddle, that wouldn't be easy. Unless he could stand up, it would be impossible. If Sawbones would lie down, it would be easier. Pete used to think Hawk was wasting his time when he taught his horse tricks. Now he wished he'd taught Sawbones to lie down on command.

He tried lifting Sawbones's hoof, but that didn't work. The horse stood patiently on three legs, expecting Pete to change his shoe or clean his foot with a pick. Pete tried pulling Sawbones's head down, but that didn't work either. He tried getting Sawbones to bend both front knees, but the horse didn't understand and moved away. Finally, exhausted and dizzy, Pete fell back. He would try again in a little while. He had to sleep. He was sure he had a concussion. Maybe someone would come along. He hated the idea of being found naked, but given the choice of being found naked alive and being found naked dead, he preferred alive.

He woke up after dark. The chill in the night air caused his teeth to chatter. His skin felt as if it were on fire. He was going to have one helluva sunburn.

He rolled over and pushed himself into a sitting position. He froze. Sawbones was lying down. If he would just stay down for a few more minutes . . . Moving was agony. Between the sunburn and his wound, Pete wondered if it wouldn't be easier to die. A man could only stand so much pain. Getting to his hands and knees, he started toward Sawbones. The horse heard his movement and turned in his direction. Pete talked soothingly to him, murmuring any words that came to mind, hoping the sound of his voice would keep the horse from getting to his feet.

By the time he reached his horse, he was so weak, he sank to the ground. He continued talking to Sawbones, occasionally stroking his withers. The animal had to stay down long enough for Pete to throw his leg over his back.

Pete knew it was going to hurt. It would probably cause him more pain than any of his broken limbs. But getting on Sawbones could be the difference between living to find the bastards who'd done this to him and dying in the wilds of the Wyoming Territory, his bones picked clean by wild animals. With that thought in mind, Pete rose to his knees, threw his leg across Sawbones's back, grabbed hold of his mane with both hands, and held on for dear life.

For a moment he thought it wouldn't be enough. Sawbones lurched to his feet, throwing Pete forward, then back. Pete held on to the mane with all his strength. He knew if he fell off now, he'd never get on the horse again. Once on his feet, Sawbones stood still, waiting for Pete to tell him what to do.

After the waves of pain had subsided, Pete muttered, "Go home."

They'd had no regular home in more than ten years, but anywhere would do. He used the last of his strength to squeeze with his legs. Sawbones started walking.

Through the endless night, Pete hung on. He had no idea how far they had traveled when the sun rose to reveal that Sawbones had come to a stop near a wagon.

"Anybody there?" Pete called. His voice sounded weak and far away in the vastness of the open plain. He got no answer. They probably couldn't hear him. He called again but still received no answer. Digging his heels into Sawbones's sides, he rode up to the back of the wagon. He looked inside but didn't see anyone.

Pete didn't understand where everyone could have gone, but he'd worry about that later. He needed a place to shield his nakedness and shelter from the sun. He leaned over and let himself fall from Sawbones's back into the wagon. He felt dull, throbbing pain when he landed on the hard wooden floor. He collapsed and went to sleep.

Pete awoke twice during the day. Finding both food and water inside the wagon, he ate, drank, and went back to sleep. He awoke and ate once during the night. By the second day, the pain from his sunburn was intense, but the pain in his head had subsided a little. Movement caused his head to pound violently, but he couldn't remain still, wondering why a wagon amply supplied with food and water had been abandoned. He could see nothing from either end of the wagon but a wide expanse of blue sky. When he sat up, he saw a distant brown ridge in the front, another even more distant behind.

After a quick look though its contents, Pete decided that nothing had been removed from the wagon. Clothes, food, weapons—everything a man needed for a trip through the Wyoming Territory—was here. He opened a trunk and looked through the clothes inside. All men's clothing in the style of an Easterner, a tenderfoot, but the clothes looked about his size. He'd apologize to the owner when he returned, but Pete didn't hesitate to take advantage of his good luck. Using almost the last of his strength, he managed to put on underwear, shirt, pants, and socks. Despite the pain of having clothes rub against his sunburn, he sighed with relief. At least now he wasn't naked.

He found a quilt, lay down, and pulled it over him. Tomorrow he'd be strong enough to climb down from the wagon. Tomorrow he'd discover where he was.

Pete leaned against the side of the wagon as he looked down at the body of a young man who had been dead about two days. The body lay near the front of the wagon, invisible from the direction Pete had ridden in from. Pete figured he'd been killed the day he himself had been shot. Pete couldn't figure out why the man had been killed and the wagon left on the trail. Or why nothing had been taken. The man looked like an Easterner. He wore a suit too fancy for anyone out here. His hair had been smoothed with Italian oil, his face shaved close. He had every appearance of a dude, a man who would be out of place in the Wyoming Territory.

Being careful not to move too quickly, Pete knelt down and opened the man's coat. Much to his surprise, the man's wallet was still in his pocket. It held $200. Searching the other pockets, Pete found a small bundle of letters addressed to Peter Warren, Springfield, Illinois. Even the man's pocket watch and chain had been left, the name Peter Warren inscribed on the back of the watch. Pete felt uncomfortable wearing a dead man's clothes, but it was obvious Peter Warren wouldn't need them.

Pete felt like he'd stepped into the middle of a game with new rules. Every killer he knew would do nearly anything for money. Yet the men who'd killed Peter Warren had left over two hundred dollars in the wallet, a trunk full of clothes, a perfectly good wagon, supplies, and equipment worth more than a thousand dollars. Someone very powerful had ordered this killing, someone powerful enough to enforce the order that nothing be removed from the site.

Pete put the wallet and letters inside the wagon. After he fixed himself something hot to eat, he would search the wagon more thoroughly. He hoped to find something that would tell him what this man was doing in Wyoming and why someone would want to kill him.

Afterwards, he'd figure out how he was going to bury him.

That afternoon Pete searched the wagon systematically, paying special attention to the trunk. He found nothing there but more clothes, personal items of jewelry, a large family Bible, and several dozen letters tied together with a string. He combined them with the ones he'd found in Peter's coat pocket, put them in order according to the dates, and read them all straight through.

After he'd finished, he sat deep in thought for nearly an hour before reading them all through again. Now he knew what a twenty-six-year-old hardware store owner from Illinois was doing in Wyoming Territory. He had inherited the Tumbling T, a large cattle ranch started by his uncle. If Peter didn't want the ranch, or didn't show up by noon on September 4, 1886, the ranch would go to a relative of his uncle's wife.

Or anyone strong enough to hold it. Pete knew what it meant if the rightful owner didn't show up. A range war to claim some of the best grazing land east of the Big Horn Mountains.

Someone obviously didn't want Peter Warren to inherit. But Pete still didn't understand why nothing had been stolen, why all the identification had been left on the body. Obviously the murderer wanted whoever found Peter to know who he was. Pete couldn't figure out how that could benefit anyone, but it must somehow.

Instinct urged Pete to collect food and weapons and head down the trail as fast as he could. But the manner of the killing bothered him. Peter Warren's gun belt was rolled up behind the wagon seat. A rifle lay on the wagon floor. Clearly the man hadn't been expecting trouble. Nor had he realized he faced it before he was killed. He'd had no opportunity to reach for his weapons.

That argued that someone he knew, possibly a friend, even a member of his family, had killed him. That bothered Pete even more. You couldn't depend on much in life, but a man had to be able to depend on his friends and family.

What should he do?

He could turn everything over to the nearest sheriff or law officer, but there wasn't one nearby. Besides, they might start thinking Pete had killed this stranger. The fact that he was wearing Peter Warren's clothes wouldn't help his position.

Besides, it was quite possible no lawman would care about a stranger. The sheriff might just keep the money, sell his belongings, and pocket the money for them as well. That went against Pete's principles. According to the letters, Peter's young wife was expecting him any day now. She might need his money. Now that he was dead, she might need it even more. Few things were important to Pete, but family was sacred. His had been killed by Indians when he was five. He had never stopped missing them.

It was obvious Peter had wanted his uncle's ranch. He had meant to show up on time. Pete had heard rumors of rustling in this area, but he hadn't paid any attention. He'd quit ranching when he left Texas and never intended to start again. But rustling was common. If a man couldn't protect his own cows, someone would rob him blind.

Still, Peter's wagon and food had saved Pete's life. He felt he owed Peter Warren something. Maybe he would try to find his wife, tell her what had happened, return the money, letters, and other personal items. But the main thing occupying Pete's mind was finding the thieves who'd shot him and getting his money back. He'd worked too hard and too long in too many goldfields to let some sneaking cowboys take the profits. He wasn't as good with guns as a couple of the orphans he'd been raised with, but he was good enough.

Still puzzled as to why the killer had wanted Peter's body found and identified, Pete decided he would burn the wagon and bury Peter where no one would find him. Tired from so much thinking and planning, Pete went to sleep.

He spent all the next day looking for a place to bury Peter. He spent the next two days digging the grave, a third day moving the body. He spent the next day in complete rest. His sunburn didn't hurt any longer, his wound had continued to heal, and his headaches were reduced to a dull throb. He had been fortunate to survive the gunshot. Sean had always said Pete was the most hardheaded man alive. Well, his hard head had saved his life.

He made a meticulous study of the area around the wagon, wondering what had happened to the two mules that had drawn it. He found the prints of two riders, presumably the men who'd killed Peter. He studied the hoofprints until he felt certain he would know them again no matter how imperfectly made.

The day after that he harnessed Sawbones to the wagon. The horse objected to such treatment, but Pete finally convinced him to pull the wagon to a clump of willow and boxelder that bordered a stream. He discovered the missing mules grazing there. He decided to leave them there and burn the wagon. He couldn't take a chance on being hanged as a horse thief. Though it went against the grain, he would use Peter's money until he caught up with the thieves. But he would pay it back. Pete had done a lot of things he wasn't proud of, but he'd never stolen from a dead man and didn't intend to start now.

Pete had another important task. He had to go back to his camp and see if he could discover anything that might help him identify the men who'd robbed him and left him for dead. Taking all of the food and clothing, he headed north.

What he found convinced him the men who'd robbed him had also killed Peter. That made no sense, but hoofprints didn't lie. The same horses had been in both places. Pete headed south.

Anne Thompson fought as hard as she could against her Uncle Frank and Cyrus McCaine, the wretched excuse for a man to whom her uncle had sold her, but the two men were much stronger than she was. The other men sitting their horses in front of the Tumbling T ranch house didn't intervene.

"You can't force me to marry him," Anne said to her uncle. "I'm already married to Peter."

"That's a lie," her uncle replied. "You haven't seen that boy in more than ten years."

Anne wrapped her hands around the step railing. "I married him by proxy. I signed the documents three months ago."

"Then where is he?" Cyrus McCaine demanded. "He was supposed to be here before today if he wanted this ranch. I say he doesn't want it. I say he doesn't want you, either."

Cyrus was fifty-four, rich, and mean-tempered. Anne's uncle had sold her to him to become his third wife. Cyrus's first wife was said to have died of a blow to the head she received when she fell from a horse. His second wife had run away and divorced him from the safety of St. Louis. Anne had no intention of becoming the third Mrs. McCaine.

Even though she hadn't seen Peter since she was seven, Anne remembered him as her only real friend. When it became clear her uncle meant to marry her off to the man willing to pay the most money, Anne had asked Peter to marry her. Marriage to a man she barely remembered was better than being the wife of Cyrus McCaine.

"You can't force her to marry a second husband," Dolores said. The ranch housekeeper and cook had tried to protect Anne from her uncle, but Belser held Dolores back.

"She ain't going to have a second husband," her

uncle growled. "She's lying, like she always does when she doesn't want to do something."

"She's not lying about signing the papers," Dolores said. "I saw them." She tried to break away from Belser, but she couldn't.

"It's illegal to force me to commit bigamy," Anne said. "The sheriff will arrest you if you try."

"You ain't got no husband," her uncle repeated. "If he was going to be here, he'd be here to get this ranch, not because he wanted to marry some—"

Anne let go of the post long enough to slap her uncle. "Don't say it! Don't ever say it again. If you do, I swear I'll kill you!"

Apparently the fury, the pure hatred she felt for him, surprised him so much that he closed his mouth. He didn't dare hit her in front of so many men. They wouldn't lift a finger to keep her from being forced to become the wife of a savage old bastard like Cyrus, but they wouldn't put up with his hitting her. Anne didn't understand that. She'd rather be beaten regularly than have to spend one night under the same roof as Cyrus McCaine, much less in his bed.

Cyrus gave a tug, but Anne had renewed her hold on the post. She was only seventeen and petite, but she was strong.

But not strong enough. Cyrus held her while her uncle pried her fingers loose from the post.

"You wouldn't do this if the foreman were here," Dolores said again. "It's not lawful."

"We're the law out here," Cyrus said, "and what we say goes."

Anne was all too aware of the truth of that statement. The Wyoming Territory was thinly settled, mostly by powerful men who owned large ranches. They had long ago become accustomed to taking the law into their own hands to deal with rustlers, thieves, and property disputes. It was only one step further to dealing with women.

Anne could see only one end to this struggle, but she intended to fight every step of the way. She still had half an hour. Peter could still arrive, though she'd lost hope he would.

He was supposed to have arrived eleven days ago. When he was a week overdue, she feared he wasn't coming. She didn't understand. His letters had promised her he would arrive in time to claim his inheritance. By the time Cyrus and her uncle arrived that morning, she'd given up hope.

Peter had probably decided that running a hardware store, even one that was losing money, had to be easier than running a ranch. He had been her last hope. With her father killed by a grizzly and her mother dead from pneumonia, she was at her Uncle Frank's mercy. He'd never treated her like a cherished niece, only someone to be ashamed of. From the moment her mother died, he'd thought of nothing but finding her a husband . . . for a price.

Anne's father had been Carl Warren's foreman. The two men had come to Wyoming together, established the ranch together. After her parents' deaths, Carl had given Anne a home, let her call him "uncle." She had been safe as long as he lived. He was dead now. If Peter didn't show up, Belser, Carl's wife's nephew, would inherit the ranch. He didn't like Anne. He wouldn't care if she were forced to marry Cyrus.

Anne was fighting so hard against the two men pulling at her, she took only the most momentary notice that another man had ridden up. She heard the newcomer talking, but she paid no attention until he dismounted, walked up to her uncle, and hit him so hard in the face that he fell to the ground. Cyrus turned to attack the man, but he was sent sprawling just as quickly.

"My name is Peter Warren," the man announced. "This woman is my wife. I'll kill the next man who lays a hand on her."

When the man had broken Cyrus's hold on Anne, she stumbled backward, lost her balance, and fell to the ground. She sat there, stunned at Peter's last-minute arrival, at her miraculous escape. She looked up, but the sun was in her eyes. She could only see the shape of the man who'd rescued her. From her position on the ground, he looked huge and strong, with broad shoulders and powerful thighs. There was nothing of the shy, rather timorous boy she remembered. This was a man in the full powers of his maturity, certain of his own strength, apparently afraid of nothing.

Anne fell head over heels in love with him in an instant.

"Let me help you up," the man said.

She had to stop thinking of him as *the man*. He was Peter Warren, her childhood friend and confidant, her husband.

His hand was strong and calloused. He pulled her to

23

her feet in one effortless motion. She didn't know what kind of work hardware store owners were called on to do in Illinois, but Peter had obviously worked long and hard to have developed into a man such as this.

"Did they hurt you?" he asked.

"N-no." She couldn't think straight. Even his voice had changed. It sounded much deeper, more forceful. Of course it would. He was fourteen when she last saw him, twenty-four now. Everything about him had changed. For the better.

She hadn't realized he was so tall until she found herself staring at the buttons in the middle of his chest. She was used to being told she was a dab of a girl, used to men towering over her, but he was taller than any man present. She didn't remember Peter being very tall, but she'd been very young when he left.

"Who the hell are you?" Belser demanded. He'd come up without Anne's being aware of his approach.

"I already told you."

"You can't be," Belser said.

Anne was aware of a sudden hardening of Peter's gaze, of an abrupt feeling of dangerous tension in the air.

"Why would you say that?" Peter asked

"You don't look like you're supposed to," Belser said.

"How am I supposed to look?" Peter asked.

"Like your father's picture," Belser said. "And you don't act a thing like Uncle Carl said you would."

"I take after my mother's side of the family," Peter said.

"I don't give a damn who you are or who you favor,"

Anne's uncle said, getting to his feet. "That's my niece, and she's marrying Cyrus here."

"That would be bigamy," Peter replied succinctly, "and that's against the law."

"I want to see some proof she's married to you," Cyrus said.

"I don't have it," Peter said, directing his gaze back to Belser. "Someone tried to kill me on my way here. They burned my wagon and stole my papers."

"You're lying, too," Cyrus shouted.

"Maybe you'll believe this." Peter took off his hat and pushed back his straight, brown hair to disclose a wound that couldn't have been more than two weeks old.

"Anybody could have shot you," Belser said.

"True, but that doesn't change the fact that my death would have enabled you to inherit this ranch."

"I didn't shoot you," Belser said. "I haven't been off the place in weeks. And I still don't believe you're Peter Warren."

"I am, and I can prove it, but you'll have to wait until I can write my lawyer."

"That could take a couple of months," Cyrus exclaimed.

"Probably."

"I'll take charge of my niece until then," her uncle said.

"Anne is staying right here. And the first man who lays a hand on her will get a bullet in him."

Pete looked around at the assembled horsemen, who had watched in silence. "What are all these people doing here?" he asked Anne.

"They're here to see that Belser didn't take over the ranch until twelve o'clock," Anne explained.

"Why should they care?"

"I wanted to make sure Carl's nephew wasn't cut out of his chance," a particularly large and powerful man said.

"And who are you?" Peter demanded.

"Bill Mason. I own the 3-Bar-3. My range runs alongside the Tumbling T."

"He wants to take over this ranch, too," Belser said. "He wants to control all of northeastern Wyoming."

"Not that much," Mason said. "But I did offer to buy the place after Carl had his accident."

"You could buy it for a whole lot less after you rustled half our cattle," Belser said.

Bill Mason's power and position in the county were unquestioned. Anne supposed that was the reason Belser's hotheaded accusation evoked little more than a faint, pitying smile.

"Everybody knows rustlers will hit a ranch the moment a bear like Carl is wounded," Mason said. "That many cows is too much temptation to resist."

"For you to resist, you mean," Belser said.

"I don't need your cows," Mason replied.

"I think you meant to say *my* cows," Peter corrected him. "I promise you, the rustling will stop. Anybody I catch gets hanged on the spot."

He'd just issued a challenge. Anne didn't know how Peter had the nerve to do such a thing to these hard men. They'd fought Indians, wild animals, and each other to build their ranches. They didn't back down from anybody.

But apparently neither did Peter. She continued to be amazed at his transformation.

"Exactly what I would do," Mason said. "Having a ranch without a strong leader encourages rustlers. That affects all of us."

The look he directed at Belser contained enough scorn to have abashed a man twice as prideful as Belser. It seemed to just bounce off Belser's armor of anger and frustration. His face was flushed, and the veins in his neck stood out like taut ropes.

"I'm strong enough to take care of the rustlers," Belser said.

"They're still here," Mason pointed out.

"That's because I couldn't do anything until twelve o'clock today," Belser said.

"Now that Carl's nephew is here, you don't have to do anything at all," Mason said.

"I still don't believe he's Peter Warren," Belser said.

"What you believe doesn't matter," Peter said.

"It sure as hell does when I'm the one getting cheated out of this ranch."

"You never had the ranch," Peter said. "And if you don't back down and shut your mouth, I'll throw you off it."

Nobody had ever threatened to throw Belser out, not even Carl. Anne expected him to bellow his fury. Much to her surprise, he struggled visibly to get his temper under control.

"We'll see," Belser said. "You're not the only one with a lawyer."

"I'll be going," Bill Mason said. "Let me know if I can do anything to help."

"I might be calling on you to lend a hand with this rustling," Peter said.

"Come over any time," Mason replied. He nodded in the direction of Anne's uncle and Cyrus "You want me to take them with me?"

"No. I can handle them," Peter said.

Anne would have felt better if Peter had let Mason take care of her uncle and her prospective bridegroom. She didn't especially like Mason—he was too rough and unfeeling—but she had complete confidence in his ability to handle her uncle.

At a signal from him, Mason's men turned and followed him out of the ranch yard.

Peter turned to her uncle. "I'll send someone into Big Bend tomorrow with a letter for my lawyer. I'll let you know when I get the marriage papers."

"I'll have the sheriff out to you before then," her uncle threatened. "We don't allow men to carry off our women."

"I'm not carrying Anne anywhere. There's no better place for a man's wife than at his side."

Her uncle swore viciously. "She's not your wife!"

"I say she is. Now unless you want me to knock you down again, you'll take your friend and get out of here."

"You'll hear from me," Cyrus said. "I'm a powerful man. I—"

Peter pulled his gun and fired into the ground at Cyrus's feet. Anne jumped, and her hand flew to her mouth to smother a small shriek.

"You'll be a dead man if you don't get off my land," Peter said. "I don't think a Wyoming jury would find it at all out of the way if I was to kill you for trying to carry off my wife."

"I wasn't trying to carry her off."

Peter turned to Dolores. "Didn't it look to you like he was trying to carry her off?"

"It certainly did," Dolores responded vigorously.

"Didn't it look the same to you?" Peter asked Belser.

Belser hesitated but finally nodded his agreement.

"That's three of us," Peter said. "I imagine Mason would back us. That ought to be enough for any judge."

Anne could tell her uncle knew he had been outmaneuvered.

"I agree with Belser," he said. "I don't believe you're Peter."

Anne could tell her uncle knew this was a groundless objection. He could see the money he'd hoped to get from Cyrus disappearing, and it made him furious.

"I don't give a damn who you are," Cyrus said. "I want that woman."

Peter turned his gaze on Cyrus, and Anne watched a coldness grow in his expression. "I would say she's more a girl than a woman," Peter said. He turned to Anne. "How old are you?"

"Seventeen."

"Well, that makes you a woman out here." He turned back to Cyrus. "She's still much too young for an old lobo like you. Now get off, both of you, while I still have some control over my temper."

They watched in silence as her uncle and Cyrus mounted up and rode off. Anne could hear them quarreling, threatening each other, but she didn't care. She was safe. She was married. Peter had returned, and he was more of a man than she'd ever dreamed possible.

"And what's your place around here?" Peter said, turning to Belser.

"If you were really Carl's nephew, you'd know."

"I know what Carl thought," Peter said. "I want to know what you think."

Anne knew Belser had counted on having the ranch. He'd been trying to give orders for weeks, telling the men he'd fire them the moment he got control if they didn't do what he wanted. Only the foreman's determination had prevented Belser from taking over.

"Carl let me live in the house and eat with him, but I'm just a hand," Belser finally said.

"I'll do the same as long as you don't kick up any dust," Peter said. "Now I suggest you set about earning your wages."

Belser looked as though he wanted to say more, but he turned and stomped off toward the corral.

"Tell me what's going on around here," Peter said, turning to Anne. "It looks like I've landed in one hell of a mess."

Chapter Two

Pete told himself he was crazy. What chivalrous impulse had caused him to tell everybody he was Peter Warren? For all he knew, they had nothing in common but their first names. Was that the reason he'd decided to pretend to be someone he wasn't? He'd better clear things up right away and get the hell out of here.

But he couldn't do that. He'd trailed the killers to this ranch. It didn't surprise him it was the Tumbling T. He'd already decided that someone in Peter's family had killed him. One of Mason's cowhands had told him what Anne's uncle was trying to do. Pete had realized that pretending to be Peter would give him reason to stay and an opportunity to search for the killers. They had his money, all the gold he'd managed to mine in his five years in Montana. He wasn't about to let anybody steal it from him. If they'd moved on, he'd clear things up and go after them.

But he couldn't just yet. Anne's uncle would be back in five minutes to force her to marry that dried-up old husk of a man. Belser would get a ranch Pete had already decided he'd committed murder for— or hired someone to commit the murder for him. It went against the grain to let anybody get away with such a cold-blooded swindle.

No, he'd continue as Peter Warren for a little while yet, though there was one small problem. Anne. From the look in her eyes, she adored Peter. Pete didn't know what he was going to do about that, but he couldn't take advantage of her. Even if his own conscience would have allowed it, his adopted mother's teaching wouldn't. He wouldn't put it past Isabelle to somehow know what he'd done and come all the way from Texas to hang him out to dry.

Anne was a pretty young woman, exactly the kind to go in for hero worship. He didn't know if Peter was worthy of her high regard, but Pete had to find some way to tell her gently that he wasn't Peter. But he couldn't do that either. She looked the kind who couldn't tell a lie. Probably couldn't keep a secret, either.

"Everything will be all right now that you're here," Anne said, gazing up at him with big eyes filled with wonder.

Wouldn't Sean laugh to hear that? Sean had been getting Pete out of trouble ever since they met in the orphanage. It would never occur to Sean that Pete could take care of himself. Most of the time, it hadn't occurred to Pete, either. He'd just barreled ahead, knowing if he got himself into a situation that required muscle, he could depend on Sean. If it was guns, there was always Luke.

But that was years ago. Sean had gotten married and gone back to Texas. Luke had vanished into California. Pete was on his own, and having this young woman look up at him as if he was Paul Bunyon and Wild Bill Hickok rolled into one didn't help.

Still, it was a real nice change. He'd had more than enough of his adopted brothers being irritated at having to help him out of scrapes. Isabelle said he didn't think things through properly before he acted. Jake said he was plumb loco. It was a relief to discover Anne didn't think any of that. He squared his shoulders and stood a little taller.

"That may be so," he said, "but I'd like to know what's going on just the same. You never can tell when trouble might start up again."

She ducked her head, acting demure. "You ought to ask Eddie about that. He wouldn't like me talking about the ranch."

"Who's Eddie?"

She looked surprised. "Eddie Kessling. The foreman."

"Can't remember everybody's name," Pete mumbled, wondering how long it would be before he gave himself away. "We'll leave that for the moment. Tell me about yourself."

She looked really startled this time, as if she'd expected him to know everything. "I don't mean what was in your letters," he said quickly. "There must be lots of bits and pieces you didn't tell me. Seeing that man about to haul you off gave me quite a turn."

"My uncle never liked me. He didn't want Papa to marry Mama. After Papa was killed, he was mean to us. After Mama died, he threatened to sell me."

"Looks like he did sell you to that burned-up-looking scrap of a man. Wouldn't be surprised if he gives his horse a bad fright every morning."

Anne giggled. "He is old and little, but he owns a big ranch. Eddie says he's very rich."

"Only in cows and sagebrush. How long has your uncle been trying to marry you off? I know you wrote and told me, but my memory's not too good. I forget all kinds of things."

"Is that why you weren't doing so well in the hardware business?"

"What? Oh, yeah, something like that." He was going to have to start paying close attention to what he said. Belser was just waiting for him to make a mistake.

"Why didn't Belser stop him?"

"He doesn't like me. He said I'd have to leave anyway when he took over."

"That's just the kind of cowardly double-cross he'd pull," Pete said.

"I've lived here ever since my parents died. Uncle Carl said I'd always be safe. I was until he died. I told my uncle you'd married me, that you were coming soon and you'd have the sheriff put him in jail if he so much as laid a finger on me. But when you didn't come and didn't come, he decided I was lying. Why are you so late? I was afraid you'd decided you didn't want to marry me after all."

"What? And give up a ranch for such a paltry reason as that?"

Anne's face registered shock.

"I mean I'd have given up the ranch before I'd have done anything like that. A promise is a promise. I would have been here on time if I hadn't been shot."

Her quick smile was like the sun coming out from behind a cloud. "I should have known something terrible happened. You always were very nice to me."

Pete got the feeling he was sinking deeper and deeper into a pool of quicksand of unknown depth. It seemed every time he opened his mouth, he landed on unsound ground. He'd done the chivalrous thing so he could find his money. But being a husband was getting complicated already, and he hadn't been married for thirty minutes. He didn't know how people stood it for years at a time. If he didn't get things straightened out soon, he would put his head in a noose.

"I was terribly sorry to hear your brother had been killed," Anne said.

"Huh?" Pete didn't know anything about a brother. How much more family could Peter have?

"I said I was sorry to hear Gary died in that blizzard," Anne said. "I know you two hadn't seen each other for years, but it must have been very painful."

"Yeah, sure." Hell, he didn't even know his brother's name. He wondered about the whereabouts of his father and mother. Other brothers and sisters. He could have a biblical tribe on his heels right now. Why hadn't Peter written all of that stuff in his Bible?

"I never liked the way Uncle Carl preferred him to you. He was going to leave the ranch to Gary, not leave you a thing. I know Gary liked the ranch, but he was always quarreling with Uncle Carl. If he hadn't lost his temper so often, he wouldn't have run away, and he wouldn't have died. I'm sorry about Gary, I truly am, but I'm glad you got the ranch."

"Why was Uncle Carl going to do that?" Pete asked before he had time to think. "I mean, I don't think anybody ever told me. Not exactly."

"I don't suppose you remember it. Or want to. I remember every word he said. 'You're a soft, weaselly, fella,' he told you that day. 'You don't like work, you're afraid of cows, and you haven't got the sense God gave a woman. I'd be a fool to leave you so much as a foot of this ranch.' "

"A crabby old coot, wasn't he?"

"You told him you didn't like him and wouldn't have his filthy cows if he gave you every square inch of the place. Mama said it wasn't a smart thing to say, especially with you having a shiftless pa and your ma being dead as well as disowned by her family for marrying your pa, but I was proud of you."

She was besotted. And any fella with a shiftless pa, a dead brother, and a disowned ma was a fool to throw a whole ranch in the teeth of a rich uncle. He didn't know how he was going to tell her the silly fellow was dead.

"It must be terrible to be the last one in your family. Sometimes I feel lonely, too. That's why I was so glad you agreed to marry me. I couldn't think of anything else."

36

"A man of honor couldn't do anything else," Pete said. "Now I'd better unsaddle my horse and turn him out in the corral. Want to come with me?"

Thank God Anne was young, nervous, and willing to talk. He didn't want a chattering female on his heels, but if he could keep her at it long enough, he might learn enough to keep both their necks from being put into the noose. Apparently Peter hadn't been on the ranch in years, hadn't made a very good impression when he was here, and hadn't been much of a success in business, so Pete could depend upon everybody thinking him something of a dolt. That wasn't going to do his pride any good, but he figured he could stand it until he found his money and left.

And he would leave. He was anxious to get to Colorado. Or maybe he'd go to Arizona or New Mexico. He liked the freedom to wander from one place to another, and he was tired of bitterly cold winters. Arizona sounded good.

He couldn't leave without doing something about Anne. She was a pretty young woman, charming, trusting, and really rather adorable. She was too young for a twenty-nine-year-old miner, even if he did look five years younger than that, but she was just the right age for some fuzzy-cheeked cowpoke eager to start his own spread.

So Pete let Anne walk with him to the corral, chattering away about everything that had happened since Uncle Carl died. He was going to have to ask her why she called this guy her uncle when she hadn't mentioned being related to him at all. He stopped her when she mentioned the rustlers.

"Whoa! Back up to the rustlers," he said. "I want to hear more about that."

"I told you about them in one of my letters."

Damn. He wished Peter had had enough sense to keep all those letters together. Knowing Anne as he did already, she must have written him at least a hundred times. "I told you I'm terribly forgetful. I couldn't concentrate. You know, the business failing and all of that."

"I guess it would be hard to worry about things here when you had creditors beating on your door demanding payment. Where did you hide?"

"Hide?"

"When they came after you. Uncle Carl said when your pa lived here, he used to go off to the hills where nobody could find him. He'd take a saddlebag full of whiskey and not come back until he'd drunk it all up."

"It wasn't as bad as that," Pete said. "I'd pay them a little something. It would keep them off my neck for a few weeks."

The ranch was well appointed. The corrals were constructed of sturdy poles, pine and cedar. A couple of roomy sheds were piled high with hay for the winter. The bunkhouse was a large structure of sturdy logs. There was even a blacksmith shop and a low, rambling barn. Clearly the Tumbling T was a successful ranch. The large amount of glass used for windows was further proof of old Carl's success.

"Let's get back to those rustlers." They'd reached the corral. "When did it start?"

"I'm not sure. Uncle Carl didn't like to talk about business until after Dolores and I left the room."

Uncle Carl wouldn't have gotten away with that if Isabelle had been around. She'd have filled his ear good and proper. "Guess."

"I think it started soon after Uncle Carl got hurt. He couldn't ride anymore. He said the wolves always started to close in when the grizzly went down."

Sometimes they didn't wait that long. "Have they taken much?"

"Eddie says it's hard to tell. He's worried because the cows are thin this year. They can't find enough grass because we didn't get any rain the whole summer."

If he didn't start worrying about the rustling, there might not be enough cattle left to worry about. "I'll talk to him later. Anybody gotten hurt?"

"No."

Then things couldn't be too serious. At least not yet.

He stripped the saddle and cloth off Sawbones. The horse trotted away, squealing with delight. He found a bare spot of ground and immediately knelt down and started to roll in the dust.

"It'll take a half hour of brushing to get him clean now." But Pete didn't mind. Sawbones was probably the only reason Pete was alive now. Which reminded him of why he'd come to the ranch in the first place. The killers' trail had led him here, but he'd lost it before he·reached the ranch buildings. The killers had probably come through here ten days ago. Lots of riders had used the trails since then.

"I want to take a look around before supper," he told Anne. "Do you know if these horses belong to anyone in particular?" He gestured to several horses in the large corral.

"I don't think so," Anne said. "Uncle Carl always complained he had to provide everything for his men—horses and saddles as well as beds."

"Why do you call him uncle? You're no relation." He hoped he hadn't put his foot in it again.

"He said he'd always wanted to marry my ma, that he would have if my father hadn't beaten him to it. He said since I couldn't be his daughter, I could be his niece."

"He should have left the ranch to you."

"Uncle Carl would never leave anything to a woman," she said, apparently shocked at the idea. "He said women didn't know a thing about taking care of themselves, much less a ranch."

It was obvious Uncle Carl had never met women like Isabelle or Pearl. Not to mention Marina, Hannah, and Melody.

"Then he could have left it to you and Peter together . . . I mean to you and *me* together."

"Uncle Carl said women didn't have any sense when it came to property, that they'd waste it on the first handsome face they saw."

"Since you were already Pet—my wife, I don't see how he could say that."

"Uncle Carl said what he wanted."

That's what came from being set up as a king in a little bitty kingdom. Isabelle would have straightened him out in five minutes.

"I'm going for a ride. Tell Dolores not to serve supper without me."

"She never would. It's your table."

"That's going to take some getting used to. Seeing

as how all I had before was a hardware store," he added.

It wasn't going to be as easy to be a property owner as he'd thought. Just remembering he was supposed to own a couple hundred thousand acres of grazing land was a bit staggering. It was a good thing this Peter fella whose shoes he'd stepped into was a real dunce. Pete had a whole lot to learn himself.

But one thing he did know about was tracking. He'd gotten Hawk to teach him when they were both still living with Jake and Isabelle. Pete had himself two killers to find. After he did that, he'd figure out what to do about Anne, the ranch, Belser, and her miserable uncle. Then he'd get the hell out of Wyoming.

"I can hardly worry about rustling for worrying about what we're going to do to help the cattle we do have get through the winter," Eddie was saying. "There isn't any grass. It seems like every week I hear of somebody else bringing in a new herd."

Pete couldn't figure out the man's attitude. He seemed angry, confused, unable to concentrate. If he was like this all the time, Pete would have to get a new foreman.

"It's all that Eastern money," Belser complained. "They think the grass is endless, that all they have to do is bring in a thousand cows—or twenty thousand—and they can make twenty-five percent profit a year."

"Can they survive a tough winter?" Pete asked.

"That depends on how tough."

"I came along the Missouri and down the Yellowstone to the Powder," Pete said. "The Indians say the signs are bad. They're preparing for the worst winter within living memory."

"We won't survive anything like that," Eddie said.

"Then round up everything you can and sell it."

Eddie looked startled, but Belser looked shocked and angry. "I knew you were a fool. Those steers are fifty pounds underweight. They won't bring what they're worth."

"They won't bring anything dead," Pete said.

"Uncle Carl wouldn't have sold early," Belser said. "You know what he used to say?"

"Of course he doesn't," Anne interrupted. "How could he, being in Illinois all this time?"

"He always said the same thing," Belser said, glaring at Pete. "I don't think you know what it is."

"He said never send a steer to market until both the weight of the steer and the prices on the market are as high as you think they can go," Anne said.

Belser had been doing this all evening, tossing out things he seemed to think Pete ought to remember, trying to catch him. Anne had come to his defense from the beginning, answering Belser's questions, often adding information to help fill in Pete's knowledge of a past that wasn't his own. Pete just sat there smiling and letting Belser get more and more angry. It didn't surprise Pete that no one on the place seemed to like Belser. Pete was becoming more and more convinced Belser was responsible for Peter's death. Pete couldn't figure out any other reason he should be so certain Pete was an imposter.

"Selling now is a pretty big gamble," Eddie said.

"I'll ride out with you tomorrow," Pete said. "We'll decide then."

"You've got no right doing anything like that," Belser argued.

"He owns the ranch," Anne said. "I can't think of anybody who has a better right."

Belser looked as though he was bursting to say something, but he bit his tongue. "You'll have to tie him to the saddle to keep him on his horse. From what Uncle Carl said, he not only can't stay on a horse, he's afraid of them."

"That horse in the paddock doesn't look like the mount of a man who's not very good in the saddle," Eddie said, then looked angry at himself for defending Pete.

"Ten years can make a big difference," Pete said to Belser. "A man can learn to do all kinds of things. Now," he said, turning back to Eddie, "I want to hear more about this rustling."

Pete listened carefully as Eddie outlined what had been happening over the last year. It seemed as though it had started as a small-time operation—a few steers now and again. But this summer it had turned into a regular problem.

While Eddie and Belser argued over solutions, Pete took stock of where he stood. Except for Belser, everyone at the ranch took him at his word that he was Peter. But sooner or later he'd foul up somewhere, and his deception would be discovered. There was no point in fighting it. It was going to happen. He had to figure out how to get as much done as he could before that happened.

He kept asking himself why he was doing this. Any sane man would have simply tried to stop Anne's uncle from dragging her away. It would never have occurred to him to pretend to be her husband.

But having done so, Pete now found himself playing a false role. He was determined to save her, but he didn't know how. So he had to keep up the pretense until he could find an answer.

"I want to see the books," Pete said. He rose without waiting for Eddie to respond. "I'd like to know how we stand before I look at the herd."

"You can't wait to get your hands on Uncle Carl's money, can you?" Belser asked.

"It's his money," Anne said. "Or have you forgotten Uncle Carl left the ranch to him?"

"How the hell could I forget anything like that!" Belser shouted. "It was supposed to be mine. He promised."

"He only said you could have it if Peter didn't want it. I heard him say over and over again that he wanted it to go to his blood kin, even if he didn't think Peter deserved it."

"It should have been mine!" Belser shouted. "I worked for it. I deserve it."

"You're not kin."

"I'm his nephew."

"Great-nephew," Anne corrected, "on his wife's side. You're not blood kin. I heard him say that many times."

"He paid you a better wage than the others," Eddie

said, "and he let you live in this house. You can't think you've been treated badly."

"I've been cheated!" Belser bellowed, his face purple with rage. "But I'll have this ranch yet." He pointed an accusing finger at Pete. "You wait and see if I don't. And when I do, I'll hang you from the nearest tree."

"I don't know what's gotten into him," Eddie said as Belser stormed out of the room. "He's always had a temper, but he's never acted like this."

"It's because he was so close to getting the ranch and then it was snatched away from him," Anne said.

Eddie shrugged his shoulders, seeming to dismiss the problem. "We'd better get to those books," he said. "If you want to check the herd, we're going to have to get started early in the morning."

"What do you think of him?" Dolores asked Anne. "From all the things I heard Carl say, I was expecting him to stumble over his own feet and keep well back from any horse or mule."

"He's very handsome," Anne said. "And he's grown very tall."

Though Dolores Moreno was unmarried and eleven years older than Anne, they had formed a close friendship years ago, sharing confidences as a matter of course.

"I wasn't talking about his size and appearance, though that's a pleasant surprise as well. It's not every orphaned gal who finds herself suddenly married to a rich man who's handsome to boot."

"I didn't marry him because he would be rich," Anne said.

"Everybody knows you've adored him for years. Folks also know you were desperate to escape your uncle's plans to sell you to the highest bidder. Still, you've got to admit things look like they're turning out remarkably well."

Anne couldn't deny that. From the moment she'd looked up to see Peter looking magnificent and twice as big as life, things had gone way beyond anything she'd ever hoped for. She'd never imagined Peter being able to stand up to her uncle or taking over the ranch as though it was the most natural thing in the world. Belser's repeated insistence that he was an imposter didn't bother Peter in the slightest. Peter was perfect, everything a girl could dream of in a husband.

And that was the problem.

The Peter she'd known all those years ago wasn't perfect. He was nice and sweet and kind, and he never said any of the terrible things his brother and other people said. He comforted her when she cried, but he didn't rescue her from danger.

He'd been only fourteen at the time, but his character seemed to have been formed. At least everyone else seemed to think so. Uncle Carl had been relieved when Peter and his father went back East. Gary had remained at the ranch. But when Gary was killed and Peter was the only heir, things changed. Uncle Carl's determination to leave his ranch to his only blood kin never wavered, but he complained constantly that it would be Peter.

Whenever he was out of temper, he'd say, "He'll

lose everything I've spent my whole life trying to build up." Anne had always defended Peter, but she couldn't help fearing Uncle Carl might be right.

But the man who'd showed up to rescue her showed none of the shortcomings Uncle Carl had feared. He seemed a little unsettled by the circumstances, but no more so than any man walking into a strange situation. Give him two days, and Anne expected he'd have everything under control. She'd have a wonderful, wealthy, perfect husband and a secure, rosy future.

That was why Anne couldn't shake the nagging suspicion that, as much as she tried not to think about it, Belser might be right.

Her new husband was just too good to be true.

An hour later Pete emerged from the ranch office with an entirely different perspective on the situation. Carl Warren had been a very rich man. He could understand why Belser was so upset at losing the ranch. He could understand why Peter had given up the hardware store and come to Wyoming to take on a job nobody thought he could handle. He could understand why Anne was anxious to marry a man she hadn't seen in years, a man who even as a child she must have sensed didn't measure up to the challenges of the West. He could also understand why Bill Mason was so interested in the ranch. Carl had grabbed the best land in the area, nearly flat grazing land watered by creeks that flowed from the Big Horn Mountains and some timber-covered foothills. Those who came later got second-best.

Anne and Dolores were still in the sitting room when he emerged from the ranch office.

"Did you find everything you need to know?" Anne asked.

"I found far too much to absorb in one evening," Pete said. "I didn't realize the Tumbling T was such a big ranch."

"The biggest in this part of Wyoming," Eddie said proudly.

"Do you want some coffee?" Dolores asked. "It won't take but a few minutes to make more."

"No. I've had enough for one night. I'll think I'll turn in."

Dolores grinned. "I rather thought you would. After all, it is your wedding night."

Pete had forgotten that, but it was clear from the white, frightened look on Anne's face that she hadn't.

"With all that's happened today, I haven't had time to give it much thought."

"Anne has," Dolores said, grinning. "She's been thinking of nothing but this night for months."

"I've been thinking of his coming," Anne admitted. "A woman should always think of her husband."

But not think of their first night in bed together, Pete finished for her in his mind.

"You'll have to tell me where to sleep," Pete said. "I'm afraid I don't remember the house that well."

"You'll sleep in your Uncle Carl's room," Dolores said.

"My room is right next to it," Anne said.

"*Your* room is now your husband's room," Dolores said. "I've already moved your things."

The last trace of color drained from Anne's face. Pete didn't know what was so frightening—he'd never considered himself very formidable—but Anne was clearly petrified of the idea of sleeping with him. He figured that despite the fact that she had adored Peter for years and probably thought herself half in love with him, she really didn't know him. Now, brought face-to-face with a live, very real husband and told they were to share the same bed, she was reeling. She probably connected him with that disgusting pork rind who had tried to buy her. Pete didn't think he was that bad, but he was older than this Peter fella.

"Come on," Pete said, extending his hand to Anne. "You can help me unpack. I'm depending on you to keep Uncle Carl's ghost at bay until I can prove I'm not such a good-for-nothing as I used to be."

Chapter Three

Anne shrank from Peter's outstretched hand. She'd looked forward to being his wife for the last several months, not only as something she wanted, but as the only way to save herself from her uncle, her chance to be something other than a piece of property to be handed from one man to another, to have a husband she could love, a home and family of her own.

She hadn't realized until now that she'd continued to think of Peter as the boy she knew, grown up in size but still shy, sweet, and mild-mannered. It wasn't just Peter's body that had grown and matured. He was no longer the same person inside or out. He seemed so much bigger than she'd imagined, so much more virile, so much more intimidating. The idea of going into a bedroom alone with him frightened her. The idea of its being Uncle Carl's bedroom petrified her.

"Don't be shy," Dolores prodded. "You're a married woman now."

"I don't feel married. It all happened so suddenly."

"It's not half as sudden as being hauled off by Cyrus," Dolores said. "He'd have wrestled you down in the dust before you'd gotten a mile from here."

The truth of that statement didn't make Anne feel any better.

"You can sleep in your own room tonight if that'll make you feel better," Peter offered.

Anne brightened immediately and opened her mouth to gratefully accept his suggestion.

"She can't do that," Dolores said. "Nobody will believe she's married if she doesn't sleep in your bed."

"They won't know," Peter said.

"It'll be all over the ranch by noon tomorrow. Belser would like nothing better. He doesn't like Anne, and he hates you. It would support his argument that you're not Peter and you didn't marry Anne."

"But I did," Peter said.

"But you can't prove it, not without those papers you've got to send for."

"How will Belser know where we're sleeping?" Peter asked.

"He'll listen at the door," Anne said. "If you don't lock it, he's liable to come in and look. He sneaks around the house, prying into everything when he thinks no one is looking."

"Anybody who opens my bedroom door without knocking and being invited in is liable to get shot."

"You could lock your door," Eddie said.

"I'm not locking my bedroom door," Peter said. "Especially in my own house."

Anne could tell he added that last as an afterthought. She guessed he was having trouble getting used to the idea of owning the ranch. Strange, but after all these months of hoping and planning, waiting anxiously and praying Peter would arrive in time, now that it had actually happened, it didn't seem real to her, either. Maybe that was why she felt so reluctant to sleep in the same bed. She'd been a fool to think seeing Peter again would be like picking up where they'd left off ten years before, but his letters had seemed so much like the Peter she remembered, that was exactly what she had expected.

But Peter in person was quite different from Peter in a letter. She didn't feel she knew him at all.

"I guess there's nothing else to do but go up together," Peter said, holding out his hand again.

Anne hesitated.

"Go on with him," Dolores urged. "I know it seems strange to actually have him here after waiting all these months, but you'll soon get used to it."

Peter smiled reassuringly. "I promise I won't do anything you don't want me to do."

"You can't do that!" Dolores exclaimed.

"I can do anything I want," Peter said. "It's my house, my bride, and my wedding night."

"Come on," Eddie said to Dolores. "Let's leave them to figure out things for themselves."

Dolores looked reluctant to leave, but Eddie pushed her from the room. Anne felt as though her last support had vanished.

Peter picked up the oil lamp, the only light left in the room. "You're going to have to lead the way," he said. "I don't remember where anything is."

Anne led the way into the hall and up the stairs. Each step seemed to take her irrevocably closer to something she'd thought she wanted but now found frightening.

"Who sleeps in these rooms?" Peter asked.

"I slept in one, Belser one, and Uncle Carl one. The other two are for guests."

"Did he have many guests?"

"Lots. Belser had to sleep in the bunkhouse all the time."

"I'll bet he didn't like that."

"No. It made him real mad."

She paused before the door to Uncle Carl's room. She couldn't force herself to open it.

After a moment, Peter stepped past her and opened the door. "Doesn't seem to be stuck. Opened easy as pie."

He walked into the room and turned when she didn't follow. "You know you have to come in, don't you?"

She nodded.

"Are you afraid of me?"

She shook her head, but she was certain he could see the fear in her eyes.

"You don't have to be. I know I'm nothing like you remember, but if you give me a chance, you'll see I'm really not very different."

Anne felt like a fool for being so hesitant. Here was the man she'd begged to marry her, who had agreed to marry her, she was certain, only because he felt sorry for her and wanted to help her, and *she* was acting as if she had something to be afraid of. "I don't know what's gotten into me." She came to a halt three steps inside the room.

"It's probably that wolf bait you call an uncle coming in here and trying to palm off that half-dead old man on you. That's enough to cause any female to go off in a dead faint."

"I never faint."

"Good." He looked sincerely relieved. "Ticklish females make me nervous."

After the way he'd stood up to her uncle and Cyrus, she couldn't imagine Peter being nervous about anything.

"You are scared of me, aren't you? At least you're frightened at the idea of sleeping in the same bed with me."

She didn't answer.

"Come on, tell the truth. We're not going to do well together if we start hiding things from each other."

"Yes, I am a little afraid."

"Okay. Now we're getting somewhere. Do you know what's supposed to happen tonight?"

"Yes . . . no." She couldn't live on a ranch and not know what happened, but everybody acted so secretive when it came to what went on between a married couple, she figured they'd left out something important.

"Well, it's not going to happen tonight," he said. "So you can stop looking scared to death and take a deep breath."

She felt as if a tremendous weight had been lifted from her heart. She felt almost giddy with relief. But her moment of comfort was brief. Didn't he like her? Did he find her unattractive? Would he make her leave? "Don't you want me?" she asked.

He looked a little embarrassed. She couldn't imagine why. Men weren't supposed to be nervous about bedding a woman. From all she'd heard, they practically had to be forced to wait a decent interval.

"I like you just fine," Peter said. "You're very pretty, but we don't know each other. Well, hardly anymore, that is. You've had a very upsetting day. It wouldn't be right to rush into something like this right away." He waited a moment. "Don't you agree?"

She nodded.

"Okay. Why don't you show me where Dolores put my clothes. While I get my things organized, you can get ready for bed."

Anne froze. There was only one bed in the room. He couldn't mean they were to sleep in the same bed, not after what he'd just said. He was busy opening and closing drawers.

"Seems like everything here is yours," he said when he turned to her. "You sure have a lot of clothes."

"Some of them belonged to my mother."

He held up one brown dress and frowned. "It looks too large."

"Mama was bigger than I am. Uncle Carl said I'd grow into them, only I didn't."

"There's certainly a lot of them." He looked at his own clothes and frowned. "We'll have to see about getting me something else to wear. I don't think these are suitable for working around the ranch."

She thought he looked very nice. She liked him

dressed up. "Dolores said she put your clothes in the chest of drawers."

"Probably because she couldn't find any room in the wardrobe." He looked at her a moment. "Something wrong?"

She couldn't keep her gaze from turning to the bed. Feeling herself flush, she brought it back again.

He smiled. "Oh, that's what's got you ready to scurry up a tree. It's a big bed. You'll hardly know I'm in it."

She'd have to be dead not to know he was in the same bed with her. She might be seventeen and inexperienced, sheltered and all that, but she was enough of a woman to know Peter Warren was more man than she had seen in her life. What's more, he was exactly the kind of man guaranteed to turn a woman's thoughts to things besides sewing and housekeeping. She felt herself flush.

Odd that she'd never thought about this aspect of her relationship with Peter. With other men it was unavoidable, but Peter . . . well, now it was unavoidable with him as well.

"Surely you don't think I'm going to attack you after I promised to leave you alone?"

"No. I trust you." And she did. She didn't know why, since merely being in the room with him made her nervous, but she did.

"Well, you can't go on being so afraid you're practically trembling. You'll never get a wink of sleep."

She didn't expect she would. She couldn't imagine how she could.

"Here, take your clothes and change in the bathroom."

She grabbed some clothes from one of the drawers and hurried into the bathroom and closed the door behind her. The room was pitch black. She couldn't see a thing. A soft knock sounded at the door.

"You'll need a light."

Embarrassed, she opened the door and accepted the bedside lamp he handed her.

"You've got to stop being scared of me," Peter said. "I'll never intentionally do anything to hurt you. And call me Pete. I can't stand Peter. It makes me think of a preacher I once knew."

"I'll try," Anne said.

He chucked her under the chin. It comforted her, but it also made her a little angry. She wasn't a baby. *How is he to know that? That's exactly what you've been acting like.* Okay, so she had been foolish, but she still wasn't a baby. He was older than she was. Lots of women got married a lot younger, and to older men. She knew one woman her age who had two children already.

She poured some water in the basin and washed her face.

She was going to have to start thinking of herself as a woman. Uncle Carl had always treated her like a little girl, requiring her to help Dolores in the kitchen and with the housework but never letting her be responsible for anything.

She unbuttoned her dress and let it drop to the floor. She unlaced her corset and discarded it as well. She stepped out of the shift and reached for her nightgown. She hadn't paid any attention to what she was getting when she'd reached in her drawer. She'd gotten a faded gown made of sturdy cotton. She'd look like an old woman, but there was nothing she could do about it. She pulled the gown over her head. Clutching her clothes in her arms, ignoring the feel of her naked skin under the rough cotton, she opened the door and reentered the bedroom.

"I was beginning to think you'd escaped out the window," Peter said. Pete. She had to remember he'd asked her to call him Pete. It fitted him better now. A name like Peter was too stodgy for him.

"I forgot. I'm not used to anybody waiting for me to finish."

"No problem. After having to wash in a stream or a water hole, a bathroom is going to seem like an extravagant luxury. I may not come out for hours."

As soon as the door closed behind him, Anne hurried to put away her clothes and get into bed. The idea of being caught standing in the middle of the room with nothing on but a nightgown unnerved her, but the thought of sharing the bed with him had her entire body rigid with fright.

She climbed into bed and pulled the covers up to her chin, but that didn't give her any sense of comfort. Every time she moved the slightest bit, every time she took a deep breath, the bed made a sound. And that made her even more conscious of the fact that she was in a bed waiting for her husband. The coolness of the sheets, which was always a comfort after a warm summer day, seemed ice cold and unfriendly tonight. Her body seemed strange and unfamiliar. Sensations didn't register as they used to. She felt as if she was coming down with a fever, then with the chills.

She was being stupid, letting her nerves get the better of her. She would relax. Peter—Pete—had promised not to touch her. She believed him. She really did.

She wished she had the courage to blow out the big lamp he'd brought from downstairs. He must have gotten it while she was in the bathroom. She would have preferred to wait for him in the dark. At least he wouldn't be able to see the fear in her face.

The bedroom door burst open, and Belser strode into the room. "Couldn't wait to get in his bed, could you?" he shouted.

She could tell he'd been drinking. Not enough to be drunk, but enough to be unpleasant.

"He's my husband," she managed to say, her voice a harsh whisper. "It's where I'm supposed to be."

"I don't believe he's your husband. Even a sap-sucker like Peter wouldn't marry *you*. Not that I think he's Peter."

"He wants us to call him Pete. He says Peter reminds him—"

The bathroom door slammed open, and Pete strode into the room. He was naked from the waist up. Anne felt the blood rush to her face.

"What the hell are you doing here?" he demanded of Belser.

"I came to see—"

"I didn't hear you knock. I didn't hear Anne invite you in."

"I never knock. I—"

Pete's fist shot out, made contact with Belser's face, and sent him reeling back through the doorway.

"Don't ever come into my bedroom without knocking and being invited," Pete said. "Next time I'm liable to shoot first."

"Son of a bitch!" Belser shouted, holding his hand to a nose that dripped blood. "You've broken my nose."

"Your nose will heal," Pete said. "A bullet through the chest is a little trickier. Now get out of here. The sight of all that blood is liable to upset Anne." He closed the door in Belser's face. "Sorry about that," he said to Anne. "He won't do it again." Then he disappeared into the bathroom once more.

Anne lay in the bed, her mouth agape. Nobody had ever stopped Belser from bursting into rooms. Uncle Carl had given up, but it was clear Pete wasn't going to put up with it. She feared Belser might get a gun and come back, but after a series of curses that turned Anne's ears pink, his voice faded away down the hall. A moment later she heard the door to his room slam. The tension left her body and she collapsed into the pillows.

She felt exhausted, utterly wrung out, mentally and physically. She had thought the tension of waiting for Pete, not knowing when—or if—he would arrive, and worrying about what her uncle would do next had been difficult. None of that equaled the few hours since Pete's arrival. She didn't know what she'd expected, but this wasn't it.

Yes, she did. She'd expected to see her old friend of ten years back again. She'd expected to fall into the same brother-sister relationship she'd enjoyed so much. She'd expected to have to encourage him to stand up to Belser. She'd expected to feel that she was important to him, that he needed her.

Instead she'd gotten a man who not only shattered any remaining vestiges of their brother-sister relationship, but acted as if it had never existed. He clearly didn't need her to stand up for him. He was more than capable of taking care of Belser and anybody else.

Including herself. Suddenly Pete seemed very male, very sexy, very physical, even dominating, much like all the other men in Wyoming. That made her think of what was supposed to happen on a wedding night. Any other man in Wyoming would expect it, wouldn't understand—or accept it—if she felt reluctant. He'd think it his right to force her.

That was what scared her. She was suddenly thrown into a relationship she hadn't expected and didn't understand. Dolores would tell her to throw herself into his arms and let him do with her as he wanted. She couldn't do that. It would be like throwing herself over a ledge without knowing where she would land.

She wanted the old Peter back, not this new Pete. She wanted to sit next to him, hold his hand, have him put his arm around her without having to experience any of this disturbing physical turmoil. She wanted the quiet, easy relationship she remembered. This new Peter—no, Pete, she had to remember that—had thrown all that out the window. He was totally foreign, totally unexpected. But he was exciting. He was attractive. He was big, he was strong, he was . . .

She didn't have all the words yet. It was as though she'd been a girl all her life and in one afternoon she'd been told she had to become a woman. Peter might be happy with a girl, but a man like Pete, simply by who he was, demanded a woman. She didn't know if she could be that woman. She didn't know if she had the courage.

She wasn't sure what it meant to be a woman. Right now it felt uncomfortable. Frightening. Demanding. Dangerous. But she knew she couldn't turn back. Everything had changed this afternoon. She could never be the same again, not even if she wanted to be. And she didn't. The change alarmed her, but it thrilled her as well.

She'd never really understood the distinction before, but for the first time in her life she was beginning to *feel* like a woman. She'd have to talk to Dolores. She would know what to do.

But first she had to get through this night. And Pete was coming out of the bathroom.

If he'd looked overwhelmingly male before, he positively exuded masculine energy now. He'd stripped down to the bottom half of his long underwear. While the garment provided an effective cloak for the most private parts of his anatomy, it put the rest of his physique in strong relief. Unlike every other man she knew, his upper body was deeply tanned rather than white. She didn't know how he'd gotten a tan working in a hardware store. Nor why he should be working with his shirt off. But her questions were quickly forgotten as her attention was drawn to his powerful chest and well-muscled arms. He must have lifted a lot of heavy boxes.

But all that was a brief, quickly forgotten thought. She was primarily conscious of the magnificent image and the terrifying effect it had on her own body. She felt a thousand tiny shocks being administered at random all over her. She pulled the covers up higher, clutching them tightly in her hands. But that action brought her forearms into contact with her breasts, and she realized that her nipples had become sensitive to touch. The shock amplified all the other feelings until she felt like a hysterical mess.

"I didn't know I was inheriting such a modern house," Pete said. "A real bathroom with water fed from a cistern in the attic. I can't wait to take a bath in that tub. It looks big enough for both of us."

Anne blushed down to her toes. Whoever heard of a man and a woman taking a bath together? The idea was preposterous. Yet the idea settled in some corner of her mind and refused to go away.

"Are you going to sleep under all those covers?" he asked.

She nodded. She hoped he wouldn't take them away from her. She didn't know why he would, but she didn't know what men did to women when they slept in the same bed. At least not ordinary men. Belser had enjoyed himself frightening her with what Cyrus would do. She had been certain the Peter she used to know wouldn't have done anything like that. She wasn't sure about Pete.

"You'll wake up in a sweat. It's not that cold yet."

"I like lots of covers."

"Fine by me as long as you don't shove them off on me. I'm used to sleeping in the open."

"But you wrote me you lived in a nice quiet rooming house."

"That was in Illinois. I got used to sleeping out on the way here. Much more invigorating."

"Weren't you afraid of wild animals?"

He blew out the light, leaving them in the dark. She felt the bed sag under his weight, and she forgot all about any animals but the very large male in the bed next to her.

"Wild animals won't bother you. You've probably been listening to Belser spin tales just to make himself seem like a big fearless fella. There's nothing out there half as dangerous as another human."

"Does your wound still hurt?"

"No."

"Did it hurt at first?"

"Like the devil."

"Weren't you afraid?"

"Why? I was still alive. I had a horse, food, and my guns. What else does a man need?"

Anne could think of so many things, she hardly knew where to start. "I'd have been afraid."

"Naturally. You're a female."

She wasn't sure she liked that. Somehow it made her sound inferior. She probably was—Belser always said she wasn't worth as much as a ten-year-old boy—but she'd depended on Peter—Pete—to take her part.

"My parents would never let me go very far from

the house when they were alive," she said. "And Uncle Carl was even worse."

"A female ought to get out once in a while. You can't be afraid of the rest of the world. Isabelle started across Texas with nothing but a wagonload of orphans to keep her company."

"Who's Isabelle?"

"Uh . . . a woman I know. She and Jake adopted a whole bunch of orphans."

"Who's Jake?"

"Her husband. I just said they adopted a bunch of orphans. You don't expect Isabelle to live on a ranch with a man who's not her husband, do you? Isabelle's not like that. You start getting careless with the rules, and she's liable to knock you up side your head with a log to get your attention. Then she'll *really* lay into you."

"Did she lay into one of the orphans?"

"Yeah."

"Who?"

"A friend of mine."

"How did you meet him? I didn't know you went to Texas."

"I didn't. He came to Illinois. Look, are you going to chatter all night?"

"No." She nearly swallowed the word. She never chattered, but she was curious about him. He'd done so many interesting things he'd never mentioned in his letters.

"Good. We both need a good night's sleep. I've got to ride all over this place tomorrow. Then we've got to decide what we're going to do about this marriage."

"You're not going to divorce me, are you?"

Chapter Four

"Nothing like that. We just need to talk. After all, we're practically strangers."

They weren't supposed to be. She hadn't thought they would be, but Peter—she had to keep reminding herself to think of him as Pete now—was definitely a stranger. She supposed it was natural to change when you grew up, but she hadn't. Uncle Carl used to say she looked exactly the same as she had the day she was born.

Despite Pete's assurances, she was afraid he did mean to divorce her. He hadn't wanted to marry her. She didn't fool herself on that score. According to Uncle Carl, Peter didn't have the gumption to marry anybody, but Uncle Carl didn't know how he'd changed. He had plenty of gumption now, far more than she ever would. He probably wanted a wife with gumption, too.

She wondered if she could develop gumption, or if she had it and didn't know it. No, she was just a shy, silly girl who'd fallen in love with a boy years ago and hadn't grown up enough to know boys change. She'd let her need, her naivete, and his willingness to marry her convince her he would be the same sweet boy she'd known years ago. She could have believed that boy had failed in the hardware business. She found it difficult to imagine Pete failing at anything. He was so full of energy, so willing to face down anybody who got in his way. He could ride a horse, fight, use a gun . . . well, he could do just about anything a cowboy had to do.

Of course, that might have been the reason he failed at running a hardware store. She didn't imagine any of those things would be very useful in such a business. He must have spent so much time outside the store that he didn't have time to tend to business. It must have been that friend from Texas, the one the lady named Isabelle hit with a log, who taught him all those things.

She wished she knew a lady like Isabelle who could tell her how to get some gumption, or give her some of her own. Surely a lady with the courage to hit a man with a log had more than enough gumption to share. Anne sighed. She'd probably be afraid of such a woman. Besides, she probably looked like a horse. According to Dolores, pretty women didn't need gumption. They just needed to learn how to use their charms.

Of course, Anne didn't have any of those, either. She was pretty enough—people were quite willing to tell her that—but a woman of her background couldn't expect to have charm. People were quite willing to tell her that, too.

She sighed again. She had thought she had everything all worked out. Peter . . . Pete just needed to marry her and claim his inheritance, and everything would be fine. Of course, she had worried he wouldn't be able to stand up to Belser. But she had meant to help him. She'd looked forward to that. No one else had ever depended on her or even listened to her. Sometimes they talked about her as if she didn't exist. Pete had never done that. She'd counted on being important, needed. Now she didn't know if that would ever happen.

The soft breathing from the other side of the bed told her Pete was asleep. Her father used to say a man who could fall asleep quickly had a clean conscience. She was sure Peter had a clean conscience. He'd protected her from her uncle and Cyrus without hesitation. He'd stood up to Belser, and he'd kept his promise not to touch her.

But that wasn't the comfort it should have been. Maybe he didn't *want* to touch her. Maybe he was so used to women like Isabelle, women with gumption, that he wasn't interested in a female foolish enough to be frightened of her husband. Maybe he wanted a woman who wore tight dresses, had red hair, milk-white skin, and crimson lips, a woman who was more than eager to have him on her side of the bed, his hands all over her, his mouth on hers in hot, passionate kisses.

Anne's whole body trembled at the thought of Pete's hands on her, of a kiss of any kind. No man had ever touched her. She hadn't wanted anyone to—except Peter, of course. But she'd imagined holding hands quietly, his arm around her, all very brotherly; imagined his kiss would be brotherly, too. She was certain Pete's kisses would be entirely different.

The thought frightened her, but she was attracted to him at the same time. Sleeping in the same bed with him scared her, but it excited her. He was everything she wanted and nothing she'd anticipated.

She shuddered. She could almost feel his hands on her shoulder, his lips on her mouth, hot, impatient, hungry, devouring her. That wasn't what she wanted. *He* wasn't what she wanted.

Well, she did like his looks. No one could deny Pete had grown into a handsome man. And so big and strong. She'd be a fool to say she didn't find that attractive. He was certain of himself, what he wanted, what he could do, what he expected others to do. She'd liked that in Uncle Carl. It was logical she'd like it in Pete, too.

As she ran down a list of other qualities to find she liked those as well, she gradually grew more and more puzzled. What kept her trembling on her side of the bed? Those very same qualities she liked. They made him seem a little dangerous. Not the safe, biddable boy she'd expected. Pete was like a wild stallion—strong, confident, willing and able to take what he wanted.

She was starting to feel like something of an idiot. If she liked him the way he was, why couldn't she act like it?

Because she still couldn't believe Pete was real. She couldn't shake the feeling that if she tried to touch him, he'd disappear, that she'd wake up and find it had all been a dream. She didn't know why she should feel like that, but the feeling wouldn't go away.

The idea flashed into her head without warning. The impulse caught her by surprise. She turned. He was sleeping on his side, his back to her. The broad expanse of smooth, brown skin beckoned to her. *Touch me. Come on. It's all right. He'll never know.*

She had to be crazy, but once the idea thrust itself into her head, she couldn't get rid of it.

You want to touch me. I know you do. It's easy. Just reach out.

She gripped her hands together and held them tightly against her breasts. What if he woke up? What if he interpreted her touch as a signal that she wanted him to come to her side of the bed?

He's given his word. Besides, he's sound sleep.

The soft breathing continued without interruption. The more Anne thought about touching Pete, the more difficult it was to resist. She'd never had the opportunity to touch a man who was so young and strong and handsome. He was her husband. It was normal for married people to touch. Her parents had touched all the time. It was okay. It was all right.

She remembered he would let her hold his hand when they went out walking. She liked touching him. The tactile proof of his presence was comforting. He'd seemed to like it, too. His mother had died when he was a baby, and his father and brother were always yelling at him, beating and fighting him.

Maybe if she touched him—not much, just slightly—it would bring back some of the boy she remembered. Maybe all of him hadn't been swallowed up by this new person who called himself Pete.

Still unsure of herself, she unclenched her fingers. She reached out and tentatively extended her fingers. Closer and closer until they came into contact with Pete's warm, soft brown skin.

In one continuous motion, Pete threw the covers from his body, produced a gun Anne didn't even know was in the room, and leapt from the bed to his feet, crouched and ready. His reaction was instantaneous and so unexpected, it surprised a shriek out of her.

He leapt on the bed, throwing his body across hers. "What is it? What's wrong? Why did you wake me?"

Anne was too stunned to speak. She tried, but no sound would come out of her mouth.

"It's not a snake, is it?"

She managed to shake her head.

"Then what is it? I don't see or hear anything."

He got up, opened the door, and looked out into the hall, but the house was silent. A look out the window apparently offered nothing of interest.

"There's nobody here," he said as he lowered the gun. "What happened? Did you have a bad dream?"

She nodded her head. She knew something awful would probably happen to her for touching him and lying about it, but she couldn't bring herself to tell him what had really happened.

"Don't look so frightened. There's nothing wrong with that. I used to have them all the time myself. Indians. Had the same dream over and over again. They were attacking the wagon train I was on, killing everybody in sight. People screaming, blood flying, people running every whichaway. Can't stand Indians to this day."

"It was Indians," she managed to say.

"You don't have to worry about them. They're pretty much locked away on reservations. You all right now?"

She nodded.

"You think you can go back to sleep?"

"Yes."

"Good. You can wake me if you have another bad dream, but don't touch me. Just call my name softly."

"Okay."

He put the gun under his pillow—she hadn't seen him do that earlier—and got back into bed. "I'm going to see you don't have any more bad dreams. Now tucker down and go to sleep."

He turned over and was soon breathing softly again.

But Anne couldn't sleep. She didn't know if she'd ever sleep again if she had to be in the same bed with him. She didn't know how Peter could have changed so drastically. He had never acted like that. She remembered more than once having to shake him hard to wake him up. This man had been wide awake and ready to fight in the space of a second. She had never known anybody could react so quickly.

But there was something else that upset her. The nightmare. Peter had never had nightmares about

Indians, never dreamed about them at all as far as she could remember. But most important of all, he didn't hate Indians. He couldn't. She was part Indian. It was for that reason Peter had agreed to marry her.

Pete looked at Anne sleeping peacefully. He was tempted to wake her, tell her who he was and why he had come, but he changed his mind. She had probably been too scared to get much sleep last night. She had to be exhausted. His pulling a gun on her probably didn't help. She'd looked petrified. He couldn't explain to her that you had to sleep half awake to survive in a gold camp. Men had been killed for nothing more than their equipment and supplies. Only his watchfulness had kept him alive.

He was certain this Peter Warren wouldn't have done anything like that. He probably had to be shaken awake. From the way people acted, he must have been a real dolt. Pete hoped he didn't run into an adult who remembered him clearly. He might be able to fool Anne—she couldn't have been more than six or seven when she last saw Peter—but he'd never be able to fool an adult. Except for the color of their hair, they didn't look all that much alike.

Pete tiptoed to the bathroom. After years of shaving and washing in ice-cold streams, this was an unexpected luxury. He wondered how they kept the water from freezing in the winter. As he washed his face and put on his clothes, he turned his attention to the problem of finding the men who'd shot him and taken his saddlebags. The trail was old, the tracks lost in the welter of hoofprints made in the ten days since.

He hadn't found any hoofprints in or near the corral that matched the tracks he'd followed, but he was certain the men were here. Or close by. That bothered him. It made him certain that whoever had ordered Peter killed was also here at the ranch.

Belser desperately wanted the ranch. Though he'd never seen Peter, he had declared right from the first that Pete was an imposter. The best possible way to know that would be to know you'd killed Peter, or had him killed. Pete wouldn't mind proving Belser guilty of murder. The man was easy to dislike.

But Pete had to face the fact that others at the ranch could have wanted Peter dead. Maybe the foreman feared he'd lose his job. Maybe someone in the vicinity other than Belser didn't want Peter to inherit the ranch. After all, Belser could be involved with the rustling and his partners could want Peter dead so they could go on with their stealing. It didn't make a lot of sense, but it was never wise to ignore any possibility.

Whether he wanted to admit it or not, there was always the possibility that Anne was involved. After all, if Peter was the complete idiot everybody thought, maybe she didn't want to be married to him. Maybe she wanted to inherit the ranch from her dead husband, then marry a man capable of holding the place against rustlers and greedy neighbors. Bill Mason looked like an obvious choice. Pete had discovered that the man's wife had died a few years back, that Mason was known to be interested in marrying again. What would be better for both of them than to marry and combine their ranches? Mason gave the appearance of a man quite able to hold his own.

But most likely Belser was the villain. If so, and if

Anne was really married to Peter, she was in as much danger from Belser as her husband had been. Pete muttered several curses. He should have waited and taken the steamship down the Missouri. Then he wouldn't have been shot, wouldn't have lost his money, and wouldn't have found himself in the middle of a murder plot with all the guns aimed at him. He didn't like it one bit, but he couldn't leave Anne to the mercy of an unknown killer, especially if that killer was sleeping only two bedrooms away.

But he was in even more danger. If they'd tried to kill Peter once—and he didn't know that there hadn't been other attempts—they'd try again. He would have to tread very carefully if he wanted to stay alive.

Maybe he would lock his bedroom door tonight.

"You look like you've been in a fight," Dolores said when Anne entered the kitchen the next morning. She smiled wickedly. "It must have been some wedding night. You going to tell me about it?"

"It's not what you think," Anne said, pouring herself a cup of coffee and taking a big swallow of the hot liquid.

"From the looks of you, it's a lot more."

Anne sat down at the table. She needed time to still her shaking limbs. She'd finally dropped off to sleep sometime during the night, but her entire body ached. She'd been relieved to find Pete gone when she woke. "Where's Pete?" she asked.

"He and Eddie rode out at dawn. If that man intends to get up this early every morning, we'll have to start going to bed earlier."

"Did Belser go with them?"

"No. He came down later. He was in a foul mood. From the look of him, he got in a fight and lost."

"He burst into our bedroom last night without knocking. Pete punched him in the face, knocked him right back into the hall."

"Belser didn't come back fighting?"

"No."

"Your Pete has turned out to be a real eye-opener. From what your uncle said, I was worried Belser would run you both off inside a month."

"Pete's changed."

"He must have."

"He said he takes after his mother's side of the family."

"Must have been a handy bunch of people to have around. Now tell me about you. I can tell you didn't get much sleep."

It was on the tip of Anne's tongue to tell Dolores she suspected Pete might not be Peter. But if he wasn't, where was Peter? What had stopped him from arriving at the ranch as he'd promised? Something must have happened to him, but she couldn't believe Pete would hurt Peter. If she did, she couldn't have slept in the same bed with him.

She'd lain awake for hours trying to decide whom to tell, what she ought to do. But now that it was morning, she hesitated. She had to admit that worry for her own position was at the root of it. If she swore Pete wasn't Peter, then he would be thrown off the ranch and Belser would inherit. Belser would throw her off, too. The minute that happened, her uncle would haul her off to old man Cyrus.

The consequences of telling on Pete were certain. He would have no future at the Tumbling T, but she wouldn't have one either.

What if she didn't tell on him? What if no one ever found out? She was no longer lying frightened in the dark, next to a man she didn't know. She'd had time to think. She didn't know what Pete was doing there, but wouldn't it be better to try to find out? Maybe Peter had sent him. It didn't seem like something Peter would do, but it was obvious Pete was better at handling difficult situations than Peter would have been. Maybe Pete *was* the man from Texas Isabelle had hit with the log. That would explain why he knew so much about ranches.

Peter must have sent him. Pete knew a lot about everything.

"Pete said we needed time to get to know each other," Anne said. "He said he wouldn't claim his marriage rights until I was ready." He hadn't said anything about claiming them at all. Didn't that mean he was sent by Peter, that Peter was coming later when all danger was past?

Dolores's disbelief was obvious. "I never heard of a man doing such a thing. You sure there's not something wrong with him?"

There was absolutely nothing wrong with Pete. "No, he's just a gentleman. I told you he was."

"Your uncle said he was a spineless clod. He never said a word about him being a gentleman."

77

"That's because Uncle Carl wasn't much of a gentleman himself," Anne said. "Papa used to tell Mama never to let herself be caught alone in the house with Uncle Carl."

"Everybody knows that," Dolores said. "I had a few close calls myself."

"You did?"

"We're not talking about me," Dolores said. "I want to know more about this husband of yours."

Anne didn't know what she could tell Dolores. Just about everything she remembered about Peter contradicted what she saw in Pete. No matter who he turned out to be, Pete had saved her from Cyrus. She owed him something for that.

"I can't tell you much more. He's changed so much, I hardly know him myself. He said the same thing himself last night."

"Well, I'm real impressed with him. Belser was certain he could take the ranch right out of your Pete's hands. No wonder he's trying to convince us he's not Peter. Though it seems like a silly thing to say. I mean, all he has to do is produce his papers and there's no question about it, is there?"

"No."

What would happen if he produced the right papers? Then he'd *be* Peter.

And she would be his wife!

A feeling totally unlike anything she'd ever felt for Peter before ran through her. Last night she'd been too afraid, too confused to pay much attention to anything but fear. But now, with Pete many miles away and Dolores comfortingly at her side, Anne could tell this was a new feeling, a kind of anticipation she'd never experienced before. She'd never felt anything remotely like this for Peter.

She cautioned herself that no matter how attractive, no matter how exciting it might be to think of being married to such man, she didn't know who he was. She didn't know why he was here. She didn't know where Peter was. She was married to Peter, not Pete.

She shivered. The thought made her toes curl. She'd never dreamed of a husband like Pete, but now that the possibility existed, she admitted it excited her. It was like a magnet drawing her forward when she wanted to hang back.

There was, however, a very strong possibility she was wrong, that Peter had dreamed of Indians but never told her, that he had changed so much, nobody would know he was the same man. She had no proof, only suspicions based on the ten-year-old memories of a seven-year-old child. She could be wrong.

And if she were, then Pete was Peter, and she was his real, legal wife.

She decided she had let the unexpected events of the last twenty-four hours confuse her. She'd been further upset by lying awake for long hours in the dark. Pete probably had a perfectly logical explanation for all her fears. She had only to ask. He would explain everything.

Suddenly she felt better, no longer frightened. Pete *was* Peter. He would explain all her doubts away. Then he'd produce the documents, and no one would have any doubts. She would have a husband, a ranch, safety for the rest of her life.

"You're one lucky woman," Dolores said. "You used to complain that nothing exciting ever happened to you. Being rescued at the last minute from being sold to an old man by a handsome young man who turns out to be your husband is enough excitement for the rest of your life."

"Too much," Anne said. "I'll never complain again."

Dolores winked and grinned. "I have a suspicion you won't have to. Even gentlemen don't hold themselves in check forever."

"I've made up my mind to round up everything we can and sell it immediately," Pete said as he and Eddie neared the ranch after a hard day of riding. "The herd isn't in good shape. We'd lose a lot of them in a bad winter."

"You'll lose money selling now," Eddie said.

"Jake always said go with what you have, not what you might have."

"Who's Jake?"

He was going to have to watch his tongue. At this rate, he'd have blabbed about his entire family before the week was out. They'd only have to compare notes to be certain he was the imposter Belser claimed him to be.

"A man I knew," Pete said. "He lost nearly everything he had during the war. He didn't believe in waiting."

"I didn't know there was any fighting in Illinois."

He was going to have to sew his mouth shut. "There wasn't. He was from Texas. He moved to Illinois after the war." The mere thought of leaving Texas, especially to go someplace like Illinois, would cause Jake to choke.

"Anyway, I want you to start making preparations for a roundup. If we get them to market quickly, we'll get in ahead of anybody else."

"Everybody around here is waiting as long as possible, hoping the steers will put on a little more weight."

"They won't. There's no grass. And that reminds me of something else. We've got too many strays from other herds on our land. Tell the boys to chase back anything that isn't ours."

"That's going to make people angry."

"They're welcome to run mine back in this direction. In fact, I'd be obliged. It'll make the roundup easier."

"I never heard of anybody doing this."

"That's one advantage of being the foreman and not the owner. You still get paid if I make a mistake."

Eddie half grinned. "Okay, you're the boss."

"Good. Now let's get cleaned up. My stomach's already growling at the thought of the supper Dolores has cooked up."

After years of cooking his own meals over a campfire, or getting what he could at a local saloon, a properly prepared meal was a treat.

Pete looked around quickly as they neared the corrals. Belser hadn't shown up all day. He felt uneasy not knowing where he might be. He wasn't comforted by not finding Belser's horse in the corral. That meant he'd been gone most of the day. There was more than enough work to do on the ranch, but Pete didn't think it was work that had kept Belser out of sight.

Dolores stuck her head out of the kitchen as they rode by. "I'll have the food on the table by the time you've unsaddled the horses."

"Give us fifteen minutes. I've got to wash up and change my shirt," Pete called back.

This was almost like being back at the Broken Circle with Jake and the rest of the boys—Isabelle cooking mountains of food, everybody crowding around the trough so they could wash up and get to the table first. He'd hardly had time to unsaddle his horse when Belser rode up. He looked dusty and tired.

"You'd better hurry and wash up," Pete said. "Dolores said she'd have food on the table in twenty minutes."

"I eat like I am," Belser growled.

"Not anymore."

"What do you mean?"

"I mean you wash and change your shirt before you come in to eat. It's one way to show your appreciation for the work it takes to put a good meal on the table."

"Dolores is paid to cook. She don't need my appreciation."

"Then there's the fact that the sight of perspiration running through the dust on your forehead offends me. As does your odor."

"I'll be damned if I'm washing just to eat."

"Then you can eat at the chuck wagon. Be sure to sit downwind. I wouldn't want you ruining the men's dinner."

Belser dismounted and walked up to Pete. He wasn't quite as tall, but he outweighed him by at least fifty pounds. "You telling me you're throwing me out of the house if I don't wash up?"

"That's about the sum of it."

"Uncle Carl never made me wash."

"Uncle Carl is dead."

They stood facing each other.

"I could kill you," Belser said.

"You could try."

Pete hadn't expected Belser to challenge him so openly, but he was ready when the big man charged him, fists waving in the air. Pete nearly laughed when he saw what Belser considered fighting style. If he'd had to survive twelve years in the gold-mining camps of Colorado, Montana, and the Black Hills, he'd know what real fighting was. Pete sidestepped Belser's first charge and tripped him. He went down with a whoosh of air from his lungs and came up with a roar.

"If you want to fight, stop waving your arms in the air like you're brushing off flies," Pete said. "You'll never hit me like that."

Belser rushed him again. Pete figured Belser thought his size would carry the day. He didn't know Pete had honed his skills on his best friend, Sean, who was five inches taller than Pete and heavier than Belser. Pete sidestepped the second charge and hit Belser in the temple as he rushed by.

He hit the ground with a thud. He didn't get up so quickly this time.

"It would be a lot easier to wash up," Pete said. "You're going to have to do it anyway."

Belser came at him again, but he was more careful this time. He managed to connect on one blow, but he swung his arms around in a giant circle, which took away a lot of the force of the blow. Pete easily recovered and moved straight in, pounding Belser with a rapid series of sharp blows straight to the stomach, ribs, and jaw. Belser wasn't fat or out of shape, but he didn't have any real fighting skill or stamina. He sank to his knees in a matter of minutes.

"Wash up and change your shirt, or eat at the chuck wagon," Pete said, breathing hard from his exertions. "That's the way it's going to be tonight and every night from now on."

He started toward the house.

"I wish you hadn't done that," Eddie said.

"I could see it coming from the moment I got here. Now maybe he'll think a little before he goes off half-cocked."

Pete wasn't surprised when Belser came down in time for dinner, and wearing a clean shirt. He had figured Belser would rather not eat at all than have to join the chuck wagon crew and explain his humiliating loss.

"I've decided to round up all the beef that's in reasonable shape and sell it," Pete announced. "The range is in poor shape, and the predictions are for a hard winter. We don't have enough hay to carry over the full herd. If we sell off what we can, we might make it through in decent shape."

"I don't think you ought to sell," Belser said.

"You're welcome to your opinion, but it's my ranch."

"It's not your ranch because you're not Peter."

"You said that before." Pete didn't look up from the steak he was cutting. He figured it would look better if he appeared totally unfazed by Belser's accusations.

"But now I have proof," Belser said.

Chapter Five

Pete felt a chill of apprehension. What kind of proof could Belser have? Where had he been all day? It wasn't possible for him to have traveled back to the spot where Peter had been killed. Even if he had, Pete had been very careful to camouflage Peter's grave and burn the wagon. Trying to appear totally unconcerned, Pete surveyed the faces at the table. Dolores appeared curious more than anything else. He couldn't quite decipher Eddie's expression, but he doubted the foreman would look forward to working under Belser.

Anne looked as white as a sheet. He could only guess at the reason, but he was certain she dreaded the prospect of Belser's inheriting the ranch.

"Everybody's anxious to hear your proof," Pete said. "Don't keep us waiting." He directed his gaze back to his food. If this was his moment of exposure, there was little he could do to stop it. He would just explain what he was doing there and bow out as gracefully as possible.

"Carl said Peter couldn't fight. Peter could never have beaten me, so you can't be Peter."

Pete breathed an inward sigh of relief. If this was Belser's idea of proof, it was safe to let him keep making accusations. After a while, no one would believe anything he said.

"That's ridiculous," Anne said. She had turned toward Belser, her cheeks now spotted with color. "Anybody can see Pete has changed since he left here. It's only natural that he learned to fight. All men do."

Pete hadn't expected Anne to support him with such vehemence. From her pallor, he figured she was more afraid of losing her security than her husband. After all, she'd been willing to marry a man she had last seen as a child.

"He wouldn't have decided to sell the herd," Belser said, ignoring Anne. "Uncle Carl said he didn't know anything about cows. That he didn't like them."

"You don't have to like cows to know you have to sell them to make money," Pete said. "I *was* thinking about selling everything on the place, going back to Illinois, and opening up a really big hardware store this time."

"That sounds exactly like something Peter would do," Belser said.

"Which disproves your own argument," Anne said. "If that's exactly what Peter would do, then this must be Peter."

"He's not, you little fool," Belser exploded.

"I don't really care who you think I am," Pete said, "but you call my wife a fool again—even a little one—and I'm going to knock you through that window. Then you can take up permanent residence in the bunkhouse."

"That's something else Peter wouldn't do," Belser said. "He didn't have the courage of a coyote."

"I always thought coyotes were right brave," Pete said. "They're little, but they'll attack an animal twice their size. Smart too. I don't mind you comparing me to a coyote. Just watch what you say about Anne. You got to treat ladies differently."

"She ain't no lady," Belser exploded.

A silence fell.

"You can explain that statement, or you can apologize for it," Pete said. "But only one choice is going to allow you to keep all your teeth."

Anne turned her unbelieving gaze on Pete. He got the feeling she wasn't used to anybody taking her part. If that was true, it was too bad. She was a nice young woman. Any fool could see she tried hard to be liked. Probably nobody had thought to do anything but make her feel like a burden. He'd have to see what he could do about that before he left.

"I mean she's a girl," Belser said. "She's not old enough to be a lady."

"But you're sure she will become a lady the minute she's old enough, whenever that is." Every eye in the room was on Belser. The silence seemed to stretch a little too long. "I don't think Anne heard your answer," Pete said.

"Probably. You never can tell about women," Belser said.

"That's a cheap apology," Pete said. "It wouldn't have cost you a penny to say something nice. Everybody would have thought well of you. Now all we see is a mean-spirited, poor loser who'll say anything he can to get a ranch he never had any right to in the first place."

"I had more right to it than you do!" Belser exploded. "I don't know who you are or how you got here—"

"I'm Pete Warren. I got here on horseback. I intended to arrive by wagon, but somebody burned that after they tried to kill me."

"You're not Peter!" Belser shouted. "You probably killed him and showed up in his place."

"Don't be ridiculous, Belser." Dolores spoke for the first time. "He couldn't possibly know as much as he does and be anyone but Peter."

"Pete," Anne said. "He wants us to call him Pete now."

"How do you explain his wound?" Dolores asked Belser.

"How do I know? Maybe Peter shot him before he got killed."

"And he somehow knew enough to find his way here on the last day before he would lose the ranch," Dolores said.

"He—"

"And he knew who I was," Anne pointed out. "He rescued me from Uncle Frank before anybody had a chance to say a word to him."

That wasn't true. Pete had talked to one of Bill Mason's cowhands, but Pete didn't figure it would help his case to say that.

"Anybody could have told him who you were," Belser said. "But we don't know anything about him. Nobody's asked him any questions. Peter would be fool enough to let anybody walk into his camp, tell them just about anything they wanted to know. He'd be easy to kill. I say we see just how much this one knows."

"I don't see why you can't wait for his papers," Dolores said.

"That'll take weeks, maybe months," Belser said. "He could have the herd sold and be gone with the money before we find out who he is."

"I'm not going to sit here answering a bunch of questions," Pete said. "However, I will promise not to spend any money on myself until I can prove who I am." That wasn't a problem. He didn't plan to use the money anyway.

"I don't see why you should have to wait," Anne said.

"I'm not going anywhere," Pete said. "I don't mind."

"You're tricking us," Belser said.

"How could I be doing that?" Pete asked, beginning to get irritated.

"I don't know, but you're not Peter. You know you can't prove you are. So if you're willing to wait, there must be a trick somewhere."

Pete lost patience. "The only *trick* is pretending I don't mind putting up with you. I *do* mind, and I'm not

89

going to continue doing it. If you can't stop throwing up your crazy theories every time you see me, you can move into the bunkhouse and eat with the crew. If you still insist on running your mouth, you can clear off the place."

"You saying you'll fire me?"

"I don't know why the old man put up with you, but you're not related to me. I don't owe you anything."

"Peter would never call Uncle Carl *the old man*."

"I've done a lot of things different since I left here."

"Like going broke," Belser added, sneering.

"Not quite, but that needn't concern you. Just remember what I said. Now, if you'll excuse us, ladies, Eddie and I have plans to make."

"When are you planning to send for those papers?" Belser asked.

"Anne and I are going into Big Bend tomorrow. I'll send off a telegram then."

"You didn't say anything about going into town," Anne said. She looked surprised but pleased.

"What with having to close down that windbag," Pete said, scowling at Belser, "I haven't had a chance. You don't mind, do you? I'm depending on you to show me around, introduce me to people, warn me who to watch out for."

"How would she know that?" Belser asked. "She doesn't have any more sense than a goose."

"You have a very short memory. I guess I'm going to have to help you lengthen it a bit."

"What are you talking about?" Belser asked, looking uneasy.

"I told you to be careful what you said about my

wife. Comparing her to a goose is not my idea of being careful."

"Everybody's always saying something like that."

"I don't like it. Neither does Anne. Don't do it again."

Pete pushed back his chair. He wanted to get out of the room before he had another conflict with Belser. "You ready?" he said to Eddie.

"Sure."

"How about dessert?" Dolores asked.

"Sounds good," Pete said. "How about bringing some with coffee in about an hour?"

"You really going to throw Belser off the place?" Eddie asked as they left the dining room.

"If he keeps up this nonsense about me being an imposter."

"He's angry he didn't get the place. He's just trying to make trouble."

"He's trying to do more than that. After being nearly killed once, I don't mean to set myself up for a second try. If he doesn't stop, he leaves."

"You can't think Belser shot you."

"Somebody did. Who had more reason to want me dead?"

"He never left the ranch."

"It was a hired thing. Two men came after me."

"You never said that."

"Nobody asked."

"Did you see them?"

"They shot me from the dark. I didn't regain consciousness until the next day."

"Then how do you know—"

91

"I followed their trail."

"Do you know where they went?"

"I know they came this way. Their trail disappeared after that."

Eddie looked stunned. "Nobody here would do a thing like that."

"Not even for money?"

"No. That'd be cold-blooded murder."

"It almost was. Or do you doubt I was shot?"

"No. You didn't get the scar on your forehead falling off a horse."

"Keep that in mind when you defend Belser. Now, let's see about organizing this roundup."

Anne was sitting up in bed when Pete entered the bedroom. Almost immediately she put her arms under the covers, pulled the covers up to her shoulders, and slid down in the bed until she was barely visible. Obviously she wanted to draw as little attention to herself as possible.

Pete had no intention of mistreating a woman who not only wasn't his wife but whom he would leave before long. However, her acting like he was the closest thing to a marauding savage left a sour taste in his mouth. Why was she so reluctant even to come close to her husband in the bedroom? She hadn't seemed frightened of him downstairs. He wished she'd stop looking at him as if she expected him to ravish her on the spot. He didn't know what she knew of men, but if Belser and old Clyde were examples of the available men, she probably had good reason to expect just that.

"You sure you don't mind going into town with me

tomorrow?" he asked as he started to undress. He might not take advantage of her, but he refused to hide in the bathroom. She might as well get used to what a man looked like, at least in his underwear. Then when she finally did get married, maybe she wouldn't act like a scared rabbit.

But there was no denying she was a pretty woman. He'd always had a weakness for women with dark hair and black eyes. It made them seem mysterious, dangerous. Not that Anne was either mysterious or dangerous. But you never knew what was going on in a woman's mind.

"No. I'd like to go to town," she said.

"We'll have to get up early."

"I don't mind."

"Before dawn."

"I know."

"I forgot to ask if you can ride."

"No."

"Why not?"

"Uncle Carl said ladies don't ride horses."

Hell, they'd have to use the buckboard. That would take all day. "Do people know I was coming, that we were married by proxy? Belser's bound to have told somebody I'm an imposter. It won't be nice for you if people believe him."

"I told everybody we were married. It was the only way to keep Uncle Frank from forcing me to go with Cyrus."

"We're not going to be expected to go to parties or anything like that, are we?" He'd just thought of that. The prospect was unnerving.

"No."

He was relieved, but she might as well have been talking about buying a horse or a new blanket for all the emotion she showed. Being shy and nervous and unsure about what to do with a new husband was one thing. Appearing to have no emotional involvement with him was quite another. Why should she defend him so fiercely against Belser's accusations unless she was more worried about her position on the ranch than she was about whether he was Peter or an imposter? Could she have married Peter for his money and position without loving him at all?

He didn't want to believe that. He liked Anne even though she wasn't his type. She was too young, too innocent, too shy. He liked a more mature type, a bold, assertive woman who knew what she wanted and wasn't afraid to go after it. He didn't really know what to do with a timid girl.

He didn't want to believe she was so mercenary.

"Do you know a lot of people in this town?"

The question seemed to make her nervous. "No. I never went to town very much. Uncle Carl said a woman's place was on the ranch."

That didn't make a lot of sense to Pete. Why had Carl kept her out of sight? Maybe that was why she was so shy.

"I like to see women in town," Pete said. "I like to see them all dressed up, sashaying up and down the boardwalk, looking smart, knowing all the men are staring at them with their tongues hanging out."

"Nobody would stare at me."

He could tell she was hoping he'd contradict her.

"Everybody would stare at you, especially if I bought you a fancy dress."

"Would you do that?"

Her excitement was palpable. Pete hadn't thought a thing about dresses or parading up and down the boardwalk. He was just talking to fill up the silence, but it was clear he'd hit upon something important to Anne.

"I'll buy you two or three dresses," he said. Hell, he didn't mind spending old Carl's money, as long as he wasn't spending it on himself.

"One would be enough," Anne said, but the excitement in her eyes was contagious.

"We won't stop at dresses," Pete said. "There's all kinds of things a female needs. I'll ask one of the women in the store to take you under her wing. She'll know what to do."

"No, you've got to come."

He didn't know what he'd said that was wrong. All the brightness, the anticipation, had disappeared to be replaced by something awfully close to fear. "I'm no good with female things," he protested.

"You've got to come. I won't know what to do."

He didn't either, but for some reason, she was afraid to go by herself. Probably more of Uncle Carl's belief that women weren't worth very much. He'd have to see what he could do about that before he left. Anne was much too nice to spend the rest of her life being afraid of her shadow. She was liable to let some man walk all over her.

"Okay, but I'll stand in the corner."

"That's okay. Just as long as you're there."

He wondered what she thought he could accomplish by his presence. Or prevent. He'd have to find out. He didn't like the idea that she would marry Peter without feeling anything for him, but he liked it even less that she was afraid to go anywhere alone.

This might turn out to his advantage, though. He'd have even more time to talk to her, learn enough of his own history to keep from falling into trouble. Everybody knew women couldn't think of what they were saying when they were looking at clothes. She'd be liable to say all kinds of things she'd never remember. Yes, a shopping trip with Anne just might be the thing to save his scalp.

Pete had expected Anne's spirits to rise as they got closer to town. Instead, she got quieter, hardly speaking unless he asked her a direct question. She no longer seemed excited about the prospect of buying new dresses. Pete had never known any woman not to be interested in clothes. Even Isabelle had a distinct weakness for shopping. Jake used to say she only wanted to know how much money he made each time he sold a herd so she would know how much money she could spend.

"You not feeling good?" he asked.

She looked startled by his question. "I'm feeling fine."

"You're about as talkative as a corpse."

"I don't have anything to say."

"You chattered like a magpie when we first started. You tired?" They'd been in the buckboard for nearly six hours. Pete was so used to working long hours in the goldfields, he didn't realize a woman used to staying in the house all day would probably be exhausted by now. "You *are* tired, aren't you?"

"A little."

"You mean you're about to keel over. Why didn't you ask me to stop?"

"That wouldn't help. It would just take longer to get to town, and you wouldn't like it."

Did he come across that ruthless? "I'm not used to being around women. I don't know what they think, what they feel, or what they need. You'll have to tell me."

"Is that why your store failed?"

"Huh?"

"Not understanding women. I would imagine women did most of the shopping. From what I can see, men don't like it much."

"Probably." He wondered if he'd ever learn to think before he opened his mouth. This business of pretending to be somebody else was tricky. Just as soon as he could find those men and get his money back, he was going to light a shuck to anywhere south of Wyoming Territory.

Only abandoning Anne still bothered him. Getting the papers that proved she was married to Peter was the only way she'd be safe. But he couldn't even be sure she'd be safe then. Women like Anne needed a man to take care of them, especially in a place like Wyoming. Men generally wouldn't work for a woman. And if she found one who would, he'd probably steal from her. He ought to stay until she got proof she was Peter's widow. Then, before he left, he could make sure she had a good foreman. Of course it meant he'd have to actually run the ranch until then. It wasn't something he'd planned to do—he'd vowed to have nothing to do with cows when he left Texas—but it wouldn't be hard. Jake had taught him well. He might even like it enough to stay.

What man wouldn't like stepping into ownership of a huge ranch, becoming a wealthy man overnight? He didn't mind the work. It couldn't be harder than working in the goldfields. Having his own bathroom made it look even better.

A man could get used to being rich. Peter Warren was dead. Belser didn't deserve the ranch. As far as Pete was concerned, if he decided to stay, he wouldn't be stealing anything from anybody. His conscience tried to tell him otherwise, but he wouldn't listen.

But even as the idea occurred to him, he knew it wouldn't work. First, he didn't want to be married. He liked his freedom. After a dozen years of wandering where he wanted, doing whatever he liked, he wasn't about to give it up for the shackles of married life. Second, if he did want to get married, he didn't want an innocent like Anne, even though she was very pretty. He liked strong women. Last of all, he wanted to find the men with his money.

He couldn't put off looking for the men much longer. Even though he was certain Belser had hired them to do the killing, he didn't want to give them time to leave the area with his money.

"You got some friends in town?" he asked Anne.

"No."

"I thought all women were friends. There aren't enough of you to have enemies."

"I don't have any enemies," Anne said, her eyes downcast. "I don't know anybody because neither Mama nor I went to town much after Papa died. It's too far, and Uncle Carl didn't want to bother with us. He said he could buy us anything we needed."

"I suppose that's why you have so many ugly clothes."

Her smile was faint. "He didn't think a woman should draw attention to herself."

"What have clothes got to do with that?"

"Uncle Carl thought a woman ought to work hard for her keep. He thought nice clothes made women think too much of themselves, set too much importance on what they wanted, what they thought. He said if a woman had nice clothes, she wouldn't work very hard for fear she'd mess them up."

"I'm surprised he ever got married."

"Uncle Carl was very rich. Lots of women wanted to marry him."

It made him smile to think what Isabelle would have said about such a man.

"Do you find that funny?" Anne asked.

"No. Just thinking about something else." They were approaching the town of Big Bend. Not that it deserved such a grandiose name. The bend was in a creek, and it was little more than a hook to the right. Besides, there wasn't enough water in the creek to deserve the name.

"You hungry?" Pete asked.

Anne shook her head, but Pete didn't believe her. They'd been too hurried to do more than get a few swallows of coffee before leaving.

"Well, I'm starving. You ought to eat more. Maybe you wouldn't be so little."

That remark seemed to upset her. He had to be careful what he said. She appeared to be sensitive on a whole lot of subjects. He figured that meant somebody had been picking on her for a long time. He didn't like that. It wasn't much of a man who went around picking on a woman to make himself feel big.

"We'll see about getting a room in a hotel first. I'm just about ready to get down from this buckboard. How about you?"

She nodded with a weak smile. "I must admit I haven't ridden in one all that much."

"I'll fix that. No point in your being stuck in the house all the time. You ought to get out, get to know the ranch. How would you know what to do if something happened to me and you suddenly had to run it?"

She looked stunned, as though the idea had never occurred to her. "I don't know. I guess I'd let Eddie run it."

"I'm sure Eddie's a great foreman, but Jake says you ought never to let anybody know more about your own business than you do. Unless you want to lose it."

"Who's Jake?"

"Isabelle's husband. Remember, the pair that adopted all those orphans?"

"Oh. You talk like he's somebody you knew."

Clearly he was never going to learn to think before he opened his mouth. He was just going to have to be more nimble at inventing lies. He hoped he could remember all of them. "I feel like I know him. My friend, the one from Texas, talked about him all the time."

"Oh. I thought you might have gone to Texas yourself, maybe met him there."

Why hadn't he thought of that? No reason why this Peter fella had to stay closed up in a hardware store in Illinois for all those years. Besides, he lost the store, didn't he? Maybe he was off somewhere else.

"I did, for a while. That's where I learned about ranches. Of course, Texas ranches are different from ranches in Wyoming."

"I thought all cows were the same."

"Cows are. The land isn't."

Before Pete had time to explain, the sound of a bullet splintering the wood floor of the buckboard was followed instantly by the boom of a rifle. Somebody was trying to kill him again!

Chapter Six

"Get down!" Pete shouted as a second bullet smashed into the buckboard. Anne sat frozen on the seat. Pete thought he was the target, but he couldn't be certain. He pushed Anne from the seat onto the wooden floor. She tumbled to her right, hitting her head. He hoped she wasn't hurt, but right now he was more concerned about getting off this trail alive. If they could just get out of rifle range, they'd be safe.

Pete dropped to the floor and whipped up the reins. The horses didn't need much encouragement to break into a gallop. He looked around as best he could, but a thick growth of juniper covered the low hills on either side of the trail. He could see no sign of the rifleman.

Rifle fire followed them along the trail, but the bushwhacker didn't hit the buckboard again. Still, Pete didn't pull the horses out of a hard gallop until he was a thousand yards down the trail. He climbed up on the seat so he could look back, but as expected, he didn't see anyone following. He pulled back on the reins, and the horses gradually slowed. When they finally came to a halt, he reached down to help Anne back up on the seat.

"Are you hurt?" he asked.

She shook her head. She hadn't moved from where she had fallen. Pete lifted her back onto the seat. All the color had drained from her face. She didn't look scared. She looked petrified.

"Let me see where you hit your head," Pete said.

She didn't move. Pete took her face in his hands and gently turned her head. He didn't see a bruise or broken skin. Apparently her hat had protected her.

"Does your head hurt?"

"No."

Her voice sounded small, unsteady. She turned to look at the two holes in the floor of the buggy.

"That man was trying to kill you, wasn't he?" she asked.

"It looked that way," Pete said. And he would give odds that if he had been killed, the bushwacker would have then turned his fire on Anne. As Peter's wife, she stood to inherit the ranch on his death.

"He came very close."

"Naw. Anybody good with a rifle would have gotten me with the first shot." Which told him that the bushwhacker wasn't one of the two men who'd killed Peter and nearly killed him. Those men had been deadly accurate.

103

"But why would they want to kill you?" Anne asked.

"To get the ranch."

"But it would be my ranch if you died."

"They probably think you'd be so anxious to leave, you'd sell it for a low price. You've got the best grazing land in the area. Any one of fifty people could want it." He didn't want her to realize how close she might be to becoming a target.

"If they killed me, they wouldn't have to buy it, would they?"

"I expect they would prefer to buy. Much less trouble that way."

"Then why don't they offer *you* money?"

"I don't know. Maybe they think I saw them when they tried to kill me the first time."

"Did you?"

"No. It was dark, and they were coming up to the campfire. I didn't see anything but shadows." Boots and spurs, but nothing he could remember. He started the horses moving again. "We're safe now. He won't try again."

"What are you going to do?" she asked.

"Go on into town, get a hotel room, and eat. I don't know about you, but I'm starved."

"You're just going to forget it?"

"No, but there's nothing I can do about it. I can't go after that man. I don't have a horse. Besides, he'd be gone long before I got there. There's no use telling the sheriff. He won't know any more than we do."

"But you've got to tell the sheriff. Owen is a good man. He'll go after him."

Pete knew there was nothing to go after. The ground was covered with needles under the junipers. There wouldn't be any prints. If the bushwhacker picked up his spent shells, there wouldn't be any evidence that there'd even been a bushwhacker. Except for the holes in the buckboard.

"Okay, I'll tell the sheriff. But first let's find a hotel so you can lie down and rest. You're worn out from riding in this contraption. Having to dodge bullets can't have made you feel too chipper."

Her laughter was unexpected.

"No, not chipper, but I'm also not scared to death. I thought I would be, but I can't be scared with you acting like you get shot at every day. Does this sort of thing happen a lot in Illinois?"

Not in Illinois, but it did in the goldfields. "No, but it's happened a lot since I got to Wyoming." He had been so busy worrying about her, he'd forgotten Peter would probably be having a fainting spell about now.

"You must have the luck of the Irish."

"Sure do. Got it straight from an Irishman, my old partner, Sean O'Ryan. He said I'd need it to survive without him."

"I didn't know you had a partner."

Damn! Him and his big mouth. "I didn't for long. Now it's time to stop asking me questions and decide on a hotel."

The town of Big Bend owed its existence to an army fort two miles away. Saloons and houses of prostitution stood side by side with merchants, blacksmiths, and lawyers' offices. The town boasted two banks but no church. All the business was congregated on either side of the main street. Private homes occupied the few streets that fell away from the main street. The Big Horn mountains in the background formed a beautiful backdrop.

They'd reached the Grand Union Hotel. It looked like a decent place. "This hotel all right with you?"

"I wouldn't know. I've never been here."

"Well, if you don't like it, we can go someplace else, but it looks fine to me. As soon as we get our rooms, you can freshen up while I look after the horses. After that we'll get something to eat. Then we'll see about doing some business."

"Won't somebody at the hotel take care of the horses for you?"

"That's something else Jake used to say. Always take care of your own horses, and you'll never be left stranded."

Anne seemed to have heard enough of Jake and Isabelle that she no longer questioned references to them. Now he had to figure out why Anne seemed to be drawing into herself. She was small enough already. If she kept shrinking, she'd soon disappear.

Pete put his arms out to lift her down from the buckboard. His hands almost met around her waist. She put her hands on his shoulders, leaned her weight against him. He felt her tremble. He couldn't understand why she should be afraid. Certainly not of him.

He, however, would have to start being a little afraid of himself. He was beginning to find her too attractive. She was tiny and she was young, but she was a woman. A very pretty woman. He would have to be dead not to think her pretty, not to think of doing more than treating her like a brother.

He'd do better if he didn't let himself think about that.

He picked up the saddlebags he'd borrowed from Uncle Carl's closet and headed toward the hotel.

The lobby was typical. A lounge area was to the right as they entered. Overstuffed chairs and tables were covered with magazines, a few books, and an occasional newspaper. A profusion of spittoons and cuspidors indicated that the patrons were mostly male. The desk was on the left, the stairs just beyond that. A restaurant at the back of the hotel could be seen through a set of doors with glass panes.

Pete walked up to the desk. "I want a room for the night," he told the man behind the desk. "Make it a nice one. I just got married. This is my wife's first trip to town."

The man, probably on the shady side of forty, smiled at Anne with a look that in other circumstances Pete would have called a leer. "Your wedding night, is it?"

"No, but it's close enough."

Anne blushed rosily, but at least she didn't turn white. That was an improvement.

"I can give you number six," the clerk said.

"Does it have a private bath? I don't want to be sharing with every stranger on the hall."

"It has its own bath," the clerk said, offended. "It's our best room. It's on the back corner, so the street noise won't disturb you." He grinned broadly and directed another look at Anne. Much more, and Pete was going to have to have a talk with him. "How many nights will you be staying?"

"Just one."

The clerk looked disappointed. Pete took the key from his resisting grip.

"We'll take good care of it. Now where do I find it?"

"It's on the second floor," the clerk said, clearly annoyed. "Take the stairs to the first landing. It'll be at the end of the hall."

"Come on," Pete said to Anne. "I'm starved."

It took only a matter of minutes to reach their room. "Not bad," Pete said when he unlocked the door. "I've stayed in a lot worse."

He was pleased to see that Anne appeared impressed with the room. A huge mahogany bed competed for dominance with an equally huge wardrobe. Two chairs with a table and lamp provided an inviting corner for relaxation. Tables with extra lamps flanked the bed. Pete dropped the saddlebags on the bed and opened the bathroom door. He was pleased to see a washstand and bathtub with a mahogany surround.

"I'm off to see about the horses and drop in on the sheriff," he said to Anne when he came back into the room. "I'll leave you to wash the trail dust from your face." He rubbed his finger along her cheek. "Fix yourself up pretty. I want to show you off to all the locals. Sort of rub it in. After all, one of them could have caught you if they hadn't been so slow."

Anne watched the door close behind Pete, her hand on her cheek where he had touched her. So many conflicting emotions bombarded her mind that she couldn't think clearly.

She was still shaken by the attack on the road. It was one thing for Pete to tell her he'd been shot. She could even empathize with some of the suffering he had endured while his wound healed, but it was all remote, unreal, something she'd heard about. The shots this morning had been real. There was nothing imaginary or remote about them. In case she forgot, she had only to look at the holes in the buckboard to remember how close they'd come to being killed.

She found it difficult to think of herself as being in the middle of a murderous plot to take the ranch from Pete. Nothing like this had happened on the Tumbling T since she'd been born. Uncle Carl's rule had been supreme. Now Uncle Carl was dead and someone had twice tried to kill Pete.

Only they had failed. Pete was still alive. She found that hard to explain.

The Peter she remembered would never have had the strength to get on a horse and stay on, conscious, until he reached someone who could care for him. The Peter she remembered would have panicked if anyone had shot at him. He certainly wouldn't have shoved her to the bottom of the buckboard and calmly driven to safety. Neither would he have known when they were out of rifle range. He would have raced all the way into town.

The horrible suspicion that Pete couldn't be Peter reared its hideous head once again. How could Pete be completely different from the man she remembered and still be Peter?

But he wasn't completely different. She had adored Peter because he treated her kindly, listened to her, never acted like she wasn't there. Pete did that, too. He'd promised to buy her new clothes. He'd promised to give her time to get to know him better. He'd defended her against Belser. He was just as kind and thoughtful as Peter ever had been.

And she liked Pete a lot, just as much as she liked Peter. She wasn't a fickle woman. She couldn't possibly have loved Peter for as long as she had and then transfer her affections to a complete stranger. No, if nothing else should convince her, her feeling for Pete should tell her that he really was Peter. True, he'd changed in many ways. He must have stayed in Texas a long time. That probably accounted for his losing the hardware store.

A wave of heat swept over her, and she felt terribly disloyal for doubting Pete. He'd done everything she'd ever hoped he would do. And more. He'd treated her like Cinderella, pulled her out of the corner and set her at the head of the table. She ought to be ashamed to consider Belser's accusations for even a minute. She made a promise to herself right then that she'd never do it again. She was a very lucky woman. She ought to be intelligent enough not to throw away her good fortune.

She looked around her at the luxurious hotel room and felt uneasy. She wasn't used to being the focus of attention. Coming to Big Bend with her new husband, she was certain to attract attention wherever she went. She should have stayed at the ranch. She felt comfortable there. Except for Belser, everybody liked her, accepted her as she was. It felt like home. She was happy there.

She didn't know anybody here. She could recognize a lot of people—her father and Uncle Carl had brought many men to the house while they were alive, but she didn't really know them. And they didn't know her. She didn't think they were going to be too happy about an Indian girl marrying the owner of the biggest ranch in the Powder River basin. But their reluctance to accept her would be nothing compared to their wives' coldness.

Many white men had taken up with Indian women, especially in the early days when trappers came to the mountains or when the first of the ranchers grabbed land in what was Indian Territory. Her maternal grandfather had been a French trapper with noble connections. He had taken up with a beautiful Crow woman, then deserted her when he returned to France. Anne's father and Uncle Frank were the only survivors of a New Orleans family that lost everything during the War Between the States. Her father had come West to start over again. Her uncle had come, too, bringing his hatred and his lust to regain the wealth and power of his youth.

He had been infuriated when his brother married a half-breed Crow woman. It didn't matter that she was the niece of a French count. All her life Anne had been told she was worthless, a *breed*, that her mother was nothing more than the spawn of a whore.

Despite her black hair and eyes, Anne had inherited her looks from her French grandfather. She knew she was pretty. She knew because men lusted after her. But they wanted only her body. To them she was still a breed, someone to use and discard.

Her father had met up with Carl when he came to Wyoming, had helped Carl establish his ranch. As a reward, he had been Carl's foreman until his death. Anne had been born on the ranch, considered it her home. She was there when Peter's family came to spend those two years with Uncle Carl.

Peter was different. They became best friends right away. He didn't care that she was part Indian. He got angry when his brother Gary called her a breed. They got into fights. Peter always lost. His brother was older, stronger, and a better fighter. But Anne loved Peter for defending her.

Even after his family went back to Illinois, she didn't forget Peter. When her uncle started threatening to sell her, she thought of Peter. He'd liked her and had always been kind. If they married, she would take care of him. She would never have to leave the ranch, the only home she'd ever known.

It had seemed the perfect plan—until Peter arrived. Not Peter, Pete! Now everything felt different. From the first moment she'd been attracted to him in a way she'd never felt about Peter. She wondered if this was the way her grandmother had felt when she left her people to go live with the French trapper. Surely it wasn't the way normal, respectable women felt toward their husbands. It was too disturbing, too uncomfortable, too . . . She wasn't sure what it was. But she knew it was going to make it very difficult to continue sleeping in the same bed with Pete.

* * *

"It's good to get the money stuff straight," Pete said to Anne as they walked out of the bank. The owner of the bank had been reluctant to advance Pete any money at first. But Pete's assurance that he wouldn't authorize any major expenditures until he received his papers relieved the banker's worry. "Now we have to find a lawyer's office. Know anybody to recommend?"

"How about him?" Anne said, pointing to the office of John Langley. It was across the street. "He's one of the men who used to visit Uncle Carl."

"Know anybody else?" The office was on the other side of a street ankle-deep in dust and horse droppings. It would be impossible for Anne to cross on foot.

"No."

"Then I guess I'll have to carry you across."

"No!" Anne sounded startled.

"You can't walk. There's nothing wrong with a man carrying his wife across the street."

"But you're—"

"Strong enough to carry two of you," Pete said as he scooped Anne up. "You don't weigh more than a newborn calf."

Anne had never been picked up by a man. The sensation was beyond words. She wrapped her arms around Pete's neck and held on tight. He acted as though she didn't weigh anything. He just picked her up and marched right into the street. At first Anne was too startled to do anything but hang on. But once she got the courage to look around, she noticed two smiling soldiers.

"Nice package you've got there," one of them called out.

113

"You going to unwrap it as soon as you get home?" the other asked. They both burst out laughing.

"Pay no attention," Pete said. "They're just jealous."

Anne couldn't believe that. Nobody had ever been jealous of her before. But the idea intrigued her. Warmth flooded through her. She hoped he was right.

"Here we go," Pete said as he set her on her feet on the boardwalk. "And not a spot on you."

"What about you?"

"That's what boots are for. Now, about this lawyer."

Anne looked around and came face-to-face with two women staring at Pete. For a moment she didn't understand their look. Then it hit her. They were admiring Pete, just as men admired women. She could hardly believe it. The notion was so new. Living in a nearly all-male society, she'd never had the opportunity to see women ogling men.

Then they looked at her. She had no trouble telling the women were jealous of her. It wasn't something she could explain. She just knew. She couldn't recall even one time in her life when anyone had been jealous of her. It made her feel almost like a real person.

"Are you going to answer me or not?"

Anne came out of her fog. "What? I didn't hear you."

"I asked if you remembered the name of my lawyer in Illinois. I guess I'm still suffering from that concussion. I'm sure I'll remember in a few days, but I don't want to have to come back to town."

"Of course I know his name. He sent me the marriage papers I had to sign."

"Good. We'll get him to send us copies of our marriage certificate. Then there won't be any question of my being an imposter. I don't want anybody disputing my claim to the ranch."

Anne watched and listened as Pete explained to the lawyer what had happened, what he wanted, and how to go about getting it. He said he wanted confirmation that Anne and he were married sent by telegraph. The sooner that question was cleared up, the better. He wanted certified copies of all the relevant papers as soon as it could be arranged. He also sent a letter to a man she didn't know. She'd heard her father and Uncle Carl speak of Monty Randolph. They said he was one of the most important cattlemen in Wyoming.

Pete wrote that letter in his own hand. He said it was personal.

He also wrote another paper he said was personal. Anne didn't object. She'd never expected to be privy to any of the business he transacted.

She had never been allowed to be present when Carl conducted business, but she was impressed with Pete. He seemed to know exactly what he wanted and how to get it. He didn't let the lawyer intimidate him. And every time the man had an objection, Pete found a way around it. She couldn't help admiring him. He was so capable.

And so attractive.

She really shouldn't think so much about his looks. It made her feel like a vain and shallow female. Everyone knew that a person's looks often had nothing to do with their inner qualities. Everyone also knew that handsome men and beautiful women were vain, expecting to be flattered, pampered, and spoiled. But Pete wasn't like that.

Besides, no female could ignore a man as handsome as Pete.

"Now let's go see about buying you some new clothes."

She'd been so busy with her own thoughts, she hadn't noticed that Pete had finished his business and risen from his chair. He whisked her out of the lawyer's office and headed her toward the largest clothing emporium in Big Bend.

"I don't need any new dresses," she said.

"Nonsense. Everything in your wardrobe is dowdy or looks like it was made for a little girl. You're a woman, and you ought to dress like one."

That thought pleased Anne, but uneasiness continued to be her overriding emotion.

"No one ever comes out to the ranch. It won't matter what I wear."

"We'll soon have parties with lots of important guests," Pete said. "People will come just to look at you."

"Me!"

"You're very pretty now. I might even say extremely pretty. But this is nothing compared to what you're going to be in five or ten years. You'll be the most beautiful woman in the Wyoming Territory."

"Me!"

"Don't tell me nobody has ever told you that you were pretty."

"Yes, but—"

"You still have a girlish look now. Simple and

pretty, exactly the kind of look that matures into true beauty. I've seen it happen before. I know. You'll have men coming by all the time just to sit and stare at you. I'll have to hire extra hands just to keep them off."

She couldn't imagine anything so preposterous. No one had ever paid that kind of attention to her. Cyrus wanted her, but he was a vile, lecherous old man who would take advantage of any young, defenseless female. She'd noticed the cowhands sneaking a peek at her occasionally, but she didn't put much store in that. The poor boys went whole weeks without seeing a female. It was only natural they would stare when they got back to the ranch. She was sure they stared at Dolores just as often.

"I'll buy you a bigger mirror," Pete said. "Obviously the one you have isn't very good."

"I'd like that." Her mirror was quite small and covered with spots where the silver had turned black. It was impossible to see more than a small portion of her face at a time. She had asked Carl for a new one. He had said it was a useless extravagance.

"How many dresses do you think you'll need? Three? Five?"

The idea of having five new dresses astounded her. She'd always made her own clothes. She wasn't very good at it, but she accepted the necessity. However, it was very difficult to get anything but the plainest material, virtually impossible to get buttons and other ornamental things to make the dress look different, special.

"I'm sure one will be quite enough."

"Only one?"

"Well, maybe two, if they're not too expensive."

"Come on. Let's see what they've got."

Anne had been nervous, even a little frightened, about entering this store, which called itself The Emporium. But she forgot everything at the sight of the dresses and hundreds of other items for sale. She couldn't believe other women took all of this for granted. She wandered down aisles where counters groaned under bolts of more beautiful cottons, linens, wools, taffetas, satins and silks that she'd ever imagined. The selection of hats, pocketbooks, shoes, gloves, stockings and undergarments seemed to be endless. In one corner of the store drawers contained an endless assortment of buttons, ribbons, buckles, beads, fans, colored silk thread, lace, feathers of all kinds, and appliques—more things than she'd ever imagined could be used to decorate a dress.

"Do you see anything you like?" Pete asked.

The choice was too great. Anne couldn't possibly make up her mind quickly. There were too many things to consider. She could spend days in the shop and still not see everything.

"I don't know where to begin."

"Let's start with a dress. How about that grayish-bluish thing over there? It looks rather nice."

One of the clerks approached them. Her manner was cold. She didn't even look at Anne.

"Are you certain you're in the right place?" she asked.

Anne felt ice in her veins. Instinctively she reached out to grasp Pete's arm.

"Do you sell women's clothes and stuff here?" Pete asked.

"Yes. We have the widest selection in the Territory."

"Then we're in the right place. I want that dress over there."

"I think the hardware store down the street would be more suitable for your needs."

"I'll be the judge of what I need," Pete replied.

Anne could tell he was getting short of temper. "Maybe we'd better go," she said quietly. "I don't think I like that dress all that much anyway."

"I do," Pete said. "Besides, I remember passing that hardware store. I didn't see a thing I liked."

"The Emporium caters to the wives of the army officers and the families of the wealthy ranchers," the woman said.

"Then we're in the right place," Pete said. "I'm a wealthy rancher and she's my wife. Now get that dress down. And while you're at it, bring down a few more suitable for a pretty young wife, something pink or yellow or one of those bright colors women are so fond of wearing when they go to parties."

"I can't imagine that your wife would be going to any parties around here," the clerk said.

Anne felt Pete's body stiffen.

"Do you mean something in particular by that, or are you just naturally a rude, vicious old biddy?"

The woman looked as though he'd slapped her.

"I mean people around here aren't in the habit of inviting Indians into their homes."

Chapter Seven

"What the hell do you mean by that?" Pete thundered.

"I mean your wife, if she really *is* your wife, is an Indian."

The woman couldn't have shocked Pete any more if she'd pulled a gun from under her apron and shot him. *An Indian!* Anne couldn't be an Indian. He'd have known by the time he came within ten feet of her. No one could hide anything like that from him.

"You're either blind or insane," Pete said. "I don't care which. But if you go around spreading rumors about my wife, you'll wish you were anywhere but here."

The woman turned indignant and appeared ready to blister Pete with her reply.

"No point in blowing up like a toad, even if you're as spiteful as one. Now get down those dresses. And if you don't do it on the double, I'll speak to your employer. Move!"

The order was so peremptory, so unexpected, that the woman jumped. It also brought another woman from the back of the store.

"Is there some problem?" she asked.

"Yes, there is. I came in here wanting to buy some clothes for my wife. Your clerk seems to feel she can tell Indians at a glance. She also seems to feel she won't serve them. Is that the policy of this establishment?"

The woman looked from Pete to the clerk to Anne and back to Pete.

"Our usual customers are the wives of the officers and soldiers at the fort," she said coolly. "Our clothes are chosen to suit their tastes and their pocketbooks. If your wife feels our goods will suit her, she's welcome to see anything she likes."

"Well, I like that gray dress. And we'd like to see several more in bright colors suitable for a young woman."

"Certainly. Judy, help me choose some dresses for the . . . you didn't give me your name, sir."

"I'm Pete Warren. This is my wife, Anne."

"We'll have several dresses for you to choose from in a moment, Mrs. Warren. Please look around to see if we have anything else that might interest you."

Pete was pleased to see the owner had put this Judy person in her place right off, but he didn't like the feel of things. The owner, whatever her name was, was as cold as a dead fish. And angry. Not in the way Judy was angry, all hot and turning red in the face. No, she was cold angry, the kind that never lets you forget it.

121

That didn't bother him much. Women were always getting upset over things men would hardly notice. But they'd upset Anne, and that made him angry.

"Don't let it bother you," he said when the two women had left. "I don't know what set that Judy woman off. Just because you have black eyes and black hair doesn't make you an Indian."

"But I am an Indian."

"What!"

The word exploded from him. He couldn't have stopped it if his life had depended on it. The one kind of human being he hated most in the world, and here he was pretending to be married to her, holding her arm, sleeping in the same bed with her.

"I'm a quarter Indian," Anne said. "My grandmother was a Crow."

He kept standing where he was, Anne still grasping his arm, a smile still pinned to her face. "It wouldn't matter if you were full Indian," he said finally. "You have a right to buy anything you want from any store."

His mouth was saying things he didn't want to say, things he didn't believe.

But Judy came back carrying the gray dress and something in pink. The undisguised anger in her eyes, the mottled red of her cheeks, the obvious effort she was making just to serve Anne made Pete furious. He didn't know why. He didn't understand it. He just knew he couldn't embarrass Anne in front of this poison-tongued clerk. The owner followed with two more dresses.

"We have to return to our ranch tomorrow," Pete

said. "Can you make any alterations in the dresses by then?"

"If they're not too extensive. Maybe your wife has a sewing machine and could do up the hems herself. Since she is rather short, they'll all have to be altered."

"Do you have a sewing machine?" Pete asked.

Anne nodded.

"Good. Try on as many dresses as you like. Look through all the rest of this stuff. Get yourself some of everything you need." Anne looked at him as though she couldn't believe he meant what he said. "No telling when we'll get back to town. This may have to last you for a whole year." He didn't care how much money she spent. It wasn't his.

He couldn't keep his mind on the dresses she put on for his approval or the coats, hats, blouses, or other endless items of clothing, enough to outfit half-a-dozen women. He said yes to everything because he didn't really see anything they showed him. He only saw the massacre when the Indians killed his parents, his brothers and sisters, everybody in the wagon train except himself. He wouldn't have escaped if he hadn't been crouched in a dry wash a short distance away taking care of nature's call.

He could still hear the battle cry of the Indians as they exploded from a dry wash on the other side of the trail, hear the screams of the victims as they fell, one after another, to the arrows, hatchets, spears, clubs of the Comanche who were determined the white man wouldn't take their land. He had cowered in that wash knowing there was nothing a child could do to stop the slaughter, knowing he would become a victim himself if they discovered him.

He'd hidden there for hours, long after night had shrouded the grisly scene in dark shadows. When he finally came out, it was to drive coyotes away from the bodies. All night long he stood watch, protecting what was left of his family.

Some hunters found him two days later. They buried his family and took him to the nearest town. They sold the wagons and their contents and gave the money to a family to take care of him. When the money ran out, the family turned him over to an orphanage.

He'd never been able to forget hiding in that wash, shaking with fear, not daring to cry in case one of the Indians might hear him, wanting to do something to help, knowing he couldn't. That helplessness had left him with a tremendous feeling of guilt that he hadn't somehow saved his family, guilt that he had somehow survived and they hadn't, guilt for being too afraid to move. It didn't matter that he *knew* he couldn't have done anything to help, *knew* they would have killed him if they'd found him. The guilt remained. No amount of reasoning, no broadened perspective that came with age, no accumulated knowledge that came with maturity had been able to get rid of it.

"You can't like everything I show you. You've got to choose something," Anne said.

Pete jerked his mind from the dark corridors of his past. "What?"

"You've said yes to everything I've shown you."

"Then take them all."

"That's nearly a dozen dresses. I can't possibly use that many."

The possibility of such a tremendous sale seemed to have gone a long way toward making the two women more willing to be cooperative. That was when Pete noticed the pile of shoes, purses, and dozens of other items, some of which he didn't recognize.

"Those yours, too?"

"Yes. You really must choose."

"Nonsense," Pete said, gathering his wits. "They're your clothes. You choose. Have them pack up anything you like. I'll settle the bill when I return."

He had to get away, if only for a few minutes.

"Where are you going?"

Fear—or was it panic—showed in her eyes.

"Outside to get some air. I've been closed up too long."

He forced himself to walk at a normal pace. He couldn't decide whom he was trying to protect, Anne or himself, but at this point he hardly cared.

"You look like you're escaping from an Indian attack."

Pete whirled to find himself face-to-face with the banker. "Just from an hour helping my wife shop for clothes," he replied.

The banker laughed. "That's nearly as lethal. I always make my wife take her sister."

"My wife has no sister. No mother, aunts, or cousins either."

"Then I'm afraid you're stuck."

No, he wasn't stuck. He had already sent for the papers that would prove Anne had married Peter before he was killed. The ranch would be hers. He didn't have to protect her any longer. He couldn't believe he'd defended her. He'd done *more* than defend her. He'd sprung to her defense with the eagerness of a medieval knight. He hated Indians. He always had. He refused to have anything to do with them. He—

His brother was an Indian.

He hadn't thought of Hawk like that in years. He used to attack him whenever he got the chance. Isabelle had threatened to bar him from the table if he didn't stop. Jake had sworn to chain him to the horse corral. But Pete had stopped *wanting* to attack Hawk. When? Why?

When he'd finally been able to separate Hawk from the Indians that killed his family, when he had come to terms with the fact that folks are individuals regardless of skin color. He'd done the same thing with the Indians he met in the mine fields, in the saloons, the Indians who warned him of the coming winter. He'd stopped hating them, too. He just thought he did because he'd been in the habit of saying "I hate Indians" for so long, he hadn't stopped to asked himself if he really did hate them.

But when had he stopped?

When he finally got over the need to feel shame, the need to blame himself for not being able to prevent the slaughter of his family. He was a child then, thinking as a child, feeling and reacting as a child, striking out against the world like a child. Jake and Isabelle had given him a home, love, understanding—had helped him realize he didn't have to keep on carrying the burden of that tragic morning. He could still grieve for the loss and horror of his family's murder, but the world was different now. He was different.

He was a man.

Pete felt the pressure inside him ease, then go away entirely. It felt good to let go. Now he could be proud that he'd defended Anne.

He walked over to a bench in front of The Emporium and eased himself down. His hat annoyed him. It didn't fit right. He was tired of wearing another man's clothes even if they did fit nearly as well as his own. And he was tired of looking like a dude. He was going to buy himself some proper clothes, and he wasn't going to let the fact that he didn't have any money of his own stop him. Peter owed him something for saving his wife from her uncle, and for saving his ranch from Belser. A few clothes didn't seem like a high price to pay.

"We're ready for you, Mr. Warren."

Pete turned to find the owner standing in the doorway of the emporium.

"Your wife has picked out all the things she wants."

"Then add them all up."

"We have."

When he walked back inside that building, Anne didn't look any different. She looked at him with the same almost childlike innocence, her big black eyes open wide, questioning, worrying, fearful. They seemed to say "You're my only shield. Without you I feel lost." He realized that her Indian ancestry made it all the more important for him to protect her. He had managed to overcome his prejudice, but others clearly hadn't.

"I'm afraid it's rather a lot," she said.

"How much?"

"More than two hundred dollars," Judy said, her tone giving the impression that it was a mortal sin that a woman like Anne should be allowed to squander such a large sum of money on herself.

"That's nothing compared to some of the bills Pearl used to run up."

"Who's Pearl?" Anne asked. "You never mentioned her."

"Sean's wife," he said, reaching into his coat pocket for his wallet. "I'll tell you about her later. How much exactly?"

"The total is $233.68."

Pete paid and waited for his change. "Wrap everything up and send it over to the hotel by tomorrow morning."

"I'll need a wagon to get all this over there," Judy said.

"Then get a wagon," Pete said as he turned and headed out of the store.

"Where are we going now?" Anne asked, hurrying after him.

"You're going back to the hotel to take a nap to make up for the sleep you lost getting up so early this morning. I'm going shopping."

Pete was late. Anne had probably been expecting him back hours ago. He swallowed the last of his whiskey and considered ordering another. No, better not. He had to keep his wits about him. If anybody found out who he really was, he'd be in jail five minutes later. He doubted he'd be able to make anyone believe he was only pretending to be Peter Warren until he could find his own money. Certainly not after spending so much of Uncle Carl's cash.

And if anyone found Peter's body—and that was always a possibility—he'd probably be hanged for murder.

He took his time walking back to the hotel. He was glad he'd had his new clothes sent back to the room. It would have been very awkward to carry such a large package through the streets. He entered the hotel at 7:08 P.M. He would be late for dinner. He hoped the dining room hadn't closed. He hoped Anne hadn't waited for him.

But she had.

She rose from the chair by the window when he entered the room. The vision that met his gaze caused him to stop in his tracks.

"You had me worried," she said in her soft voice. "I was afraid something might have happened to you."

His tongue lay like a dead thing in his mouth. He couldn't speak. She had always been pretty, but in his absence, she'd turned into a vision. She was beautiful. She was wearing the deep-red gown. He remembered her showing it to him, but he didn't remember seeing her wear it. Surely he couldn't have forgotten something like that.

"What have you done to yourself?" he managed to ask.

"You don't like it?" She was instantly fearful, crushed.

"No. It's very nice. In fact, it's more than very nice. It's stunning. But what happened? How did you change?"

He had the distinct feeling that a suave, clever man who understood women and knew how to flatter them would have stated that very differently.

"I met a woman here at the hotel who knew my mother. When I told her I'd bought all these new clothes and didn't know what to do with them, she offered to help me."

"Your hair. What have you done to it?"

"Do you like it?"

Didn't the woman have a mirror? Couldn't she tell she was beautiful? He walked across the room, took her by the shoulders, turned her around, and marched her toward the mirror that covered about two feet of one wardrobe door.

Always before she'd worn her long, heavy tresses in a loosely confined mantle down her back. Now they had been braided and coiled atop her head like a crown. A series of silver-tipped ivory combs he didn't remember held them in place. She looked regal, queenlike.

"Look at yourself," he ordered. "You don't have to ask my opinion to know you're beautiful. You came here looking like a pretty woman. You've turned yourself into a beautiful one."

Anne smiled broadly. "I hoped you'd be pleased. Mrs. Dean said you would be."

Pete wasn't very good at describing women's

clothes. His primary concern over the past decade had been how to take them off as quickly as possible. Anne's dress was the kind a man admires as much as he respects the lady wearing it. It had a full skirt and ruffles at the bottom. But it was the top that made it unique and made Anne look special. It hugged her waist, outlining its slimness as well as the shapeliness of her hips. It opened at the front to show a white blouse and enough of the top of her breasts to get him aroused.

It was completed by a little jacket—something like he'd seen one of the bullfighters wear when he was in Mexico several years before. It had long sleeves and a high collar and was lavishly decorated with black braid.

"Any man would be pleased to be seen with you. He'd be the envy of every man he met."

Anne turned pink with pleasure. "If it's going to cause people to stare, maybe I should change back into my old dress."

He'd have had to be ten times as insensitive as he was not to know that changing back into her old dress would crush Anne's spirits. "Stay just as you are. I'm the one who ought to change."

"You look very handsome," Anne said. Then she blushed a little more. "You always do."

Pete wasn't used to thinking of himself as hand-some. Growing up with Matt, Chet, Luke, and Will— especially Will—that had been impossible. The notion that any woman could consider him handsome made him wonder if she was trying to wheedle something out of him.

"Come off it," he said, trying to convince himself he didn't care if nobody thought he was handsome. "I don't scare the cows when I ride by, but that's about the best you can say. Sean always said—"

He stopped in mid-sentence. When was he going to stop talking about people Peter Warren couldn't possibly have known? "Never mind what Sean said."

"If he said you weren't handsome, he was wrong," Anne said. "Dolores commented on it the day you arrived. She said I was fortunate to have got myself a man who was tall, handsome, and sensible."

"I think it's about time we stop complimenting each other. We'll have such big heads, we won't be able to get through the dining room door."

"We'd better hurry," Anne said, suddenly agitated. "They stop letting people in after seven-thirty." She grabbed her purse—a beaded, sacklike thing that dangled elegantly from her wrist—and a black lace shawl Pete was positive he hadn't seen before.

"You should have gone without me," Pete said as he draped the shawl over her shoulders.

Anne turned to face him, her expression one of surprise. "Why would I do that?"

Pete realized that the clothes had proved she had a woman's body, but her mind and emotions were still those of the same innocent Anne.

"Because my being rude enough to stay late drinking in a saloon is no reason for you to go hungry."

"I wouldn't think of eating without you," she said as he held the door for her to leave the room.

"Why not?" he asked, as he locked the door.

"You're my husband."

He kept forgetting that. He had to remember.

They descended the steps into the lobby. "Hold that door," he said to the waiter who was removing the stops that held the dining room doors open.

"You made it just in time," the young man said. He might have been talking to Pete, but his eyes were glued to Anne.

"I hope you saved some food," Pete said. "I'm hungry enough to eat a horse." He hadn't eaten since breakfast. Anne hadn't either. She was probably as hungry as he was, though she hadn't had three whiskeys.

The waiter seated them at a table in the center of the room. It would have taken just a few minutes to clear one of the tables in a more secluded spot, but Pete decided the waiter wanted to position Anne where he could look at her. Pete could understand, but he wasn't sure he liked that. She wasn't his wife, but as long as he kept up this pretense, she was his responsibility.

He was amused to see that most of the menu was in French. He was certain there hadn't been a real Frenchman in Big Bend since the beaver gave out in the Big Horns fifty years earlier.

"I can't read anything," Anne said.

"What do you want to know?" He almost told her that he'd spent so many years in mining camps, eating wherever he could, that he'd gotten to the point that he could read almost anything in French, German, or Spanish, as long as it had to do with food. For once he managed to think before he spoke. Maybe he would survive after all.

They ordered their meal. He even ordered a glass of

wine for Anne to be brought to the table immediately. He ordered a whiskey for himself. It amused him to watch Anne's tentative sips, the face she made when she got the first sharp taste of the dry red wine.

"It's bitter," she exclaimed. "Why would anybody pay money to drink something like this?"

He laughed. "It's like coffee, an acquired taste."

She took another sip and wrinkled her nose. "I'd rather taste your whiskey."

"You wouldn't like it."

"I might."

"It's not suitable for a lady to drink whiskey. People will think . . . well, it's just not suitable."

Anne blushed. She looked more charming than ever. Her cheeks glowed with heightened color. She looked excited, young, and extremely lovely.

The food arrived. A smile of quiet pleasure wreathed Anne's face.

"What are you grinning about?" Pete asked.

"This will be the first meal I've eaten in a very long time that I didn't have to help cook."

"I thought Dolores did all the cooking."

"When Uncle Carl brought me to stay with him, he said I would have to help Dolores to earn my keep. I didn't mind. After Papa died, Mama and I needed somewhere to stay. But Mama was too ill to work. I couldn't expect Uncle Carl to keep us for nothing."

Clearly Uncle Carl wasn't made of the same stuff as Jake and Isabelle. They'd adopted Pete and ten other orphans just because they had no place to go. They had to work, but neither Jake nor Isabelle made them think they worked for their keep. They worked for the family, for themselves. Clearly nobody had ever made Anne feel like that.

"When did your mother die?"

"When I was nine."

"Do you have any other family?"

"Not that I know about."

So she'd been an orphan, just like him. He supposed that didn't feel any different, no matter whether you were Indian, French, Spanish, or a mixture. He was about to ask her about her father when a very well-dressed old woman approached the table.

"Well, my child, I'm glad to see you got down before the dining room closed. I thought for a while you might have to go to bed hungry."

"I'd never let that happen," Pete said. "If they wouldn't open up again, I'd have taken her someplace else. There must be other restaurants in town."

"Several, but this is the nicest. You'll have to introduce me to your companion," the woman said to Anne. "I had thought you would be dining with Peter."

"But I am," Anne said. "This is Peter."

The woman looked startled. She looked at Pete, then at Anne, and back at Pete. "What trick are you trying to pull, Anne dear? I knew Peter as well as anybody. This man can't possibly be he."

Chapter Eight

Pete wondered how many more bullets he would have to dodge. Calling Belser a liar, when it was obvious he was enraged over not getting the ranch, was easy compared to facing an elegantly dressed woman who appeared to have nothing to gain from his exposure.

"Of course he's Peter," Anne replied immediately. "I know he's changed. I was rather shocked myself at first, but he was only a boy when he left."

"He may have been a boy," the woman stated, "but boys develop definite characters by the time they're fourteen. I knew Peter. He was a weak-willed, nervous fellow, never able to stand up for himself. I was in The Emporium a short time after you. From what I understand, this man more than stood up for you."

Anne lowered her gaze before raising it again. "They didn't want to serve me because I'm Indian."

"You're not an Indian," the lady declared, "certainly no more so than half the people in the Territory, and I told them so in no uncertain terms. However, that doesn't change the fact that this man is not Peter."

"There's at least one person who disagrees with you," Pete said. He pulled his hair back to expose the scar made by the bullet. "I was shot on my way to Wyoming. Someone tried again this morning."

"Why should anyone want to shoot you?" the woman demanded.

"To keep me from inheriting the ranch."

"Who would do that?"

"The most obvious choices are Belser, so he could get his hands on the ranch, and Anne's uncle, so he could sell her to that old leacher, Cyrus McCaine."

"That man ought to be shot."

"Who are you trying to get rid of now, my dear?" a man asked as he came up to join the woman at their table.

"Cyrus McCaine."

"I don't much like him myself, but I don't see what he's done to you."

"He hasn't done anything to me."

"Then why are you trying to convince this young man to shoot him?"

"I'm not. But he's been trying to get Anne's worthless uncle to force her to marry him."

"Don't do it, child," the man said. "He's rich, but you wouldn't like being married to him."

Anne laughed. "I can't marry him. I'm already married to Peter. He wants people to call him Pete now he's grown."

"See there, my dear," he said to his wife. "Nothing to worry about. She's already married to this fella."

"Horace Dean, do shut up and listen. I've just been telling Anne that this man is not Peter."

"He must be, my sweet. She just said she was married to him and his name was Peter. Heard her say so myself. Can't be two young men in the room named Peter. Don't imagine Anne would forget which one was her husband if there were."

His wife's disgust was so patent, Pete had to struggle to keep from smiling.

"Horace, it will always be a mystery to me how you got to be a colonel in the army. I declare, if I hadn't been around to watch out for you, you'd have been cashiered long ago."

"Always knew you were smarter than I am," her husband said, his affability unimpaired. "I tell everybody. Quite proud of you."

His obvious pride didn't smooth his wife's ruffled feathers.

"Forget about all that. Forget about Cyrus, too."

"I had forgotten about him. You brought him up."

"Well, I'm not going to mention him again."

"Good. Never did like Cyrus much."

His wife took a deep breath—apparently to keep hold of what was left of her temper—and started all over again. "Do you remember Carl's nephew, the young one? His name was Peter."

Her husband's dazed expression gave Pete hope that he hadn't the slightest idea whom his wife was talking about.

"Well, this young man says he's Peter."

Her husband smiled and stuck out his hand. "Glad to meet you again, young fella. I thought you'd gone back East. Good thing you didn't."

"Horace, if I thought it would do the least good, I would brain you with the first solid object I got my hands on. This man is *not* Peter Warren. He just says he is."

"Well, if he says he is, I think you ought to believe him, my dear. After all, he really ought to know who he is."

Pete felt rather dazed. He'd braced himself to be exposed, at the very least to endure a harrowing few minutes, and the whole thing had turned into an absurd exchange between this harridan and her doddering old fool of a husband. Though thankful that all the other diners had already left the dining room—even the waiters seemed to be elsewhere—Pete was certain the entire conversation would make its way through Big Bend before morning.

"Young man," the woman said, turning on him with the light of battle blazing in her eyes, "do you know who I am?"

A dozen answers sprang to Pete's tongue, but he thought it better not to utter any of them. He was certain this woman could be a very dangerous enemy. "No, I don't," he said, quite candidly. "But before you jump on that as proof of what you say, let me tell you that I don't remember half of what I should. I'm still getting over the effects of a concussion."

"That's no excuse. I say you're not Peter."

"Really, he is," Anne said. "He knows all kinds of things he couldn't know if he weren't."

"Such as?"

"I can't remember exactly. But we've talked about lots of things, and he remembers nearly everything."

"How did you travel here?" she demanded of Pete.

"I went to St. Louis and took a steamboat to Miles City."

"What did you go there for?"

"Business. After that, I bought a wagon and headed south. Two men ambushed me and left me for dead."

"Why didn't they make sure of the job?"

"I don't know. I wasn't conscious at the time."

She clearly didn't believe him. She took him by the chin and turned his face from one side to the other. "It's all wrong," she announced. "You've got the wrong bone structure. Peter would never have been as handsome as you."

"Thank you."

"I didn't mean it as a compliment. You're a fraud. I don't know what your game is, but I must say, Anne, I'm extremely disappointed to find you going along with it."

"There's no game at all," Anne insisted, clearly distressed by the whole situation.

"I can understand your talking him into marriage to protect yourself from that penny-pinching uncle of yours," the woman said. "I certainly can't imagine Peter having such a sensible idea on his own. Nor can I imagine you loving such a dimwit. I had hoped you'd outgrown your fascination with him. You deserve better."

"He's not a dimwit," Anne said. "Eddie said he

shows a remarkable understanding of the ranch for being here such a short time. He says it's in capable hands."

"Then I *know* he can't be Peter Warren. Horace, we must inform the sheriff at once. I'm sorry, Anne dear, but I can't let you delude yourself with this man. He's a much better catch than Peter ever would be, but you can't have him. Come, Horace. I must speak to Owen immediately."

She turned and sailed away without looking back to see if her husband followed. Pete was certain he always had.

"Sorry about this, young fella. She's got you mixed up with this other Peter. Bea doesn't usually get the wrong end of a stick. She's a sharp one, Bea is." He saluted and toddled off after his wife.

"You've got to stop her from talking to the sheriff," Anne said.

"Who is she?" Pete wanted to know.

"Mrs. Dean. She was the only woman who ever came out to the ranch. We've got to stop her. If she talks to the sheriff—"

"There's no way I can stop that woman from doing anything she wants to do," Pete said.

"But we can't let her talk to Owen."

"What harm can it do?" It could do a lot of harm, but he didn't want to tell Anne that.

"People will talk."

"People always talk. Don't pay any attention to them. As long as you believe me, there's not a lot anybody can do. Besides, we're going back to the ranch

141

tomorrow. It won't matter what anybody thinks. Now finish your dinner. I expect they're waiting for us so they can close up."

But Anne was no longer hungry.

"We'll go for a walk before we go to bed."

"No," Anne squeaked. "We can't possibly be seen."

"If we hide in our room, people will think the worst. If we go parading about the town as proud as peacocks, what they'll see is a beautiful young wife and a man who considers himself very fortunate to be her husband. They'll think we couldn't possibly be walking about so openly if we weren't telling the truth. Unless I'm mistaken, your Mrs. Dean is a busybody who's ruffled more than a few feathers in her time. I imagine there'll be lots of people only too glad to believe she's got the wrong calf by the ears this time."

Anne didn't look convinced.

"Besides, you don't want to miss this chance to show off your new finery," Pete said. "You'll turn every man's head, and the women will seethe with envy."

"They won't."

He could tell she hoped they would.

"If they don't, we'll go straight back to that store first thing in the morning and buy another half-dozen dresses. We'll keep on buying dresses until we find one that will make every woman in this town green with envy."

Anne's eyes shone with happiness. "You never used to be so bold. I was the one always getting in trouble. You didn't say such pretty things, either."

"No fourteen-year-old boy is able to appreciate a

woman. Now come on. We don't want to waste the light. Nobody can see you in the dark."

But as they walked along the single street, looking in store windows, making a point of speaking to everyone they met, Pete wondered if maybe that bullet hadn't affected his brain after all. He certainly wasn't acting like himself. Words of flattery poured out of his mouth as though they were natural to his speech. He kept falling over himself to reassure Anne, to make sure no one hurt her feelings, to shield her from anything that might make her unhappy.

He'd never done any of that before. He had fallen in and out of love with a dozen women, been crazy about them for a morning, or as much as a week, then forgotten all about them. He wasn't in love with Anne. He couldn't even tell her who he was. Yet he was watching over her like a protective older brother. He guessed that was what it was. She was so young, so sweet, so innocent, and so alone, he couldn't help wanting to look after her.

That was okay. Isabelle had always insisted the boys do everything they could to protect defenseless women, but he had to remember his neck was on the line. He had to think less about how adorable she looked when she giggled and more about where to find his saddlebags. His neck wouldn't be safe until he was a long way from Wyoming Territory. If the killers were in the area, they would want to kill him. It wouldn't matter to them whether he was Pete or Peter. They would want him dead either way.

He had to think of a way to look for his saddlebags without making himself a target.

* * *

"Did you enjoy that?" Pete asked Anne when they returned to their hotel room.

"It was sort of fun to see the whole town, to talk to everybody, daring anybody to say you aren't Peter," she replied. "But I was scared the whole time. If I hadn't been holding your arm, I could never have done it."

"There's nothing to be scared of," Pete said. "They're just people."

"But they're important people."

"No more important than you."

That notion was so completely beyond her ability to conceive, she couldn't do anything but stare back at him.

"Well, look at you," Pete said. "You're young, beautiful, and the wife of the richest rancher in this part of Wyoming. If anything happened to me, you'd be the *owner* of the richest ranch in this part of the territory."

Anne wanted to protest that nothing would happen to Pete—she didn't even want to think about the attack outside of town—but she couldn't think of that for the picture of herself Pete had painted. Except for her parents, she had always been the little girl nobody wanted and everybody was ashamed of. Even Uncle Carl ordered her to keep out of sight when he had visitors. Mrs. Dean might insist she was different, but she had never seen either Anne or Peter as real people, just kids she had to champion because she was a woman, and women were supposed to be interested in children.

Even Eddie and Dolores treated her more like a daughter than an adult. She couldn't imagine anybody at the ranch, especially Belser, treating her like an owner, like a *boss*.

"People will soon be after you to sign petitions, form committees, head up projects," Pete said. "They'll seek your advice and solicit your support."

"I couldn't do that," she said, unnerved by the thought of standing up and giving her opinion to a group of women like Mrs. Horace Dean. "I don't know anything."

"Of course you do," Pete said. "And you can learn even more." He'd started to undress and spoke to her from the bathroom. "None of those women we met today knew any more than you when they started." Pete stuck his head outside the bathroom door. "And you're smarter than they are, so it won't be any time at all before you know twice as much as they do."

His head disappeared and Anne heard him pour water into a basin. She ought to be undressing, preparing for bed, but she couldn't move. No one had ever thought she was smart. No one asked her opinion. No one listened if she managed to get up the courage to offer it. She'd been ignored all her life, taken for granted, always present, always ready to be of use when wanted.

And always, at the back of everything else, was the knowledge that she was part Indian, that she was inferior.

"I wouldn't let them talk you into anything just yet," Pete said, still invisible in the bathroom. "We may decide to live in town during the winter, but you'll want to spend most of your time on the ranch. It's too far to drive in more than a couple of times a year, and you don't want them coming out." He stuck his head out again. "Can you imagine being locked up in the same house with Mrs. Dean? She'd probably expect you to give up your bedroom."

His head disappeared again, and Anne sank into a chair. She'd never considered the possibility of entertaining Mrs. Dean as an equal. The thought terrified her. The idea of having to entertain the owner of The Emporium was equally intimidating. She didn't believe anybody would want to ask her opinion or solicit her to form committees, but she definitely would refuse if asked. She couldn't do any such thing. Fortunately, living on the ranch would make it a practical impossibility.

But no sooner had she reached that comforting conclusion than she became aware of a very different feeling. She didn't want people to keep thinking of her as that little Indian girl, as a young woman with no opinions worth notice. She liked having people stare at her in admiration, even envy. She liked being noticed, her comfort considered, her wishes consulted. Nobody had considered her before except Peter—Pete.

She used to have to protect him. Now he was protecting her. She liked that, too.

"You haven't even started to undress."

Pete had come out of the bathroom. He had changed from his fancy clothes—that was what he called them—into the clothes he'd bought that afternoon. He looked more like a cowboy than a rancher, but she decided she liked him better that way. He looked younger, more like the boy she remembered.

His pants fitted his slim hips and powerful thighs more tightly. The shirt and vest fitted snugly across his chest. Now that they weren't partially hidden by his

146

loose coat, she could see just how broad his shoulders were when compared to his waist, how powerful his arms were. She couldn't imagine what he'd done to develop such a powerful body, but she liked the results. He might say she was the most beautiful woman in town—she didn't believe him, but it was nice of him to say it—but there wasn't any question she had the most handsome husband of any woman in Big Bend. She imagined the women in The Emporium were just as upset about that as they were about her having the money to buy clothes they considered too good for a breed.

Pete was looking at her with concern. "Are you feeling all right?"

She practically jumped to her feet. "I'm fine."

"You looked a little funny. Your stomach isn't acting queer, is it?"

"My stomach is fine," she said, grabbing a few things before heading to the bathroom. "I was just thinking."

Pete grinned. "Never do any hard thinking before you go to bed. It'll give you nightmares."

"I almost never have nightmares."

"I do."

About Indian massacres. She remembered. "I won't be very long."

"Take your time. I'm going out. I need to talk to some of the other ranchers about the best way to get our cows to market."

She felt pleased that he talked with her about the ranch. She'd never felt she was capable of being responsible for anything. Even the clothes she wore, the food she ate, had been chosen for her. She wasn't quite ready for the new vision of herself Pete was creating, but she meant to be soon. Until Pete showed up, no one had ever felt she was capable of anything more complicated than cleaning a room or helping cook dinner. She wasn't sure how she was going to do it, but she was determined to prove herself worthy of Pete's faith in her.

She felt a little disappointed he was leaving, but she really hadn't expected him to spend his whole evening talking to her. Uncle Carl always said no woman had enough to say to interest a man for more than ten minutes. Pete was showing signs of being pretty smart, maybe as smart as Uncle Carl. She was lucky he'd spent as much time with her as he had. "When will you be back?"

She shouldn't have asked. Men hated it when women wanted to know what they were doing.

"It depends on how long it takes to get the information I need. Don't wait up for me."

She would.

"Now that I'll be out of the room, you can take a long bath. The clerk said we're the only people here tonight, so there ought to be plenty of hot water. Cover yourself with powder. Pamper and cosset yourself all you want. We'll be going back to the ranch tomorrow, and it'll be a long time before you get to spend the night in a hotel again."

Pete was surprised at himself for returning to the hotel so quickly, but he was honest enough to admit it had little to do with the fact that he'd gotten more than enough information about the condition of the range, along the shipping routes, from the first man he talked to. The whole time the man was talking about the lack of rain, the stupidity of ranchers in dumping new herds on range that was already overburdened, the advantages and problems associated with various routes to a railhead, Pete kept thinking of Anne.

In a bathtub.

When the man invited him to join several others in a convivial gathering of ranchers and local business leaders, he'd declined the invitation, saying he wanted to be up early in the morning, that he needed to get his business finished so he could reach home before dark. And all the time he kept thinking about Anne.

In a bathtub.

The man had laughed and made a bawdy comment about newlyweds. Of course Pete didn't tell him his situation wasn't anything like what the rancher supposed.

Even before he reached their room, Pete heard the sounds of someone singing softly. The singing stopped abruptly when he opened the door. "It's just me," he called out.

She didn't answer.

"Are you in the bathtub?"

"Yes." The answer came after a moment of hesitation.

"How long have you been in?"

Another hesitation. "I'll get out."

"Stay as long as you like. I'm in no rush."

Quiet. He couldn't even hear sounds of the water as she moved about in the tub.

"What were you singing when I came in?"

149

"Just a song."

"It was pretty. Why don't you finish it?"

"I don't want to bother you."

"It won't bother me. I like it. You've got a pretty voice."

Pearl, his best friend's wife, was the only singer he'd ever really paid attention to. She had been the star attraction of her own saloon when Sean met her. She had a big, robust voice, one that could float the high notes and hammer out the low notes, all with a power and energy that made it impossible to sit still.

Anne's voice was light and sweet, the sound almost feathery. It had none of Pearl's assertiveness, none of her bold confidence. It almost apologized for itself. Yet it was that lack of self-assurance that made it so compelling. It practically begged you not to pass it by in favor of bigger, brassier, more colorful sounds.

Pete could have ignored big, brassy, and colorful. He'd heard it all too often. It was the plaintive quality that tugged at him in a way nothing else had before.

She started to sing again, softly, tentatively. He crossed the room and stood just outside the bathroom door. He leaned against the wall and let the moist, aromatic heat tease his sense of smell as it wafted its way into the bedroom. Sound and smell. Together they began to weave a spell around him in which there were no stolen saddlebags, no accusations of being an imposter, no murdered husband who stood between them, a spell in which the attraction between them grew stronger and stronger until it became like a physical pull.

Anne's voice cut off abruptly in a squeak. He found

himself inside the bathroom, staring at her in the bathtub. She looked like some black-haired sprite buried in a mound of bubbles.

"What do you want?" She looked and sounded fearful.

"I thought you might like me to wash your back." He had no idea where the words came from. Clearly that thought hadn't occurred to Anne, either. She looked at him wide-eyed, surprised, shocked, and he thought . . . hoped . . . just a little bit intrigued.

"I never heard of a man washing a woman's back," she said. "My father never did anything like that."

"Jake does it all the time," he said. "At least that's what my friend says. He says Isabelle would be upset if he didn't."

Her look implied she couldn't believe him, that such a thing was too far from her experience to accept, but that a small part of her was strongly attracted to the idea.

"We're married," Pete said. "It wouldn't be improper. If you don't like it, I'll stop."

He couldn't imagine why he was doing this. He'd never washed a woman's back before. Well, not a *nice* woman's back. He had no intention of letting any kind of feeling warmer than friendship develop between them. She was married to someone else. He was crazy to be standing in the bathroom, staring at her. He was insane even to think about washing her back, much less offer to do it.

What did he think he was going to do—wash her back, get himself completely stirred up, then go quietly to bed *with her lying only inches from him?* That bullet must have addled his brain. He would back out of there as fast as he could. Forget how adorable she looked, her big black eyes wide with shock, wonder, and . . . he was certain of it now . . . expectation.

"Okay."

Too late! One word, and he was lost.

Chapter Nine

Anne couldn't believe she'd given Pete permission to wash her back. Who'd ever heard of such a thing? Dolores had never mentioned it. She was certain her father hadn't done it. She wondered if all men outside her circle of acquaintance did things like this, or if Pete was the only one. It seemed terribly daring, even immodest.

You're married, you foolish girl. This man is your husband. There can't be any impropriety in a husband washing his wife's back. He just told you Jake did it for Isabelle all the time. For all you know, they're the most respectable married couple in the whole world.

But Anne realized that up until this moment she had never felt as if Pete was her husband. Everyone treated them as husband and wife. They slept in the same bedroom, in the same bed. As soon as the lawyer sent it, they would have a piece of paper saying they were married. Yet, she'd continued to feel that they were just friends, like when they were children, only this time Pete had taken the role of leader.

Thinking of Pete as her husband rather than her friend changed everything. She wanted him to find her attractive. She liked his talking to her as an adult, sharing information about the ranch, but she wanted a different kind of sharing, too. She wanted to be close to him, and being close meant touching.

Pete stepped into the bathroom and started rolling up his sleeves. "Where is the soap?"

She felt around in the water until she found it. "Here," she said, holding up the dripping bar to him.

"Would you rather I use a brush or my hands?" he asked.

A brush sounded too rough, his hands too intimate. "Your hands."

She couldn't believe what she was doing, what she was saying. How could she let a man—even though that man was her husband—wash her back?

She wasn't sure when it happened—she'd been totally unaware of it at the time—but her feelings toward Pete had changed. Maybe it came from his letting her buy practically anything she wanted. Maybe it was when he paraded her through the town. No, it must have been when he told her she was beautiful, that he was proud to be her husband. No woman could keep from falling in love with a man who said something like that.

That phrase exploded on her consciousness. Falling in love! Wasn't she already in love with Pete? She thought she'd been in love with him for years. She'd never thought of any other man as being her husband. Never wanted any other man. She had felt repulsed by Belser and Cyrus. She'd thought about Pete and dreamed about him for years. Yet what she felt now was different.

She jumped when his hands touched her skin.

"Is my hand cold?"

"A little."

He swirled it around in the water behind her back. "It'll be warm in a minute."

She leaned forward, scooted down a little more to make certain her breasts stayed hidden under the bubbles. She couldn't be certain his hand was cold. Or hot. The electric shock that blazed though her at his touch seemed to sear her nerves. Yet her body shuddered. Anticipation of his second touch made it hard to breathe.

"This is supposed to relax you"—she flinched when he touched her again—"not tie you in knots."

"It's the first time a man has touched me," Anne said. "I can't help it."

"Then we'll talk," Pete said. "That will help take your mind off it."

Anne didn't think she had enough presence of mind to answer a direct question, much less carry on a conversation. Pete's hand was moving back and forth over her right shoulder. Every nerve seemed to have suddenly moved to that part of her body.

"What makes all these bubbles?" Pete asked.

"Bath soap," Anne managed to reply. "The lady at The Emporium said the army wives bought it all the time."

"It smells good."

"It's lavender. She said it was an English herb."

"I wonder if the whole country smells like this?"

"She didn't say." She couldn't imagine a whole country smelling this good. Pete shifted his attention to the other shoulder. Nearly all her nerve endings followed him, but a few remained, giving the freshly scrubbed shoulder a tingling sensation.

"I don't suppose it does. I've met a lot of Englishmen. I think they'd have mentioned something like this."

"Where could you meet so many Englishmen in Illinois?" She could have sworn she heard him curse under his breath.

"They were headed out to the goldfields. They would load up on supplies before they left."

"You must have met a lot of interesting people." His hand had slipped off her shoulder down to her arm. She held it up so he could get to it more easily.

"What else did you buy this afternoon?"

"I bought some powder that smells like this soap."

"I guess I'll feel like I'm sleeping in a bed of lavender tonight."

The possible implications of that statement caused Anne to flush and her skin to burn.

"Lean forward so I can get to your back," Pete said.

Anne leaned so far forward, her nose nearly touched the bubbles.

"Don't disappear," Pete said. "I'd have to crawl in and fish you out."

Anne hadn't thought she could flush any warmer, but she was wrong. She was certain the water would be hotter when she got out of the bathtub than when she got in.

"There's not enough room," she said.

"A tight fit would make it all that much more fun."

Anne decided people did things in Illinois they simply knew nothing about in Wyoming Territory. She very much wanted to ask Pete if he'd ever gotten in a bathtub with a female, but she hadn't the courage. She didn't know what she'd do if he said yes . . . or if he asked to get in the bathtub with her.

Yes, she did. She'd faint. Drown. And that would be the end of that.

"Don't panic. I'm not going to jump in with you. I'd ruin my new clothes."

The old Peter would never have considered such a thing. She doubted the new Pete would be deterred by much of anything, certainly not a few wet clothes. The more changes she discovered in him, the more she marveled that one man could have changed so much. Uncle Carl had always said that keeping him on the ranch would have made a man out of him. Apparently Illinois was able to do just as well.

"You must have bought something besides soap and powder," Pete said.

It was hard to think with Pete's hand moving over her back in slow circles. It did nothing to reduce her temperature or ease the tension in her muscles. Or clear the mush out of her brain. She couldn't remember half the things she'd bought. "I bought some body oil. The woman said it would make my skin soft and smooth."

"It's already soft and smooth. It feels like silk."

Anne had never seen or felt silk until that morning when the lady brought out a dress made of a deep-green material that moved and shimmered like a shaft of emerald light. The material felt so soft, so smooth. Anne thought it was wonderful that Pete would compare her skin to that magical material.

"I'll rub some on your back after you get out of the bathtub," Pete said.

Anne was certain she didn't have the strength to get out of the tub. "I don't know . . . "

"You can't reach your back. All of you ought to be soft and silky."

Anne didn't trust her sensory perceptions anymore—nothing in her body was working like it should—but she was certain Pete's voice had changed in quality. He spoke more slowly, deliberately, at a lower pitch, with more breath in the sound. If she hadn't known better, she would have said he was just as strongly affected by the situation as she. But that couldn't be. Pete knew all about two people in the same bathtub. She couldn't even imagine such a thing.

Much to her surprise she found she could. In fact, she was imagining it at that very moment.

"A little bit more, and we'll be done," Pete said.

He was washing low down on her back, so low she felt his fingertips on her hips. She thought she felt his breath on her shoulders. She hoped not. If she did, she might faint for sure.

"There, all done." He stood up and dried his hands on the towel. "Do you need me to help you out of the tub?"

"No! I can do that myself."

That would expose all of her body to his view. She was certain she couldn't stand that. It didn't matter that he was her husband, that they had slept in the same bed together. What really mattered was that she'd just become fully aware of the physical nature of his presence, and it had shocked her nearly witless. She would need time to recover, to get used to the idea that a husband had the right to put his hands all over his wife's body.

To get used to the idea that she wanted him to touch her.

At the moment, she was inclined to think the second thought was the more shocking of the two.

Pete practically staggered back into the bedroom. He couldn't say just why he'd volunteered to wash Anne's back—his mind was acting too peculiarly for him to know just what was going on with it—but he did know it was a crazy thing to have done. And what on earth had prompted him to tease her about crawling into the bathtub with her? He was losing control of a situation that required the most careful management if he was to get out of it with a whole skin.

He sank down on the bed but got up almost immediately. The vision that sprang into his mind was guaranteed to keep his mind and body in turmoil.

He reminded himself that Anne was legally married to another man. He might be able to get away with pretending to be Peter Warren, but he *wasn't* Peter, and taking advantage of Anne would be the same as raping her.

No, that wasn't true. He would never force himself on a woman who didn't want him. It would be just his luck that any day now Anne would decide they had had enough time to become reacquainted and she wanted him to make love to her. What excuse could he offer then? More important, could he resist? He was safe during the day. He could keep his distance, involve himself in work. Other people were around.

But during the night! He didn't want to think about it.

He walked over to the window, raised the blind, and looked out. The view from the window was of the Big Horn Mountains in the distance, their silhouette outlined by the moonlight that poured down on the hills from clear, star-filled skies. He could hear occasional sounds from the street in front of the hotel, see parts of buildings outlined by the shadowy light coming from inside the various saloons that would remain open all night. Behind the hotel, the waters of Clear Creek tumbled over the rocky streambed on their way from the Big Horn Mountains to the Powder River and on north to the Missouri River.

But nothing outside the hotel could make Pete forget that Anne was in the bathroom, in the bathtub, naked, and that he'd offered to rub oil on her back.

Just the thought of it made his body swell. He cursed. Tight pants were meant to make a cowboy's work of riding and wrangling easier. They weren't meant to accommodate an aroused condition. Or disguise it. If he didn't think of something quick, he'd have to duck out the door before Anne emerged from the bathroom. Seeing him in this condition might give her heart failure.

He wondered again at her reluctance to share her body with the man she thought was her husband. He could understand her initial shyness. Regardless of how much she thought she loved Peter Warren, seeing him as a man rather than the boy she remembered had to have been a shock. She would have needed some time to readjust her thinking. Maybe a few hours. Maybe even a few days. But any girl who had grown into womanhood ought to be glad the boy she remembered had grown into manhood, especially if that boy was her husband.

If she loved him, she ought to be eager to consummate their marriage.

Anne had shown no signs of wanting to be intimate with Pete. Though he was thankful for this on one level, it worried him on another. He liked Anne. She was a beautiful woman, and he hoped things would go well for her in the future. But it tarnished his perception of her to think she might have married Peter just to protect herself from her uncle. He could understand that. He couldn't blame her. But it didn't sit well with him.

Of course, her desire to keep her distance might be his fault. She had fallen in love with another man. From everything he'd been able to learn, Peter Warren wasn't a bit like him. Anne might not know he was an imposter, but she must instinctively know she was facing a stranger, even if that stranger was supposed to be the grownup version of the boy she used to know.

Pete pulled the shade down and turned away from

the window. There was no point in racking his brain trying to figure out anything about Anne or her motives. He would leave as soon as he found his money. In a few weeks, he probably wouldn't even remember her.

"I'm ready."

The sound of her voice acted on his nerves like an electric shock. Pete jerked himself around to see Anne standing in the doorway to the bathroom, her hair piled atop her head, her body lost inside an oversized bathrobe. She held out a jar to him.

Pete felt rooted to the spot.

"It's all right if you've changed your mind."

"No," he managed to reply. "I was just thinking. You caught me off guard." She'd caught him off guard a long time ago. Thinking had just made it worse.

She smiled and his legs threatened to go out from under him. "I never had so many nice things. Thank you for giving them to me."

"It's nothing. Every woman ought to have those things." He didn't know what she was talking about. He was just blubbering. She came closer, handed him the jar. He managed to collect himself enough to take it.

"Uncle Carl didn't think so. Neither did my father from what I can remember. They thought a woman ought to be happy with one company dress, a husband, children to look after, and her own kitchen."

It was a good thing old Uncle Carl wasn't married to any of the women Pete knew. He'd have had heart failure long ago.

"A woman likes to look nice, to feel pretty, to be

pampered." He was quoting Isabelle and Pearl. He'd never thought much about it himself.

"You always did understand me better than anybody at the Tumbling T. I was very lonely after you went back to Illinois."

Pete wasn't about to get caught in a quagmire of memories he didn't remember. "Well, I'm back now. You don't have to worry anymore."

She turned her back to him, pulled the robe high against her throat, then let the neck fall, exposing about a third of her back.

"Is that okay?" she asked.

"A little off the shoulders." His voice sounded unsteady; his throat felt lined with cotton.

She giggled. "Much more, and it'll be off me altogether. Of course that wouldn't be so terrible. You *are* my husband."

Pete tried, but he couldn't articulate a response. His vocal chords had shut down altogether.

She turned around. "Did I shock you?"

He could tell she'd probably shocked herself. If he hadn't offered to wash her back—

"No," he managed to say. "As you said, I am your husband." The word caught in his throat before he managed to force it out. "Now turn back around."

Seeing her bare back was dangerous, but looking into the wide-eyed innocence of her gaze was lethal. He had good intentions and he meant to hold to them, but he was only human.

"My hand will probably be cold again."

"That's okay."

It wasn't okay for him. Just the sight of her back bare to her hips inflamed his body to the point of pain. "I don't know how much to put on. You'll have to tell me when I've got enough."

"I don't know either."

Just what he needed, a woman who didn't know any more than he did. He poured some oil on her back.

She flinched and giggled. "It's cold."

He started to rub it in. Body heat must release the fragrance. The longer he rubbed, the more aromatic the oil became.

"It smells nice," Anne said.

The effect of the lavender oil wasn't nearly as powerful as the sight of her bare back. The smoothness of her pure-white skin was intoxicating. He had never realized how soft a woman's skin could be, how beautifully warm and perfect. He rubbed the oil over her shoulders. She was so slim, he could feel each bone. In a few years they would be padded by a small layer of flesh that would round off the corners and edges to a seductive softness.

A tremor shook his body.

He poured some oil into his hand. He could feel each vertebra as his hands moved slowly and steadily over her lower back. "I can count your ribs," he said, lust thickening his voice. "We'll have to start feeding you better."

He poured more oil into his hand and rubbed it on her side.

She twisted away from him. "That tickles."

"Sorry."

She backed up to him again. He wished his body tickled. That would have been a relief from the throbbing pain in his groin. He had to get this over with before he exploded. He quickly rubbed oil over her lower back, refusing to let himself think how close his fingers came to the flare of her hips.

"I'm done," he said, stepping back and setting the bottle of oil on one of the tables. "I'm going to take a short walk. That'll give you a chance to get ready for bed."

He didn't want to give her a chance to tell him he didn't need to leave. He might stay. And in his present frame of mind, that would be disastrous. His willpower had dropped to a dangerously low level.

Neither did he intend to let himself dwell on the look of surprised disappointment on her face. He had just enough presence of mind to do what honor required of him. If he spent so much as a minute thinking she might be disappointed, he would certainly do something his conscience would never let him forget.

Anne slipped into the bed. She wondered when Pete would come back.

This evening had been a revelation to her. She liked Pete. No, she told herself, she loved him. Meeting him as an adult after so many years had been a shock. It was stupid of her not to have realized he would change. Everybody did. It had taken her a while to realize she didn't *want* Pete to have stayed the way he was as a boy. She was glad he was proving everybody wrong. She had actually begun to feel proud of him.

Despite his kindness and thoughtfulness, she hadn't felt close to him until this trip. Maybe it was the buying spree in The Emporium. She hadn't expected him to buy her more than one dress. To be turned loose in the store and told to buy anything she wanted had stunned her. He obviously really did love her. Neither Uncle Carl nor her father would have spent that kind of money on her.

Telling her she was beautiful, that he was proud to be her husband, further dissolved the reserve between them. But what had actually melted her, what canceled any desire to keep her distance from him, was his offer to wash her back.

She couldn't explain what it did to their relationship. She certainly couldn't say why it had happened, but it had the effect of making her feel very close to him, as if he were a kindred spirit. No, that was wrong. They were too different for that. He was calm, confident, and competent. She was timid, tiny, and tentative. But somehow his washing her back, rubbing oil into her skin, had brought her inside the circle of his protection.

Now she wasn't making any sense. He'd protected her from the moment he arrived on the ranch, even before by marrying her by proxy so she'd be safe until he arrived.

But there was a difference. Maybe it was all on her side. Maybe she'd finally stopped being afraid of him. She didn't know, and trying to reason it out was giving her a headache. She only knew that now she felt like his wife.

So why didn't he want to make love to her?

According to Dolores, a man couldn't wait to spill his seed inside a woman. Every man. Any woman. They weren't particular about time or place. Then why had Pete escaped into the night rather than stay with her?

He had said she was beautiful. She knew she was clean, that she smelled good, that her night dress was pretty. They had time, opportunity, the perfect place. The only conclusion she could reach was that he didn't love her anymore.

That frightened her. She wanted to be loved. She desperately needed it. No one in her life had ever made her feel loved except Peter. She'd held the two years he lived at the ranch close to her heart. They had become more precious as the world around her grew colder and more cruel. She had held tight to her little-girl memories, content to know that one person in the world loved her honestly and truly, without reservation.

When Peter agreed to marry her, she had been certain she would never be alone again. She had waited for his arrival, prayed when he was late, despaired when the last day arrived and he still hadn't come.

Then, miraculously, he was there, more magnificent and more wonderful than she could have hoped. Surely he loved her. He *had* to love her. It would be too cruel if now, when everything she'd ever wanted seemed within her grasp, he didn't.

But thinking about it wouldn't give her any answers. She'd ask Dolores. And if he didn't love her, maybe Dolores could tell her how to make him fall in love with her again. Anne had the distinct feeling she'd never be truly happy otherwise.

* * *

A light burned by the bedside when Pete entered the room on silent feet. He felt like a thief in the night, like a miserable coward, like the weak-willed ninny Peter Warren was supposed to be, but tonight he didn't trust himself to get into bed with Anne while she was awake. He was too vulnerable.

He walked around to her side of the bed to turn out the lamp. He paused. Her face was turned toward the light. She looked so damned sweet and innocent, it was enough to make a grown man cry. No woman like her should be shunned by merchants because she had Indian blood. Miserable coyotes like Belser shouldn't be allowed to yap at her heels. As far as he was concerned, her uncle and Cyrus ought to be hanged for what they had tried to do.

And she had pinned all her hopes on a poor, weak failure like Peter Warren. Didn't she understand that purity of heart and intention meant nothing in a world where both were considered weaknesses? No, she'd married Peter certain that once he arrived in Wyoming, everything would be all right. She probably had no notion that Peter's arrival would have been the beginning of a string of tragedies that would have ended with Peter's death, the loss of the ranch, and probably being married off to Cyrus.

She had no one to help her. Even that old crone, Mrs. Dean. If she was half as smart as her husband thought, she ought to have realized that a fake Peter was just what Anne needed.

Pete turned out the light and undressed in the dark. He couldn't afford to look at Anne's face any longer.

Not and keep the promise he'd made to leave her as innocent as he'd found her.

"There he is," Mrs. Dean announced as she pointed her finger at Pete. "I demand that you arrest him immediately."

With a fatalistic sigh, Pete turned. One look at the gathering blocking the door of The Emporium told him it wasn't going to be so easy to talk his way out of it this time. Belser stood at Mrs. Dean's shoulder, his smile indicating that he was certain Pete would at last be unmasked for the liar he was. Anne's uncle stood in the background, visibly quivering with excitement. But it was the banker standing right next to the sheriff who bothered Pete the most. It also bothered him that Bill Mason was present. What interest could he have in this?

"I knew he wasn't Peter the first time I set eyes on him," Belser said. "I said it over and over, but nobody believed me."

"They'll believe me," Mrs. Dean declared.

Pete and Anne had returned to The Emporium after breakfast. He wanted her to pick out a few pieces of jewelry, several pairs of earrings, a bracelet, and a necklace or two. But most of all they were there to pick out a wedding ring. He knew women put great store in things like that. Besides, with a wedding ring on her finger, people wouldn't question her marriage. They had just completed their purchases and were about to return to the hotel in preparation for their trip back to the ranch.

Pete looked at Anne. Her face had lost all its color. No more smile of pleasure when she learned he really wanted her to buy the gold earrings. No more pure joy in choosing between two expensive necklaces. No more tears of happiness when he slipped the wedding ring on her finger. That haunted, frightened, unhappy-little-girl look was back.

Pete cursed inwardly. Why couldn't they have arrived an hour later? He and Anne would have been out of town by then. He looked at Belser, grinning with triumph. Pete would have a great deal to say to him when they got back to the ranch—if he was still in control of the ranch by then.

"What have you got to say for yourself?" the sheriff asked. "Mrs. Dean has made a very serious accusation against you."

"It's not an accusation," Mrs. Dean said. "I'm stating the truth."

"Are you here as spectators or as part of the prosecution?" Pete asked the banker and Mason.

"I have to be concerned with any accusation of this nature," the banker said. "I just advanced you a great deal of money. If you're not who you say you are, I'll have to ask the sheriff to put you in jail."

"Jail!" Anne exclaimed. "You can't do that." She turned to Mrs. Dean. "I told you he was Peter. I said—"

"Stop." Pete put his finger to her lips to still her protests. "They're not going to put me in jail." Her uneasy glance at the sheriff told him she didn't have a lot of confidence in his assertions. "All they have is the word of your uncle, who's trying to get rich by selling you to an old lecher, a man who's angry he didn't get the ranch, and an unbalanced busybody."

"Busybody!" Mrs. Dean snorted. "Unbalanced!"

"Judging from the way you treat your husband, you're probably a bully as well," Pete added.

If the situation had been less serious, he would have been pleased at the sheriff's smothered smile, the amusement in the banker's eyes.

"Owen, I demand you arrest this man at once," Mrs. Dean declared to the sheriff.

"Now wait a minute, Bea. We haven't heard what he has to say."

"*I* have heard it, and I don't need to hear it again."

"Well, I've got to hear it. I can't arrest a man on your say-so."

"I say he's an impostor, too," Belser said.

"Me, too," Anne's uncle added.

"But you don't have any proof," the banker said.

"He's not a thing like Uncle Carl said he was," Belser said. "The real Peter Warren couldn't ride a horse or run a ranch. He was afraid of his own shadow."

"His bone structure isn't right," Mrs. Dean said. "My family has exceptionally fine bone structure. I've made it a study all my life, and I'm never wrong. This man is much too handsome."

"What have you got to say for yourself?" the sheriff asked Pete.

"What do you expect of other men when they come to your town and say who they are?"

The sheriff looked uncomfortable.

"We pretty much accept them for what they say they are," the banker said. "But the ownership of the biggest ranch in the area is in question now."

"I can't give you any more proof than I offered Belser days ago," Pete said. "Someone tried to kill me and stole all my papers." From the surprised expression on the faces of the sheriff and the banker, Pete gathered Belser had neglected to mention that. "Anne and I went to the lawyer's office yesterday, and I instructed him to have my lawyer send duplicate copies of everything. Until then, all I have to show are some letters Anne wrote me."

"You kept them?" Anne said, surprised.

"I've kept everything you ever wrote." Pete was certain Peter Warren would have.

"You never showed me any letters," Belser said.

"They're none of your business," Pete said.

"I guess I'd better see them," the sheriff said.

"No, you won't," Anne announced. "Nobody will see them."

Chapter Ten

"Those are my private letters to my husband," Anne stated when everyone turned to her. "I refuse to allow anyone else to read them."

From the astonished expressions all around him, Pete could tell nobody had anticipated such an outburst from Anne. Neither had he, but he noted a difference between the young woman who'd ridden into town with him the previous day and the woman who now stood at his side. Before, Anne had always been quiet and sweet-tempered. This woman was angry and didn't care who knew it. Anne would never have spoken up for herself. This woman looked willing to take on anyone who crossed her path. Anne had been uncertain, unsure of herself. This woman knew exactly what she thought.

"They seem to be the only evidence we have," the sheriff said.

"I demand that you hand those letters over to the sheriff immediately," Mrs. Dean said to Pete.

"Since they're *my* letters," Anne said, "you should direct that request to me."

"It's not a request," Mrs. Dean said.

"It doesn't matter what it is," Anne said. "No one will see those letters." She turned on Mrs. Dean. "I don't know what you expect to gain by this, but you have certainly lost my friendship."

"My dear, I'm only trying—"

"You're trying to stir up trouble," Anne said, interrupting, "just like Belser. Nobody at the ranch would listen to his ridiculous accusations, so he followed us into town hoping to find someone who would. I knew Peter better than either of you. I, and I alone, should be the one to determine his identity. I tell you here and now, this man is Peter Warren, Uncle Carl's nephew, my husband. He's just given me a ring to prove it. Isn't it beautiful?"

She held the ring out for all to see.

"That doesn't prove anything," Belser exploded. "Besides, he bought it with ranch money."

"You're fired."

The words came out so quickly, so unexpectedly, that everyone stared.

"Who are you to question my husband's identity?" Anne demanded. "You aren't a relative. You aren't a friend. As of this moment, you aren't even a hired hand. As soon as you return to the ranch, collect your things and leave."

"You can't do that," Belser exploded. "I'm Uncle Carl's nephew. I'm the one he wanted to have the ranch. I'm—"

"That's a lie," Anne said. "He didn't think Peter could handle the job, but he always meant to leave the ranch to a blood relative. You're not a relative. You're his wife's great-nephew. He disliked your whole family."

"You can't fire me," Belser said. "You—"

"Of course she can," Pete said quietly. "As my wife, she's just as much owner of the ranch as I am."

"Not if you're dead," Belser growled.

"In that event, she would own it all," Pete said. "I made out a will yesterday. I left everything to Anne in case of my death. I'm sorry I can't help you," he said, turning to the sheriff, "but the papers will be arriving soon. As for the letters, I can't hand them over. I don't have them."

"If you don't have them, then—"

"They're at the ranch. Now, if you'll excuse us, you've delayed us long enough already."

Pete took Anne by the arm, and they walked from The Emporium. He was certain the entire conversation would be all over Big Bend by evening. The two women who'd waited on them had listened to every word with rampant curiosity.

Pete felt Anne go limp the moment the door of The Emporium closed behind them.

"Don't relax now," he said. "Keep your head high and your back straight. We've got them on the run."

Anne straightened her posture, but when she turned to him, he could see the uncertainty in her eyes. "Do you really think so?"

"You were magnificent. Your infantry blunted their offensive, your reserves caught them on their blind side, and then you brought up the cavalry when they thought we had our backs against the wall."

"I have no idea what you're talking about," Anne said with a weak laugh.

"I mean you left them nothing to say."

"Does that mean you think I was right to speak up?"

He couldn't remember when he'd seen anyone more anxious for praise. He put his arm around her waist and hugged her to him.

"I couldn't have done half as well myself. I listened in awe as you masterfully destroyed Mrs. Dean and Belser."

Anne blushed with happiness, and he felt an odd sensation of pleasure shoot through him. She looked like an angel when she smiled. He couldn't understand why men wanting to court her weren't lined up at her front door.

"I probably shouldn't have spoken to Mrs. Dean like that, but she made me so angry I couldn't help myself. I couldn't believe she'd ask the sheriff to arrest you."

"Forget about her. By the way, if you're not serious about firing Belser, I am."

"I don't know if I really should," she said, uncertain again. "He is related to Uncle Carl, even if only by marriage."

"Okay, we'll let him stay one more night. Now I insist you forget about everything except how to fit all your new clothes into the buckboard. I'd offer to leave the supplies, but I doubt the men would appreciate it when the food started to run out."

She laughed again, and he swore he'd make sure she laughed every day for as long as it took him to find his money.

"You should have seen her," Pete said to Dolores and Eddie after he'd finished telling them of the confrontation with Mrs. Dean and the sheriff. "You wouldn't have recognized her. She stood up to them like a she-wolf defending her cub."

"I didn't," Anne protested. Heat suffused her cheeks. "I was so scared I could hardly talk."

"Nobody would have guessed from the way you tore into Belser. She's got very sharp teeth and claws," he said to Dolores with a wink. "You'd better watch out."

"Please, ma'am," Dolores said, pretending absolute terror, "don't beat me. I promise I won't burn the bread ever again."

"Stop it, all of you," Anne said amid the laughter. "If you keep teasing me like this, you'll deserve to be beaten."

"Aha!" Pete said. "A taste of power, and she becomes a tyrant."

Pete didn't stop, and they laughed all the way through dessert. Anne couldn't remember an evening when she'd had so much fun. Belser hadn't returned from Big Bend, leaving just the four of them for supper. It had been the best evening of her life.

For the first time, she felt included. More than

that, she felt at the center of things. Important. Everyone's attention had been focused on her almost from the moment they reached the ranch. First on her clothes, then on the other purchases she'd made. Pete had spent all evening telling them how pretty she looked, how people stared when she passed— she didn't remember anybody staring, but then, she couldn't see everything—how she'd stood up to Mrs. Dean.

After years of expecting not to be seen, rarely heard, and never attended to, Anne found it a little disconcerting to be the center of so much attention. But she liked it. If this was what things were going to be like, she would positively enjoy being the adored and beloved wife of the owner of a big ranch.

Did Pete adore her?

His treatment made her feel protected, valued. After the trip to Big Bend, she felt important, cherished.

But did he love her?

She fingered the engagement and wedding rings.

She'd never expected the clothes and other things. But as nice as they were, they weren't a patch on what it meant to have Pete slip those rings on her finger. At that moment, she had felt really married. He hadn't understood the tears, but the women in The Emporium had.

She was married. Safe. Protected. Cared for. But did Pete love her? That question had become of paramount importance because she was in love with him. She knew she was because this feeling was unlike anything she'd felt as a child. She looked at Pete at the head of the table. He seemed to belong there, naturally. There was no uneasiness, no uncertainty. He had complete confidence in himself and in what he meant to do.

He'd taken her with him. To the bank. To the lawyer, everywhere. He discussed nothing behind closed doors. He didn't say anything was too complicated or difficult for her to understand. He didn't even say it wasn't a woman's business. He'd even asked her opinion. Almost as much of a surprise, she'd had one to offer. And he'd listened.

He made her feel real, valued, important. She would have fallen in love with him for that alone.

"It's time for Eddie and me to start making plans for the roundup," Pete said, pushing his chair back from the table.

"I have to start cleaning up," Dolores said, "or I won't get out of the kitchen before midnight."

"I'll help," Anne said. "You're late because you held supper for us."

"Could we have some coffee in about half an hour?" Pete asked.

"You sure it won't keep you awake?" Dolores asked.

"After two days spent in that buckboard and battling Mrs. Dean, nothing could keep me awake. I imagine you must be worn out," he said, turning to Anne. "I'll probably be up half the night. Don't wait up for me."

"I am rather tired," Anne admitted.

He walked around the table to her chair, his hands outstretched. She took them, and he pulled her to her feet.

179

"Sleep tight," he said and kissed her lightly on the lips. "You don't have to leave a light on. Now," he said, turning to Eddie, "where do we start? I want to move these cows as little as possible. I don't want to walk off any more flesh than necessary."

Pete and Eddie walked off to the office already deep in their discussion.

Anne stood rooted to the spot. Pete had never kissed her before. It was hardly more than a brushing of the lips, but it was a kiss. He must love her. Surely he wouldn't kiss her if he didn't.

"It sounds like you had quite a trip," Dolores said as she began gathering up empty plates.

"It was very nice," Anne replied, coming out of her trance.

"Your husband buys you a ring with a diamond the size of a pea, and all you can say is *very nice*!"

Anne picked up a platter of beef and a dish of potatoes. "Okay, it was wonderful."

Dolores backed her way through the kitchen door. "I'd say splendid, magnificent, and spectacular were closer to the truth. If anything like that had happened to me, I'd still be floating ten feet above the earth. Actually, I'd be certain my husband had at least three mistresses scattered about the county and was trying to make sure that if I found out I'd be too happy to care."

"Pete wouldn't do anything like that." They set everything down on the big table in the center of the kitchen and went back for a second load. "He's too kind."

"Not to mention generous."

"I guess he is, but he's a rich man now."

"He still spent a lot of money on you."

"He said he was trying to make up for Uncle Carl not spending anything."

"In that case, he's got a long way to go."

They deposited the second load of dishes and went back again.

"Maybe he's in the habit of spending too much. Maybe that's why his hardware store failed."

"I don't know about that," Dolores said, picking up a tray loaded with glasses and cups and handing it to Anne while she wiped the table clean. "If you ask me, it must have been something else. Eddie says he's impressed with Pete's decision to sell now rather than risk a bad winter. It takes a man with a lot of confidence in himself to make a decision like that. Your husband is nothing like what everybody led me to expect. And that includes you."

"He is quite different," Anne said, passing into the kitchen while Dolores held the door. "It's taken me a while to get used to him."

"I don't know what his brother was like, but he must have been a doozie for everybody to prefer him to Pete."

"He liked the ranch and was always joking."

"Just like Pete. I thought if he made me laugh another time, I'd split my sides. Why didn't you tell me he could be so funny?"

"I didn't know," Anne said. "He was always so serious."

"Probably depressed from hearing his brother

praised all the time," Dolores said as she started putting the dirty dishes into hot, soapy water. "It would have put me into a prolonged sulk."

"Me, too."

But Anne wasn't listening. She was remembering Pete telling about Mrs. Dean and making it sound so funny even she laughed. That was definitely unlike the Peter she remembered. She was glad he'd changed, grown more confident, more knowledgeable. She'd have to ask him about the miraculous transformation. Maybe she could learn something that would make her more confident. Pete said she'd faced Mrs. Dean with courage, but that wasn't the truth. She and the sheriff were attacking Pete only moments after he'd put a wedding ring on her finger. They were trying to take from her the only person who'd ever really made her feel happy.

She couldn't let that happen. She'd struck back. She still found it amazing, but she'd do it again. There wasn't anything she wouldn't do for him.

"I think I'll give the house a good cleaning while the men are gone," Dolores said.

Anne came out of her daze. "That sounds like a good idea."

"You'll use your time better getting rid of all your old clothes. You can also start making up some of that material he bought. Where are you ever going to wear all those clothes?"

"Pete says he wants me to look nice all the time."

"You sure there aren't any more like him in Illinois? Dangle a man like that in front of me, and I'll grab him so fast it'll make his head spin."

"I thought you didn't want to get married, that you couldn't trust a man enough to love him."

"I sure could learn to love a man who wanted to spoil me like Pete wants to spoil you. I'm half in love with him myself. You must be delirious."

"I am," Anne said, looking at her rings for the thousandth time since Pete had put them on her finger. "I never dreamed I could be so happy."

"With you two making sheep's eyes at each other, I expect this place will fill up with children in no time. You'd better find somebody to help with the work. I can't do it all, especially not with you pregnant and unable to get out of your chair."

Much to her surprise, Anne realized she'd never thought about having children.

"I bet he's a wonderful lover," Dolores said. She'd paused in her washing. "Not that I'm asking you to tell me anything."

But Anne could tell Dolores was hoping she'd tell her everything. Wouldn't she be surprised—no, shocked—to learn Pete hadn't done anything more intimate than wash her back?

"We haven't talked about children yet," Anne said.

"You'd better do it soon. With you young and him healthy—well, you know what to expect."

"I'm sure we've got plenty of time."

"I'll bet you're pregnant right now."

"I'm not."

"How can you be sure?"

She couldn't admit Pete hadn't made love to her, not even once. "I'm sure I'll feel something."

Dolores laughed. "You'll feel something all right, when you take one look at your breakfast and run straight for the sink."

"Are you sure you'll need extra help?"

"Certain."

"I'll talk to Pete."

But not right away. Not until there was a reason to bring up the subject of babies.

Pete released the horse's foreleg and eased back into the shadows. There was so much moonlight tonight, he had to take extra care not to cause the horses to make any unusual noises. If one of the men should come out of the bunkhouse, he'd see Pete in a matter of minutes. He had an excuse prepared as to why he should be wandering about the corrals, checking the feet of every horse on the place, but it would be better if he didn't have to use it.

He hadn't found either of the horses ridden by the men who'd shot him and killed Peter Warren, but that didn't really surprise him. He didn't think the killers or their horses were at the ranch house. He believed the three of them were playing a game of cat-and-mouse. They wanted to kill him, but they couldn't get close because they thought he would recognize them.

He'd been keeping an eye out for those distinctive hoof marks, but it was hard to look for hoofprints when he was in the middle of a crowd and didn't want anybody to know what he was doing. That was why he'd decided to do it in the middle of the night when he had the time to make a careful and thorough search. Now that it was done, he'd be glad to get to bed. He was so tired, he was yawning.

He was certain there were other horses on the ranch he hadn't seen, probably even ranch hands who bedded down in line cabins because it was too far to make the long ride in each day. It was a shame he couldn't pin the crime on Belser, but Eddie swore Belser never left the ranch, that he hadn't seen him with anybody who wasn't a Tumbling T hand. Pete was certain Belser had somehow found and hired two men to do the killing, but he couldn't figure out how he'd done it.

Belser had come back from Big Bend drunk. Or as drunk as a man could be after a six-hour ride. Fortunately, Anne had gone to bed. If Belser had said anything more to hurt her feelings, Pete would have thrown him out of the house right then and there. Pete had let Belser go to his room to sleep it off, but the man would pack his belongings and leave first thing in the morning. He had enough to worry about without having that coyote snapping at his heels all day.

Pete carefully worked his way through the herd. He had to get back to the house without being seen.

Back to bed with Anne.

It was a good thing he was going on roundup. He didn't know how much longer he could sleep in the same bed with Anne without touching her. He'd thought knowing she was married to another man would help him keep his distance. If that failed, his conscience wouldn't let him take advantage of her knowing he meant to leave the minute he found his money.

But he'd been wrong. He'd gone from one piece of folly to another, taking her to town with him, buying her clothes and turning her into a beauty, touching her skin until he thought his body would explode. Now it was all he could do to keep his hands to himself. If things got any worse, he'd have to come up with some reason why he had to sleep in a separate bedroom.

But he couldn't think of an excuse that anyone would believe.

He had to keep reminding himself what Isabelle would do to him if she ever found out. That was it. He had to remember Isabelle. Surely it would be harder to take advantage of a woman, no matter how beautiful, with his mother looking over his shoulder.

Anne woke up with a start. It was all she could do to stifle a scream. Her heart beat so rapidly that it hurt; her breath came in short, sharp gasps. The dream had been so real, so terrifying.

She'd dreamed Pete was an imposter, that he'd killed Peter and was trying to kill her. She'd tried to hide from him, but he always found her; she'd tried to run from him, but he was faster; her dress caught on a branch, and she fell down. Belser and Mrs. Dean laughed at her. The sheriff refused to help. Eddie and Dolores couldn't reach her. She was alone and helpless. The closer he came, the more horrible Pete looked, the more his face resembled some terrible animals. She started to scream and scream and—

Then she woke up.

The relief was tremendous. As horrible as it was, as terrified as she still was, she was awake, safe in bed with Pete. Remembering his warning never to touch him while he was asleep, she whispered, "Pete."

She got no answer.

"Pete, please wake up."

Still no answer.

She fumbled in the drawer beside the table until she found a box of matches, and struck one.

There was no one there. Pete wasn't in bed.

Then she remembered he'd said he and Eddie might be up a long time talking about the roundup. Quickly, before the match could burn her fingers, she lit the lamp she kept beside the bed.

The clock across the room said 2:37 A.M. She wasn't certain she'd wound it properly, but she could hear it ticking. Pete shouldn't be up this late. He'd never be able to get up in the morning. He was working too hard, probably determined the ranch wouldn't fail like his hardware store. She'd go down and make him come up to bed. He wasn't going to fail this time.

She found her slippers and put on a robe.

Belser's door was closed. So he'd come back. She had mixed feelings about that. She felt bad about firing him. She probably would have let him stay if Pete had let her. At the same time, she was glad Pete had insisted Belser leave. He would never accept Pete's ownership of the ranch. She didn't want her children being brought up with stories of how their father had cheated Belser out of his rightful inheritance.

The house looked eerie in the dark, lamplight casting long, ominous shadows that jumped and swayed with every step she took. She told herself she was spooked because of the dream, that nothing could possibly happen to her as long as she was in the house, certainly not with Eddie and Pete still up.

But long before she'd crossed the huge living room, Anne knew there was nobody in the office. The door stood ajar. No light came from within.

Pete was gone.

She told herself not to be foolish. He was here. He had to be. She just had to think where. In the kitchen. He and Eddie probably got hungry. Or wanted more coffee. Relieved to have found the answer, she turned and hurried to the kitchen.

Empty.

Panic threatened to overcome her determined effort to remain calm. She whirled and ran out of the kitchen, up the stairs, and down the hall toward the room where Eddie slept. She stopped. She didn't need to wake him up. She could hear him snoring softly. She wasn't alone. Everybody else was here except Pete.

Where was he?

Her first impulse was to wake Eddie and tell him something had happened to Pete. Instead, she backed away from the door, turned, and headed back toward her own bedroom. She didn't know what Pete might be doing, but she was certain he'd be furious if she woke everybody up and started a search for him.

She returned to her room, closed the door, and got back into bed. Where was he? What could he be doing? Why on earth would he be out in the middle of the night? He never would have done that when he was a boy. He didn't even want to sit on the porch after dark. She was glad that had changed. She liked sitting out at night and watching the stars.

But an uneasy feeling started to grow inside Anne all over again. Pete had changed an awful lot. She had liked the changes. She had been happy he'd grown into a man capable of handling his inheritance. She had thought several times it was a shame Uncle Carl hadn't lived to see that Pete had turned out a whole lot better than he'd ever thought possible.

But now, even though she tried to push the thought away, she couldn't rid herself of the dreadful suspicion that maybe Pete had changed too much. Maybe it wasn't possible for a man to learn to be so completely unlike himself in ten years. Nobody else thought he could change. She wondered again if he might have made up that story about failing in business in Illinois. She didn't know why he would have done something like that, but maybe he'd done it to make Uncle Carl think he'd turned out to be just as much of a failure as Uncle Carl expected. Instead he'd gone to Texas and learned to be a cowboy so when he inherited the ranch, he'd know exactly what to do.

That would explain all that business about Isabelle and Jake. It would also explain why he could do everything better than anybody else.

Only one thing was wrong.

If he'd gone to Texas, how had he sent all those letters to her from Illinois? Why did the letters she'd been getting over the last ten years sound like the Peter she knew before, not the Pete who was her husband now? Had he done that intentionally, fooled her, too, so nobody would know what he was doing?

It answered everything perfectly. As long as she could believe it, she wouldn't have to doubt Pete. She could go on loving him, depending on him, enjoying being treated with kindness and thoughtfulness. She could look forward to a future as the cherished wife of a powerful rancher, as the mother of sons and daughters who would be just as wonderful as their father. She would never have to worry about having nowhere to go, about being ignored and despised because of her Indian blood.

But what if that weren't true?

She didn't even want to think of that. The possibilities were too numerous, too dreadful. If that were true . . .

She heard the faint sound of a footstep in the hall. Very quickly she turned out the light and slid down into the bed.

Moments later the door opened. She knew without looking that Pete had entered the room in stocking feet. She lay perfectly still while he tiptoed around to his side of the bed. She could barely hear the sound of his clothes as he carefully slipped them from his body. She felt the bed give as he eased his weight down onto the mattress. He gradually got fully into bed and pulled the covers over him. She felt his head relax into the pillow. A soft sigh escaped him.

"Where have you been?" she asked.

Chapter Eleven

"I thought you'd be asleep hours ago."

He sounded startled, as if someone had sneaked up behind him and yelled *Boo!*

"I was. I had a bad dream." She struck a match, lighted the lamp, and turned toward him. "I went downstairs looking for you, but you weren't there. Eddie's been in bed a long time. I know because I heard him snoring. Where have you been?"

"Outside checking the horses."

"In the dark?"

"It's not dark with all that moonlight. You can see practically as well as day."

"You used to be afraid of the dark."

"I wasn't afraid."

"You didn't like it."

"No kid likes the dark. I was just brave enough to admit it."

Nobody else had called it bravery. His father had been angry, his uncle disgusted. His brother had laughed. "How did you get over being afraid of the dark?"

"Working at night loading wagons, delivering stuff, walking home after I closed the store. Half the time I'd get to the store before the sun came up."

Why was it that perfectly reasonable explanations didn't seem enough anymore? She had no reason not to believe him. He didn't hesitate when she asked questions. He didn't seem upset or angry or even wonder why she wanted to know where he'd been. He'd probably jumped when she spoke because he'd expected her to be asleep and her voice coming out of the dark startled him.

"Why couldn't you check on them in the morning?"

"I need to do other things in the morning."

"Let Eddie do it."

"I like to do things like that myself. Then I know the kind of mounts we have and what I can expect from the riders."

"How did you learn so much about horses?"

"I told you, my friend from Texas. I spent a great deal of time with him. He taught me a lot."

"You said you went to Texas?"

He hesitated. "I hoped you'd forgotten about that."

"Why?"

"That's how I lost the store."

"Then why did you go?"

"I knew Uncle Carl had to leave me the ranch because there wasn't anybody else. I wasn't coming out here to let him make fun of me again. I wanted to know what to do, to be nearly as good as Uncle Carl was. Only he died before I could show him. I went back to Illinois to try to save the hardware store, but it was too late."

"Why didn't you tell me? From your letters, I thought things were getting worse and worse."

"They were at the store, but I didn't want you to know about Texas, in case Uncle Carl was right. I had a friend mail my letters so they'd all come to you from Illinois."

"You cared that much about what I thought?"

"I always cared what you thought. You were the only one who didn't think I was a total loss."

Even Peter's mother had preferred his brother. That must have hurt.

"Anything else you want to know?" he asked.

"No."

"Good. I've got to get some sleep." He leaned over and kissed her on the forehead. "Good night."

"Good night."

He must have fallen asleep instantly. She could hear the sound of his steady breathing almost the moment his head hit the pillow. She slid down under the covers. It made her feel really good to know her opinion had always been important, but she wished he'd told her about Texas and the store. She'd have understood. She'd been treated a lot like him. Maybe that was why he was being so nice to her now, because he knew what it was like to be ignored.

She'd rather he did it because he loved her.

She didn't know when being loved became so important. She hadn't thought about it when she asked him to marry her. She'd just thought they'd be friends the way they'd always been. But now that wasn't enough. She wanted love. She wanted children. She wanted forever.

But some little voice in the back of her head warned her to be careful. It cautioned her to pay close attention to everything he said and did. The voice said he was too different and the changes too perfect.

She wouldn't listen to that voice.

But it wouldn't go away.

Pete cursed himself for a fool. He should have known Anne would wake up and want to know what he was doing wandering about the ranch at night. He'd never thought he was such a glib liar, but the answers had rolled off his tongue. He guessed he'd picked up more about Peter than he realized.

This story about going to Texas was a good idea. At least it explained why he could do so many things Peter apparently would never have been able to do. He just hoped she wouldn't ask him any more questions. He didn't like having to lie to her. He'd have to tell her the truth one of these days, but he couldn't now.

It was too dangerous, and he had no assurance she would believe him.

"Are you sure Belser hasn't come down yet?" Anne asked Dolores.

"Of course I'm sure."

"We've been so busy, I didn't realize until now I hadn't seen him, but he never sleeps this late."

"Eddie said he was drunk when he came in last night. Maybe he's sleeping it off. No point in getting up if all he has to do is pack his gear and leave."

"I guess not, but he's got to get up. Everybody will leave before long. I don't want to have to be the one to make him leave. What would I do if he refuses to go?"

"Shoot him," Dolores said.

"I couldn't do that."

"Why not? You'd shoot a lobo wolf. Belser is just as bad."

"He's just angry he didn't get the ranch."

"He's always been a nasty man. I never liked him."

Anne was helping Dolores in the kitchen on what had been the most hectic morning she could remember. All the men had slept at the ranch the night before and eaten breakfast there in the morning. They expected to leave for the roundup by noon. Since finishing breakfast, the men had been hurrying to get their gear in order, choose their horses, make sure they were properly shod and had no saddle burns or sore feet.

The cook had been in and out of the house all day, getting supplies for the chuck wagon, setting aside what he would send for later. His temper had caused clashes with Dolores several times already. Anne would be glad to see him leave. He might be a fine cook for the men, but two cooks in any kitchen was one cook too many.

Once she and Dolores had finished putting the food away and washing the dishes, Anne confined herself to keeping two coffeepots going. The harder the men worked, the more coffee they drank. It also kept her out of the line of fire between Dolores and the maestro of the chuck wagon.

One of the young hands, named Ray, came inside. "Cookie wants me to collect that side of bacon now."

"You know where it is," Dolores said. It always irritated her to have anyone messing around in her storeroom.

"Before you do that, go upstairs and wake Belser," Anne said. "I'd go, but I don't think it's proper for a lady to go into a man's room."

Ray grinned. "Glad to oblige, ma'am. Just tell me where to find him, and I'll have him downstairs in a jiffy."

"Up the stairs and turn left," Anne said. "It's the next-to-last door."

"Clean your boots before you go into the house," Dolores ordered.

The young cowhand grinned again. "I already done that, Miz Dolores. I knowed you'd have my hide if I tracked dirt inside the house."

"Tell that to your cook," Dolores said.

"I don't tell Cookie nothing," Ray said. "I like to eat."

"That man thinks he can do anything he wants just because he's the range cook," Dolores fumed, once again on her favorite subject.

"The men say he's the best cook in Wyoming," Anne said.

"They'd be afraid to open their mouths if he was the worst. He's a tyrant."

The door opened, and another young cowhand entered the kitchen. "Ready for another pot of coffee, ma'am." He grinned. All the hands seemed to be in a great mood. They were looking forward to the roundup.

"Everybody's awfully thirsty," Anne said.

"It's stirring up all that dust that does it. Got to have something to wet down a man's throat."

"Do you think you'll need another pot?"

"It'd be nice if you could keep 'em coming until we pull out. The men sure do like their coffee. Especially the old ones."

The "old ones" couldn't have been more than twenty-four or -five. Cowhands didn't grow old. They soon looked for an easier line of work or tried to start a ranch of their own.

"I'll grind some more beans. Just let me know—"

Ray came back into the kitchen, his face drained of color. "Belser ain't coming down," he said.

"Oh, yes, he is," Dolores said. "If he thinks he'll lie in that bed all day, he's got another think coming."

"He ain't thinking nothing," Ray said. "He's dead."

"Don't be ridiculous," Dolores said. "You just have to shake him harder. He went to bed drunk as a skunk."

"He ain't drunk," Ray said. "He's dead. Stone cold. Stiff as a board. There's a knife sticking out of his back."

Anne didn't believe Belser could be dead. Nobody got killed in his own bed. Besides, no stranger had entered the house last night. The doors were never locked, but she was sure she'd have heard if anybody had come up the stairs.

197

"That's impossible," Dolores said. "You've got to be mistaken."

"Go see for yourself," Ray said. "I sure as hell ain't going up there again."

"Get Pete," Anne said to the cowboy who'd come for the coffee. "Tell him to come here right away." Ray went out with him.

Anne didn't know what Pete could do, but her first thought had been that Pete would take care of everything.

"Did you hear anything last night?" Dolores asked after both the cowhands had left.

"No."

"Me, neither. And I didn't see any sign that anybody had been in the house."

"Who would want to kill Belser?" Anne asked. "Nobody liked him much, but he was leaving."

The two women stood there, each absorbed by her thoughts, until the kitchen door was flung open.

"Ray said Belser's been killed," Pete said as he entered the kitchen, followed closely by Eddie and Ray.

"I don't know," Anne said. "Neither one of us has been up there."

"Well, we have to go now." He held out his hand toward her. "Will you go with me?"

She'd seen death before, but she'd never seen anyone who'd been killed. The horror of it made her so weak she could hardly move. The fact that it had happened in the house, in the bedroom next to where she and Pete had slept, made it seem even more horrible.

She had been sound asleep at the moment someone drove a knife into Belser's body. Just the thought caused her to shiver.

"I'll go." She knew she had to.

No one spoke as they left the kitchen, ascended the stairs, and approached the door to Belser's room.

"Did you move him?" Pete asked Ray.

"No," he answered. "As soon as I opened the door, I saw that knife in his back. I knew he weren't going to wake up."

Anne wouldn't have touched him either. Just the thought of it caused her to grip Pete's hand more tightly.

"I know you don't want to go in, but it's best we all see it. Then there can't be any question about what anyone saw."

He didn't have to tell Anne this was a murder, that there'd have to be an investigation. She knew that already.

The door to the room stood open, apparently just the way Ray had left it. They all entered the room, Pete and Anne first.

The scene looked so quiet and ordinary, and Belser looked so peaceful, it was hard for Anne to realize he was dead. He was on his stomach, his head turned toward them, his arms and legs flung out from his body, the bedclothes thrown on the floor. He had gone to bed in his underwear, his discarded clothes and boots scattered around the room.

The only disconcerting image was the knife sticking out of his back.

"That looks like one of my kitchen knives," Dolores said.

"Are you missing a knife?" Pete asked.

"I don't know. Things have been too mixed up this morning to tell. If I'm missing anything, Cookie probably has it. He's always taking what he wants without asking."

"Go check," Pete said.

Dolores left.

"Did you hear anything last night?" Pete asked Eddie.

"No. I went to bed after we finished talking. I didn't wake up until Dolores called me for breakfast."

"None of the boys did," Ray said. "Somebody woulda said something if they did."

"The horses would have waked them up if there'd been strangers about," Eddie said.

"Did you hear anything?" Pete asked Anne.

Anne didn't want to lie and say she hadn't heard anyone at all. Neither did she want to tell everyone the only person she'd heard was Pete trying to slip into their room unnoticed sometime after two o'clock. That would make everyone suspect him.

"I mean other than me coming to bed late," Pete added.

Anne breathed an inward sigh of relief. She wouldn't have to lie, and Pete didn't want her to hide the fact that he'd been up late. It also showed he couldn't have had anything to do with Belser's murder. She knew he hadn't—she chastised herself for even thinking of it, but she couldn't help it. Everybody would say Pete had the most to gain by getting rid of Belser.

"No, I heard no one," Anne said. "I'm a light sleeper. I'm sure I would have heard anyone enter the house."

"None of us heard anything," Eddie said, "but somebody murdered Belser."

Anne didn't like the way he said that, or the way he looked at Pete. She couldn't imagine why Eddie would suspect Pete, but she didn't know what else that look could mean.

"Ray, ride into town and notify the sheriff," Pete said. "I'd like him out here before nightfall if possible."

"Sure," the boy said, clearly glad to leave the room.

"The rest of us will go about our business as usual. We've got cows to round up."

"You can't mean to do that now," Anne said.

"Belser's death doesn't change the fact we need to get our cows to market before the bottom falls out," Pete said.

"But Belser's been killed."

"Stopping work won't bring him back."

"I know, but . . . " Somehow it seemed disrespectful to go about their regular work as if nothing had happened.

"It's up to the sheriff to decide what to do next," Pete said. "We can't sit here doing nothing all day. Eddie, do you mind telling the men what's happened?"

"I imagine they already know."

"Then see they get back to work. They won't do any good speculating about who did it. I still want to pull out by noon."

"You leaving before the sheriff gets here?"

Anne didn't like the way Eddie asked that question.

It was almost as if he thought Pete might know something about the murder.

"No. We were both in the house last night, so we'd both better be here when he arrives. We can ride out tonight, or tomorrow morning if it gets too late."

Eddie left. Only Pete and Anne remained in the bedroom.

"Do you know what could have happened?" she asked.

"No. If anything, I'd have thought Belser wanted to kill me. Do you know if he has any enemies?"

"He wasn't very likable, but he never did anything to make anybody want to kill him."

"One person did," Pete said.

Yes, Anne thought, and everybody is going to think it was you. She could swear he'd been in the bed with her all night. He hadn't, but she could swear it. Regardless of the changes since they had known each other as children, she was certain Peter could never kill anyone.

But was he the same man?

That thought wouldn't leave her. She could give herself lists of reasons why Belser and Mrs. Dean had to be wrong, but the question continued to nag at her.

What if Pete wasn't Peter Warren?

She refused to let herself think of that. Pete wasn't a killer. He was her husband. She was his wife. She was the only one who could absolutely clear him from suspicion in this murder.

But would her testimony do that? Some people would say she'd say anything to defend her husband. Others, some truly vicious people who hated her because of her Indian blood, would insist she'd say anything to keep her position as the wife of a wealthy rancher. They'd whisper that she was in cahoots with an imposter to defraud poor Belser of his rightful inheritance. They'd say they all knew Belser meant to throw her off the ranch the minute he got control.

He had. Belser had told Anne more than once that he considered her nothing more than a parasite. He would have taken great pleasure in making her leave.

Cold fear settled in Anne's stomach. If anything happened to Pete, she'd be at her uncle's mercy again. He'd force her to marry Cyrus McCaine. That was all the more reason why Pete had to be Peter, why he had to be innocent of this murder.

Pete sat at the desk in his office, but he wasn't getting anything done. He would be glad to get the next few hours over with. He didn't know what was going to happen, but he couldn't expect the sheriff to believe he hadn't killed Belser when his own men did.

Nobody had said anything. They didn't have to. They continued their preparations, but the mood of cheerful excitement had given away to one of moody quiet. Their conversation became subdued whenever he was around. The younger ones wouldn't look him in the eye, even found reasons to stay out of his way. When they thought he wasn't looking, their eyes followed him, quietly accusing him of what no one wanted to say out loud.

Pete refused to acknowledge the shift of feeling and continued with his work as though nothing had happened. He sat down at the same table with the men when they had their midday meal. He addressed them when they were ready to leave, telling them he and Eddie would ride out to their camp that evening or early the next morning, depending on how long the sheriff needed them.

No one had said anything, and they'd ridden away in silence.

After that there hadn't been much to do. Anne and Dolores worked in the kitchen, cleaning up after lunch, beginning preparations for a supper that could include several men in addition to the sheriff. For a while, he and Eddie worked together in the office. For the last hour he'd been alone.

A knock sounded on the door. "Come in."

Anne stood in the doorway, worry creasing her lovely face. Pete got up, crossed the room, and slipped his arms around her waist. "You've got to stop worrying. The sheriff's visit won't be much fun, but it'll soon be over."

"He'll want to know who killed Belser."

"All we can tell him is what we know."

"But he won't believe us."

"He'll probably think I did it, but he can't prove it. Now sit down and stop worrying about me. I've been in scrapes before and gotten out. I'll get out of this one."

Anne allowed herself to be seated in a captain's chair, but she didn't relax. "This one's serious."

"I know."

He was confused. He'd been certain Belser was responsible for Peter's death. No one else had anything to gain by it.

"Who would want to murder Belser?" Pete asked. "Besides me, of course."

"I don't know. Nobody disliked him that much."

"That's what I think. Which brings us back to my being the most logical person to have killed him. But since I didn't—and I'm not sure anyone is going to believe that but you and me—we'd better bend our minds to trying to figure out who did."

"How can we do that?"

"By thinking logically. I've been thinking about this for the last hour, and I can come up with only two possibilities. Someone murdered Belser because they had something to gain by his death or something to lose by his staying alive."

"What could that be?"

Maybe Belser knew who was responsible for Peter Warren's murder, and the killers didn't feel certain he wouldn't tell on them. But Pete couldn't tell Anne that. Not yet. "I don't know. But there's another possibility, one I like even less."

"What's that?"

"That someone killed Belser to incriminate me."

"But why?"

"To get this ranch, you, or both."

"Who'd want me?"

"You're very beautiful. A lot of men would count themselves fortunate to have you for a wife."

"Nobody ever thought I was beautiful except you."

"You never acted like you were beautiful until we bought those clothes. But now you know you are, and you'll never go around hiding in corners again. You've got courage, too. You haven't gotten used to the idea of using it yet, but you will." He still got angry at Carl Warren for treating her so shabbily all these years. He didn't understand why no one could see what a loyal, loving, strong woman she was.

"Who could want the ranch?" Anne asked.

"Just about anybody in the Territory. I never met a man who didn't like the idea of being rich."

"Enough to kill Belser?"

"That does reduce the size of the list, but not much."

"But how could someone have gotten into the house?"

"Now that brings the list down rather sharply. But it also leaves us once again with two choices."

"What are they?"

"Either the person killed Belser himself—unlikely because a stranger would be noticed by the hands during the day and by the horses at night—or somebody here was paid to do the murder."

Anne blanched. He didn't like to frighten her like that, but he was certain somebody on the ranch had killed Belser. Until he knew different, he had to assume Anne was in just as much danger as he was.

"Nobody here would have done a thing like that."

"Offer a certain kind of man enough money and he'll kill his best friend."

"But the cowhands are just boys, like Ray."

Anne got to her feet. She looked about her like a caged animal looking for a way out. She started to walk first one way, then the other. He got up and gripped her by the shoulders until she stopped fighting him.

"I didn't believe it when you said you were shot,"

she said. "I mean I *did* believe it because you said so, but you were so strong—as though you'd never been hurt in your whole life. We all acted like it never happened. In a few more days I might have been able to forget the attack outside of Big Bend. But I can't forget Belser."

She started to shake. He pulled her to him and put his arms around her. She resisted at first, then threw her arms around him. He held her tightly and kissed the top of her head.

"Your uncle neglected your education more seriously than I thought. Not only did he neglect to tell you that you had beauty and courage, he failed to teach you that some people will do anything for money and power. Some very nice people, people who are your friends, people you thought you knew. When a ranch like this is at stake, some people will do anything."

"But it's not at stake. It belongs to you."

"Somebody has twice tried to kill me. They may now be trying to frame me for Belser's murder. If I'm out of the way, you're the only one standing between some very determined person and this ranch."

"But I don't own it."

"You would as my widow."

"Then someone might want to kill me?"

"I don't intend to let them. I've become very fond of you."

She looked up at him with those big black eyes. "How much?"

He didn't dare answer that question. He couldn't afford to hear the answer.

"Have you learned to love me?" she asked.

That question rocked him hard. He could tell by the look in her eyes that the answer was important to her.

"You said you wanted us to remain friends, just like we used to be." He'd read that in one of her letters.

"I thought that's what I wanted, but it isn't. Not anymore."

He couldn't make her think he loved her, then leave as soon as he found his money. "I haven't known you long—as a woman, that is—but no man could know you for long and not fall in love with you."

"Could you?"

"Very easily."

Then he kissed her. Her lips were soft, her mouth yielding. Parting her lips, she raised herself to meet his kiss. There was nothing shy or tentative about her response. She clung to him, kissing him with an intensity that lit a fire in his veins. Crushing her to him, he pressed his mouth to hers, forcing her lips wider with his thrusting tongue. She wasn't a woman who needed much instruction. Her tongue challenged his. Dancing and whirling, they engaged in a sinuous exchange that caused Pete to hold Anne even tighter, which caused Anne to mold her body tightly against his.

As he roused her passion, his own grew stronger. Blood pounded in his brain, leapt in his heart, and made his knees tremble. His emotions whirled and skidded, sending shock waves throughout his entire body. His kisses deepened as he forced his mouth hard against her lips, as he ground his body against hers. The need deep within him, which he'd been denying for days, burst free from its bonds and came rocketing to the surface—hungry, greedy, ravenous for what it had been denied so long.

The door opened. "The sheriff is here," Eddie said.

Anne tore herself from Pete's arms, but he couldn't tell if her look, made up of equal parts of consternation, desire, and disbelief, was for what had happened between them or for Eddie's catching them in a passionate embrace. He knew what he felt. A few minutes more, and he'd have taken Anne right there on top of the desk. He managed to calm his racing heart, control his treacherous voice.

He put his arms around Anne as he hoped a loving husband would hold his wife. "Good," he said. "Send him in."

Chapter Twelve

Anne grabbed Pete's arm. She didn't know why she was looking to him for protection when he was the one who needed protecting.

"It's all right," he murmured. "Everything will be all right."

Things had never been all right. Every time something good came along, something else came to take it away. Now, when she'd finally discovered love, the sheriff was here to take it from her. She wouldn't let it happen. No matter what it took, she wouldn't let that happen.

"What happened?" the sheriff asked.

"I'm sure Ray has already told you as much as we know," Pete said.

"We were so busy getting ready for the roundup, we didn't notice he hadn't come down," Anne said.

"When did you notice?" the sheriff asked.

"When everyone had finished breakfast and gone outside," Anne said. "I'd fired Belser. I wanted him gone before Pete and the men left."

"Why?"

"Because I wasn't sure I could make him go."

"Where's the body?" the sheriff asked.

"In his room," Pete said. "We left everything just as we found it."

The sheriff looked surprised.

"That's what the sheriff back in Illinois said we were supposed to do."

"You were involved in a murder there?" the sheriff asked.

"We had a vagrant killed one night. The people moved him off the street so it wouldn't upset the ladies. The sheriff was real sore about that."

"He should have been," the sheriff said. "I'd better go see Belser."

"Here's the key," Pete said, taking the key from his pocket. "I wanted to make sure nobody touched anything," he said when the sheriff's eyes narrowed. "All four of us have been in the house since we found him. We can vouch that no one has gone up the stairs since."

"He's sure you did it," Anne said as soon as the sheriff left the room.

"I'm the logical suspect. Unless something turns up we don't know about, I'm the only one he has."

"But you didn't do it."

"I know that, but the sheriff is the one we have to convince."

"I can't think of a soul who'd want to kill Belser," Eddie said.

"Me, neither," Dolores added.

"The most logical explanation is that someone in the house—one of us—killed him," Pete said.

"You can't suspect me!" Dolores exclaimed.

"No, but the sheriff is bound to notice he was killed with one of your knives. If one of us didn't kill him, it almost had to be one of the cowhands. I don't see how anybody else could have gotten into the house without being noticed."

"He could have come from the hills behind the house," Eddie pointed out. "That way the horses might not have caught his scent."

"Who would know the house that well?"

"Maybe he's been here before," Dolores suggested. "Carl used to have lots of people stay here for days at a time."

"It's probably someone none of us will think of," Pete said, "but we've got to realize the sheriff is going to be sure one of us did it."

"How can you be so calm?" Anne asked Pete. Her stomach was tied in so many knots, she felt she'd be sick any minute.

"I don't have much choice. Unless one of us confesses, the sheriff isn't going to be able to solve this thing. It'll be up to us to figure out what happened."

"But we've already tried."

"Then we have to keep trying. You can be sure he'll keep trying to pin it on me."

That became clear as soon as the sheriff came back

downstairs. "I want to know where all of you were last evening," he said, but his gaze remained fixed on Pete.

Anne waited for Pete to start, but he nodded for her to relate the events of the evening. That frightened her. She was used to people like the sheriff ignoring her. She murmured a silent prayer to her French grandfather, the arrogant aristocrat who'd taken a Crow maiden to live with him, then abandoned her to return to France after he'd made his fortune. If she'd ever needed a drop of his imperious pride, she needed it now.

"We didn't finish supper until sometime after nine o'clock," Anne said, "because Pete and I were late getting back from Big Bend. I helped Dolores clean up, and the men went to Pete's office to go over their plans for the roundup. Pete told me not to wait up because they'd probably be late, so I went to bed when we finished in the kitchen."

"When did he come to bed?" the sheriff asked.

"I don't know. I didn't look at the clock." Okay, it was a tiny lie, but she couldn't tell this man the truth. If he found out Eddie had gone to bed long before Pete, he'd be sure Pete had killed Belser. "I do know that after he came to bed, he never left again."

"How can you be so sure?"

"I'm a light sleeper. I'd know if he got up during the night."

The sheriff didn't look pleased. "What about you?" he said, turning to Dolores.

"Pretty much the same thing," Dolores responded. "I went to bed after we finished in the kitchen."

"When did you get to bed?" the sheriff asked Eddie.

"About twelve-thirty."

"Did you see Pete go to his bedroom?"

"No. I left him in the office."

"Did you see Eddie go to his bedroom?" the sheriff asked Pete.

"No."

"How long did you stay in your office?"

"Only long enough to put the maps up."

"When did Belser get back?" the sheriff asked.

"After the women had gone to bed," Pete said. "He was drunk. I wanted to throw him out of the house right then, but I didn't because of Anne."

"And why was that?"

"She felt sorry for him. She'd even asked if I didn't think we ought to give him his job back."

"What did you say?"

"I said we'd let him have his room for one more night, then he'd have to go. Now I'm sorry I didn't throw him down the steps the minute I saw he was drunk."

"You didn't like Belser."

"I wouldn't like anybody who kept calling me an imposter. Would you?"

"It's not a question of what I would do," the sheriff said. "Anybody recognize that knife?"

"I think it's from the kitchen," Dolores said. "But with Cookie helping himself to anything he wants, it's impossible to tell what's missing."

"Have you checked Cookie's knives?" the sheriff asked.

"Are you crazy?" Dolores said. "You go asking to see what he's got in his chuck wagon and see what kind of reception you get."

"I'll ask, and I'll find out."

Once more he fixed his gaze on Pete, and Anne's chill of apprehension deepened. She was certain the sheriff was going to take Pete to jail.

"Do you have any more questions?" Pete asked. "The ladies have suffered quite a shock. They'd probably like to lie down. I know Anne needs to rest."

He put his arm around her. She didn't know how he could have so much strength.

"I'm fine," she said. Though she would dearly love to run to their room, close the door, jump into bed, and pull the covers over her head, she couldn't leave Pete to face the sheriff alone. Besides, her future was at stake. She didn't know what she'd do without Pete. She'd always liked him, but during recent days she'd decided that most likely her original feelings had been primarily thankfulness that he liked and accepted her as she was. No one else had.

But what she felt for Pete now was something completely different. He was like a dream come true, and he was *her* dream. Not somebody she'd read or heard about. *Her husband!* She still found that hard to believe.

It was just as hard to believe the way he felt about her. He thought she was beautiful, and she felt beautiful when she was with him. It wasn't the dresses or the jewels or even the nice things he said about her. It was the way he looked at her, the way his gaze lingered on her shoulders, or her lips. The way his eyes grew warm, his expression heated. He not only liked her and thought she was beautiful, he desired her.

It had frightened her when Cyrus McCaine desired her. It excited her to know Pete wanted her. She had no experience in love, but she knew instinctively that what the two men felt for her had nothing in common. Cyrus made her feel cheap, worthless. Pete made her feel cherished, like the most beautiful, the most valued woman in the world.

"The ladies can go about their work or do anything else they want," the sheriff said. "I want you men to stay here until I talk to your range cook."

"He's gone," Pete said. "They left for the roundup camp shortly after noon."

"Now why would you have them do that?" That suspicious look was back in the sheriff's eyes. It was obvious he thought Pete had killed Belser and was trying to cover his tracks.

"Because we're starting a roundup tomorrow."

"It's still summer."

"Late summer," Pete corrected.

"Still, nobody goes on roundup for another month or six weeks."

"The range is bare and overcrowded. The signs for winter are ominous."

"I haven't seen any signs," the sheriff asked.

"I traveled up the Missouri River and came down from Montana. The Indians say the signs point to the worst winter in memory."

The sheriff snorted. "Nobody pays any attention to redskins."

"Why not? They occupied these plains long before we got here."

"That still doesn't explain why you're starting roundup so soon. Your cows will be underweight. You won't get much for them."

"I'll get more than if they're dead. The herd isn't strong enough to stand a severe winter, and there's not enough food to carry them over. I'm taking them to market while I still can."

"That's a big gamble."

"If I lose, I won't lose anybody's money but my own."

The sheriff's expression indicated he wasn't at all sure it was Pete's money. Or his ranch. His expression also indicated frustration.

"I'm going to take Belser's body back to town with me."

"I appreciate that," Pete said. "Naturally we'll pay for the funeral arrangements."

"Don't be so forward. I don't know when he'll be buried."

"We'll pay for the funeral, whenever it is."

The sheriff couldn't argue with that.

"I want all of you to stay here where I can find you."

Again his gaze fixed itself on Pete.

"I don't plan to leave Wyoming, if that's what you're saying," Pete said, "but I have to go on the roundup."

The sheriff pointed an angry finger at Pete. "I want you in this house."

Much to Anne's surprise, Pete actually smiled. She didn't know where he found the courage.

217

"I know you think I killed Belser, and you're frustrated you can't prove it," Pete said, "but at least give me credit for a little intelligence. If I had wanted to kill Belser, I would never have done it in my own house, in the next bedroom, with a knife from my own kitchen. I certainly wouldn't have done it in the house where my wife was bound to know I'd left the bed and any one of three people would hear Belser cry out if I didn't get him in the heart with the first knife thrust."

Stated like that, it didn't sound at all like anyone could believe Pete had killed Belser. Anne suddenly felt a whole lot better.

"Okay, you can go on the roundup as long as I know where to find you if I need you," the sheriff said, still not pleased.

"I had Eddie draw up a map of my range. I plotted where I expect to be each day. If you need me, Anne will be happy to show you where I am."

Anne had never seen a map of the ranch. She had no idea how to read one, but it made her feel wonderful that Pete automatically assumed she'd know what to do. Uncle Carl had always assumed just the opposite.

The sheriff turned to leave, then turned back again. "Don't think you've heard the end of this," he said to Pete. "I'll get you yet. We don't like killers in Johnson County. We especially don't like killers who aren't who they say they are. You watch him, Eddie. If you see him trying to sneak off, shoot him. I'll tell the judge you had my permission."

"I won't try to sneak off," Pete said. "And if anybody shoots me, it'll be murder. Or have you forgotten somebody's tried twice already?"

"That's what you say. Nobody saw it."

"I saw it," Anne stated, furious at the sheriff. "I was in the wagon when the shots were fired. Are you going to call me a liar?" He wouldn't dare. Pete would knock him down. "We all saw his wound when he got here. It was obvious it was quite recent."

"It could have been for other reasons," the sheriff said. "Him being an imposter and all, you can never tell—"

"Leave my house!" Anne ordered. "I have no intention of trying to impede the law, but I won't have you calling my husband a murdering imposter and me a liar and a fool. Get out!" she said when he just stood there staring at her as though she'd gone berserk.

"I'll be back."

"You'd better have proof, not just prejudice and suspicion."

The sheriff turned and stalked out, muttering "crazy redskin" under his breath. Anne grabbed hold of Pete when he started after the man.

"I don't care what he says. What you think is all that matters."

"I think you're a mighty classy lady," Pete said. "I don't know why everybody's yammering about me changing so much when you're changing just as much right before their eyes."

"That's right," Dolores said. "She'd never have had the courage to do that a month ago."

She hadn't had any courage at all a month ago. Or any confidence. Pete's belief in her had been responsible for the change. It had given her the courage to believe in herself. She loved him for that, too.

219

* * *

Anne moved restlessly about the sitting room. She looked out the window, but the brown landscape was unchanged from the last time she'd looked out. She listened, but silence shrouded the house. With just the two of them at home, the quiet was eerie.

"If you don't stop fidgeting, you're going to stick yourself with that needle," Dolores warned.

Anne put her work aside. "I can't concentrate on sewing, not when I'm wondering what the sheriff is going to do next. He's certain Pete killed Belser."

"Like Pete said, as long as you'll swear he never left the bed, there's no way he can pin it on him."

Anne had told herself that over and over again, but she had never known men to let logic and facts get in their way when they were determined to do something. And the sheriff was determined to hang Pete for Belser's murder. She wouldn't be able to rest easy until the real murderer was caught.

"I'm afraid the sheriff will never find out who killed Belser," Anne said to Dolores. "Then everybody will spend the rest of their lives being certain Pete did it. I couldn't stand that."

"I'm sure Pete will think of something. He seems like a very resourceful man."

"Yes, but even he can't conjure killers out of thin air."

And that was the problem. The killer had disappeared into thin air, something Anne knew was impossible. Yet the only other explanation was that someone in the house had killed Belser. She knew that was impossible.

"Listen."

Anne stopped her pacing. "It sounds like a buck-board," she said.

"Who would be using a buckboard?"

Both women hurried from the room, down the hall, and to the front door. They flung open the door and ran out to the porch. Both stopped dead in their tracks, stunned by what they saw. A buckboard had come to a halt in front of the house. The driver jumped out to help Mrs. Horace Dean down.

"I've come to support you in your hour of trial," she announced. "No young woman should have to watch her imposter of a husband be hauled away to the gallows without the support of friends."

Fear clutched at Anne's heart. She looked down the trail to see if the sheriff was following Mrs. Dean. The emptiness of the landscape provided little reassurance. He could have gone straight to the roundup.

"Has the sheriff found any evidence?" She couldn't believe she could control her voice enough to speak.

"No, but he soon will," Mrs. Dean said as she climbed the steps to the porch. "Bring my trunk in," she directed the driver. "Dolores will show you where to put it. And now, my dear, you must allow me to comfort you. You must be near fainting from thinking of your near escape."

"How could we have escaped? You just said the sheriff was going to hang Pete."

"I mean your escape from a murderer who took advantage of your ignorance to claim to be your husband. I certainly hope you're not carrying his child. That would be a tragedy."

Anne had never understood how anyone could be

angry enough to commit murder, but she was beginning to.

"My husband is not an imposter and he's not a murderer. If you've come here to say so, you can turn right around and go back to Big Bend. I will not have a guest in my house slandering my husband."

Anne didn't know where those words had come from. When she opened her mouth, she hadn't intended to throw down a challenge to Mrs. Dean, but she would not allow anyone to say such things about Pete.

"As to that, my dear, the future will tell. Now direct your servant to show this man where to stow my trunk. I'm exhausted and want to lie down before dinner. Afterward we'll talk."

"Dolores is not a servant. She's my friend."

"One should never make a friend of servants, child. It's a mistake."

Mrs. Dean sailed right past them into the house as if Anne hadn't spoken. The woman was impervious to hints, even openly stated prohibitions.

"Put her in my old room," Anne said to Dolores. "No matter what you do, don't show her our room. She's liable to move right in."

"Not if I tell her Pete's likely to come home in the middle of the night and crawl into bed expecting to make love to his wife."

The two women broke into giggles.

"I don't know what you can find to laugh about in such a situation as this," Mrs. Dean intoned from inside the house.

Dolores rolled her eyes, and Anne recaptured her dignity.

"I ought to put her in Belser's bed and hope the killer comes back," Dolores said.

"Don't say that, not even in fun. Now go before she comes out demanding to know why I haven't learned to exercise better control over my servants."

"I know you don't like to think about it, my dear," Mrs. Dean said to Anne as they sat over supper, "but you've got to consider all possibilities. There's something very wrong about this whole affair, and I mean to get to the bottom of it."

After getting up from her nap, Mrs. Dean had refrained from mentioning Pete or Belser's murder. Instead, she'd taken Anne over the entire house, inch by inch, telling her how she should redecorate it now she was mistress. Irritated by the constant stream of criticism, Anne had asked her how she could be mistress of the house if her husband was an imposter about to be hanged.

Mrs. Dean had ignored the question.

Having exhausted Anne's patience and prevented her from helping Dolores with the supper preparations, she led Anne to the table with the aplomb of a queen in her own home. Once at the table, however, she'd reversed herself and concentrated on Pete's guilt.

"You have to consider every possibility." That was her reply every time Anne objected to one of her presumptions, or assertions, or out-and-out fabrications. "This thing is a great mystery. The solution may be something quite beyond even my powers of imagination."

Anne didn't believe that was possible. Mrs. Dean

seemed capable of imagining anything, regardless of how absurd it might be. Such as the scenario she was propounding just now.

"Even you have to admit it covers all the particulars," she was saying. "This man who calls himself Pete meets up with the real Peter Warren on his way here. Peter was such a dolt he'd tell anybody anything and not suspect a thing. It would have been child's play for this man to have pumped him for as much information as possible, then murdered him in his sleep."

"Pete was never that bad, not even as a boy."

Mrs. Dean ignored her interruption.

"Then that man shows up here pretending to be your husband. It's entirely understandable how you could be fooled, my dear. I'm the first to admit he's more handsome than poor Peter would ever have been."

"He looks just like what I thought Peter would look like as a grown man," Anne insisted.

"You overlook the bone structure," Mrs. Dean said. "Never overlook bones. They don't lie."

Anne didn't know how she could forget about the bones, as much as she would like to, with Mrs. Dean forever flinging them in her face. Nobody could tell what a boy's face was going to look like at maturity, not even Mrs. Dean.

"It's perfectly logical he should want to put an end to Belser's insisting he was an imposter," Mrs. Dean continued. "I imagine he would have liked to murder me as well if he dared do such a thing."

Anne was beginning to wonder if there weren't a lot of people who would like to murder Mrs. Dean.

"And if all the things I've said were true, there'd be

GET UP TO
4 FREE BOOKS!

You can have the best romance delivered to your door for less than what you'd pay in a bookstore or online. Sign up for one of our book clubs today, and we'll send you **FREE* BOOKS** just for trying it out...**with no obligation to buy, ever!**

HISTORICAL ROMANCE BOOK CLUB

Travel from the Scottish Highlands to the American West, the decadent ballrooms of Regency England to Viking ships. Your shipments will include authors such as CONNIE MASON, SANDRA HILL, CASSIE EDWARDS, JENNIFER ASHLEY, LEIGH GREENWOOD, and many, many more.

LOVE SPELL BOOK CLUB

Bring a little magic into your life with the romances of Love Spell—fun contemporaries, paranormals, time-travels, futuristics, and more. Your shipments will include authors such as LYNSAY SANDS, CJ BARRY, COLLEEN THOMPSON, NINA BANGS, MARJORIE LIU and more.

As a book club member you also receive the following special benefits:

- **30% OFF all orders through our website & telecenter!**
- **Exclusive access to special discounts!**
- **Convenient home delivery and 10 day examination period to return any books you don't want to keep.**

There is no minimum number of books to buy, and you may cancel membership at any time. See back to sign up!

*Please include $2.00 for shipping and handling.

YES! ☐

Sign me up for the **Historical Romance Book Club** and send my TWO FREE BOOKS! If I choose to stay in the club, I will pay only $8.50* each month, a savings of $5.48!

YES! ☐

Sign me up for the **Love Spell Book Club** and send my TWO FREE BOOKS! If I choose to stay in the club, I will pay only $8.50* each month, a savings of $5.48!

NAME: _____

ADDRESS: _____

_____

TELEPHONE: _____

E-MAIL: _____

☐ **I WANT TO PAY BY CREDIT CARD.**

☐ VISA ☐ MasterCard ☐ DISCOVER

ACCOUNT #: _____

EXPIRATION DATE: _____

SIGNATURE: _____

Send this card along with $2.00 shipping & handling for each club you wish to join, to:

**Romance Book Clubs
20 Academy Street
Norwalk, CT 06850-4032**

Or fax (must include credit card information!) to: 610.995.9274.
You can also sign up online at www.dorchesterpub.com.

*Plus $2.00 for shipping. Offer open to residents of the U.S. and Canada only.
Canadian residents please call 1.800.481.9191 for pricing information.
If under 18, a parent or guardian must sign. Terms, prices and conditions subject to change. Subscription subject to acceptance. Dorchester Publishing reserves the right to reject any order or cancel any subscription.

JOIN NOW!

nothing easier than to steal into poor Belser's room in the dead of night and kill him. Being drunk, he couldn't offer any resistance."

"I've told you repeatedly, Pete didn't leave again after he came to bed," Anne said.

"You were asleep. How could you tell?"

"I'm a light sleeper. I would have woken up."

"You'd had a long trip from town, my dear. You were exhausted. I'm sure you slept like the dead."

"Not quite. I did wake up when Pete came to bed. And he was tiptoeing in his stocking feet so he wouldn't wake me. I heard him outside the door." Mrs. Dean didn't need to know she had already been awake. "He couldn't possibly have gotten out of bed and into it again without waking me."

"He could have murdered poor Belser before he came to bed."

"No, he couldn't. He told the sheriff he only stayed downstairs a few minutes. Belser had just gone upstairs. He wouldn't have been asleep yet."

"I'm sure he could find a way. I will admit he's a clever man."

"Much too clever to kill a man under his own roof," Anne said, repeating Pete's rationale. "Now I'm tired of talking about Belser's death. There must be something else of interest going on in Big Bend. Are you in charge of the ball at the fort this year?"

The annual officer's ball was the highlight of Mrs. Dean's year. She had been placed in charge of arrangements eight years before when the fort was moved to Big Bend, and she hadn't let her husband's retirement force her to give it up. Anne could relax for the rest of the evening knowing that once started, Mrs. Dean wouldn't stop talking about the ball until bedtime.

Anne rose from bed on the third day of Mrs. Dean's visit in the certain knowledge that she couldn't stay in the house with that woman another day without committing murder herself. She couldn't send her back to town because there was no one at the ranch to take her. Pete had left Ray at the ranch with strict orders not to let Anne out of his sight for any reason. When he flatly refused to take Mrs. Dean to Big Bend, Anne was marooned. She had been forced to listen to even more theories about why Pete was impersonating Peter Warren and how he'd managed to kill Belser without anyone knowing.

It didn't matter that some of her theories were completely implausible. She was certain Pete had killed Belser. Such a man could do many things ordinary people couldn't.

Anne had to get away from her, but there was no place Mrs. Dean wouldn't follow her. Yesterday, hoping to escape for at least a short while, Anne had said she wanted to collect anything Belser might have left in the bunkhouse. It hadn't worked. Mrs. Dean had followed her. Anne was desperate, but what could she do?

An idea occurred to her. It was rather bold, perhaps too bold, but she was desperate. The more she thought about it, the more she liked it. With a smile of satisfaction, she jumped out of bed and started looking through her closet for something she could use for riding clothes.

She was going to join Pete at the roundup.

Chapter Thirteen

"The roundup has gone slower than I expected," Pete said to Eddie, "but I think we can finish up tomorrow."

They were standing on a slight rise, upwind from the herd, where they could watch the cowhands cutting out the animals to be sent to market without having to breathe the dust stirred up by thousands of hooves. The weather had turned cold. The ceaseless wind cut through Pete's clothes like a knife. He thought longingly of the warm clothes the killers had taken when they shot him and stripped his camp. He had a big score to settle with those men when he found them.

If he ever did.

Under the pretense of checking the condition of the horses, he'd made a careful inspection of all the horses in the remuda. He hadn't found either of the horses ridden by the men who shot him. If he'd found any newly shod horses, he'd have suspected they'd pulled the old shoes. But only the horses kept at the ranch had visited a blacksmith in the last month.

"When you take the herd to the railhead, I want you to buy any hay you can find," Pete said.

Eddie looked surprised. "It'll be expensive."

"I know. But if the winter's as bad as the Indians predict, it might be the edge we need to bring the herd through."

"You put a lot of stock in what those Indians say, don't you?"

"Like I told the sheriff, they lived on these plains for hundreds of years before we got here. A lot of people think they're not very smart, but they survived. And without log houses and nice warm stoves."

"I'm not sure I can get any men to stay. They usually head south after roundup."

"I'll only need a couple to help with that hay."

Eddie went off to talk with the men, leaving Pete to enjoy the view from the rise. He wondered how Anne was getting along back at the ranch. He'd hated to leave her, but to have stayed away from the roundup— even to protect and support his wife—would have been interpreted as a sign of guilt. He couldn't afford to do anything that might weaken his precarious position. By coming on roundup and doing his work with the confidence of a man with a clean conscience, he had changed the cowhands' minds about his guilt.

Besides, he couldn't find his money by staying at the ranch. Despite his lack of success so far, his instinct told him the horses were still around somewhere. The men, too. He didn't know how or why, but he had a gut feeling that whoever killed Peter had killed Belser as well. He just hoped he would find them before they found him. He'd made a point during the last two weeks of being sure he wasn't an exposed target as he had been on the trip to Big Bend. He tried to keep himself in the midst of a group of men. When he was in an exposed position as he was now, he made certain he could see far enough to know no one could shoot him from ambush. Except along the streams and some of the foothills closer to the mountains, the plain was barren of anything except miles and miles of grass. He had every intention of heading south with his money and his hide in one piece. But he had to admit, the longer it took him to find his money, the smaller his chances of success.

There was another reason he needed to find his money and leave. If he didn't get out of Wyoming soon, he was going to do something he'd be sorry for. Every hour, every minute he spent in Anne's company made it harder to keep his hands to himself. More important, he had started to like Anne. Still worse, the thought of staying at the ranch kept popping into his head. He wasn't the marrying kind. He wanted to be free to roam. Only freedom didn't look so inviting when it meant leaving Anne behind. It was difficult to understand how she had taken such a hold on his feelings in such a short time. He'd been infatuated before, but this wasn't the same.

His fantasies about women had always started and ended with sex. But while thoughts of making love to Anne kept ruining his sleep, it was the dreams of taking her back to Texas, seeing her with her own daughters, growing old alongside her, that let him know this was more than infatuation. He was in very great danger of falling in love with a woman who was married to another man. The fact that the man was dead wasn't going to make any difference. He'd lied to her over and over, urged her to support him against her friends, tied her credibility tightly to his statement that he was the Peter Warren she married by proxy.

When she found out what he'd done, she'd hate him. If he didn't find out who'd killed the real Peter Warren, she'd probably believe he'd done it.

She'd probably think he killed Belser, too.

She knew perfectly well he'd had plenty of time to commit the crime. Once he admitted he'd lied to her so many times before, it would be impossible for her to believe he hadn't lied one more time. After all, if he'd kill Peter Warren to inherit his ranch, what difference would it make if he killed Belser? They could only hang him once.

Pete knew it was highly unlikely he could get out of Wyoming with his reputation intact. He'd be doing well if he got out with his hide in one piece. Still, it hurt to know he would leave with Anne knowing he was a liar and an imposter, and thinking he might be a killer as well. He wanted her to understand, to know he'd done it all for her.

Well, almost all of it. He still intended to find his money. Despite the danger, it wasn't easy to give up the result of five years in the goldfields. He and Sean O'Ryan had started out together. Now Sean had his ranch, a wife, a blond stepdaughter, and three red-headed sons who promised to grow up to look just like him. Lately he'd found himself thinking it might not be so bad to have a couple of brown-haired, black-eyed tots of his own. It was an infallible warning that time was running out. If he didn't escape soon, he might leave his heart in Wyoming.

He had turned to join Eddie when he noticed a horse and rider top a rise in the distance. The rider was coming from the direction of the ranch. Immediately Pete worried something might have happened to Anne. The rider was much too far away to recognize, but he was too small to be Ray. At almost the same moment he realized the rider was a woman, not a man.

It couldn't be Anne. She wouldn't know how to find her way across the trackless plain. Yet he felt certain it wasn't Dolores, either. There was something about the rider that said it couldn't be anybody but Anne.

He considered returning to camp to get his horse, then changed his mind. She might think he didn't want to see her and turn back. He waved both hands in the air, and started toward her. By the time she turned her horse in his direction, he had recognized Anne's flowing black hair. She must have found Carl's wife's saddle. It was so old, it was in danger of falling apart. Riding sidesaddle struck him as out of place in Wyoming. It seemed something women did in cities and other civilized places where husbands weren't killed and left for the wolves, and cowhands weren't knifed in the next bedroom.

He started running toward her. He didn't mean to. He just couldn't help it. When he reached her, she let go of the reins and threw herself into his arms. She nearly knocked the breath out of him. She did knock him off his feet. They tumbled to the ground, laughing like two young fools.

He pulled her roughly, almost violently, to him. Gathering her into his arms, he held her snugly. It felt good to have her in his arms. She fit. She belonged there.

Their kiss was immediate, natural, necessary. His mouth covered hers hungrily. This was no gentle kiss, tender and searching. It was an assault, a ruthless ravishing of her mouth. Wriggling her body about until she lay atop him, Anne returned his kiss with equal urgency. There was nothing tentative about her now. She was a woman who knew what she wanted from her man, and she meant to take it.

Pete gave in gladly. Tomorrow he would remember he had to keep his distance. Tomorrow he'd come up with a reason why she had to go back to the ranch while he stayed with the roundup.

"What are you doing here?" he asked when he finally broke their embrace.

"You're not angry, are you?"

"No, but I was worried when I recognized you."

"I had to come. Mrs. Dean is at the house."

Pete sat up. He couldn't think while lying down. "Mrs. Dean?"

"She said she had to support me in my hour of travail, but she's really trying to make me doubt you."

"How?"

"She kept coming up with reasons why you aren't Peter. She had it all worked out, how you met him on the trail, learned he was to inherit a ranch, killed him, and arrived here to take his place. She said you killed Belser to keep him quiet."

The heat abruptly faded from Pete's body, and he felt the chill of danger. That line of reasoning was all too believable. "And you didn't believe her?"

Anne sat up. "Of course not. I know you'd never kill anybody."

"But everybody says I've changed an awful lot."

"You still couldn't kill anyone." She put her arms around his neck and kissed him. He responded more gently this time. "No man could kiss like that and be a murderer."

"But you don't know any murderers. Maybe they can do all sorts of things you don't expect."

"That's true, but no woman could be that mistaken about the man she loves."

Anne's reaction to her words took Pete by surprised. She blushed furiously, then averted her gaze. He didn't understand why she should suddenly be so self-conscious. She'd loved Peter Warren all her life, and everybody knew it.

Unless . . .

He didn't let himself pursue that thought. He didn't want to know the answer. "Tell me how you found your way out here," he said, anxious to divert both their minds from a thought that clearly made both of them uneasy. "I thought you didn't know your way past the corrals."

"You told the sheriff you'd left a map of the ranch in your office. I figured if he could find your camp by studying the map, I could too. It wasn't easy. Buttes and ridges don't look at all like they do on the map when you're riding around them. And most of the creeks were hardly more than a dry crack in the ground."

Pete laughed. "I think you're a genius to have found us. Wait until I tell Eddie."

"It wasn't anything special."

"Getting on a horse and coming out here was special. Finding your own way was incredible. You must be the smartest woman in Wyoming. I already know you're the most beautiful."

"Do you really mean that?"

Her earnestness touched his heart. "Of course, I do. I've told you so many times."

"But people often say things they don't mean. I don't mean that you'd lie—I know you wouldn't—but lying isn't the same as exaggerating."

Pete felt his gut twist into a knot. If she only knew how many times he'd lied. But he wasn't lying about her looks. "I don't have to exaggerate even the tiniest bit. You are the most beautiful woman I've ever seen."

"Now I know you're lying."

"In Wyoming."

She laughed. "You've hardly seen any women here at all."

"Then you're easily the most beautiful."

She laughed and kissed him again. "I wish we didn't have to go back to the ranch or see the sheriff and Mrs. Dean. I wish we could stay out here forever. It's so beautiful and peaceful."

"It won't be beautiful or peaceful when there's two feet of snow on the ground, the temperature is thirty below zero, the wind is strong enough to knock you off your feet, and wolves are howling all around."

She shivered. "How do the cows survive it?"

"I don't know, but they do. Now before Eddie sends someone up here to see if I've been kidnaped, we'd better go down to the camp. You'll have to start back to the ranch soon if you're to make it before nightfall."

"But I want to stay here with you."

"We're not set up for women. There's no privacy, no place for you to sleep."

"Where do you sleep?"

"On the ground."

"Then I'll sleep on the ground, too."

"There'll be men all around you."

"Then I'll be well protected."

"They'll be embarrassed."

"I won't look when they get dressed."

Her eyes twinkled with merriment. He'd never seen her look so happy, so free of worry. He hated to spoil her fun.

"A roundup camp is no place for a woman. Your presence will upset everybody."

"I won't go back while Mrs. Dean is at the ranch." Her chin jutted stubbornly. "All she does is tell me how you're an imposter and a murderer. I even started dreaming about the things she says. If I have to listen to her for five more days, I might murder her."

"Five more days!"

"She told her driver not to return for a week. I couldn't stand it any longer. Please, let me stay. I won't go anywhere near the men."

He didn't have the heart to send her back to face

235

Mrs. Dean without him there to support her. He certainly didn't intend to let her make the trip across the plain by herself. When he got back, he intended to find out why Ray hadn't accompanied her.

"We'll see. Now let's go shock Eddie."

Eddie wasn't the only one surprised at Anne's presence. Every man within sight stopped to stare.

"Is this what you do?" she asked as she watched the riders keeping the two herds separate.

"What do you mean?" Pete asked.

"Ride around the cows," she said. "It doesn't look very hard."

Eddie looked offended. Pete broke out laughing. "It wouldn't be if the cows liked being separated into two herds or driven from their favorite part of the range. They're wild animals used to defending themselves against wolves, bears, and cougars. Any one of them can kill a man or gore a horse."

"Then why do you do this?"

Pete laughed again. "Because nobody's figured out how to make them go to market on their own."

"I'm serious. I didn't know it was so dangerous."

"Just about any way a man chooses to make a living out here is dangerous. Which is why you're never to leave the ranch alone again."

"I was perfectly safe."

But he couldn't be sure of that. She had more to fear than wild animals.

"The men don't act like I've upset them at all," Anne said.

"That's because it's dark. They can't see you now, and I've kept you away from them most of the day."

They'd finished the evening meal more than an hour ago. The men not on duty had already crawled inside their bedrolls. Their turn on night watch would come soon enough. The only sound from camp was the faint murmur of Eddie's voice as he talked to the cook. The cows had stopped bawling and milling about and were lying down, chewing their cuds and waiting to be allowed to return to their favorite feeding grounds.

Pete had taken Anne to a curve in Crazy Woman Creek shaded by a grove of cottonwoods, ash, and box elder. They sat in the shadows, invisible to prying eyes. It wasn't his cowhands that worried him, but the unknown killers. He was certain he was the next target. He feared Anne was a target, too. If he had thought his going would have protected her, he'd have left now, even without his money.

He would have to tell her of the danger, explain his lie and why he'd told it. Soon. But not yet. He asked only for tonight. He'd tell her when they returned to the ranch.

"I never realized it could be so beautiful out here," Anne said.

They looked out over the treeless hills that formed the drainage basin of the Powder River, the best grazing land in Wyoming. The brilliant moonlight had turned the landscape tawny beige, the cows into honey-colored lumps casting inky shadows. The ceaseless wind rustled the leaves above their heads. Soon the first frosts would strip the branches, turning them into a network of charcoal lines against a blue-gray sky.

"It is beautiful. But like all beautiful things, it can be dangerous, too."

"I know. Grizzlies, mountain lions, and wolves."

"That's why you're never again to take out across the plain alone." He put his arm around her waist and pulled her to him. "Promise?"

"I promise. In all normal circumstances," she added quickly. "Mrs. Dean is worse than grizzlies, lions, and wolves."

He laughed. "Not that bad, but close."

She put her arms around his waist and held him tightly. "If you like Wyoming so much, why did you tell Uncle Carl you never wanted to come back?"

They were on dangerous ground. He didn't know enough about Peter Warren to start discussing his motives.

"Young men say a lot of things they don't mean when they're angry. But I don't want to waste all this moonlight talking about Uncle Carl."

"You always were so sweet," Anne said. "Much sweeter than your brother. It made me angry when Gary made fun of you."

More relatives he knew nothing about. "I don't want to talk about my brother, either. Let's make a deal. We won't talk about relatives or the past."

"What will we talk about?"

"Us."

"I think that's a very good idea. When we get back to the ranch—"

"Not the future, either. Just now. Tonight." That was all he had.

"What can we talk about?"

"About how beautiful you look in the moonlight. Did you know your eyes shine like black pearls?"

She giggled. "Pearls don't shine."

So much for romantic sweet talk. "Then what do pearls do?"

"They have a luster."

"Your eyes do much better than luster. They shine. What's black and shines?"

"I don't know."

"Onyx. Your eyes shine like onyx." He thought he remembered Isabelle saying something about onyx being black.

"Are you sure onyx is black?"

"Positive. It practically glows in the dark." After all the lies he'd told, a few exaggerations were nothing.

"That sounds nice. What else do you like about me?"

"Your hair. It's black as a raven's wing and as rich and warm as sable."

"Where did you learn to talk so nice?"

"Running the hardware store. You have to learn to talk pretty to the ladies, or they'll take their business elsewhere."

"Well, I don't know how you failed. I'd have gone to your store just to hear you talk."

He was going to have to be careful. He'd already told her he didn't know much about women. He didn't want to be caught in a contradiction, but he couldn't be expected to remember everything he made up. It

239

seemed even his last night would be strewn with obstacles. He could easily stumble badly.

"They had husbands who weren't particularly pleased to have other men compliment their wives."

"Would you be upset if other men complimented me?"

"I'd be upset if they didn't."

"Really?"

"Really. Now stop begging for compliments and kiss me."

"I'm not begging."

"Yes, you were."

"I was just asking. A woman can't find out things unless she asks."

"If she kisses a man just right, he might tell her anything she wants without having to ask."

"Is that a bribe?"

"Yes."

"I wish you'd bribed me before now."

"I guess that's why I failed in the hardware. I never knew when to start."

Or stop talking before he put his neck in a noose. He put his hand under Anne's chin, tilted her head upward, and kissed her firmly on the mouth.

"Know what I like about your lips?" he asked when he broke the kiss.

"What?" She kept her eyes closed, her head upturned.

"They're so soft and kissable. I've never found a pair of lips so kissable."

"Have you kissed a lot of women?"

"Not many." He'd kissed hundreds of women, but

he figured Peter wouldn't have kissed more than two or three.

She opened her eyes, a satisfied smile on her lips. "I don't believe you. I think you've kissed hundreds."

"Not nearly so many."

"You're very good at kissing."

"Have you kissed a lot of men?"

"Only you."

"Then how do you know?"

"A woman knows."

They all said that, like there was some vast, cosmic information source all women could tap into when they stopped wearing their hair in pigtails. Men didn't have anything like that. He'd had to learn everything one painful lesson at a time.

"Then a woman knows a man prefers kissing to talking any time."

"Nobody ever preferred kissing me."

"That's because Uncle Carl kept you locked up. He knew the minute men got an inkling of how good you could kiss, they'd be lined up at his front door every day of the week. He'd never get any work done for having to hold them off. Now kiss me and prove Uncle Carl was right."

He seemed to have found the right key at last. She kissed him and seemed quite content to do it over and over again without saying a single word.

She fit very nicely in his arms. Odd that no matter how they came togther, they seemed to fit perfectly. All the more reason to clear out. Before long, he'd start thinking they were supposed to fit.

"Nobody ever told me kissing could be so much fun," she murmured against the side of his neck.

"They were afraid that once you found out, you'd never want to stop."

"I don't." She leaned back until she lay on the ground. She pulled him down with her.

She was so innocent, so adorable. She had no idea of the danger that hovered around her. Pete didn't know how he was going to stand leaving her. She was like a fragile flower unfolding. For the first time she was discovering what it was to be a woman, to be attractive, to have confidence in herself. He was watching her come to life. He'd been largely responsible for it. In a way, he felt he'd created her.

She was his. She didn't belong to anyone else.

But she wasn't his. He was living a lie. He had tonight and nothing more.

Pete's arms encircled her, one hand in the small of her back. He rolled over until Anne lay atop him. Her soft curves molded themselves to the contours of his lean body. "Kiss me," he whispered into her hair. "Kiss me like you're never going to see me again."

"I'll see you every day for the rest of my life."

"I know, but I want you to kiss me like there is no tomorrow, only tonight."

She kissed him on his nose. "I always wanted to do that." Then she kissed him on his eyes, his forehead, his chin, cheek, eyebrows, peppering him with teasing kisses until he couldn't stand it any longer. He took her face in his hands and brought her mouth down to his in a long, satisfying kiss.

"That's what I mean," he whispered, his voice

hoarse with passion. She radiated a vitality that drew him like a magnet. He felt the weight of her body on his, her breasts pressed against his chest, his groin fitted snugly into the space between her thighs. The sweet, intoxicating scent of her body sent a delightful shiver of wanting through him. He prayed the heat generated between them wouldn't inflame his body to the point that she would notice and lose her spontaneity, but he was losing the battle. Her nearness caused his heart to pound an erratic rhythm. Heat radiated from him as if he were a locomotive climbing a mountain. He rolled until they lay side by side. It was all he could do to keep his hands from covering her breasts.

He nestled her head in the crook of his arm. "I could lie here looking at you all night," he said.

"It's so dark you can't see me."

"I can see the moonlight on your skin. It's more luminous than pearls." He cupped her face in his hand, trailed his fingers down her cheek, her jaw, the side of her neck, across the top of her breast.

"You're just saying that. My skin turns brown every summer."

"The moonlight has turned it white as alabaster."

"Is alabaster pretty?"

"It's beautiful and rare and prized by men the world over. Just as you should be."

He rolled her over on her back. He trailed his fingers down the hollow of her throat, following with a line of slow, thoughtful kisses. Raising his head, he gazed into her eyes.

"Your skin has the luster of opals," he whispered, "but it has a creamy softness, the smoothness of silk."

Anne sighed, turned her head to one side so he could more easily kiss her neck and throat. But Pete was in the throes of an urgent need that was rapidly moving beyond his control. His hand moved to cover the mound of Anne's breast as his lips covered hers with hot kisses. Anne's body arched against his hand, filling it with her warm softness. Unable to stand it any longer, Pete undid the top buttons of her dress and let his hungry mouth place kiss after kiss on the tops of her breasts.

But a taste was not enough. He needed to feast until this merciless hunger could be satisfied. As he roused her passion, his own grew stronger. His need seemed to die down and then flame hotter than ever. He undid more buttons, loosened the tie on her chemise until he could slip his hand inside. Anne's gasp sent hot desire boiling through his insides, causing him to shudder like a naked man in a blizzard. His touch on her bare skin brought a quick, ragged intake of breath from Anne, but she didn't shrink from him.

She reached her hand behind his neck and pulled him closer.

Pete didn't need another invitation.

Having tasted her body, her willingness to yield herself to him overpowered Pete's self-control. He knew himself for a heel, but he was in the throes of a passion unlike anything he'd ever experienced. This wasn't merely a desire to spend his seed inside a woman; this wasn't merely a wish to satisfy his ego's need to know a beautiful woman desired him. This was a need to belong, to join, to become a part of her, to demonstrate his adulation.

Chapter Fourteen

Anne's body shuddered convulsively when Pete lifted her breast out of her chemise. He leaned down and kissed her gently, repeatedly, until she felt she would explode. She'd come to escape Mrs. Dean, not in hopes he'd make love to her. But in this moment, she knew she'd come to Pete in the eternal sense. She'd come face-to-face with the fact that she loved him and had accepted it, rejoiced in it. Despite the affection she'd always felt for Peter, despite her innocence about the relationship between men and women, some part of her sensed there was more. Even while she'd reached for what she knew, for what was safe, she'd hoped for more. She was profoundly thankful she'd found it. She had fallen in love with her husband. She loved him completely—heart, mind, and body. She wanted him to love her just as completely.

Her own eager response to the touch of his lips shocked her. Her body was chaste, untouched, unloved. She'd seen quick kisses and held hands, but she hadn't anticipated anything like Pete's kisses. There was nothing polite and gentlemanly about them. They practically turned her inside out. They invaded her mouth, seared her lips, ignited a fire deep in her belly, set her body a-tingle, made her want to get as close as possible to him, to crawl inside his skin.

She'd heard talk of cuddling on a cold winter night. But in her naivete, she'd assumed it was as much to keep warm as anything else. When she asked questions, everyone said she would be told when the time came. Well, no one had told her, and the time was here. Now!

Being held in Pete's arms was wonderful. Being kissed, heavenly. But having his lips on her breast! A revelation! Pete's tongue teased her nipple until it became firm and upright. She didn't know men did things like that. Or that a woman could like it. She hadn't known that the touch of the man she loved could excite her to such an extent that she felt like throwing herself on him, begging him to do more, to do anything as long as he never let her go. She couldn't describe the sensations that radiated from her breast to the rest of her body. It was like an increasingly pleasurable ache, an uncontrollable tremor, a focusing of every nerve ending in a single spot, their combined sensitivity making her rigid with pleasure.

When Pete took her nipple into his mouth and began to gently suckle it, Anne thought she would scream from pleasure so exquisite it was almost painful. She hadn't known anything could feel like this. Why had-n't someone told her that her body was a gold mine of unexplored, untapped, unnamed sensations? Why had they allowed her to believe a woman had to "suffer" a man's attentions for the sake of children or because of a man's "base needs"? If she was any judge, her needs were very much of the same nature and extent as Pete's. She suspected that helping him satisfy his needs would do exactly the same thing for her.

She didn't know if a wife could be called a loose woman because of the feelings she had for her husband, but she didn't care. Every respectable matron in Big Bend was welcome to ignore her for the rest of her life as long as Pete worshiped her body.

His hand delved into her chemise once more, cupped her other breast, and gently kneaded it in rhythm with the movement of his lips. Anne's moans of pleasure, her arching body against him, seemed to stoke his need. He started to unbutton her dress, doing it so quickly he tore a button loose. Her nimble fingers took over, doing it twice as fast. He pulled the draw-string of her chemise, and the soft material fell away, exposing her breasts and shoulders to his heated gaze. She felt no hesitation, no reluctance, though every-thing was new to her, unexpected, almost frightening. She wanted him to love every part of her. It made her feel beautiful in a way words and clothes never could.

For years no one had wanted her. People had told her that she was worthless, contaminated, inferior. The covert gazes she'd begun to notice during the last year only intensified this feeling. That people could only look at her out of the corner of their eyes made her feel unacceptable, as if they only looked at her out of pity, lust, or disgust.

Pete had changed all that. His glances were frequent and forthright. He didn't mind staring at her, nor did he apologize for doing it. He said he liked looking at her. He liked buying things for her, kissing her, holding her. When he continued to keep his distance, she'd begun to wonder if he meant what he said. Now she didn't have to wonder anymore. Surely no man could do what he was doing to her body and not think her beautiful.

His tongue and teeth continued to caress and torture her sensitive, swollen nipple while his hand fondled her other breast, its pink nipple marble-hard. His gentle massaging sent currents of desire racing through her. She wanted to kiss his mouth, to crush to her own the lips that were creating such havoc with her tortured breasts. She took his face in her hands and tugged until he took her lips in a harsh, greedy kiss that stoked the fire of need within her. She drove her tongue deep inside his mouth, reaching to satisfy her craving for a connection, a sense of attachment. The need had suddenly risen to the surface from a corner where it had been hiding, denied and ignored.

Now, in the swelling tide of Pete's love, it could feed and grow content.

Pete wrapped his arms around Anne and rolled over until she again lay atop him, her breasts pressed against the roughness of his shirt, his swollen groin cradled between her legs.

"We shouldn't be doing this," he whispered into her

hair. "You deserve something better than cold ground and a bed of leaves."

She'd forgotten they were outside. She'd only been aware of Pete and her own body. "I'm not cold." She felt alive with the fire he'd ignited in her veins. "I like it here. You look beautiful in the moonlight."

Pete looked surprised at her words. Maybe you weren't supposed to say a man was beautiful—maybe you were supposed to say he was rough, craggy, even homely in an unusual and rather attractive way—but Pete was beautiful to her, the most beautiful man in the whole world. She wanted to make him feel as beautiful as he made her feel.

She cupped his face in her hands and kissed him gently. "You've given me what everyone else tried to take away, confidence in myself, in my own worth. You've made me feel beautiful, like a woman, like a human being equal to all other human beings. I'd think you were beautiful for far less than that."

"You were already that and more."

"But I never felt it before. Now I do. Now don't talk. I want you to kiss me and kiss me until the world goes away."

And it did. But just before it vanished, she wondered if Colonel Dean had ever kissed his wife the way Pete was kissing her. A giggle escaped her.

"I thought I was doing better than that."

"You are," Anne assured him. "I just wondered if Colonel Dean ever kissed his wife like this."

That started them both laughing and rolling over with first one, then the other on top. Very quickly all thoughts of the Deans disappeared to be replaced by a keen awareness that their bodies were entwined like two vines, each trying to climb the other. Pete's hands moved gently and inexorably down the length of her back, first massaging her shoulders, then the small of her back. When they moved to cup the swell of her buttocks, her body trembled, causing Pete's swollen groin to settle more deeply between her legs.

The stroking of his fingers sent pleasant jolts radiating throughout her body. The churning fire in her belly seemed to draw additional heat from Pete's body, gradually causing the focus of her sensations to shift center. It was an odd sensation, pleasurable yet making her uncomfortable, restless, unable to remain still.

Pete rolled over until she lay on her back.

She missed the feel of his body against her own, of his heat burning through their several layers of clothes. But the feel of his hand on her breast, moving across her abdomen, down her side, and along her thigh generated a whole new line of fires in her, fires so hot she thought she would burn up. She reached out to unbutton his shirt so she could touch his skin, but it was nearly impossible to think with his hand exploring parts of her body that hadn't been seen or touched by anyone since she was old enough to bathe herself.

Yet as much as it unsettled her, it excited her, made her want to be closer to Pete, to become part of him. She pressed her body against him, kissing him with ardor and excitement. His explorations didn't cease. With one hand he traced the shape and contour of her thigh from knee to hip, from side to front. With the other hand, he unbuttoned her dress down to the waist.

The feel of his fingers moving against her belly made her squirm.

Pete sat up. "I'm going to take your shoes off."

She felt bereft. The faint sensations coming from her feet couldn't compare with having his body in her arms, his hands on her belly and thigh. But the heat index shot up when his hands moved under her dress to remove her stockings. When his fingers touched the heated, bare skin of her inner thigh, she thought she would rise up off the ground. The sensation was unique, intimate, incendiary. His fingers seemed to linger on her thigh, the back of her knee, her calf, her ankle as he slowly removed her stocking.

Then she had to go through it all again. When he finally removed the second stocking, she let her breath go in a huge *whoosh* that left her feeling exhausted. She wiggled her toes, and the sense of freedom invigorated her.

"Take off your boots," she said. "I want to feel your toes."

"I never heard of any woman wanting that," Pete said as he quickly complied.

"I never heard of anything you're doing to me, but I know I don't want you to stop."

Pete looked worried. "I ought not—"

She sat up, quickly cut off his words with her lips. "Tonight we think of no one and nothing but ourselves. Tomorrow will come soon enough." Not that she was afraid of tomorrow. She wanted lots more tomorrows to spend in Pete's arms, lots more tomorrows to explore his body as he had explored hers. "Now unbutton your shirt. I want to touch your skin."

Pete's chest was bare, a wide expanse of soft skin spread over ribs she could count as her hand moved down his chest. She kissed his chest and felt the heat in his body nearly burn her lips.

"You're hot," she whispered.

"You're about to make me burn up."

She liked knowing she could do that to a man. She especially liked knowing she could do it to Pete. But she didn't get much chance to enjoy her power. He buried his face between her breasts while his hands started to work her dress over her shoulders and down her waist. He didn't have to ask her to lift her body so he could move the dress past her hips. Her body responded of its own will.

She expected the frostiness of the night air to penetrate her chemise and chill her body. Instead it felt delightfully cool against her skin. The heat coming from inside her was more than enough protection against the bite in the air.

Anne moaned softly as Pete's hands lightly traced a path over the skin of her waist and her hips. The thin fabric of her chemise annoyed her. She wanted nothing between her skin and Pete's touch. She had loved the feel of his hands and lips on her breasts. She longed for him to make love to the rest of her body as well. She twisted beneath him until she got the straps of her chemise off her shoulder and pushed it down to her waist. She lifted her body and Pete removed it entirely.

She lay before him, naked, vulnerable, ready.

"Take off your clothes," she whispered. "I want to feel your skin against mine."

Anne didn't know where she got the courage to do

what she'd done, to say what she'd said. It seemed to happen all by itself, as though there were another person inside her, a person who knew what she was doing and what she wanted. Instinct told her she wanted to be able to touch Pete all over. She fervently hoped he would touch every part of her aching, yearning body. He had created a voracious appetite within her that had to be satisfied.

Pete stood to remove his clothes, and Anne marveled again that such a tall man could desire a small woman like herself. Her uncle had said she was only a dab of a woman, but Pete said she was more than enough woman for any man. Tonight he'd made her feel that way.

Until he removed the last of his clothes.

Then she wondered if she'd ever be enough woman for him. She'd never seen a naked man, never had any idea what happened when they were aroused, but she did know her body was supposed to encompass him. She didn't know if she could. When Pete lay back down beside her, her apprehension increased. He slid his hands up and down her arms. She shivered with pleasure.

"Don't be afraid," he said.

"I'm not." She wasn't afraid he would hurt her. She was afraid she might disappoint him. He must have been with women who had lots of experience in pleasing a man. She didn't know anything, and she desperately didn't want to disappoint him. She wanted to be wonderful for him, so wonderful he'd forget all those other women. She wanted him to think womanhood began and ended with her.

Pete let his fingertips trail across her breasts, tease her nipples, massage her belly before moving across the line of her hip. She drew in her breath when his hand moved to the inside of her leg.

"Relax," he said. "It won't hurt."

She didn't think it would, but she couldn't force her body to relax. The anticipation of what he would do next seemed neverending. He rubbed her belly again, and the churning sensation caused her to tremble from head to foot.

"Hold me," she said, and rolled up against him, only to find his swollen groin pressed hard against her thigh. She tried to draw away, but his arms closed around her.

"I won't hurt you."

"I know you won't." But now she wasn't sure.

The spiral of excitement in her body and the all-consuming heat burned away any reluctance. Every feeling, every instinct, every primitive drive urged her toward him, toward a union she could sense would change her forever.

When his hand moved between them, she didn't draw away. When she felt his fingers enter her, she gasped and stiffened. But she didn't draw away. When he gently touched a nub that threatened to raise her body off the ground, she gasped and clenched her teeth. But she didn't draw away.

She couldn't. Her body craved more, urged her to impale herself on his hand, to force him deep inside her, where the throbbing need stayed just out of reach. She breathed in deep gasps as his expert touch sent her to even higher levels of ecstasy. Involuntary tremors and fire spread from her belly throughout her body, igniting every nerve, making each acutely sensitive to touch. Her desire for him overrode everything else as the dormant sexuality of her body awoke, shuddered to life for the first time.

Heat rippled under her skin. She couldn't disguise her body's reaction, didn't want to. When his fingers continued to rub that tiny nub, that endless source of rapture, she couldn't control her outcry of delight. She yielded to the searing need that had been building in her, and a moan of ecstasy slipped through her lips. Desire flooded her entire being. She felt as though she would lose touch with solid ground, with reality, with everything except the sensations that encircled her body like a silkworm's soft, luxurious cocoon. Everything in her tightened, stretched, expanded, clamped down until she was certain she would be torn apart by the magnitude of the forces that had taken possession of her body.

She quivered uncontrollably, shaken to and fro by surges of passion; then everything flowed from her like water from a stream falling into the sea. She sighed with exhaustion, ready to sink back into Pete's arms.

Then she felt him enter her. She felt herself stretching and stretching. Before she reached her limit, he withdrew, then slowly entered her again, farther this time. He repeated the process once more.

"This might hurt."

Before she could tense, he drove deep inside her. A sharp pain cut through her haze of pleasure with the keenness of a knife but disappeared almost immediately, leaving her aware only of the weight of his body, of the fullness of having him inside her.

Exultation surged through her. Her body melted against his and her world was filled with him.

Within moments the crescendo began to build again within her. Her body felt as though it was half ice, half flame, as waves of ecstasy throbbed through her. She rose to meet him. Hungry desire spiraled through her, exciting already sensitive nerve endings to hypersensitivity. Once again she felt herself going out of control, out of contact with the corporeal world. She abandoned herself willingly, and an amazing sense of completeness filled her.

The feel of his skin against her, the sound of his rapid breathing, the musky smell of his passion-heated body served to lift her to levels of even more exquisite pleasure than before. Her body began to vibrate with liquid fire; a tremor inside her heated her thighs and groin as she felt herself soar toward a shuddering ecstasy. She felt passion rising in her like a hot fire, clouding her brain, rendering her incapable of doing anything beyond feeling. She abandoned herself to the whirl of sensations.

The waves of passion grew even more turbulent than before. Anne felt tossed about until she wanted to cry out for release. Electricity arced through her until she felt positive she glowed from incandescent heat.

"Please," she murmured.

As before, the release came without warning, and she felt all the tension, the ache, the turbulence flow from her in a single rush. They fell apart. She was too exhausted to speak.

The waves of erotic sensation died away, leaving

her tired but exhilarated with the knowledge that she and Pete were finally joined as man and woman, husband and wife. No matter what happened in the future, no one could take that away from her.

Mrs. Dean was waiting at the ranch when they returned. So was the sheriff.

"Thank heaven you're back," Mrs. Dean exclaimed as she enfolded Anne in an embrace which clearly closed Pete out. "I was certain you'd been kidnaped. I sent Ray for the sheriff immediately."

"I left a note saying I was going to visit my husband at the roundup," Anne said.

"I supposed that was a subterfuge to allay my fears until it was too late to retrieve you. Child, no respectable woman goes to the site of a roundup. There's nothing but men there."

Pete had waited until Eddie and the men started the herd toward the railhead. Eddie was going along to head up the drive. It would be several weeks before they returned. Pete expected to be gone before then. He hadn't found his money, and he was beginning to suspect he never would. He was tempted to stay here long enough to wring it out of the ranch. It wouldn't take long. Old Carl might even have enough money tucked away already, and Peter owed him something.

But he knew he wouldn't. He'd told enough lies already.

Then, of course, there was Anne. He'd already taken advantage of her once. He couldn't fool himself into thinking he would stay on his side of the bed tonight.

The longer he stayed, the more they made love, the more deeply she would fall in love with him. He had no right to do that to Anne. He had to leave.

"Well, don't stand here arguing," Dolores said. "I held supper back hoping you'd get here before it got cold or dried out."

"We have things to discuss," the sheriff said.

"Then discuss them at the table," Dolores said. "If you don't eat now, I'm going to throw it out."

So they ate supper. Anne and Pete took their places at opposite ends of the table. The sheriff and Mrs. Dean sat on one side, Dolores and Ray on the other. Pete and the sheriff were soon talking about the roundup and conditions on the range. For once Mrs. Dean didn't seem anxious to force the issue. Pete decided she thought it was improper to discuss important matters in front of the help. For once, Pete was glad of her snobbery.

But it couldn't be postponed forever. By the time dinner was over, Anne was trying to suppress yawns. Pete felt sorry for her. She hadn't gotten any rest last night. She wasn't used to sleeping on the ground or outside. She'd started at noises all night. She'd kept him awake as well. He was nearly as tired as she was, but he wasn't the least bit sleepy. In a short time they were going to be in their bed together, alone. After last night, he knew he couldn't keep his hands to himself. Even now he could remember the feel of her skin as though he were still touching it. He would remember the taste of her until his dying day.

"It's time for you to seek your bed," Mrs. Dean said to Anne. "You've been yawning for the last quarter of an hour."

"I am tired," Anne confessed. "I never realized riding fifteen miles on horseback could be so tiring."

"I'm surprised you aren't prostrate from fatigue," Mrs. Dean said. "I know I wouldn't be able to rise from my bed for at least a week."

"I can't afford to stay in bed that long. Dolores wants to give the house a good cleaning while the men are away."

"Good. That will keep your mind off wondering what will happen to you when this man"—she directed a hostile look at Pete—"is shown up for the imposter that he is."

"She won't have to worry about that no matter who this man proves to be," the sheriff said, reaching into his pocket.

Every eye turned to the sheriff.

"I haven't had a chance to tell you, but a sworn affidavit to Anne's marriage to Peter Warren ought to be coming in a few days. Once I have that, whether she's Peter Warren's wife or his widow, this ranch will be hers."

"She's only seventeen," Pete said. "If anything were to happen to me, would her uncle have control over her again?"

"No. Out here a married woman can take control of her own affairs, no matter how young she is."

A weight lifted off Pete's shoulders at the same time a screw in his belly tightened another couple of turns. Anne would be safe. The ranch belonged to her. He could leave now.

"That's all nonsense," Anne said. "The ranch belongs to Pete. I'm not a widow."

"How do you know?" Mrs. Dean asked. "He probably killed your husband. I've told you—"

"I know what you've told me, but I don't believe it. Even if for some reason Pete weren't Peter, he still wouldn't be a murderer." Anne looked down the table, love shining in her eyes. "I love him. I trust him with my life. I know he couldn't kill anyone."

Pete's heart leapt into his throat. Agony and ecstasy fought for supremacy. While ecstasy won now, he knew it would be agony that would ultimately claim the victory.

"You can't love that man!" Mrs. Dean exclaimed. "I forbid it!"

"It would be wise to keep your feelings in check for a while yet," the sheriff said. "He's still under suspicion of murder."

"He didn't kill Belser. I told you he never left the bed that night."

"What about Peter?" Mrs. Dean asked. "We don't know where that man has left poor Peter's body."

"He didn't kill Belser, and he obviously didn't kill himself," Anne said, her voice rising. "The sheriff says this is my house. If it is, I can do anything I want. I won't have anybody here who keeps saying my husband is an imposter and a murderer. If you can't stop, you can leave immediately."

"It's pitch black outside," Mrs. Dean declared. "You can't expect the sheriff to start back to town at this hour."

"I meant you, too."

"Me!" It was clear the idea that she should control

her tongue or be forced to leave had never crossed Mrs. Dean's mind.

"Yes," Anne said, not backing down. "I appreciate your coming here to watch out for me, but I don't need it. And, I won't have you calling my husband a murderer."

Every eye in the room remained focused on Anne. Apparently no one was able to believe that the mild-mannered girl they knew had turned into such a force-ful woman. Pete smiled with pride. Though his inten-tion had been honorable in the beginning, he hadn't cut a very chivalrous figure during these last days. Still, he could take pride in knowing he'd had a crucial part in helping Anne come out of her protective shell, in helping her find her place in her home and in local society. She was smart, beautiful, and determined.

She'd do.

Pete pushed his chair away from the table. "Before we fall into a wrangle, let me suggest we all go to bed. Anne is tired. Mrs. Dean and Dolores have had a try-ing time worrying about Anne, the sheriff made a long ride, and I've been through a roundup. Only Ray here isn't yawning into his fist."

Ray blushed.

Mrs. Dean got to her feet and moved to Anne's side. "I hope you don't think you're sleeping in Anne's bed." As she said that, she put her arm across Anne's bosom as though to protect her from a frontal attack.

"As a matter of fact—"

"We don't know who you are. Until we do, I can't allow you to compromise Anne any further."

"Really, Mrs. Dean, I think I can sleep with my husband without compromising myself."

"The sheriff hasn't gotten his papers yet," Mrs. Dean said. She didn't move or moderate her glare, which challenged Pete to defy her.

"After Mrs. Dean said you were an imposter, I wired for a physical description," the sheriff said. "The lawyer said it ought to be here in a day or two. We'll know then."

"Until then you must maintain separate bedrooms," Mrs. Dean declared.

"No," Anne said.

"I don't see any reason—" Pete began.

"I'll stand at her door all night," Mrs. Dean declared. "I'll throw myself across your bed if necessary, but you will not violate this child until you can prove you are truly her husband."

"This could be several days," the sheriff said.

"This is ridiculous," Anne said. "I will not be bullied."

But Mrs. Dean was insistent. She called upon Dolores and the sheriff to support her. When she didn't get the unqualified support she wanted, she turned to Ray. The poor startled boy blushed from neck to hairline and remained inarticulate. Finally she appealed to Pete's better nature.

"I don't think imposters and murderers have a better nature," he said. "Except for mothers and sisters, they probably want to ravish every female they see. It isn't that they don't want to have a better nature. They just can't help it."

"Young man, I will not be made fun of."

Pete had had enough. Mrs. Dean was probably

Providence in disguise come to keep him from doing what he knew would be wrong. He ought to take the chance he'd been given, accept it gracefully, and get out before he did something he'd really regret.

"I won't sleep with Anne," Pete said. "I'll sleep in Belser's old room."

"I won't have an unidentified man sleep under the same roof with me," Mrs. Dean said.

"This is my house," Anne said. "I'll say who sleeps where, and I want my husband to sleep with me."

"It'll just be until the description comes," Pete said.

"But—"

"It's not worth fighting over," Pete said. "The sheriff and I will sleep in the bunkhouse with Ray. That way you can lock the doors, and Mrs. Dean can feel perfectly safe."

"This is ridiculous. How can you let—"

Pete put his finger over her lips. "I don't like it either, but we've got years ahead. It seems a lot now, but you'll forget it before long."

"I'll never forget it," she said. "Or forgive it," she added, directing the last to Mrs. Dean.

"I still have my bedroll," Pete said to the sheriff. "You ready?"

"Sure. I hope you don't snore."

"He doesn't," Anne said, directing a triumphant look at Mrs. Dean. "He breathes very softly while he's asleep. I've listened to him often."

Pete was glad Mrs. Dean had the good sense to keep her mouth shut for once. He didn't know what Anne meant to say to her later, but the glitter in her eye made him regret he wouldn't be there to hear it.

"That was decent of you," the sheriff said as they walked toward the bunkhouse.

"No point to putting people's backs up unnecessarily. Are you really expecting the description by tomorrow?"

"It should have been here with the affidavit."

"What about the other papers?"

"It'll take a while before they get here."

"Can Anne do business for the ranch in the meantime?"

"I don't see why not. Her claim isn't in dispute."

That was all he needed to know. He'd tell her tomorrow. No, he'd wait until Mrs. Dean left. Hearing the truth was going to be hard. Making Anne listen to it front of that woman would be cruel. "I hope you don't mind sleeping in the bunkhouse," Pete said to the sheriff "It's not fancy."

"I've slept in worse. I bet you have, too."

Worse was about all he was going to have for a long time to come. There were no luxuries in the goldfields.

"Mrs. Dean wishes to return to Big Bend today," Anne announced as soon as they'd finished their breakfast. She turned to the sheriff. "I'd be obliged if you'd escort her."

"Sure, but I thought—"

"I'm being thrown out, Owen," Mrs. Dean said, her brow even more thunderous than it had been during the meal. "Anne said I'm no longer welcome in her home."

"I'm surprised you thought you would be," Anne said. "You've lost no opportunity to call my husband an imposter and a murderer. Last night you had the effrontery to drive him from his own house."

264

"I was only trying to protect you."

"I'm a grown woman. I can protect myself."

"You're still a girl."

"I'm a married woman. This is my home. You are no longer welcome."

Mrs. Dean flounced from the table. "Be so good as to see that my box is placed in the buckboard," she said to Ray. She completely ignored Pete. "I will be ready as soon as I get my coat." She turned back to Anne. "Before long, young woman, you will look back on this day and wish to God you could do it over again."

"You didn't have to leave. All I asked was that you stop slandering my husband."

"The man is a liar and a killer," Mrs. Dean declared. "It is my duty as a Christian woman to see he is unmasked."

"Then you ought to be satisfied."

Anne had thought she'd be quaking in her boots when the time finally came, but she felt quite calm. She'd been so angry the night before when Mrs. Dean drove Pete to sleep in the bunkhouse, she'd lost her temper—and her fear of the formidable woman—and told her she was surprised she'd stooped to slander and innuendo to find something interesting to fill her dull days. The resulting argument only served to make Anne angry enough to conclude by saying Mrs. Dean would have to leave in the morning.

But she'd spent the night tossing in her bed being angry at Mrs. Dean, missing Pete, and regretting she'd lost her temper. By morning, she'd almost made up her mind to apologize. Mrs. Dean's continued attacks on

Pete's character overwhelmed that impulse. She was actually glad to tell Mrs. Dean to leave.

The silence that followed Mrs. Dean's departure to her room nearly unnerved Anne. Fortunately, Pete came over, took her hand, and gave it a squeeze.

"You didn't have to do that," he said. "I don't care what she says."

"I do. She has no right."

He kissed the top of her head. "People are going to do all kinds of things they have no right to do. It'll drive you crazy if you let it. Just ignore them."

"I don't know how you can."

"I'm a lot older. I've been called a lot of things in my life."

"You won't be if I have anything to do with it."

"My, but you've turned into a fierce little kitten."

"Kittens are babies. I'm a lioness. I'm not afraid of anybody." And much to her surprise, she found she wasn't. If she could stand up to Mrs. Dean—a woman who frightened every woman and half the men of Big Bend—she could stand up to anyone.

Mrs. Dean came down carrying her coat and a small suitcase. "You will be sorry, young woman. Mark my words."

Anne and Pete followed Mrs. Dean outside. As they watched silently, the sheriff settled Mrs. Dean into the buckboard. Before he could reach for her luggage, they heard first one shot and then another come from somewhere beyond the hills east of the ranch buildings.

"Are we being attacked?" Mrs. Dean asked.

Chapter Fifteen

"I think it's an advance signal," Pete said. "Somebody must be in trouble."

Everybody waited. In country as empty as the Wyoming Territory, everybody had to help everyone else. You never knew when you'd be the one needing help.

A short time later, Cookie, driving as fast as his two mules could go, pulled the chuck wagon around to the front of the ranch house and jerked it to a stop.

"What's wrong?" Pete asked.

"The herd's been rustled," Cookie said, jumping down from his seat. "The boys are out chasing down their horses. I got Eddie in the wagon. He's hurt bad. He needs a doctor."

"Eddie!" Dolores practically threw herself down the steps to the man who lay in the bed of the wagon. He didn't respond to her entreaties to open his eyes and look at her, to say something.

"Let me see," Mrs. Dean said. "I'm a trained nurse."

Anne was surprised Mrs. Dean had been trained to do anything except intimidate people, but she told herself not to be small-minded. Even cruel people could have good qualities.

"What happened?" Pete asked.

"They was ready for us," Cookie said. "Eddie had just called everybody in for a meeting to reorganize their positions during the drive. Not a soul was near a horse. The rustlers came over the rise shooting and yelling like painted redskins. Everything on four legs except my mules was gone in a flash. They did a lot of shooting, but Eddie was the only one got hurt."

Mrs. Dean emerged from the wagon. "This man needs a doctor immediately."

"The sheriff will take him," Dolores said.

"I'm riding in the buckboard," Mrs. Dean announced. "There's no room."

"Cookie can take him in the chuck wagon," Pete said.

"I'm going with him," Dolores said, climbing into the wagon. "Drive as fast as you can," she ordered Cookie.

Cookie whipped up his mules, and the wagon started down the trail toward town.

"He'll never make it," Mrs. Dean said. "He's been shot with a rifle. He'll be dead within two hours. This is all your fault," she said to Pete.

"People have been rustling herds ever since there

have been cows in Wyoming," Pete said. "Even Carl had trouble."

"I warned you," she said to Anne. "This man will destroy you."

With that pronouncement, she let the sheriff help her into the buckboard and they started down the trail after the chuck wagon.

"Shouldn't the sheriff go after the rustlers?" Anne asked.

"He can't do anything by himself. Besides, they can't get far. I'll send Ray out with some extra horses. After the boys round up their horses, we'll go after the rustlers."

"Won't that be dangerous?"

"Facing people willing to steal or kill is always dangerous, but they'll rob you blind if you don't. While I talk to Ray, you check on how much food we have. We'll pack everything in our saddlebags." He gave her a quick kiss. "Don't look so worried. With luck we'll be back inside a week."

It was nearly dark when Ray returned. When Pete saw he'd brought back the horses, he knew they were in for trouble.

"They won't come back," Ray said. "They said you were an imposter, that they were going to kill you. They said if any of the boys came back to the ranch, they'd kill them too."

"Who said that?" Pete asked.

"It was written on a piece of paper nailed to a tree."

"Was anybody else hurt?"

"No. But there's something strange about that. The boys said there was a lot of shooting going on. They didn't think anybody was trying to hit them. I heard Mrs. Dean say Eddie was shot by a rifle, but the boys swear there weren't no rifle in the group they saw."

If Pete had had any doubts, he didn't any longer. Somebody had planned to steal the herd some time ago and had laid very careful plans. The only reason he could figure that Eddie would be the only one shot—and with a rifle, which indicated somebody had shot him from hiding—was to keep his mouth shut. But what could Eddie tell?

"They're going to attack the house," Pete said.

"How do you know?" Anne asked.

"Somebody is after this ranch. They've killed P— tried to kill me twice, killed Belser, and now tried to kill Eddie. I don't know all the reasons, but that's got to be what's happening. Ray, take the horses and hide them in that canyon behind the ranch house. Then you can leave."

"I'm not going."

"You know what that letter said."

"I don't run because of no letter."

"Thanks. If we get though this, I'll remember that."

"What are you going to do?" Ray asked.

"Pack up enough food to last a few days. If they attack us, they'll try to make certain we can't reach town. That means we'll have to find a place to hide."

"I know a cabin up in the hills, in the timber," Ray said.

"Can you take us there?"

"Yeah."

"Okay. We'll start loading the food. Anne, pack some warm clothes for both of us. The first snow could come any day."

But Anne didn't move. "I don't understand. Why should anybody want to attack us? Why should we leave?"

The time had come to explain everything.

"The food is in the kitchen," he told Ray. "Pack what you can in fifteen minutes, then leave. If you take the horses down the canyon behind the house, no one will see you. We'll be right behind you."

"Pete, what is going on? I insist you tell me."

"I will, but you're not going to like it." He took her by the shoulders, sat her down in a chair in front of the fireplace, and pulled another up close to her.

"Why?" she said when he'd sat down and was looking at her intently.

"Because I'm an imposter."

Anne's complexion turned white.

"Listen to every word I have to say before you make up your mind about anything," Pete said. "I'll make this quick. We may not have much time.

"My name is Pete Jernigan. I've been working in the goldfields of Montana and Idaho for the last five years. About a month ago I decided to take my money and head south. I had already made camp for the night when two men rode up and asked to join me. I invited them to get down. Next thing I knew, I woke up buck naked with a concussion from a gunshot to the head. They took everything I had, stripped my camp bare. I

271

don't know how my horse got back. I managed to get on his back and start him walking, hoping he'd take me to the nearest ranch.

"He stopped at a wagon abandoned along the trail. Someone had taken the mules, but they'd left the body of the owner sprawled out on the ground."

Anne's swift intake of breath told Pete she'd guessed who the man was.

"I was nearly unconscious, but I managed to climb into the wagon and sleep. Later I woke up, ate some of the man's food, and went back to sleep. I did this for eleven days, until I was strong enough to ride again. In the meantime, I searched the man. I found his wallet and dozens of letters from you. I wondered why everything had been left on him, why the wagon had been left in the open where it could be seen from miles away. Now I know. Someone was supposed to find him so Belser could inherit the ranch. It was pure chance I discovered him first."

Anne's expression was blank. He wished she'd say something, give him a hint of whether she believed a word he was saying.

"I used to think Belser killed Peter, or at least hired those two men to do it, but now I don't think so. Anyway, I read all the letters. That's how I knew Peter was coming here to claim his inheritance. But I wasn't interested in that. I meant to turn everything over to the first sheriff I found. I wanted to find the men who stole my saddlebags. Every bit of the money I had to show for the last five years was sewn inside the lining. As soon as I was strong enough, I went back to my camp. The hoofprints of the killers' horses were easy to see.

The men who'd robbed me and left me for dead were the same men who killed Peter."

Still no reaction. He couldn't tell if Anne was feeling shock or disbelief.

"Their trail led me here. I arrived just as your uncle was trying to haul you away. I realized the only way to protect you was to pretend to be Peter. Since I was sure the killers were hiding on your ranch, pretending to be Peter would also give me a chance to find my money. So that's what I did. You know the rest."

"You're not Peter." She looked dazed from the shock. Worse than that. She seemed paralyzed, devastated, as if he'd destroyed her whole world.

"No."

"But I let you . . . we . . . "

She didn't look at him. Rather, she looked at her hands as though she'd somehow gotten them dirty. He could excuse everything else he had done, but not that.

"You lied to me." She looked up, pain in her eyes. "Why?"

"I did it to help you."

"Everybody told me you were lying, but I wouldn't believe them. I was certain you were honest and true and good."

"Maybe I'm not as good as I ought to be, but I never meant to hurt you. I just wanted to keep you from having to marry Cyrus. But you were so sweet and charming and trusting, I couldn't help but like you."

"You thought I was a gullible child who wouldn't care whom I married as long as I was safe from Cyrus McCaine."

"I thought you were a lovely young woman who'd

been mistreated by the very people who ought to have valued her. At first I stayed only so I could find my money. Later I stayed to make sure you'd be able to keep the ranch after I left."

"I don't believe you. You're lying again." She said it quietly, calmly, as though it didn't mean anything to her anymore. "You know that description isn't going to prove anything one way or the other. Peter's clothes fit you. You even look alike. There never was any money or saddlebags. You want this ranch, and you're banking on my being so afraid of Cyrus that I'll back your claim."

"If that was true, I wouldn't have told you anything."

She paused, but only for a minute. "You're afraid somebody will find Peter's body. What did you do with it?"

"I buried Peter where no one will find him and burned the wagon." He shouldn't have told her that part. Now she'd be certain he wanted to steal the ranch.

"Did you kill Peter?"

"No!" He'd been afraid she might think that, but hearing the words were a shock. They hurt.

"Were you the one who came up to his camp, asked to join him? He would have let you. Peter wouldn't have suspected you meant him any harm. He never could see the bad in people. He thought they were all innocent, like him. You wouldn't have had to read those letters. He'd have told you everything if you just knew how to manipulate him."

"He was dead when I found him. I was shot in the head, remember?"

"Maybe Peter's the one who shot you. Maybe he realized, before you killed him, what you meant to do and made one desperate attempt to save himself."

"That's Mrs. Dean's story. You told me you didn't believe it."

"She was right about you being an imposter. Why shouldn't she be right about everything else?"

"Look, Anne, I'm sorry I lied to you. If I'd had time to think, maybe I would have done something else, but it was all I could think of on the spur of the moment."

"Why didn't you tell me that first night?" Her chin was up, defying him to tell her anything she'd believe.

"If I'd told you then, I'd have had no excuse to stay here to find my money. You'd probably have thought I killed Peter, just like you do now."

"Why should I believe anything you say? You're a very practiced liar. Whenever I had questions, you always had an answer ready. Did you plan out your answers ahead of time, or did you think them up on the spur of the moment? That would be real genius if you did."

She was doing her best not to cry. He wanted to reach out and touch her, take her in his arms, comfort her with a kiss, but he knew he couldn't touch her. Her control was very fragile. The attack on the ranch could come at any time. He couldn't afford to have her hysterical and out of control.

"I never knew what to say. I depended on you to tell me enough about Peter's background so I wouldn't make a mistake."

Tears shown in her eyes. "So I helped you lie to me."

"I just wanted to stay long enough to find my money. I was going to tell you everything when I did."

"But in the meantime, you decided to have some fun with this little Indian girl from Wyoming, this breed who didn't have enough sense to know a scared little boy couldn't grow into a fancy cowboy. I was so stupid, I fell for it." In an angry gesture, her hand flew to her face to dash away a tear that had started down her cheek. "I was so dazzled by your good looks, your ability and confidence, your telling me I was beautiful, that I was ready to believe anything you said. Buying me all those clothes, giving me this ring"—she fingered it nervously but didn't look down at it—"it was a small price to pay for my steadfast devotion."

"I didn't do it to bribe you. You *are* a beautiful woman. I wanted you to know it, to feel it. You're Peter's wife. You deserve those rings."

"What did you intend to do when I finally figured out you weren't Peter? And I would have figured it out. Sooner or later you'd have made some mistake. Did you hope I'd be pregnant, or have two or three children by then, and wouldn't turn in my husband for the lying, murdering imposter he was?"

"I wasn't going to let you have my children. You were too sweet, too innocent, too—"

"If you mention my sweetness and innocence once more, I'm going to scream and start throwing things. You mean I was stupid and naive, so anxious to believe I was pretty and a man could like me that I would believe anything, swallow any horror, help you cover any crime—"

He couldn't contain himself any longer. He reached

for her. She tried to avoid him, but he gripped her by the arms. "You *are* beautiful. You *are* sweet and innocent. But you're also intelligent, strong, and very loyal. You are a wonderful woman, and one day you'll make some man a wonderful wife. I always knew I couldn't be that man, even though living with you has made me want to be, but I knew you'd never forgive me for what I've done."

"You're right about that. I hate you. I never want to see you again."

"Blame me for lying, for violating your emotions and trust, but I didn't kill Peter, and I never meant to steal your ranch. I never meant to make love to you. Good God, I tried not to, but—"

"So I'm to praise you for—"

A shot broke the window at the front of the house. Pete threw Anne and himself to the floor.

"What was that?" she asked.

"Somebody's outside." They had waited too long. The attack had already begun.

"Peter Warren," a voice called, "or the man who calls himself Peter Warren, come out."

"Who wants me?" Pete shouted.

"Bill Mason."

Nothing made sense. What was Mason doing there? "What do you want me for?"

"I know you're an imposter, that you killed Peter Warren. I'm taking you in to Big Bend to stand trial."

Something wasn't right. If the sheriff had proof Pete was an imposter, he'd have come after Pete himself.

"You don't have any proof to back up such a claim," Pete said.

"We found where you buried Peter. We found where you burned the wagon, too."

The only way anybody could have known he'd burned the wagon was to know exactly where it had been left. The only way they could have found Peter Warren's grave would have been to have spent days looking until they found the piece of sod Pete had removed and carefully replaced.

And the only person who could have done that would be the man who'd murdered Peter Warren.

"Bill Mason killed Peter Warren," Pete whispered to Anne, "or rather had those two men kill him."

"That's the most ridiculous thing I ever heard."

"He couldn't know all of what he's saying unless he knew where to look. I hid everything very carefully."

"To cover your tracks."

"No. To protect Peter's body from wild animals."

Clearly Anne didn't believe him.

"I can't leave the ranch without an owner," Pete shouted. "Rustlers will clean us out in no time."

"There are no rustlers."

"Then who stole my herd?"

"I stole the herd to protect it for Anne."

"Did you kill Belser to protect Anne, too?"

"I didn't kill Belser. You did."

"Why did you shoot Eddie?"

"That was an accident."

But it hadn't been an accident. Eddie had been shot, maybe killed, by a rifleman firing from a distance, a man who didn't want to be seen.

"What will happen to Anne?" Pete asked.

"I'm going to marry Anne," Mason said. "That's

what I was going to do the day you arrived pretending to be Peter Warren."

"Did you know Mason wanted to marry you?" Pete asked Anne.

"Yes, but I told him I had already married Peter."

"What did he say when you told him that?"

"Nothing. He came by even more often afterward."

"Did he ask you about Peter?"

"Yes. He said they'd been friends years ago, that he was looking forward to seeing him again, that he wanted to know all about what had been happening to him in Illinois."

"Did he know when Peter was arriving?"

"Yes. He wanted to go meet him, but he got busy and couldn't."

Suddenly Pete understood it all. "Mason had Peter killed so he could marry you and get the ranch."

"That can't be true. If Peter didn't inherit, Belser would."

"He had Belser killed, too."

"How?"

"Eddie. Eddie worked for Mason. I don't know why, but he did."

"Eddie didn't kill Belser. I know he didn't."

"He's the only person who could have. Neither you nor Dolores would have had the strength. I know I didn't do it, so that leaves Eddie."

"I don't know you didn't do it," Anne replied.

He had expected her to say that. "That explains why Eddie was the only one shot when Mason rustled the herd. He wanted to make sure Eddie couldn't tell what he knew."

"There's no end to the lies you'll tell, is there?" Anne asked. "Are you going to keep lying about everybody I know until I believe you?"

"I'm not lying. Everything I said fits the facts."

"Everything Mrs. Dean told me fits the facts, too. It's incredible how you can think all this up in a matter of seconds."

"Anne, I want to marry you," Mason shouted. "I'll protect you from people like him. Come on out. If he's holding you inside, we'll kill him."

"He could be lying," Pete said. "He's already killed three people to get this ranch. Do you think he'll let a breed stand in the way of his getting it now?"

"So now I find out what you really think of me," Anne said.

"No, but you said everybody in Big Bend treated you like dirt. Do you think the man who plans to be the richest man in the whole area would saddle himself with a wife who was an outcast? He'd find some way to get rid of you after you were married, probably a riding accident."

Anne started to get up. "I've known Bill Mason for years," she said. "I trust him to protect me."

Pete pulled her back down beside him. "Haven't you heard a single thing I've said?"

"I won't believe any more of your lies."

"Think! If what Mason says is true, he doesn't have to attack the house. All he has to do is wait for the sheriff. But that won't work for him because he's got to find a way to stop me from talking and of making sure you marry him. He can't be sure the sheriff won't believe my story, or that some proof won't turn up. He also can't be sure that once he gets you to town, you'll marry him. This way he can be certain of both."

But Pete had lost his credibility with Anne.

"I won't believe anything you tell me ever again, but I don't want your death on my head. I'm going with Mr. Mason. I'll find a way to stall him until you have time to get away to the horses. If you can't escape after that, then I'm sorry."

"You can't go to Mason. He'll kill you."

Anne struggled to break his grip. "Leave before I change my mind and let him capture you."

Pete knew it was no use arguing further. Anne was too hurt to believe him, no matter how logical his reasoning. There was only one thing to do. Clamping his hand over her mouth so she couldn't cry out in warning, Pete picked Anne up and ran out the back of the house with her.

"I can't believe Ray let you carry me off," Anne complained. "When I get back to the ranch, I'm going to fire him."

"Apparently he doesn't trust Bill Mason very much either," Pete said.

They had arrived at a cabin in the foothills of the Big Horn Mountains under cover of night. He hoped they'd gotten away at least ten minutes before Mason discovered they were gone. He also hoped Mason wouldn't be able to follow their trail. Little more than twelve feet square, the cabin was a single-room affair with bunks on opposite walls, a table and two chairs, and a stove that was used for both cooking and heating. The catalogue pages that plastered the wall served to keep out the cold as well as provide reading material on freezing winter nights. A shed had been attached to the back of the cabin. A small corral had been laid out in a protected clearing among the pines. A tiny spring emerging from a rock outcropping twenty yards away provided them with fresh water.

"Why did you send Ray away?" Anne asked.

"I sent him for the sheriff."

"I don't believe you. That would expose you for the liar you are."

"But it will keep Mason from getting his hands on you."

"I don't know why you keep talking like Mason is a killer."

"Because I know I'm not," Pete said, tired of defending himself. She wouldn't believe him innocent. But he had to convince her Mason was dangerous. It could cost her her life if he didn't. "Somebody did those killings."

"You did."

"Just once assume everything I'm telling you is true. Don't argue," he said when she started to open her mouth in protest. "There's always a chance I'm telling the truth. Even if it's only a very small chance, we're talking about your life. Doesn't that make it worth considering every possibility?"

She didn't answer. But she continued to look at him as though he was a rattlesnake and she'd give her right arm for a shotgun.

"I know you can't trust me after what I've done. Just don't take everything Mason says on face value. He's your neighbor. Your uncle had the best grazing land within a hundred miles. Mason can't help but want it for himself."

"Bill Mason isn't like that."

"Three people have been killed, Anne. Somebody wants something mighty bad, and the only thing at stake is your Uncle Carl's ranch."

"He had an accident."

"Wasn't it a peculiar accident for a man of his age and experience?"

She didn't answer.

"Now Peter Warren and Belser Wilmot are also dead. The only person standing between Mason and that ranch is you. He figures you'll have to marry to hold it, so he corners you at your ranch and says he's going to marry you to protect you from me. Maybe he does love you. Maybe he's nursed a secret passion for years. Or maybe his secret passion is for your uncle's land. I can't prove what I'm saying, but you've got to consider it. If you make the wrong decision, it could cost you your life."

"Why should I listen to you when I know you're a liar and an imposter? Probably a killer as well."

"Why *probably?* I thought you were certain of it."

"I didn't actually see you."

"You're too generous."

"I don't want to talk with you anymore. I'm going to sleep. I hope you will come to your senses by morning and let me go."

"If I'm the desperate killer you think, I can't afford to let you go. I'll have to take you hostage."

"You already have."

"Believe it or not, I brought you here to protect you.

I wanted one last chance to convince you Bill Mason is dangerous."

"Well, you haven't, so you can save your breath. Tomorrow morning I'm going to town. I don't want to marry Bill Mason, even if he does have a secret passion for me. What are you going to do?"

"Try to find another place to hide. I don't trust Mason not to know of this cabin."

"If I were you, I'd head south while you still have the dark to hide you."

"But you're not me," Pete said. "I haven't done things like I should, but Jake taught all his boys never to run from trouble. He said once you start running, you got to keep on."

"I thought you made Jake up."

"He's real. So's Isabelle. You ought to be glad they are. They're the only reason I'm still here. Isabelle pounded into our heads that we had to take care of any woman we found in trouble—old, young, pretty, ugly, rich, poor, even women just plain too stubborn and hardheaded to believe the truth. I don't know how, but I'll get you out of this mess. Then I'll head south as fast as I can."

Chapter Sixteen

Anne couldn't sleep. Though she tried to block it out of her mind, she couldn't forget what Pete had said. It seemed impossible he could be innocent. Everything fit too well—the meeting with and murder of Peter, pretending to be her husband, killing Belser, rounding up her cattle early so he could steal her money. That didn't explain why rustlers had stolen the herd and shot Eddie, but she was sure she'd find out why before long. In any case, Pete had to be the man who'd killed Peter.

Then why wasn't she frightened of him?

He'd lied to her, kidnaped her, was holding her hostage. If she believed Pete had killed three people, why didn't she believe he'd kill her?

Because he needed her? Maybe. Mrs. Dean could trumpet her objections to the whole of Big Bend, but it wouldn't matter. As long as Anne's public faith in her husband never wavered, he would be accepted as Peter Warren without having to produce any incontrovertible proof.

She wondered what he would do to convince her to continue to support his lie. With Peter dead, there was no one to prove they had ever been married. Without that, she couldn't inherit anything as his widow. She would have no money, no place to live, nowhere to go. Would Pete threaten to turn her over to her uncle and Cyrus McCaine? Wouldn't marriage to Pete, even if he were a murderer, be better than a lifetime sentence as Cyrus's wife?

Anne refused to let herself consider such an option. Nothing could be worse than being married to a murderer.

Pete had been kind to her. He'd treated her better than anyone had ever treated her, including Peter. He hadn't forced himself on her that first night or any of the nights after that. When she'd made love to him, she'd done so because she wanted it more than anything else in the world.

Love! How could she use such a word! How could any woman love a man who'd done what he'd done?

But he'd been sweet and charming and thoughtful. He'd bought her clothes, a beautiful ring, told her she was beautiful, *treated* her as if she was beautiful. He'd even acted as if he loved her.

She was thinking like a fool. She'd been starved for love and affection for so long that she was willing to defend the first man who gave it to her, even if he was a criminal. She had to get her emotions under control.

She didn't know anything about killers. She'd always assumed they were vicious. But it would seem logical that any man who wanted to pretend to be someone he wasn't would have to be charming enough to make the victims want him to be that person. Dozens of little things had warned her, had made her question whether Pete was Peter.

But he'd been so charming, sweet, generous, considerate, appreciative, capable, masterful, big, strong, handsome—all the things a woman wanted in a husband—it was no wonder she'd wanted to believe he was Peter.

She couldn't imagine any other man spending so much time or money making certain she found just the right dresses to flatter her face and figure. Nor had he quibbled at all the extras she bought to make herself beautiful. He'd given with a free hand.

And the ring! She could still remember the tears she'd shed when he'd slipped it on her finger.

Fool! Why shouldn't he be generous? It wasn't his money. And every penny he spent made her more determined than ever to believe in him. She didn't doubt him even when Mrs. Dean said he was an imposter. She didn't believe anyone until Pete himself told her he wasn't Peter.

That didn't make any sense. Why should he have told her he wasn't Peter? He needed her support now more than ever. As far as she could see, he had everything to lose and nothing to gain.

But he'd only told her when he came up against Bill Mason and his armed cowhands. Maybe he thought that by confessing to the smaller crime of being an imposter, she wouldn't believe him guilty of the bigger one, killing Peter and Belser. But why confess to any crime? Why not go on pretending complete innocence? After that night in his arms, she would have believed anything he said.

She tried not to remember that evening, but it was impossible. She had been certain she'd found love, a place to belong forever. She'd thought she had finally been transformed from a girl into a woman. She doubted Pete was in love with her yet, but she was certain he soon would be.

She wasn't experienced in love. But she couldn't believe a man could make her feel that wonderful, so totally re-created, unless he cared deeply. She wasn't very good with the physical sensations connected with love—they were too new to her—but she was an expert in feelings of the heart. She knew when people disliked her, looked down on her, didn't think her worth considering.

Pete cared. No matter what he'd done, she knew he cared.

And she cared about him. She couldn't deny that. How could she not care for a man who'd made her feel wanted, valued, safe, beautiful, intelligent—all the things Uncle Carl and the other men she'd known had made it a point to deny. For the first time in her life, she'd felt good about herself. She'd felt confident enough to stand up to Mrs. Dean, to fire Belser, to ride ten miles across the plains to the roundup when she'd never been more than a hundred yards from the ranch house in her life. She'd even felt confident enough to stop apologizing for being part Indian.

But none of that should count when set against the horrible crimes he'd committed. There was no telling how many men he'd killed before he ran into Peter Warren and realized what an opportunity had fallen into his lap. For all she knew, he could be a notorious killer, wanted all over the West for dozens of horrible crimes. She was lucky he hadn't killed her. She'd have to escape.

She got out of bed and checked the door to the cabin. Locked. That didn't surprise her. She'd expected it. But he couldn't lock her in all the time. There would be times when he wasn't watching, when her horse would be ahead or behind his, times when she would need to disappear into the woods to be alone. She just had to be ready to take advantage of the opportunity when it came.

Yet as she climbed back into her bed and pulled the rough covers over her, a part of her couldn't admit Pete was a murderer. A part of her brain said no man who'd treated her as he had could be such a vicious criminal.

What if Pete was telling the truth?

But that was impossible. There was no point in trying to make him innocent. She just had to think of him as two people. One of those people was a wonderful man who was on the verge of falling in love with her. The other was a vicious killer willing to do anything to get his way. She just had to keep reminding herself that she couldn't have one without the other.

Pete had awakened to look out on a ground stiff with frost. Sudden snows could come at any time of the year in the higher elevations. By the time the sun had melted the frost, he'd fed and watered the horses, loaded the packhorse, and saddled the others. He didn't want to stay here too long. This cabin looked too well used. He was certain someone would think to look here. He wanted to be gone before that happened.

He woke Anne, but she refused to speak to him, look at him, or eat any of the food he offered. He supposed she would become a little more accommodating when she got hungry, but he didn't have time to wait. Right now he wanted to get on the horses and leave. The sun had disappeared, the wind had picked up, and the sky had turned a dull blue-gray. It looked like snow.

"You need to get dressed and packed," he said when it became clear Anne wasn't going to eat.

"Why?"

"I'm sure Mason or his men will think to check this cabin before long."

"Good. I want them to find me. I want them to shoot you."

"Well, I don't, so oblige me by being ready in five minutes."

"No."

"Do it."

"What will you do if I don't, beat me?"

He stomped out of the cabin, afraid he'd say something unforgivable. Though why he should worry about that now he couldn't say. If she really did want Mason to shoot him, he didn't have an awful lot more to lose. He'd made a mistake in telling her the truth.

He hadn't gone ten steps from the cabin before movement on a distant slope caught his attention.

Riders. Six of them. He didn't need binoculars to know they were Mason's men. He raced back to the cabin.

"Riders are coming. We've got to leave now."

"You go if you want. I can't stop you, but I'm staying here."

"Mason wants your ranch. He intends to marry you to get it. If you don't say yes, he'll take you to his ranch and keep you there until you do. Once you're pregnant with his child, you won't have much choice."

He'd expected her to show surprise, shock, even a little fear. He saw none of those—only anger.

"I'd rather be pregnant with his child than yours."

Pete hadn't thought of the possibility that she might already be carrying his child. It was a slim chance, but the notion nearly unmanned him. He'd never thought of children except as belonging to someone else. Even then he wasn't too high on them. They were always underfoot, always demanding something, needing something. Their parents couldn't seem to talk about anything else.

But the possibility that he and Anne might have created a child together raised the concept of fatherhood to quite a different status. He couldn't think of giving up his kid. Even less could he accept the idea that his son might be raised by another man. Especially a man like Bill Mason, who would have no interest in seeing that the child of another man lived to grow up.

"Are you pregnant?" Pete asked.

"No. I mean, I don't know. You know it's impossible to tell this early."

He didn't know. It was something that had never concerned him.

"Well, I'm not letting Bill Mason get his hands on you until we know for sure."

"I told you I'm not leaving here."

"I'll carry you over my shoulder if I have to, but you're coming with me."

"No, I'm not."

"They'll be here before long. We've got to leave."

"No."

He didn't have time to argue. "I'm sorry, but you made me do this."

She tried to dodge him when he moved toward her, but there wasn't enough room in the cabin. He reached out when she tried to dash by, caught her arm, and pulled her to him. She struck out at him with her fists, but he caught her arms and pinned them behind her.

"We don't have to do it this way."

"You do if you plan to take me out of this cabin."

She struggled against him. But after years of back-breaking work in the minefields, he was far too strong for her. He picked her up and carried her outside.

"You can't leave all my things inside."

"I'll get them once you're on your horse."

She didn't say a word when he lifted her into the saddle. But the instant he turned back to the cabin, she jumped off the horse and started to run. He caught her before she'd gone twenty yards.

"I'm not going," she said, panting heavily from her exertions.

"Yes, you are, so you might as well stop fighting."

"I'll just run away again as soon as you turn your back."

"Then I guess I'll have to tie your hands behind you."

"You wouldn't dare."

"I'm trying to save my neck. Whether you believe it or not, I'm trying to save yours as well. I'll do anything I have to."

She fought like a little tiger, but he had her hands tied behind her back in a trice. "Now if you try to jump off your horse, you'll fall."

"Help!"

The scream caught him by surprise. The mountainside threw it back at him.

"Stop, you little fool. They'll hear you."

"That's what I want." She screamed again.

Pete clamped his hand over her mouth. He studied the group of riders nervously. They showed no signs they'd heard her cry for help, but they'd soon be close enough to hear.

"Don't do that again."

She stared defiantly at him.

"I'm going to uncover your mouth. If you—"

She screamed before he had fully removed his hand. He could tell from the look in her eyes that she was going to scream every chance she got.

"I'm sorry to do this, but you give me no choice." He pulled his handkerchief from around his neck and gagged her.

She looked shocked. More than that, she looked absolutely furious.

"I hate to do this, but I can't trust you not to scream again."

She fought him hard, but with her hands tied behind her back, there wasn't much she could do.

He lifted her into the saddle. "In case you are stubborn enough to throw yourself from your horse again, I'm going to tie your feet below the saddle. No point kicking," he said when she did her best to kick him in the head. "I'm ten times as strong as you. You might as well give in and wait for a better chance to escape."

Apparently she agreed, for she stopped struggling the moment he tied her feet. "I have to collect the rest of our things. I don't want to leave any signs we've been here." Just in case she decided to spur her horse in an effort to run away while he was inside, he tethered the horse to the rail. She rewarded him with an evil glare.

It took precious minutes to collect Anne's belongings and return the cabin to its previous look of neglect. Once outside, he did his best to erase the hoofprints the horses had left around the cabin. A line rider could account for a few tracks but not all that their three horses had created since yesterday.

"I don't know where we're going," he said to Anne when he mounted up. "If we get lucky, we might find another line cabin. If not, Ray says there are caves up in those mountains. They might have to do."

Anne didn't show any response, but then he couldn't expect much with her hands and feet tied and a gag in her mouth. He didn't know how she would react to hiding in a cave. He wouldn't like it much, but he'd lived in worse conditions at more than one mining camp. All he asked was that water didn't drip from the ceiling.

The first snowflakes started to fall as they rode away from the cabin. Finally, a piece of good luck. The snow would cover the hoofprints. With luck, Mason's men would decide they'd never been here and stop searching this part of the ranch. Pete didn't know how much they knew about these hills. The land belonged to the Tumbling T, but he figured Mason already considered it his own.

Pete pushed hard to reach the place where the trees grew thick enough on the low hills to provide cover. The last time he saw Mason's men, they were still a mile from the cabin, but he didn't slow his pace. There were only a few places where he could find cover before he reached the more dense forest of the mountain itself.

He dropped down into the canyon created by Crazy Woman Creek as it came out of the mountains. Following an ancient buffalo trail alongside the creek made travel much easier. Cottonwood, willow, ash, box elder, water birch, and mountain alder provided a band of cover about fifty feet on either side of the creek through a canyon covered mostly with sage, greasewood, rabbit brush, and sumac. Further up, juniper, maple, aspen and ponderosa pine provided a dense cover Pete hoped would hide him until he could find a cave, a temporary refuge until he figured out how to get them safely to Big Bend.

The temperature dropped significantly as they climbed higher and higher into the Big Horn Mountains. He wanted to be certain Anne was warm, but she refused to respond when he spoke. He also wanted to get as far away from the cabin as possible before stopping.

All through the morning the snowfall continued heavy enough to cover the ground but not heavy enough to make travel difficult. Except for the cold. The temperature continued to drop.

At midday, Pete pulled his horse to a stop. "I'm stopping here to fix something to eat."

She grunted when he untied her feet and lifted her from the saddle. He was certain her muscles hurt from the unaccustomed position of riding astride, but there was nothing he could do about that now. He built a small fire, heated the beef he'd fixed for breakfast, and took it over to Anne.

"If I untie you, can I trust you not to run away?"

Anne shook her head.

"I have to take your gag out to feed you."

She still looked mutinous.

"It would be dangerous to try to escape," he said. "You'd get lost. Besides, you couldn't make it back to the cabin on foot. You'd probably die of exposure if you had to spend the night outside."

She didn't say a word. He didn't know if she believed him or thought he was just trying to scare her. He couldn't take the chance. He removed the gag, but she refused to open her mouth.

"You might as well eat. I know you're hungry."

She just glared at him.

"We can't stop again until evening. You need something in your stomach to keep you warm."

Still no response.

"If you're carrying a baby, you've got to eat. You can hate me, but you can't hate your baby."

"I refuse to be carrying your baby," she said.

He grinned. "You probably aren't. But if you are, I especially don't want you to fall into Bill Mason's hands. I don't think he'd be very good to it."

"From the experience I've had with men so far, I'd prefer to remain unmarried."

Pete held out a spoonful of beef, and she finally opened her mouth to accept it.

"You might not have much choice," he said while she chewed. "Until we get confirmation that you married Peter, you don't have any money or a home. Your uncle can do what he wants with you. Your other choice is to marry Mason and hope he meant it when he said he'd protect you."

"I don't need anybody to protect me."

He stopped her talking by putting more food into her mouth.

"Mason doesn't mean to give up the Tumbling T. If you're Peter's widow and his heir, marrying you would make his seizure legal."

"I told you I won't marry Mason."

He put more food in her mouth.

"Once his hold on the ranch is secure, I don't trust Mason not to do something to get rid of you."

"You shouldn't judge everybody by yourself," she said.

"If I did, I'd never have figured out what Mason did. I spent twelve years working in the goldfields with murder and theft rampant all around me, yet I never killed anybody for anything. I worked for my money."

"Where is that money? I've never seen it. I might think you were telling the truth if you could show it to me."

"I told you, it was stolen."

"Like all the other evidence to support your claim," she said. "Whoever heard of robbers taking a man's clothes and leaving him naked?"

"Nobody. They ought to be hanged. Do you know what would have happened if anybody had come by? I'd have had to hide. I couldn't let them know I was naked. A man could die from something as embarrassing as that."

"Just like a man to let his pride kill him."

"It's what you're trying to do. You're so damned mad that you stood up for me against everybody, you're willing to throw yourself into the hands of the first man who comes along, even though I've talked myself silly trying to show you that you're in more danger with him than me."

"He hasn't killed anybody."

"Neither have I. Now eat the rest of this beef. We've got to be on our way. I want to get to those hills. I'm hoping I can find a cave to give us shelter and concealment. I have a feeling we're going to need both." He helped Anne to her feet. "I'd like to untie you. Can I trust you not to try to escape?"

He saw her glance at the snow that had already begun to filter down through the covering of trees. She obviously figured this wasn't the time to escape. She nodded.

"Good. I don't like seeing you so miserable."

"Then you shouldn't have killed Peter."

"When will you get it through your head that I'm not after this ranch? Even if I had decided to take it, the trouble started long before I got here. I think it started when your Uncle Carl got hurt and he appeared vulnerable for the first time. Eddie couldn't hold this place. He might be a good foreman, but he doesn't have the guts to stand up to men like Mason. I think Belser would have killed for it, but he wasn't smart. He let himself be suckered, and it got him killed."

"You know I don't believe a word you're saying."

"Yeah, I know. But when I figure out how to get you to Big Bend without getting myself killed, I'm getting out of here so fast, you won't see anything but dust. You'll have to make your own decisions. I'm hoping I can at least make you question everything Mason says before you stick your head too far into his noose."

"I'm not falling into anybody's noose," Anne insisted.

Pete ignored her interruption. "Quite frankly, I don't think you'll ever get your ranch back, not unless you have proof of your marriage to Peter and a very good lawyer. Even then I think Mason would fight you for it. He'd probably try to convince the other ranchers you couldn't hold the ranch on your own, that it needs to be controlled by a man to protect all of them from rustling. And he'd be right."

"I'd hire a foreman."

"You'll have a hard time finding a cowman out here who'll work for a woman. That gives Mason all the excuse he needs to kidnap you and keep you on his ranch until you agree to marry him. The women wouldn't like it, but the other ranchers probably wouldn't say anything. Once you were married—and that could be arranged even without your consent—there wouldn't be anything anybody could do."

For once she didn't fling a hot-tempered response back at him. Good. Maybe she was beginning to think. If he could keep this up for a few days, maybe she'd have a chance. "Enough talk. We'd better be going."

Traveling became harder as they climbed higher into the mountains. The leafy cottonwoods gave way to scattered water birch and patches of currants, raspberry, and chokeberry. The bitterly cold wind drove the snow directly into their faces. Pete stopped twice to make certain Anne's hands and face were covered.

They climbed steadily toward the belt of lodgepole pines still a couple of thousand feet above them. Before long they came to a place where ancient rivers had cut a canyon through rock that rose nearly perpendicular around him. This was the best place to look for caves hollowed out millions of years ago. Leaving the comparative shelter of the streambed, they rode out into the open and started up the steep mountainside.

The sharpness of the wind made him huddle deeper into his coat. Once again he cursed the men who had robbed him of the clothes that had kept him warm through Montana winters. If he ever found them, he'd take great pleasure in stripping them naked and driving them out into the teeth of a storm.

Pete soon found an area where small caves were plentiful. But finding the right kind of cave wasn't that simple. He needed one deep enough to provide shelter from the wind and snow. He needed enough deadfall close by to build fires for cooking and heat. He needed a belt of trees to screen movement in and around the cave from anyone who might have followed them. He needed open meadow so the horses could find something to eat. Finally, there had to be a stream close by for water.

The afternoon wore on, and still Pete couldn't find a cave to suit his requirements. With the snow getting deeper and the wind getting colder, he had to abandon the search and head toward the pine forest above. He would have to settle for building a shelter of pine boughs. They reached the trees a little before dusk.

"We'll stop here," Pete said. A natural park in the middle of a huge stand of pines would give his horses forage and protection from the worst of the storm. A tiny stream that meandered through the park would provide water.

"This isn't a cave," Anne said. "It's woods. We'll freeze to death or get eaten by wild animals."

Pete laughed. "The wild animals will more anxious to avoid you than you are to avoid them. It'll be cold, but at least we're out of the wind."

Pete rode among the trees until he found a group of pines growing so close together that no snow had managed to filter down through their limbs.

"We'll make our camp here."

It was too dark under the trees to see Anne's face, but he heard her sharp intake of breath when he lifted her out of the saddle.

"Are your muscles sore?"

"Yes."

The way she said the word told him almost as much as the fact that she couldn't stand on her own.

"If I had you in Texas, I'd teach you to ride a horse properly."

"I never want to get on a horse again," she said.

"Hold on to the saddle for a moment." Pete took a blanket from the packhorse and spread it on the deep pine needles under the trees. He carried Anne to the blanket and set her down gently. "Don't move. I'll be back in a minute."

"Where are you going?"

"I've got to take care of the horses. If we lose them, we'll both die up here in these mountains."

"You can't leave me here."

"I have to."

"I don't have a gun. What if something comes after me?"

"It won't."

"But what if it does?"

"Have you ever used a gun?"

"No."

"Then you couldn't hit anything."

"I could scare it off."

"You'd more likely shoot yourself. Or me. Or worse still, one of the horses."

"You've got to leave me a gun."

"And have you use it on me the minute I return? Not on your life."

"I won't shoot you."

"Why not? You've been wanting somebody to shoot me all day."

"I don't now."

"I don't believe you."

"Okay, I do want somebody to shoot you, but I'm

not fool enough to shoot you while we're lost in these mountains."

"We're not lost. And I don't believe you."

"Why would I shoot you?"

"Because you're crazy enough to think I killed Peter and Belser. You probably think I'm going to kill you, too."

"No."

"No what?"

"I don't think you're going to kill me."

"Why? According to you, I've killed everybody else I've come across."

She looked stubborn. "I don't believe you'll kill me. You'd never have thought of taking me back to Texas or teaching me to ride if you meant to kill me. Now let me have a gun and go take care of the horses. I'm starved. Besides, my legs are so stiff, I couldn't run away if I wanted."

Pete told himself he was crazy, that putting a gun in Anne's hands could be the same as signing his death warrant. But he'd been crazy where she was concerned from the first moment he saw her. He handed her his pistol. "Shoot in the air. The noise will scare anything away."

Chapter Seventeen

Anne marveled at the wrenching changes that had occurred so quickly in her life. This time two days ago she was in the arms of her husband—or so she'd thought—overjoyed that he was making love to her. Any thoughts she'd had to spare had been employed looking forward to the happy years they would spend together.

Yesterday, she'd been worried about Eddie and the rustled herd, but she was confident Pete, her adored husband, would get the herd back. She was also confident he would do so in a manner that would guarantee no rustler would ever touch Tumbling T cows again.

Now she was lying in the middle of a forest deep in the mountains in a snowstorm, hoping some wild animal didn't decide to make a meal of her. To compound her dilemma, she was the prisoner of the man who had killed her husband. And Belser. She had to get up. She wasn't fool enough to try to run away, but she couldn't lie here like a corpse. If she wasn't careful, that was exactly what she might become.

But even as that thought went through one part of her head, a contradictory thought emerged from another. Pete wasn't going to kill her because Pete wasn't a murderer. It went against logic and the evidence as she saw it, but she absolutely could not believe Pete—what did he say his last name was? Jernigan?—could kill anyone.

That argument had gone through her head all day. Time and time again she'd gone over all the reasons why Pete had to be lying. Over and over she'd proved beyond the shadow of a doubt that Pete was the worst villain unhanged. And every time, her heart had refused to accept it. She hoped it was her heart. She'd hate to think her brain was that stupid.

But if he was the killer, why hadn't he tried to get away as quickly as possible? He didn't need to bring her along. He didn't need to go deep into the mountains. He could have been in Colorado by now, well beyond Mason's reach. Instead he was taking care of the horses and getting ready to cook her supper. The only way any of this made sense was that Pete was telling the truth, that all the evidence pointed in the wrong direction.

But that was more than Anne's rational brain could accept. Maybe she couldn't believe he was a killer, but she couldn't believe he was innocent either. She realized that was a stupid way to think, but she couldn't help it. She didn't know what to believe anymore.

He'd given her a gun. She could shoot him, grab a horse, and follow the creek back. Someone would find her.

She tried to get to her feet and failed. She couldn't even stand up. She certainly couldn't steal a horse and run away. She turned on her hands and knees and crawled over to a tree. Bracing her hands against the trunk—the rough bark hurt as it dug into her soft palms—she pulled one leg up until it was beneath her. Using all her strength, she pulled the other under her. The pain was terrible. She thought she would scream. She waited without moving until the abused muscles began to relax. Then she waited a little longer. She knew the next part would be the hardest, the most painful. She heard Pete enter the trees. She was determined to be standing when he reached her. Taking a big breath and gritting her teeth, Anne forced herself to stand up.

At first she thought she couldn't do it. Her muscles simply wouldn't respond. She willed them to lift her, but nothing happened. Then, gradually, they lifted her inch by inch toward a standing position. If the pain had been awful before, it was excruciating now. But Pete was coming closer. She was determined to be on her feet. With one last superhuman effort, she made it upright.

She was standing.

"I told you not to move," Pete said. He raced to catch her before she fell. "You shouldn't have done this. You could have hurt yourself."

Hurt didn't begin to cover the situation. Half kill

herself was a lot closer. Pete settled her back down on the blanket.

"Now lie down. I'm going to massage your muscles to get some of the kinks out."

"I had to stand up," Anne said. She couldn't explain why she couldn't lie there waiting for him to come back and take care of her. She had to do something for herself. It hadn't been much and it had been futile, but she'd done it. She didn't expect him to understand, but it seemed he did.

"Stubborn. It's a good sign in a woman. Not a comfortable one, mind you, but good."

Anne decided she didn't understand Pete at all. He continued to act as if they were married, continued to treat her much the same way he had before she told him she hoped Mason or his men would shoot him. Why didn't he get mad at her? Any normal person would. Instead, he was kneeling on the blanket preparing to massage the stiffness out of her muscles.

"Turn over on your stomach."

She couldn't move. She was mortified that he had to turn her like a baby in its bed. He raised her skirt above her knee. The cold air on her skin was both a shock and a relief at once. Maybe if she got cold enough, she'd be too numb to feel the pain.

"This may hurt a little at first," he said. "But once I get the knots out, you'll feel a lot better."

With his thumbs and the side of his hand, he pressed and spread the muscles in her right calf. It did hurt. Her calves felt as if he was cutting them open with knives.

"I used to have to rub Sean's muscles," Pete said while he continued working. "He was my partner when we first started looking for gold. A huge fella with muscles like an ox, but he was determined to find all the gold he needed in one year. He'd work too hard and end up so sore he could hardly move. Once it took me nearly an hour before he could relax enough to sleep."

Anne couldn't imagine any man putting himself through this kind of torture every day. "He must have been crazy."

"No, just determined to get back to Texas as soon as possible. He loved ranching and hated mining." Pete switched to her other calf. The pain was just as bad. "Then he met Pearl, and he nearly got himself killed."

"Who are Sean and Pearl?" she asked, glad to be distracted from the pain, "Somebody else you made up along with Jake and Isabelle?"

"I told you, Jake and Isabelle adopted eleven of us."

"Nobody adopts that many children." He had to be lying. The story was too wonderful to be the truth.

"Sean was a lot older than me when I came to the orphanage. He was big and clumsy, and I was little and mean. Once we combined his muscles and my sharp tongue, everybody left us alone. After Jake and Isabelle adopted us, we didn't have to do that anymore. Isabelle didn't like fighting. Besides, once she beat it into our heads that she considered us a real family and we'd better do the same, things went pretty well."

He had one hand on each calf now, massaging the last of the tension away. She liked the feel of his hands on her body. Their warm strength was comforting. Despite the awkwardness of her position, she had almost relaxed when he moved to her right thigh and the cycle of pain started all over again.

"Why isn't this Sean with you now?" She didn't believe his fairy tale, but she'd listen to anything as long as it took her mind off the pain.

"He fell in love with Pearl. They got married and went back to live in Jake's valley in Texas."

"You said he nearly got killed." He couldn't stop talking now. It was all she could do not to moan aloud.

"Pearl was mixed up with some gambler who was determined to get Sean's gold. Only he made the mistake of kidnaping Pearl's daughter. Sean didn't stop until he got his money and Pearl's daughter back."

Anne was thankful the story made no sense. The effort to untangle it was all that enabled her to lie still when Pete started on her left thigh. She didn't know why anybody would ever want to ride a horse.

"Why aren't your muscles hurting you?" she asked, jealous that Pete seemed to be absolutely fine after spending all day in the saddle.

"I'm used to it. Besides, I know how to ride. Don't worry. I'll teach you." Their gazes met, and he stopped abruptly. "I guess I won't, but it's not hard. Sean learned to ride when he was still so uncoordinated he could hardly walk. I ought to warn you—this is going to hurt."

"What?" If he didn't think what he'd done already had hurt, then what he was about to do now would probably kill her.

"I'm going to massage your buttocks. You've got chafed skin as well as sore muscles."

"Maybe you ought to wait until tomorrow."

"It's better to do it now. At least you'll be able to sleep."

"How can I sleep in the middle of the woods?"

The man was actually cruel enough to laugh.

"You'll be surprised how easy it will be."

"If I see one pair of eyes staring at me out of the dark, I swear I'll scream."

Then she did. Well, not exactly scream, but moan. How could hands that had made such magic only two nights before cause such agony? "Tell me some more about Sean."

"What?"

"Anything! Have you seen him since he got married?" She didn't care about Sean, only half believed he was real, but she'd listen to anything to make the pain more bearable.

"Several times since. Last time, Pearl had just had their third son. All three look just like Sean. I told him it was a shame he didn't have a bunch of girls. Pearl is a beautiful woman. Jake said he'd just as soon not turn the valley into an armed camp with Sean trying to keep out all the young men trying to court his daughters. Isabelle told both of them not to be fools, that daughters had a way of marrying the men they wanted despite the well-meaning but misguided efforts of their male relatives."

Pete had moved to her other buttock. "It sounds like Jake and Isabelle fight all the time," she said, barely able to get the words out.

"No, they're too much in love. You'd think they wouldn't have anything in common—Isabelle was raised fancy by a rich aunt in Savannah, Georgia, and Jake came up on a poor dirt ranch in Texas—but Isabelle's as tough as old leather. None of us boys could ever get around her, and I promise we tried."

"She sounds like a bully."

"I guess she is in a way, but she bullies us because she loves us. Jake adores her. There's not one of us boys that wouldn't hunt down and kill any man who laid a hand on her."

Anne couldn't conceive of how a woman could win such devotion. In her experience women were treated almost as possessions, often not very valuable ones at that. Pete had to be making this whole story up. Nobody like Isabelle could exist, not even if she came from Savannah. But it was a nice story. It would be even nicer if something like that could happen to her.

It did. That's exactly how Pete treated you.

He'd rescued her from her uncle, showered her with gifts, told her she was beautiful and intelligent and desirable. Now he was risking his own safety to protect her from danger.

He had turned her into an Isabelle, and she hadn't even realized it.

And now he was turning her into a ball of molten desire.

The pain had receded. Only now did she have any spare thoughts to realize that Pete had pulled her skirt and her petticoat up to her waist. Only her drawers remained between his hands and the bare skin of her bottom. He continued to massage slowly as he talked about his family in Texas. But she heard very little of what he said. She became more and more acutely aware of his hands on her body, of the feelings that were growing in her belly and threatening to spread through the rest of her.

She fought them off with all her might. She couldn't possibly allow herself to be seduced by his touch, not even if her body was a willing—nay, eager—participant. This was a man who'd killed, cheated, lied, done enough evil to warrant being sentenced to hang. She had to remember that. There was a good side to him. She could no longer deny that. Nor could she deny that the good side was so attractive, it made her want to forget the bad things. But that wasn't possible. No decent person could do that.

Her body, however, seemed to have no qualms. It liked what Pete was doing and wanted more.

"That's enough," she said. "I feel much better now." She pushed his hands away and began to readjust her petticoat and skirt.

"Are you sure? I don't mind."

That was the trouble. She wouldn't mind it, either. "I'm certain. I'm cold and tired. I want to eat and go to sleep."

"It won't take me long to fix something to eat."

"You fix the coffee. I'll fix the food." She wasn't going to lie there and let him do everything. She couldn't accept that kind of treatment when she meant to see him hang for killing Peter.

"You're still too sore to stand up."

"I'll manage." She struggled to her feet. She wasn't

steady, but she felt much better. "Now tell me how I'm supposed to start a fire in a snowstorm."

Pete laughed. "Sit back down. I've done this a thousand times."

"Then you don't need to learn. I do. Show me."

"I never knew you were this stubborn. I thought you were a shy, biddable young woman."

She used to be. Then Pete came into her life, and nothing had been the same since.

"We all have to grow up," she said. "I guess it was my time."

"Okay. The first thing you have to do is find something dry. You can almost always find dry twigs except in the worst rain. Look under fallen trees or piles of leaves. Sometimes you can strip the bark from a dead branch and find wood dry enough to burn."

He explained everything he did in detail. He showed her how to start the fire and keep it small so it wouldn't burn up all their wood or create so much smoke that someone could discover their position. He also explained the kinds of food that were easiest to prepare outdoors with no equipment. They all resembled soup or stew.

"Occasionally I've cooked a rabbit or a sage hen," Pete said, "but it takes a long time to cook fresh game."

They had all evening, but they didn't have any fresh game. She cooked a stew made with beef jerky and dried vegetables. She'd never realized how difficult it was to cook without a kitchen. Next time Cookie wanted something from the ranch pantry, she'd give it to him without argument. She appreciated his talents a lot more now.

The snow had continued to fall. By the time they had finished eating and cleaned up, the snow was so heavy, clumps fell through the trees from time to time. The temperature kept dropping until Anne's hands felt too numb to hold the spoon. The hot food did little to keep her body warm. She thought wistfully of her soft bed and the thick quilts that kept her warm on even the coldest nights. They hadn't had time to take blankets and warm clothes. Carrying a resisting female off into the night didn't leave arms free to carry blankets and heavy coats. If they hadn't sent the food on the horses with Ray, they wouldn't have had anything to eat.

She wouldn't let herself feel guilty. She had to escape.

"I'm going to make a shelter of pine branches," Pete said. "It won't keep us warm, but it'll keep the snow and wind away."

She watched, fascinated, as he fitted the trunk of a fallen tree between two other trees to serve as the ridge pole of his shelter. Then he cut dozens of limbs from the trees and wove them together to create a slanting roof. When he finished, it looked very much like a large green tent.

"I'll make your bed," Pete offered.

"I can do that." She had to do something. She hated feeling useless.

"We don't have much to cover you with, just the blankets in the bedroll."

"I'll be warm enough." She didn't know why she

314

had to sound ungrateful. Maybe it was guilt that it was her fault they'd both be cold. "Where are you going to sleep?"

"Right next to you."

It relieved her to know he wouldn't be far away. It unsettled her that he would be so close.

"Don't take off any clothes," he said. "You'll need everything to keep warm."

She hadn't thought of that.

"How will you keep the fire going all night?" she asked.

"We won't need to do that."

"But what if some animal . . . " She didn't want to finish the sentence. She didn't even want to hear herself voice her fears.

"The horses will let us know if there's anything around."

After the misery they had inflicted on her, she didn't know if she wanted to entrust her safety to the horses.

"Are you coming to bed now?"

"No. I'll tend the fire a little longer."

He didn't have to watch the fire. He couldn't start a forest fire in this storm. He was giving her time to get to sleep before he came in. She didn't know why she should be surprised. He'd always been thoughtful. He wouldn't have insisted they sleep in the same bed if Belser hadn't accused him of being an imposter. Even then, he hadn't taken advantage of her. In fact, he'd made every effort to make sure nothing happened between them. If they hadn't both gotten carried away that evening by the stream, she'd still be a virgin.

She had to stop thinking about his good qualities. If she didn't, she'd soon be unable to believe he'd killed Peter and Belser.

He didn't. He's not a killer.

She drove that thought from her mind. If she believed it, everything would be upside down. She wouldn't know what to do then.

She crawled inside the shelter. She had few hopes the bedroll, which was made up of a large piece of canvas and two blankets, would do much to cushion the thick bed of pine needles. She spread the canvas over the pine needles and wrapped herself in one of the blankets. It wasn't enough to keep her warm, but she couldn't take the second blanket. Pete might be a killer. He definitely had brought her out here against her will, but he had tried to take good care of her. She couldn't deprive him of the only blanket left. She'd just have to be cold.

Anne awoke because she was shivering too hard to stay asleep. She had to clench her teeth to keep them from chattering. She'd never been so cold in her life. She didn't seem to have any clothes on or a blanket wrapped around her. She felt as though she'd been laid naked on a sheet of ice. She drew her body into a tight ball, but that didn't help. She could hardly feel her feet. She wondered if she was getting frostbite. The possibility of losing her toes frightened her. She reached down to massage her calves and ankles, hoping it would encourage the blood to flow into her toes, but it didn't seem to help.

"Are you cold?"

The unexpected sound of Pete's voice frightened a small scream out of her.

"No," she lied. "I'm just trying to get more comfortable."

"I know you're cold because I am," he said. "Here, take my blanket."

"No. Then you'll freeze to death, and I'll never get out of this godforsaken place."

He chuckled. She didn't see how he could laugh. There wasn't anything remotely funny about their situation.

"I survived much colder winters in Montana."

"I don't think it can get any colder." She tried, but she couldn't stop her teeth from chattering.

"You're freezing," Pete said.

"Yes, I am. But there's nothing we can do about it, so there's no point in reminding me of it."

"Yes, there is."

"I respectfully decline to be roasted over a fire, no matter how small."

He laughed again. The man was insane. Maybe killers thought weird things were funny. After all, they couldn't be normal if they went around killing people.

"I wasn't going to suggest building a fire under you."

"I don't want you to build one in here, either. You'll catch the roof on fire, and I'll still roast to death."

She couldn't blame him for laughing. She sounded remarkably silly. She wondered whether it was the effect of the freezing cold.

317

"I wasn't going to burn the shelter down over our heads. We should sleep together and share our body heat."

"No."

She didn't want him that close to her. She wouldn't remember she was supposed to hate him, to be afraid of him.

"You don't have to be afraid I'm going to try to take advantage of you. I like my women to be willing, not clawing my face."

She'd been willing that night by the creek. She'd practically forced him to make love to her.

"I don't think we should—"

"This is no time for false modesty." He tossed his blanket over her and moved closer. "Back up against me," he said.

She hesitated for only a moment. He was right. Who could think of sex when Mother Nature was threatening to turn them into blocks of ice?

Apparently she could. That was all she thought about from the moment she realized they weren't going to sleep back to back. Pete had pulled her to him, his arm around her middle just below her breasts, her derriere snuggled up against his groin. Clearly Pete knew what he was doing. Her temperature jumped at least ten degrees in half that many seconds.

She wondered how many times he'd done this before. With whom? If he had half the money he said he did, he could get just about any woman he wanted.

Now why should that thought make her envious? She couldn't possibly be jealous of some soiled dove who would hop into bed with any man who had the price. She didn't know any such women, but they couldn't be very pretty. Or nice. That was stupid. Being pretty and nice would enable them to command an even higher price. The prettier and nicer, the more men who'd want to spend time with them.

She wondered if they ever liked any of the men they met, if they regretted that one special man didn't want them to give it all up just for him. She guessed they couldn't afford to feel that way. It would be bad for business.

Anne was appalled at the thoughts running through her head. She couldn't understand what had gotten into her. She wasn't like those women. She didn't have any idea what they were like, what they would feel, what they would want.

Or had she begun to wonder if she wasn't like them after all, at least a little bit, somewhere down deep inside where it didn't show? She was nestled in the arms of the man who'd killed her husband and she didn't want him to let her go. She couldn't stop herself from remembering the night he made love to her. Nor could she stop herself from wanting him to do it again.

She had to have the heart of a soiled dove. No other kind of woman could feel this way. She made up her mind to sleep by herself and freeze to death. At least then she wouldn't be torn apart by the battle going on between her heart and body and her mind.

Then he kissed the back of her neck.

Her temperature shot up five more degrees, and she forgot all about freezing to death.

"Don't," she said. She didn't mean it, but she managed to say it.

"I can't hold you in my arms and not kiss you."

"Then let me go." She didn't mean that either.

"I can't."

"You must." She didn't know why she kept telling him to do things she didn't want him to do. He lifted her hair and kept kissing the back of her neck. He apparently knew better than she what she wanted him to do. "You've got to stop."

"It's keeping me warm. How about you?"

She couldn't deny that she didn't feel the least bit cold now. Even her toes seemed to be safe from frostbite.

"I'm warm enough."

"I'm not." His hand moved up to cup her breast. "Are my hands too cold?"

It was impossible to tell anything about his hand through the several layers of her clothing, but she had no doubt about its effect on her body. Her temperature spiked a few more degrees.

"Turn to face me," Pete whispered.

"No." To do so would be tantamount to surrender.

"I love you."

She stiffened. She hadn't heard him right. She couldn't have.

"I said I love you."

She didn't want him to love her. It would force her to admit she still loved him. If she did, she couldn't keep on believing he was a liar and a murderer.

"Aren't you going to say anything?"

She shook her head.

"I didn't want to fall in love with you. I'm not the

marrying kind. Seeing how things have turned out, I guess it's just as well."

It wasn't just as well. It was cruel. No woman should be allowed to find the one man she could love only to be told she couldn't have him.

"Loving you sneaked up on me. You were so anxious to be loved, so grateful for any attention, I couldn't stop doing things to put a smile on your face. Then suddenly you turned into a whole different person. You weren't a scared little girl anymore. You were a woman, ready and able to fight for your man. You might have been afraid, but you faced down anybody who threatened me. I think I fell in love with you when you refused to let anyone read the letters you wrote to Peter. I didn't know it until you followed me to the roundup. I had vowed I would leave without touching you, but I couldn't stop myself. I'm not sorry for anything else I've done, but I am ashamed of that."

She wasn't ashamed. It was the most wonderful thing that had ever happened to her.

"I couldn't let you go to Bill Mason. I know you don't trust me, don't believe anything I say, but you've got to believe I love you too much to let anyone hurt you. I can't leave until I know you're safe in Big Bend. I know you don't love me anymore, but I'll never stop loving you."

"I do love you." She spoke the words so softly, she wasn't certain she'd actually said them.

"What did you say?"

Why not say it? It was impossible. It would be over soon. Confess it, give in to it. Maybe then she would find some way to put her life together after he had gone. "I said I love you. I shouldn't, I don't want to, but I do."

Before she knew what he was going to do, he climbed across her body. Her back felt chilled by the sudden absence of his warmth, but the rest of her more than compensated when he pulled her so close that she felt her breasts pressed up against his chest, felt his swollen groin against her body. She knew she ought to move, but her body rebelled. She knew she ought to protest, but he took her mouth in a greedy kiss.

All resistance collapsed.

She was ashamed to admit there hadn't been much in the first place. He was still the most attractive man she'd ever met, the only man who could tap into this physical part of her that no one else had ever managed to touch. She didn't know how he did it. Right now she didn't care. She just cared that he did.

As for being a killer, no woman could believe the man in her arms could be evil. Not when his kisses, just his touch, could set her senses on fire.

Abandoning any attempt to justify what she was doing, she pressed herself against Pete and kissed him with a passion born of the raging conflict within her. It seemed to startle him, but only for a moment. Immediately their bodies were a tangle of intertwined legs and arms. He struggled to open her coat, her dress, to reach her breasts. She struggled to help him. She was no longer aware of the cold, of the howling wind and blowing snow, of their isolation in this distant stretch of forest. She had no room in her mind for anything but the man who was just as desperate to make love to her as she was that he should.

The feel of his lips on her breasts was like a benediction. She arched against him, wanting the sweet agony to become unbearable. She didn't have time tonight for a slow buildup, for a thorough pleasuring of her body. Her desperate need demanded almost immediate satisfaction. She took his hand and moved it down her body. She moaned when he worked his way through the tangle of material to the warm flesh of her inner thigh. She whimpered when his fingers parted her flesh and entered her.

But that wasn't enough. She had to have all of him, and she had to have him now.

"Please," she said, "don't make me wait."

He didn't. Despite the clothes bunched between them, the blankets tangled around them, he was soon inside her, driving her to the edge of madness. Suddenly she no longer feared the howling wind, the brutal cold, the majestic solitude of the forest. She felt a part of it. She welcomed the frenzy overtaking her body. She rushed toward it, embraced it, rejoiced in being consumed by it. When she felt her body would be destroyed, shattered into a million tiny bits, she willingly offered herself up for sacrifice.

Chapter Eighteen

They stayed in the forest four days while the blizzard
howled around them. Pete used branches to sweep the
snow from their camp area and spent hours each day
helping the horses find food under the deep snow. He
also broke the ice in the stream twice a day so they
could drink. On the third day, the stream froze to the
bottom and he had to melt snow over the fire.

When Anne tried to bring water from the stream for
cooking, it froze before she could get it back to camp.
It was simpler to melt snow over the fire they kept
going all day. After they used up all the firewood
nearby, Pete used the horses to drag wood from a distance. They had nothing to cut up the larger trees and
limbs, so Pete would put one end in the fire and keep
moving the tree trunk or limb into the flames until the

whole thing burned. Then he'd start on another. Anne decided he probably kept warmer from the work he did than from the heat of the small fire.

She, on the other hand, depended on the fire to keep her from becoming a human icicle. She had never known people could survive under such conditions. She had been certain she couldn't. It still surprised her that she had. The worst part had been trying to keep her feet and hands warm. She'd been certain she was going to lose them to frostbite until Pete taught her to put rocks in the coals of the fire. Once a rock was warm, she could take it out of the fire and put her feet directly on it. While warming herself with one rock, she'd have two or three more in the fire so she'd have another ready when the first one got cold.

It was so cold, their food froze almost before they could eat it. It was a race to eat quickly and often. Only a steady intake of hot food provided enough fuel for their bodies to keep warm. Pete had said he thought the temperature was probably down to zero.

The only time Anne got really warm was at night, when she and Pete crawled into their pine bower. Pete made love to her every night. It wasn't languid love. It wasn't leisurely love. It wasn't even thoroughly satisfying. It was too cold for that. But it was wonderful, and she looked forward to it from the moment she crawled out of their tent in the morning.

Her mind told her she was an idiot, that she was acting like a crazy person, that no woman in her right mind would make love to the man who'd killed her husband. She could only respond by telling herself the world around her was crazy. Normal people didn't live in pine bowers in the forest in the middle of blizzards. An ordinary woman didn't have to sit on hot rocks all day just to keep her feet from freezing. Ordinary people didn't have to melt snow to have drinking water or eat stew that was boiling in the middle and freezing around the edge. Nor did they have to sleep with their clothes on, bundled up next to another person to keep from freezing to death in their sleep.

When her world returned to normal, she'd try to sort things out. Until then, she'd have to do the best she could. And the best she could do right now was hang on to Pete. He was her lifeline.

Pete came back from the meadow leading the horses. "I think we ought to try to get to Big Bend," he said.

"How can we leave now? The snow must be several feet deep."

"I know, but we're running out of food. If we stay longer, we might get caught by another storm."

She had no attachment to the pine bower, even though she was certain that at some time in the future she would look back on it and smile in remembrance. For a few days she'd been able to push her problems, conflicts, and contradictions out of her mind. She'd allowed herself the privilege of thinking only of the here and now, of Pete and herself, of their feelings for each other.

He loved her. He'd told her so over and over again. He made no promises, offered no excuses, gave no explanations. He said he loved her and that he always would. Despite being stranded in the middle of a forest by a dangerous blizzard, she felt loved. She could see it in his eyes when he looked at her. She could feel it when they sat close to the fire, Pete holding her wrapped inside his coat so their shared body heat could keep them warm. They'd sat that way for hours at a time, sometimes talking about nothing in particular, sometimes not talking at all.

She no longer told herself all the reasons why she shouldn't love and trust him. She had finally admitted to herself that all the fears, accusations, implications, made no difference. She loved him, and nothing could change that. Chance had given her an opportunity to escape the rules and restrictions of the world she lived in, a few days in which to pretend nothing was wrong, that love could, and would, triumph over all. For a few days she'd allowed herself to luxuriate in the warmth of his love, in the wonder of gradually realizing she could be the most important person in a man's life, that he would endanger his own safety to protect her.

She had reached another conclusion. Pete was not a killer. She didn't know who was responsible for the deaths of Peter and Belser, but she was certain it wasn't Pete. Not that he couldn't kill. She was certain he could kill to protect those he loved, to defend what belonged to him, but he wouldn't kill to steal from someone else. She didn't want to leave the protection of the forest, to face all the difficulties that lay ahead, but they couldn't hide forever. "When can we start?" she asked.

"As soon as we can pack everything up," Pete said. "We have a long way to go. The sooner we get started, the sooner we'll get to Big Bend."

There wasn't much to pack. They'd eaten most of their food and they wore most of their clothes to keep warm.

The horses sank to their stomachs in the snow.

"We'll have to try to stay under the trees or where the wind kept the snow from piling up," Pete said. "Some of the drifts are ten feet deep."

The bright sunlight reflecting off the snow nearly blinded her. She didn't understand how Pete could find a trail, or solid ground, under all that snow, but they traveled hour after hour without any mishap more serious than the packhorse stepping off the trail and stumbling into a creek coated in ice and covered with snow. Their progress was very slow. It was clear they weren't going to reach Big Bend that day.

Despite the cold and the pain of being in a saddle again, Anne found enough positive energy to realize the scenery was absolutely magnificent. All around her, mountain peaks rose skyward, their pink, orange, brown, and red rock strata brilliant in the sunlight. Wind kept the peaks mostly clear of snow, but patches on ledges looked like ermine collars.

Pristine blankets of snow, unbroken by footprints of man or animal, covered wide mountain meadows. Towering ponderosa pine forests bent low under their weight of snow, the green of their needles made all the more vibrant by the blanket of white.

If it just hadn't been so cold, she might have enjoyed it.

They spent the first night in a grove of cottonwood, box elder, and green ash. Some juniper trees provided a shield from the wind. They cooked dinner and ate, made love and slept, each knowing the end would come soon.

It came sooner and in a different manner than they expected.

Next morning, they made it out of the mountains and into the foothills.

"We'll spend tonight at the cabin," Pete called back to her. "It'll be warm and dry. You'll be able to sleep under a roof."

"Is it very far?"

"We ought to reach it by midafternoon."

Pete had spent hours the night before massaging her sore muscles, but they continued to ache today. She doubted she'd ever learn to like riding horses, certainly not if it continued to make her feel as if every muscle in her lower body was on fire.

"You know," Pete said, "I wonder if the men Mason hired to kill your husband are at his ranch."

"Would you recognize them?" she asked.

"Not them, but their horses."

"Wouldn't they recognize you?"

"Probably."

"Wouldn't they try to kill you?"

"Probably."

"Then what's the advantage of finding them?"

"Outside of hanging them for killing Peter Warren, there's my money and my clothes," he said. "I could have used them these past few days." He went on to list everything that had been stolen from him. "But what I most want to find are my saddlebags."

329

"How can you tell one set of saddlebags from another?" she asked. She had never paid particular attention to saddlebags before, but as far as she could remember, they all looked alike.

"Mine are different. There's a "J" cut into the leather, and they've got some decorative beading. I got the saddlebags made from an elk hide by an Indian woman in Montana. You'd know them the minute you saw them. I think that's why they took them."

Anne's attention wandered as he went on to describe the saddlebags in detail. The day wore on—cold, monotonous, endless. She was practically asleep in the saddle, lulled by the gentle rocking motion, when several mounted riders burst out of a gully that had appeared to be choked by wild plum and hawthorne. Almost before she knew what had happened, half-a-dozen men had converged on Pete. He fought bravely, but it was a futile effort. One man—a rank coward, Anne was certain—rode up behind and hit Pete over the head with a gun butt.

Pete tumbled from the saddle into the snow.

Anne urged her horse forward only to find a man at her side, his firm grip on her mount's bridle preventing her from moving.

"You don't have to run away," Bill Mason said. "These are my men."

Her mind was in turmoil. She'd known she had to return to the real world, that she had to face the charges against Pete, come to grips with the fact that she didn't have a shred of evidence to support her belief in his innocence. But she'd expected to have more time. This sudden attack threw her off stride.

Her actions were purely instinctive, and instinct said she had to do anything she could to protect Pete. "I wasn't going to run away," Anne said, trying without success to break Mason's grip on her horse's bridle. She'd never paid much attention to Bill Mason, but now that he seemed to be taking control of her destiny, she found she didn't like him. She didn't trust him, either.

"We're going to hang him," Mason said.

Panic threatened to scramble her wits entirely, but she knew she had to remain calm. She had to think. Pete needed help right this minute. If she couldn't provide it, it might soon be too late for anybody to help him. "You can't hang him," she said.

"He's a killer. He deserves hanging."

"I don't dispute that," she said, trying not to show the panic she felt. "But you've got to take him into Big Bend to the sheriff. They'll try him and decide what to do with him."

"That's a waste of time. We'll hang him now and be done with it."

"But that will make you as much a murderer as he is."

She faced Mason squarely when she said that, but it was difficult not to quail before his fierce glare.

"It's not murder to kill a mad dog."

"It is when you take the law into your own hands and hang a man who's not been convicted of any crime."

"Nobody will care. They'll all be glad to see the end of him."

331

"I'll care."

His gaze became granite. "What do you mean by that?"

"Back at the ranch, you said you wanted to marry me. Do you still want to?"

"Yes. I've always wanted to marry you."

Anne had never even guessed at such a long-standing passion, but she let that pass. "Then you have to take him to Big Bend. I will not marry a murderer."

"But you married him!" Mason exploded.

"I married Peter Warren. I accepted that man as my husband because I thought he was Peter. I did not marry a murderer, nor could I accept a man I knew to be a murderer."

"Then you admit he killed Peter?"

"I don't know what he did. That's for the court to decide on the basis of evidence. You don't have any evidence, and you aren't a court."

"I don't care. Find a limb, boys. We're going to hang him high."

"Any man who participates in this hanging is a murderer!" Anne shouted. "I know your faces, and I will find out your names. As soon as I reach Big Bend, I'll have the sheriff arrest all of you on the charge of murder." The men had slowed when she began to speak. Not one of them moved a muscle now. "I will also testify that you went ahead with this murder despite the fact that you'd been warned not to proceed, that you weren't a duly constituted court, and you presented absolutely no evidence to support your charges."

"He kidnaped you," Mason said. "That's a hanging offense."

"I'll testify that I went willingly."

"You wouldn't dare."

"If you marry me, you will become the father of my children. What kind of mother would I be if I brought children into this world knowing their father was a murderer? What man will marry my daughters? What woman will trust my sons?"

"Thousands of men will be eager to marry them. They'll be the daughters of a rich man."

"I want my daughters to marry men of character, men who marry them because they cherish and honor them, not for their wealth."

"That's why he wanted you."

"I married a man I thought I'd loved since I was six. Not this man."

"Then you don't love him?"

"No. I realized I loved a boy. Peter Warren vanished years ago."

For a moment she thought she'd lost. His chin seemed jutted in defiance of everything she said. She wondered if she could take his gun, force him to take Pete to Big Bend.

"We'll take him to my ranch," Mason said. "Once we're there, I'll decide what to do."

That wasn't the clear victory Anne had been hoping for, but she didn't dare push him further now. Mason had given her more time. She had to use it to figure out how to save Pete.

Mason's ranch came into sight shortly before midafternoon. Anne felt she was being drawn further and further into a trap. Several hours in Bill Mason's company hadn't caused her to like him any better. He was a rough, cruel man, who treated his cowhands with thoughtless disregard. His treatment of Pete was even worse. Pete had been bound hand and foot to his horse and driven over the plain at a trot that bounced him painfully and caused the rawhide to cut into his wrists. When Anne pointed that out, Mason had replied that it was better to suffer a few cuts than a broken neck.

Anne decided silence would be better for both her and Pete. If she made Mason angry by continued opposition, he would take it out on Pete.

Much to her surprise, Ray came down the steps of the ranch house when they arrived.

"I been looking everywhere for Mrs. Warren," he said to Mason. "I been waiting here to see if you knew where she was."

"As you can see, I've brought her safely home. I caught the low-down murdering dog who pretended to be her husband."

Anne had an idea. "Thank goodness you're here," she said, walking up to Ray. "I need some fresh clothes. I feel like these have grown to my skin."

"Git on your horse and go get the lady her things," Mason said.

"I need to make a list," Anne said. "I need much more than dresses. Do you have a table where I can write?"

"Inside. The cook will show you. Okay, boys, bring our prisoner to the barn. Make sure you tie him up nice and tight. I'd hate to see him get loose and have someone shoot him by accident."

He cast Anne a mocking look, but she returned it with what she hoped was unsuspecting innocence.

"I don't need clothes," Anne whispered as soon as Mason went off with his men. "I need you to ride into Big Bend and tell the sheriff that Mason has captured the man who pretended to be my husband and that they plan to hang him. Then I want you to go to Mrs. Dean's home. Tell her I apologize for doubting her, that she was right about Pete from the beginning. Then beg her to come to Mason's ranch as soon as possible to act as my chaperone. He means to keep me here until I'm free to marry him, but there's no female here to give me countenance."

"What about the clothes?"

"Take my messages to town first. Then get my clothes."

"What about the list?"

"Forget the list. Just bring everything. I don't know when I'll be able to leave here."

"You don't think he's guilty, do you?"

Ray's question went to the heart of what she was doing, of his helping her. "No, I don't, but I don't have any proof."

"I don't think he's guilty either."

"Then we've got to do our best to save him. Now go quickly, before Mason comes back."

Pete tried to shift his position so the weight of his body wouldn't pull on the rawhide that tied him to the inside of a stall. Mason had intentionally tied him in a manner guaranteed to make the rawhide strips cut deeply into his skin. Despite the pain, he had few thoughts to spare for his wrists. Anne's intervention had saved him from being hanged. He knew she loved him. That must mean she believed him.

He didn't know how a man could be happy tied to a wall with his captor itching to hang him at the first opportunity, but he had been. However, the euphoria he first felt had been replaced by calm acceptance of the fact his life was in grave danger. If he didn't do something soon, Anne was going to be in love with a dead man.

For the second time within a month.

But tied up as he was, he didn't have any options. He had to wait for an opportunity. He knew Bill Mason was going to do his best not to give him one.

Anne didn't like the way Bill Mason looked at her, as though she were prey and he a hungry predator. Mason was so happy with his capture of Pete, he'd given the men the rest of the day off. A constant flow of men had come through the house all afternoon and evening, but soon everyone would be moseying out to the bunkhouse, and she'd be left alone with Mason. There was no woman in the house. The cook was a thin, silent man who moved about the place like a shadow.

She longed to go see Pete, but she couldn't think of a way that wouldn't arouse Mason's suspicion. She'd mentioned him once during dinner—asked the foreman how the prisoner was doing—and Mason had turned on her with the speed of a striking snake, demanded to know why she should be asking about a murderer. She passed it off as idle curiosity.

"After all, I did live with the man for several weeks. I can't forget him as if he never existed."

"That's exactly what you're going to do," Mason replied. He'd then started asking about their relationship, wanting to know if they'd been intimate. Anne thought it was inexcusable of him to expect her to answer in front of several hired hands.

"I've told you before, I felt uneasy," she said. "Peter and I hadn't seen each other in years. We decided to keep to ourselves until we became better acquainted."

"Eddie said you slept in the same bed."

A bell rang in the back of her head. Pete had said he thought Eddie and Mason were somehow working together. This proved it. There couldn't be any other reason for Eddie to pass along such personal information.

"We didn't have any choice, not with Belser accusing Pete of being an imposter and me of marrying him only to get a rich husband. But Pete never once crossed the center of that bed."

The men had looked embarrassed, had kept their gazes on their plates. She didn't think Mason even noticed.

She was forced to pass the time after supper in complete idleness. Mason ignored her for his card games. Finally, in desperation, she went to the kitchen and begged the cook to allow her to prepare the coffee, serve it, wash cups, anything to keep busy.

"Okay."

That was all he would say. If she asked where to find something, he either got it or pointed to it. She gradu-

337

ally limited herself to questions that could be answered by a shake or nod of the head.

That was how the situation remained until she saw the saddlebags.

They were lying in the corner of the storage room. Saddlebags with a J stenciled on the side and decorated with Indian beadwork. Pete's saddlebags! The ones he said had been stolen by the men who shot him and killed Peter. It was the first piece of evidence she'd found that might corroborate Pete's story, might help prove he didn't kill Peter.

"What attractive saddlebags," she said to the cook, trying to control the excitement in her voice. "Are they yours?"

He shook his head.

"Who do they belong to?"

He shrugged his shoulders.

She picked them up. They were empty. Whatever had been in them had been removed. She turned the saddlebags around, pretending to inspect them. The seams hadn't been cut. If Pete really had put the money inside, it was still there.

"I think they're very pretty. I'd love to have some like this."

He looked at her with no interest.

"Who do they belong to? I want to see if he'll sell them."

"They don't belong to anybody," he said, speaking at last.

"Someone must own them. They're too nice to be cast off."

"They belonged to a man who stopped at our

chuck wagon one night. He said he didn't like beadwork."

"That's why I like them."

"He left them in the chuck wagon, said it was in exchange for feeding him and his friend. None of the
boys wanted them, so I threw them in there. I don't
want them, either, but they look too good to waste."

"Can I have them?"

"If you marry Mr. Mason, you can have anything
you want."

She wanted to take them with her, but Mason hadn't
given her a room. She couldn't explain why she'd want
to walk around clutching a pair of saddlebags all
evening. She didn't dare try to open them unless she
was assured of absolute privacy.

She'd have to leave them for now. She dropped
them back into the corner with as much nonchalance
as she could muster. "I'll leave them here for the time
being," she said. "I really don't have any use for them
just now."

But the thought of those saddlebags sitting unpro-
tected in the storage room nagged at her all evening.
She kept telling herself nobody wanted them, that
they were safe, but she knew she wouldn't be able to
relax until she had them in her possession. She could-
n't do that until she knew which room was to be hers.
When she'd asked him earlier, Mason had acted irritated, said he hadn't made up his mind yet. She decided he just didn't want the card game interrupted.
She supposed he would tell her at bedtime.

Finally the time came when the men had gone off to
their own quarters, no one wanted anything else to eat

or drink, and everything in the kitchen had been washed and put away.

When the clock stuck ten, Mason announced, "It's time to go to bed."

"I can't go yet," she said. "I don't have any night-clothes."

She could have sworn she saw a gleam in his eye.

"You won't need any. I can keep you warm."

She pretended he hadn't spoken. "I asked Ray to bring my clothes tonight no matter how late it was. I'll wait up until he comes."

"He could be hours."

"I don't mind. I'm not really sleepy. You can go on to bed."

"I don't want to go to bed alone."

That was putting things on the line with a vengeance. He wasn't going to pretend he intended to wait for the marriage vows before he deflowered her. It would take him only minutes to discover he was too late.

"You can't think I would come into this house, even as your affianced bride, and go to bed with you the first night."

"Why not?"

"It's not proper."

"I don't give a damn what's proper." He took a step nearer. "I want you. I've wanted you for a whole year."

She took a step back. "You never said anything."

"You couldn't talk about anybody but that silly fool Peter Warren. He was so pathetic, even his uncle didn't want to leave the ranch to him. He'd have been better off to leave it to Belser."

"Uncle Carl believed very strongly in blood ties." She had to talk, do anything to keep him at a distance while she tried to think of a way to escape being carried off to his bed. The thought of opening her body to him in the same way she'd given herself to Pete made her feel physically ill. It also made her furious. He had no right to force himself on any female, but especially not one he said he cared for and wanted to marry.

"Peter was his only living relative," she continued. "In his mind, he had no choice but to leave the ranch to him."

"That accident turned Carl into an old fool," Mason said. "It would have been better if it had killed him."

Another bell rang. Pete had wondered if the fall had been an accident. He said it wasn't the kind of thing that would happen to an experienced rider like Carl.

"Uncle Carl agreed with you, especially when the pain was really bad."

"I'm tired of talking about Carl. I'm ready to go to bed, and I mean for you to go with me."

She backed farther away until she backed into a table. "You can't want to disgrace the woman you intend to marry. Think of what people will say."

"I don't care what anybody says." He closed in on her. "You're a mighty tasty morsel. I always wondered who would get you first, Carl or Belser."

Anne was horrified. Such a thought had never crossed her mind.

"Or maybe they had you already."

"I can't believe you'd say such a thing," Anne said. "You call yourself Carl's friend, yet you desecrate his memory."

"Come down off your high horse, girl. It's not desecration to bed a breed and not marry her. Most respectable men wouldn't even consider marriage. I'm considering it."

Peter had said Mason didn't want to marry her, that he would do it only to gain control of the ranch, that he would find some way to get rid of her once he had legal possession.

"Now stop resisting." He reached out, grabbed hold of her wrist, and pulled her to him. "And don't think you have me believing that story about you and Pete staying on opposite sides of the bed. I bet he had his hand up your dress before the door was closed good. I bet you liked every minute of it." He grabbed her breast and pawed it roughly. "I hear breeds really like it when a man is rough. I hear it makes them really hot."

"It doesn't make me hot," Anne said, struggling to break his hold. But he was too strong. He backed her up against the table, bent her so far back, she could barely keep from falling.

"I bet I can make you hot. I'm twice as much man as anybody you ever had. Belser was a fool. Carl was senile. The only one who was any better than a piece of dead wood was that man out in the barn, the one I'm going to hang tomorrow. I bet that's why you didn't want to admit he was an imposter. After Belser and Carl—did you bed Eddie, too?—I bet you were anxious to keep him between your legs."

She struggled harder, but he pinned her against the table. He ground his groin against her.

"I know you can feel me between your legs. I'm

bigger than any of them, and I'm not even worked up yet. Kiss me, get me hard, and I'll show you what a real man feels like."

"Don't," she protested. "One of your men could walk in and—"

"Any man fool enough to come through that door now will get thrown back through it and fired on the spot. Now come here. I'm tired of playing games."

He grabbed her, pulled her to him, and kissed her hard. She fought with all her strength, but it was useless. He lifted her off her feet just as easily as if she had weighed no more than a satchel. He forced her lips apart and drove his tongue into her mouth until she thought she would gag. She kicked and used her fists, but she was powerless to prevent him from carrying her off and raping her.

"William Mason, put that young woman down this instant!"

Mason turned on Mrs. Dean with an angry snarl. "What the hell are you doing here?"

"I've come to chaperone your prospective bride. Apparently I arrived in the nick of time."

Chapter Nineteen

"Then he said it wouldn't make any difference what he did because I was a breed, that no respectable man married a woman like me."

"I've always thought it unfortunate you should have that blot in your heritage," Mrs. Dean said. "There's no disputing it causes men to look at you quite differently."

They were safely in the bedroom Mrs. Dean had insisted she share with Anne. She had stated categorically that she couldn't depend upon Mason's better nature to assert itself.

"I don't pretend to be any more than I am," Anne stated, annoyed by Mrs. Dean's remarks, "but I won't be treated like a woman of the streets."

"No, indeed. I shall remain at your side until this disgraceful business is over."

Mrs. Dean's arrival had infuriated Mason. For a moment, Anne had wondered if he might not throw her out of the house. But in the few seconds it took him to recover from his shock, Mrs. Dean had insinuated herself between him and Anne. Even in a rage, Mason had enough sense not to lay a hand on Mrs. Dean. To do so would have resulted in his being driven out of the Territory. He retired in defeat, shouting curses all the while.

"Are you quite certain you wish to marry Bill Mason?" Mrs. Dean asked.

"I'm quite certain I don't," Anne responded. "But he showed up at the ranch the night before the snowstorm, demanding that Pete give himself up and announcing he was going to marry me."

"I knew nothing of this passion for you."

"Neither did I. But after the way he treated me tonight, I think his passion is more for the ranch than for me. I have every intention of refusing to marry him, but I'm afraid he means to keep me here until I accept him."

"Not while I have anything to say about it. Tomorrow I shall send for Horace to bring a carriage from town."

"Don't forget the sheriff."

"Horace and I shall be quite enough to protect you. But my dear, what are you going to do after that?"

"I don't know. Pete says if I can prove I married Peter before he was killed, I'll inherit the ranch."

Mrs. Dean clutched her bosom. "Peter has been killed?"

Anne related what Pete had told her.

"And you believe him? You needn't bother to deny it. I can see in your eyes you do. I don't deny he's a very handsome man—I thought so myself the moment I laid eyes on him—but it will not do to be in love with a man who has committed murder."

"But I don't think he has. I found—"

"Where is the imposter?"

"Mr. Mason tied him up in the barn. He means to hang him tomorrow." She got the feeling Mrs. Dean thought that was a good thing. "I know he's done some terrible things, but no man deserves to be hanged without a trial."

Mrs. Dean didn't look convinced.

"If people could just announce that a person had committed a crime and hang him without any proof whatsoever, think of what could happen. Why, they could even accuse you."

"They wouldn't dare!"

"If they didn't have to present proof, what could you do? They could hang you before anyone could come to your rescue. For the sake of everyone in the Territory, we can't allow that to happen to Pete."

Mrs. Dean appeared unhappy to have to let go of a cherished thought, but she was a woman of principle. "You are right. We can't let them hang that man, regardless of how richly he deserves it. I will insist that Bill take him into town first thing in the morning. I will speak to the sheriff myself."

"You won't leave me?"

"Definitely not. I told Carl years ago that he needed to provide you with a proper chaperone before you got into serious trouble. I'm very sorry to say my judgment has proved to be correct."

"It might not be quite as bad as you think."

"What could be worse than thinking you were married to a man who turns out to be a murderer and an imposter?"

"He says he pretended to be Peter to rescue me from my uncle."

"That's all well and good, but you can't believe a murderer."

"I don't think he killed Peter."

"Anne, this is ridiculous. Just because he's a handsome fella, you can't—"

"It's not that. He told me he came to Uncle Carl's ranch because he was following the men who shot him and stole his money, the same men he said killed Peter. I didn't believe him at first, in spite of his wound. The evidence against him was too strong."

"I'm glad to know you have some common sense."

"He kept talking about his money. He even described the saddlebags in great detail."

"What interest can you possibly have in saddlebags?"

"He said he sewed his money into the lining, that the men who shot him took the saddlebags. He thinks someone here hired those men to kill Peter. They probably robbed Pete just because he happened to be in their path."

"A likely story. I don't believe a—"

"They're here."

"What's here?"

"Pete's saddlebags. I saw them."

"How can you be certain?" Mrs. Dean sputtered. "Saddlebags all look alike."

"Not these. Pete had them made specially for him."

Mrs. Dean took a moment to digest this information. "But how can we tell for sure? We can hardly ask him to identify them."

"If we find the money in the lining like he said, won't that prove it?"

Mrs. Dean thought a moment. "Yes, I think it would. We must get those saddlebags immediately."

"They're downstairs in the kitchen storeroom."

"Then let's get them now."

"Maybe we should wait until tomorrow. I don't want to make Mason suspicious."

"I'll go with you. If anyone asks, we'll say I wanted some water. You can say you were packing the saddlebags in preparation for moving to my house in town."

"Am I going to your house?"

"Of course. Where else would you stay?"

Nowhere nearly as safe, Anne was certain.

They took a small lamp, the only lamp they could find after Mason had stormed out of the house. They didn't meet anyone on the stairs or in the front of the house.

"His cook keeps a good kitchen," Mrs. Dean said. She held the lamp aloft while she inspected every corner of the room. "I think I will have some water. Where does the man keep the glasses?"

"I don't know if he has any. I saw only cups at dinner."

"Then I'll use a cup."

Anne had just filled the cup and handed it to Mrs. Dean when the kitchen door burst open.

"What the hell are you doing down here?" Mason demanded.

Mrs. Dean froze, her outstretched hand motionless. "I will not be spoken to in that manner. Apologize this instant."

Anne nearly laughed out loud. For one moment she wished she could be a seventy-year-old dowager with a huge bosom, prortuberant eyes, and an impressive coil of iron-gray hair. It would be wonderful to be able to bowl people over by sheer force of personality.

"I thought you were one of the hands," Mason said.

"Are you saying I look like a *man!*" She made it sound like a physical deformity.

"I spoke before I looked."

"Well, now that you have, you can go back to bed."

"I'll wait and see you to your room."

Mrs. Dean seemed to swell. "Are you implying I might take something from your kitchen? What—a ham or a side of beef I plan to devour in my room?"

"No, of course not."

"Good. Now I'm going to drink my water. Anne is going to get a pair of saddlebags the cook gave her to pack some of her things in. If it will make you feel better, you can watch us to make certain that's all we take."

"No need," Mason said, backing out of the kitchen. "You sure you know your way?"

"Certain."

He disappeared though the doorway, and Anne released the breath she'd been holding. "I'm glad you didn't have to explain why I wanted this knife," she said, holding up a knife she'd taken from a drawer just before Mason entered the room.

"I'd have told him I was keeping it by my side to make certain no one entered our room during the night. In fact, I think I shall do that. Now get those saddlebags. It's cold down here."

Anne was relieved to find the saddlebags exactly where she'd left them. Clearly no one suspected what they might contain. They retraced their steps to their room.

"Lock the door," Mrs. Dean said.

"I don't see a key."

"There must be one."

"It's not in the door."

"I'll see to that." Mrs. Dean took the lamp and disappeared down the hall, leaving Anne in the dark. After a sharp exchange that Anne could hear from her room, Mrs. Dean returned.

"He had the key in his room. Told me he kept it for safety purposes. Humph! That man is not truthful." She turned the key in the lock. "Now cut the seams on those saddlebags. You've made me very curious."

Anne had never had occasion to cut the seams on saddlebags before, but she decided these must be especially well made. The stitching was so tight, she had great difficulty inserting the point of her knife between the layers of leather.

"Here, let me try," Mrs. Dean said, impatient to see what the saddlebags contained.

"I've almost got it," Anne said. She had managed to cut the first rawhide stitch. After that she quickly widened the opening until she could put her hand inside.

"Is there anything inside?" Mrs. Dean asked.

Anne shoved her hand into the opening. "Paper of some kind. A lot of it." She gripped several pieces and pulled. Her mouth fell open when the light fell on what she held in her hand—several thousand-dollar bills.

"He did hide money in his saddlebags," she said. "He was telling the truth."

"How much is there?" Mrs. Dean asked.

"I don't know."

"Check. If he spent five years in the goldfields, he ought to have more than a few thousand."

Anne searched the cavity, but couldn't find more than fifteen thousand dollars.

"We have to take the saddlebags apart," Mrs. Dean said. "I want to know exactly how much money this man has."

"He didn't steal it from Peter," Anne said. "Peter hardly had enough money to get to Wyoming."

"I'm keeping an open mind."

Taking the saddlebags apart took nearly half an hour. Anne regretted destroying such marvelous craftsmanship. Counting the money took less time. Still, it came to more than seventy thousand dollars.

"No wonder he followed those men all the way from Montana," Mrs. Dean said.

"It proves he's telling the truth, doesn't it?"

"I think it does. But if he didn't kill Peter, who did?"

"I don't know. Pete thinks the same person killed Belser. Maybe even Eddie."

"But that's impossible unless . . . "

"I know," Anne said. "Pete thought the same thing."

"Then you, my dear, are in an extremely dangerous position."

"You are, too, for coming to help me. I shouldn't have sent Ray to get you."

"No, you were right to do that. But now that we know what we know, we have to decide what to do."

"What am I going to do with this money? I don't dare let anybody know about it. Uncle Carl said lots of men would kill for a few hundred dollars."

"Give it to me," Mrs. Dean said. "I'll pack it in with my things. No one will think to look there."

"What am I going to do with these saddlebags?"

"We'll pack those up as well."

"I wish Ray had brought my clothes."

"Oh, I forgot to tell you. I instructed him to take them straight to my house. It was entirely unacceptable they should be brought here. Now, let's go to sleep. We have a great deal of thinking to do tomorrow."

Pete had no illusions about what was going to happen to him. Bill Mason wasn't about to let him get anywhere near Big Bend or the sheriff. Regardless of how much the evidence seemed to be stacked against him, Pete could explain how that same evidence made a very good case against Bill Mason. After all, the only proof Mason had that Pete hadn't been telling the truth from the beginning was Mason's assertion that he'd found Peter Warren's body. If that wasn't true, then Mason had nothing against him. To take him to the sheriff would be a stupid mistake.

And Pete knew Mason wasn't stupid.

He had tied Pete securely, hands and feet. He refused to untie him so he could sleep.

"Don't worry," Mason had said, taunting Pete that evening, "you'll have plenty of time to sleep after tomorrow morning."

Pete knew what he meant. He didn't expect anything less from a rich man who was willing to kill three people so he could gain possession of another ranch and be even richer. He was surprised Anne had been able to stop Mason from hanging him back there on the mountain.

Anne. He'd tried not to think about her. If he could have gotten free, he'd have killed Mason before he let Anne marry him. He knew she didn't love the rancher.

But why had she talked as if she would marry Mason as a matter of course? He'd told himself over and over again that she did it to save him, that Mason would have hanged him on the spot if he'd had any idea Anne wasn't relieved Mason had rescued her. He kept telling himself she'd find a way to see him, to let him know she still loved him and was trying to figure out a way for them to be together. He could see the house from where he was tied. All the lights had gone out. She hadn't come to him.

He told himself she couldn't get away, that to be seen sneaking out of the house would have been suspicious. Yet for hours after the last light had disappeared from the window, he'd listened intently, confident that sooner or later Anne would find a way to come to him.

When morning began to turn the sky shades of gray, he realized she wasn't coming.

353

It wouldn't have done any good. At least one man had stood guard over him at all times.

With the first realization came a second. Sometimes dying wasn't such a hard thing. If you had nothing to live for, maybe it was a relief. At least he wouldn't have to go back to the goldfields. He'd wasted too much of his life there, thrown away too much gold on women interested in him only for the money in his pocket and the whiskey he could buy.

He used to like it, but everything had changed in the short time he'd known Anne. The freedom that had seemed so attractive to him, so necessary, had lost its appeal. He remembered the cold and the hard work, the miserable existence, the constant threats to his life.

Most of all he remembered the loneliness. Looking back on it now, he wondered why he hadn't left years ago, why he hadn't realized his only true home, the only place that could give him a sense of belonging, was Jake's valley in the Texas hills. He could have gone back to Texas years ago, could have had a ranch next to Sean's, could have had a batch of his own kids.

But he wouldn't have met Anne.

And he wouldn't have gotten his neck in a noose for murders he didn't commit. And he wouldn't have fallen in love with a woman who seemed ready to marry any man who offered her a life of wealth and luxury.

He told himself he was being unfair, but the angry voice inside him, the part of him that didn't want to die, reminded him that Anne had married a man she hadn't seen since childhood, had accepted a stranger in his place, and was now ready to marry the man who'd come out on top.

He'd been certain when they left the mountains that she loved him, that she believed him. He had been stunned by the calm way she explained why Mason shouldn't hang Pete, by her refusal to do more than glance in his direction. Her concern seemed to be more for Mason's reputation than Pete's life. He tried to tell himself she was doing it for him, that in some way he didn't yet know, she was working to save his life. But after virtually hanging by his arms and feet for the last twelve hours, it was hard to keep believing.

When he heard Mason shouting for the men to wake up, that they had a hanging to go to, he knew it didn't matter what he believed.

He was sorry there wasn't some way he could tell Jake and Isabelle what had happened to him. It would make them unhappy—he hoped it wouldn't provoke Sean into looking for revenge—but he would have liked for them to know. At least he was certain they loved him. He wished now he'd taken more pains to let them know how much he appreciated what they'd done for him. Almost all the other orphans had gone back to Texas, returning to the one place they had been wanted, but he'd held out, preferring to be on his own.

Now he wondered why. It wasn't good to die alone.

Mason threw open the barn doors. It was impossible to see his expression with the light coming from behind him, but he seemed eager to get to his business.

"It's a beautiful day outside," he boomed, waking the man who'd had the last watch. "We've got a chinook wind that'll melt this snow in two days. We won't have to use an ax to get you into the ground."

"I'd be glad if you'd wait long enough to be sure of that," Pete replied. His throat was so dry, he could hardly talk. He hadn't had any food or water since they'd captured him.

Mason laughed as if he enjoyed the joke. Pete didn't see anything funny about it.

"You won't have to worry," Mason said. "If it turns cold again, we'll put you in the icehouse until spring. You may be a filthy murderer, but I wouldn't let the wolves get you."

"I don't figure it that way," Pete said. "In fact, I figure you're the filthy murderer."

For only the briefest moment did Mason show any fear of what Pete might say, but Pete was certain it was there. It was all the admission of guilt he needed.

"It won't matter what you figure," Mason said. "You'll be dead in ten minutes. Cut him loose," he ordered the guard.

"I figure you started rustling Tumbling T cows the day Carl Warren had his accident. In fact, I figure you were behind his accident. You thought rustling would give you a way to kill Carl and his heir with no questions asked."

"Hurry up with that knife," Mason ordered the sleepy cowhand. "I want to see him swinging."

"But you needed an informant. I figure you tried to use Belser at first, but you soon realized he was just as determined to have the ranch as you were. So you got someone else. Eddie."

"Shut up. I won't have you slandering the reputation of a dead man."

Pete was encouraged to see that several of the cowhands were listening to what he was saying with heightened curiosity. A few even glanced surreptitiously at their boss.

"What did you tell him—that when Peter Warren lost the ranch, or got shot by your rustlers, he'd be out of a job? That Belser would fire him the moment he gained control? Did you guarantee Eddie he could keep his job? Maybe you even offered him a partnership."

"Drag him out here where we can get a rope on him," Mason shouted.

"Then you hired two men to kill Peter Warren."

Pete held on to the stable wall when they tried to drag him out.

"But you made one mistake. You hired greedy men. When you wouldn't let them take anything from Peter, they shot and robbed me, left me for dead. Only I didn't die. I trailed them back here. That's when you knew you had to get rid of me, so you had Eddie kill Belser in his sleep so the murder would be blamed on me. That would get rid of the two people who stood in your way all at once."

Mason hit him across the mouth. "Shut up. Drag him out of that stall, you weak fools. Can't you do anything right?"

Pete held on desperately.

"Then you had to get rid of Eddie so he wouldn't talk. So when you rustled my herd, you told your men to shoot in the air, not to kill anyone. But you shot

Eddie with a rifle. I saw the wound. Anybody could tell it wasn't made with a pistol."

The cowhands had become virtually motionless. Pete didn't know whether they believed him or not, but he was certain he'd started them wondering. But were they unsure enough to back away from hanging him?

"If you lazy fools can't get him out of that stall, I can," Mason said.

Pete tried to dodge Mason's fist. But the very position that had allowed him to remain in the stall despite several men trying to remove him kept him from being able to move quickly. Mason's fist landed squarely, dazing him. A second blow knocked him nearly unconscious.

"Drag him out here while I get a rope," Mason shouted.

Pete tried to hold on, but he was too weak. Two cowhands dragged him from the stall.

"You're helping a murderer hang an innocent man," he said. "He wants to kill me so I can't tell the sheriff what I know. He wants to force that woman inside to marry him so he can take her ranch. He'll kill her, too, when he gets it."

"You don't know what you're talking about," one cowhand said, but Pete could tell he was unsure.

"People out here aren't going to stand for murdering a woman. When it all comes out, and it will, because I've written it all down, you'll be held responsible, too."

"We didn't kill nobody," the other cowhand said.

"You're about to hang me without evidence. That's murder."

He could feel them hesitate, but it wasn't enough to make them go up against a man like Mason. He had to come up with something fast, or everything he knew would die with him.

And Anne would be forced to marry a monster.

"I dare you to let me tell my story to these men," Pete said when they dragged him outside the barn.

"They don't want to hear your lies," Mason said.

"They don't want to be accessories to a murder either. You men have no right to hang me," Pete shouted. "You're not a court. You have no judge, no prosecutor. You have no evidence. You're acting on the say-so of one man."

"My word's enough," Mason said. He was so angry that he missed when he tried to throw the rope over the hoist used to raise hay to the loft.

"I defy you to give even one piece of evidence to back up your claim."

"I don't have to give any evidence."

"Why? Lawyers in court do. I think it's because you don't have any evidence. And you know why—because you're lying. You had Peter and Belser killed. Then you killed Eddie yourself."

"Maybe we ought to leave him to the sheriff, boss," one of the men said. "I don't want no part in hanging an innocent man."

"He's not innocent, I tell you. He killed Peter Warren. I found his body."

"You couldn't find Peter's body," Pete said as he dodged an attempt to put a noose around his neck, "unless you knew where to look *because you killed him.*"

"It was simple," Mason said. He grabbed hold of

Pete's head and held it still. "All I had to do was follow your tracks back to the wagon. It was easy. It hadn't rained in a month."

"You're lying," Pete said as Mason put the noose over his head. "I didn't bury Peter Warren anywhere near where your killers left him. I knew somebody wanted him found, so I made sure he wouldn't be."

Mason didn't bother to answer. He tossed the end of the rope over the hoist. "Here," he said to one of his men, "tie this to that horse."

"Boss, I don't think we ought to—"

"I said tie this to that horse."

"I'm quitting right here," the man said. "I ain't taking part in no hanging."

"Me neither," said another cowhand.

"Nobody quits me," Mason said, pulling a gun. "Now get on that horse and tie the rope to the pommel."

"Boss, you can't do that," his foreman said.

"I sure as hell can," Mason said.

"You do, and I'll shoot you where you stand."

They all turned, shocked to see Anne standing not ten feet away holding a pistol on Mason. He broke out laughing.

"You won't shoot me. I don't think you even know how."

"But I do." Mrs. Dean stood behind the cowhand who refused to get on the horse. "I'm an army officer's wife. I probably know more about firearms than any of you."

She was holding a shotgun. Pete doubted whether anyone present was willing to test her resolve or her knowledge. To the stunned surprise of all, she raised her shotgun, braced it against the fence, and fired at the hoist. The blast shattered the rope and tore large splinters off the hoist. Pete wasted no time in pulling the noose from around his neck.

"It won't do you any good," Mason said as he pulled his gun. "I'm going to kill you where you stand."

"Put that gun down, or I'll shoot *you* where *you* stand."

They all spun around to find themselves facing the sheriff, two deputies, and Ray.

"Drop it, Mason," the sheriff said when Mason seemed to be considering his chances of killing Pete and living to tell about it.

"Maybe I can convince him," Mrs. Dean said. "I still have one shell."

Not even Mason was foolish enough to argue with a shotgun. He holstered his pistol.

Chapter Twenty

"I'm so sorry," Anne said to Dolores. "I didn't know you loved Eddie."

"Nobody knew," Dolores said. "I wasn't sure myself until he died."

"I should have come with you."

"You couldn't have helped, and I had Mrs. Dean. As much as I dislike the woman, I don't know what I would have done without her."

Anne continually found herself feeling the same way. True to her word, Mrs. Dean had installed Anne in her own home as soon as they reached Big Bend. Though she strained against the restrictions Mrs. Dean put on her, Anne had to admit that no one else could have compelled the local women to meet her with at least the appearance of acceptance. Anne couldn't make Mrs. Dean understand that she didn't care what the women of Big Bend thought. She was only concerned with Pete.

But Mrs. Dean had been very firm on that score. She admitted that the money did give credence to Pete's story. She also agreed that Bill Mason's eagerness to hang Pete made it look as if he had something to hide. But she was adamant that the process of deciding who was telling the truth and who was lying should be left to the sheriff. It wasn't proper for a woman to interfere.

Anne didn't agree, but so far she hadn't found anything she could do to help.

"If I had gone with you," Anne said to Dolores, "I wouldn't have been caught in the mountains during a blizzard, and Pete could have been halfway to Arizona by now."

"You love him, don't you?" Dolores said.

"With all my heart."

"Even though he's not Peter?"

Anne had talked Mrs. Dean into letting Dolores share the guest room. They relied on each other for company and support.

Anne had never seen a room like Mrs. Dean's guest room. She'd never seen a house that was less like her house.

It wasn't as big as the Tumbling T ranch house, but it was wonderfully proportioned, elegantly furnished. The house seemed to be swathed in lace and rose silk. Where it wasn't silk, it was damask, satin, velvet, or some other luxurious material. The furniture was just as wonderful. The table next to their bed was made of black walnut with a white marble top. The table by the lounge was inlaid with exotic woods of different patterns and colors. Anne was afraid to touch it. Everything gleamed and glistened with a patina that could be achieved and maintained only by two maids driven to heroic efforts under Mrs. Dean's eagle eye.

Anne wondered if she'd ever get back to the ranch and her own familiar surroundings. Unless she received confirmation of her marriage to Peter, she would have no claim on it. She would have nowhere to go. One thing was certain. She didn't intend to stay with Mrs. Dean.

"I think I fell in love with Pete because he *wasn't* Peter," Anne told Dolores. "I thought I loved Peter, but now I'm certain that was only a little girl's thankfulness for someone who never cared that she was part Indian or a weak, useless female."

"And you don't think he killed Peter?" Dolores asked.

"No. I never really did. I was shocked when he told me what he'd done. I think not believing him was a way of getting back at him for hurting me. It seems rather mean and vindictive when I think about it like that."

"Maybe, but it's understandable."

"But Pete wouldn't kill Peter. I don't say he wouldn't kill anybody. I'm quite sure he would if he or someone he loved was in danger."

"Like you?"

"I think he would have killed Mason if he could. I don't think that would have bothered him at all."

"That doesn't bother you?"

"I was ready to kill him myself if he hadn't taken that rope from around Pete's neck."

"How could you fall in love with a stranger so quickly?"

"I already thought I was in love with Peter. His letters had been so sweet. His agreeing to marry me even though I knew he didn't love me made me want to love him, made me feel I should love him. I was prepared to fight everybody to protect him.

"Then Pete arrived, and he was everything I'd hoped for and more. He knew about ranches. He took charge from the moment he got here. He threw my uncle off and told him never to come back. He faced Belser without a blink."

"That ought to have told you he wasn't Peter."

"It might, if he hadn't been even more kind and thoughtful than Peter. He told me I was beautiful. He said he was proud to be married to me. He let me buy anything I wanted. He gave me this ring." She held out her hand to show Dolores.

"I know. You show it to me at least a dozen times a day."

"He never forced me to come to him. That very first night he said we ought to take some time to get to know each other."

"You mean you never—"

"Not until the night I spent at the roundup."

"Where on earth could you—"

"In a grove of cottonwoods down by the creek."

"You didn't?"

Anne nodded.

"On the ground?"

She nodded again.

Dolores tried to hold it back, but a giggle broke out. Anne was angry at first, then she saw the humor. Both women started to laugh.

"But you were always so proper," Dolores said as she wiped her eyes. "I can't imagine you doing that."

"At the time I wanted it more than anything else in the world."

"What are you going to do now?"

"I don't know. The sheriff won't let me see Pete. They're holding a hearing tomorrow. Bill Mason is determined to prove Pete killed Peter and Belser."

"What about Eddie?"

"Pete thinks Mason killed him."

"What!"

The exclamation startled Anne, but not half as much as the look in Dolores's eyes. The older woman seized Anne by the arms in a grip so tight, it drove her fingernails into the soft flesh of Anne's shoulders.

"You won't like it," Anne said.

"Tell me."

The sharp pain in Dolores's voice made Anne hesitate. "It's only a theory."

Dolores shook Anne. "Somebody killed Eddie. I've got to know who."

"Pete thinks Mason has always wanted Uncle Carl's ranch, that he started the rustling right after Uncle Carl's accident. In fact, he thinks Mason might even be responsible for that."

"How?"

"I don't know. He thinks Mason approached Belser

first. Belser wouldn't cooperate because he wanted the ranch for himself, so Mason used me to find out when Peter was arriving so he could arrange to have him killed."

"But who killed Belser?"

"This is the part you're not going to like. Pete thinks Eddie killed Belser, then Mason had to kill Eddie to keep him quiet."

Dolores pulled away from Anne, her eyes cold and angry.

"Pete thinks Mason told Eddie that Peter would lose the ranch and Eddie would lose his job," Anne continued. "He already knew Belser would fire him the moment he got control. Maybe Mason promised Eddie he could be foreman of the combined ranches."

"He's lying."

"Is he? Neither you nor I killed Belser. Pete had no reason to because he always meant to tell me what happened." Dolores started to object. "He didn't have to tell me the truth when Mason showed up. I would have defended him." The two women faced each other. "It had to be Eddie," Anne said softly. "Pete had never set foot in the kitchen. He wouldn't have known where to find your knives." Dolores turned away, but Anne moved to intercept her gaze. "You suspected something, didn't you?"

Dolores didn't respond. Anne waited.

"No," Dolores said. "I never did. Eddie had talked about leaving. He said he wouldn't have a job no matter who got the ranch. Then he started talking about the future, like he was going to have a say in it. But why should he agree to kill Belser? Pete didn't want to fire him."

"Pete thinks Mason offered him a partnership."

Dolores seemed to collapse, to shrink inward. "Eddie would have done anything for that." Even her voice sounded defeated. "He wanted his own ranch more than anything, but I don't see how knowing this can help Pete."

"I'm hoping it can help us find the men who killed Peter."

"How?"

"Mason must have told Eddie something. He talked to you all the time. Think. Can you remember anything that might help us?"

"No."

"Any strange people, new hands, names he mentioned, cowhands in unusual places, horses disappear—"

"Yes!" Dolores seemed excited. "I heard him tell one of the hands that two men would be coming by. That he was to take them to one of the line cabins."

"Which one? Where is it?"

"It's the cabin off Clear Creek, but I don't know where it is or how to get there."

"It'll be on the map Eddie made for Pete."

"You'll need somebody to take you there."

"No, I won't. I read the map once. I can do it again. You and I can go there today."

"Me!"

"I'll need help if those men are still there."

"What can two women do?"

"I'll get Ray to go with us."

It took Anne some time to convince Dolores, but everything came apart when Mrs. Dean barred their way until they confessed what they intended to do.

"You can't do anything like that," she said. "Leave it to the sheriff."

"The sheriff thinks Pete murdered Peter," Anne said, "and Mason has hired a lawyer to prove it. I can't sit around and do nothing."

"Well, you can't go alone," Mrs. Dean said. "You don't know how to get there."

"I can read the map," Anne said. "That's how I found the roundup."

"You know nothing about firearms or capturing criminals."

"Ray is going with us."

"He's a cowhand," Mrs. Dean said in disgust. "He doesn't know any more than you do."

"We'll manage. Now you've got to get out of my way. I'm going to find those men."

Mrs. Dean opened her mouth to continue her objections.

"Nothing you say will change my mind," Anne said. "Nobody believes in Pete's innocence but me. No one else will try to save him."

"You're in love with him, aren't you?" Mrs. Dean asked.

"Yes."

"Are you going to marry him?"

"I don't know."

"What you mean is, he hasn't asked you."

"How could he when I thought he was a killer, when I wouldn't listen when he tried to tell me Mason was behind everything?"

"But you want to marry him?"

"More than anything in the world."

Mrs. Dean sighed. "Well, there's no help for it. Horace and I will have to go with you."

Anne felt as though she was leading a parade of clowns. Here she was attempting to capture two desperate killers, and she was accompanied by a cook, a beardless cowboy, a domineering dowager, and her dotty husband. She kept reminding herself that Mr. Dean had been a colonel in the United States Army, that Mrs. Dean was a crack shot, that Ray was young and strong, and that she and Dolores were attractive enough to lure the killers out of their hiding place. That ought to be enough to capture two men, but she was afraid their attack would never succeed. If they could decide on a method of attack. Mrs. Dean and her husband had been arguing since they left the ranch.

"It'll never do to launch a frontal attack," Horace Dean was saying. "You've got to outflank them, attack them where they least expect it. Destroy their fortifications with your big guns, wear them down with your infantry, and clean up with your cavalry."

"Don't be a fool," his wife said. "All you have is a few rifles, a cart horse, and three women."

"I think our best approach," Anne said, "is to pretend Mr. and Mrs. Dean got lost and we're looking for them."

"What would they be doing out here?" Dolores asked.

"You could say we're looking for Custer's battle-field," Mr. Dean said. "It's a very famous attraction."

"That makes about as much sense as saying we're hunting for elk," his wife said.

"If Mrs. Dean had a parasol, we could say they went for a walk and got lost," Dolores volunteered.

"It's too far to walk," Anne pointed out.

"I think we oughta say two dotty old people got lost, and we've come looking for them," Ray said.

"I think I know how we can do it," Anne said quickly, before Mrs. Dean could blister Ray with her retort.

"My dear—" Horace began.

"Let her speak," Mrs. Dean commanded. "You've forgotten more military strategy than you remember."

"I think Dolores and I ought to approach the cabin from the front," Anne said.

"My child, you can't put yourself in the line of fire," Horace said.

"They don't have any reason to hurt us," Anne explained. "How could two women threaten them? Anyway, while we're talking to them, Ray could come up from behind the cabin and catch them while they're not looking."

"That's not a bad plan," Horace said.

"It's better than anything you've come up with," Mrs. Dean said. There followed a long discussion as to what Ray should do. It ended with Horace and Mrs. Dean deciding to accompany Ray.

"Horace will get confused and blunder right into the cabin," Mrs. Dean said. "He'd give the whole thing away."

Anne tried to explain that Mrs. Dean was an even more illogical person to accompany Ray.

"I'm an expert shot with a rifle," Mrs. Dean said. "There were plenty of hostile Indians out here when Horace commanded his first post. All of us women learned to shoot."

Anne advanced several counterarguments to no avail. When tactfully reminded that it wasn't easy for someone of Mrs. Dean's age to climb over boulders and fallen trees, she said she'd walk around them. Anne decided that she and Dolores should have waited until the dead of night and climbed out the window. There was no hope of their capturing even the most incompetent killer with this contentious army of five.

Anne even considered abandoning the scheme. She would go back to the ranch, maybe back to town. Tell the sheriff. Hire some men to come with her. No matter what she had to do, she couldn't abandon Pete. If she couldn't prove these men killed Peter Warren, Pete would surely hang. Other schemes might offer a better chance for success, but it would be impossible to keep them secret from Mason. Slim as it was, this was her only chance.

She tried to think what Pete would have done. He had been faced with one unexpected challenge after another, and he'd always come up with a plausible explanation. He kept calm, said as little as possible, and let others do the talking. Pete said she was smart. Well, this was her chance to prove it. She just wished the consequences of failure weren't so grave.

Ray drove the wagon as close as he dared to the line of junipers that formed a woodland at the base of one of the foothills.

"We should be in place by the time you reach the front of the cabin," Mrs. Dean said. "Have you decided what you're going to say to them?"

"No," Anne replied. "I'll have to improvise. Get as close to the cabin as possible so you can hear what I'm saying." She drove away before Mrs. Dean could start offering more suggestions.

"What *are* you going to say?" Dolores asked.

"I really don't know. Do you have any suggestions?"

"No."

Anne couldn't think of anything that didn't sound stupid. During the hour it took her to circle the butte and approach the cabin from the front, she racked her brain searching for new ideas, going over old ones, but nothing brilliant occurred to her.

"Do you think they'll shoot us?" Dolores asked as they neared the cabin.

"We don't even know they're in there," Anne said. She didn't know why the men would have stayed around this long unless Mason had told Eddie to keep them around in case he needed them again. Her skin crawled at the thought that she might have been the need he was talking about.

"Somebody's in there. I can smell smoke."

But as they approached the cabin, they saw no sign it was occupied.

"They probably hid their horses in the trees," Dolores said.

That didn't make Anne feel any better. It made the killers appear all the more determined not to be found. How far would they go to keep from being captured?

Anne was still a hundred yards away when she saw the barrel of a rifle appear through one of the windows.

"Turn around," Dolores said. "They're going to kill us."

Anne's heart was in her throat, but she couldn't turn back. There was a chance she would get hurt, but Pete would surely hang if she backed down. She had no choice but to keep going. "I'll let you down," she said to Dolores, "but I can't stop."

"Go on," Dolores said. "I can't let you be the only fool out here."

As they drew closer to the cabin, Anne searched frantically for some explanation of her presence, but nothing came to mind. How could anyone possibly explain two women in a wagon miles away from any ranch?

A bullet kicked up dust in front of her horse just as the sound of a rifle split the silence. "Go away, or I'll kill you," a man shouted.

"Don't shoot," Anne called out, doing her best to act like a silly, harmless female flustered by the rifle shot. She knew it was dangerous to keep going, but she had to get closer. "We're not carrying any guns." She kept the wagon moving. She was the bait to draw the killers outside so Ray and the Deans could capture them.

"What do you want?" the man asked.

"I'm looking for my parents," Anne said. "They

came out hunting elk, but their horses came back without them." It was a silly story, but it was the best she could do.

"There's nobody around here. We heard no gunshots."

"My father's hunting with a sword," Anne said, remember the sword Mr. Dean insisted upon bringing.

"He must be a complete fool!" the outlaw said.

"My parents are from Illinois. They don't understand Wyoming."

The gun barrel disappeared from the window, and a man appeared at the doorway holding a rifle. Anne had imagined killers would look mean and ugly. She was right. The man had several days' growth of beard and oily hair, and his clothes looked as if they hadn't been changed in several days.

"My parents are rather old," Anne said, "and Father doesn't see very well, but they wanted a set of elk antlers to take back with them. Are you sure you haven't seen them?"

"Look, lady, when I say I haven't seen anybody, I mean I haven't—"

"You've got to help us find them," Anne said. "It'll soon be dark. My mother will start to scream if she's caught out in the dark."

"Mrs. Dean will kill you," Dolores whispered, giggling softly. "She prides herself on being able to handle any situation."

A second man had come out of the cabin. He looked just as unkempt as his partner, but he had cold, cruel eyes. Anne was relieved to see he hadn't brought a gun, but she didn't like the way he looked at her and

Dolores. She didn't know much about killers, but she didn't want to learn by becoming their next victim.

"I don't know how she's going to handle this situation," Anne whispered. "Look at those men. They're big and healthy."

"Why did you come here?" the second man asked, clearly suspicious.

"Because of your cabin. You must have horses somewhere. My parents would want to buy them so they could return home."

"We ain't selling our horses to nobody," the first man said.

"But we might consider it, if the price is right," the second man said. "Why don't you get down and come inside? We can talk it over. Who knows—your parents might show up before we settle on a price."

"We ought to start looking for them right now," Anne said. "Mother," she called as loudly as she could, "can you hear me?"

Dolores made a sound that Anne could only compare to a coyote's wail. "They'll hear that a lot better," she said.

"Here, stop that!" the first outlaw said. "You'll have every four-legged animal within five miles coming this way."

"Mother!" Anne called again. "Please come if you can hear me. She's frightened of four-legged animals," she told the outlaws.

"Then what the hell is she doing out here looking for elk?" the outlaw asked.

"She wants Papa to have his antlers," Anne explained, "but she doesn't realize they must first be attached to an elk."

The outlaws approached the wagon as she pulled to a stop in front of the cabin.

"You'll have to get down," the second one said. "You'll never find them sitting up there screeching like a prairie chicken."

Anne didn't want to get down. She knew what that outlaw had in mind, but she couldn't figure out how she was going to do anything sitting in the wagon either. She handed the reins to Dolores. "You hold the horse," she said, "while these men help me look for Mama."

"I'm going with you," Dolores said.

"No," Anne said.

"She ought to get down, too," the second outlaw said.

"Why?" Anne asked.

"We can split up. We'll find them a lot faster that way."

Anne didn't want to split up. That would make it virtually impossible to capture both men. She and Dolores got down from the wagon and started walking quickly toward the trees that came up to the back of the cabin.

"Wait," the second outlaw said, clearly angry that things weren't going according to his plan.

Anne didn't slow down. "If my parents are lost in those trees, Mother will be so frightened she won't be able to move. It'll take both of us to coax her out."

The outlaws hurried after them. "Wait up," the second outlaw called. "I don't think it's a good idea for you ladies to go into them woods." He took hold of Anne's arm with a grip that didn't allow for argument. "Now let's go inside and talk about this."

Just then Mrs. Dean came stumbling out of the trees, her hair flying in all directions, her clothes looking as though she'd come through a briar patch backward. "Praise be to the saints," she cried out as she sank to her knees. "Horace, we're saved. Our daughter has found us at last."

Both outlaws stared open-mouthed at Mrs. Dean. Anne was certain they never expected—or intended— to look for anybody. Anne was relieved to see that Mrs. Dean kept a firm grip on the rifle she carried.

Anne tried to pull away, but the outlaw didn't release her. "You've got to help her," she said. "We've got to take her to your cabin until she recovers."

Just then Mr. Dean darted out of the trees looking just as demented as his wife, brandishing a sword at some imaginary foe. He looked around as if he had no idea where he was or what he was doing there.

Anne broke from the outlaw's slackened hold and hurried forward to Mrs. Dean.

"Get them both to come help me up," Mrs. Dean whispered when Anne reached her. "You must get both of them."

Anne and Dolores attempted to help Mrs. Dean to her feet, but she collapsed rather dramatically, still holding tightly to her rifle.

"Can't you get the old cow to her feet," the second outlaw scoffed.

"She's exhausted," Anne said. "We need your help—both of you."

"We ought to shoot her and put her out of her misery," the second outlaw said. He appeared to be weighing in his mind the possibility of getting rid of Mr. and Mrs. Dean and having Dolores and Anne to himself.

"Don't say things like that," Anne said. "You'll frighten Mama."

"Oh, hell!" the first outlaw said. "Let's get her in the wagon and out of here."

The two outlaws bent over to help Mrs. Dean to her feet. As they did so, Anne and Dolores wrenched the rifle from the first outlaw's slackened grip. At the same moment, Mr. Dean attacked the second outlaw with his sword. The outlaw managed to deflect the sword point, but the two of them went over in a heap.

Mrs. Dean lurched to her feet, her rifle on the first outlaw. "Don't move, or I'll put a bullet in you. Horace, you fool, let go of that man."

"I'm holding him for you, my dear," Horace said as he was flung against a tree. Ray came out of the woods at that moment, his gun drawn and pointed at the second outlaw. But Horace staggered to his feet and into his line of fire. The outlaw, unarmed, grabbed Horace for a shield.

"Pull that murderer off Horace before he kills him!" Mrs. Dean cried.

Ray tried fruitlessly to draw a bead on the outlaw, but he hid behind Horace. Holstering his gun, Ray attacked the outlaw, head first. They all went down with a series of grunts.

"Don't try to help your partner," Mrs. Dean warned the first outlaw.

He ignored her, and she put a bullet in his thigh. The man screamed and fell to the ground clutching his bleeding leg.

"My leg is broken," he cried.

"I doubt it, but if it is, it serves you right. I warned you," Mrs. Dean said. "I'm very good with this rifle."

"I'll kill you," the outlaw shouted to the accompaniment of grunts and groans from the three men wrestling on the ground.

"Not until you can walk," Mrs. Dean said, then turned her attention to the other man, who seemed to be holding both Ray and Mr. Dean down at the same time.

"Hit him with something," she said to Anne.

"What?"

"Anything."

Anne had nothing except the first outlaw's rife. She was reluctant to do anything as violent as hit a man on the head with a rifle stock. Then she thought of Peter and Pete. Those men had shot them in cold blood and left their bodies in the open for wild animals to tear to pieces. Cold anger that anyone could be so cruel and coldhearted ousted any feeling of sympathy. Gritting her teeth, she raised the rifle into the air and slammed the butt into the back of the outlaw's head.

He subsided into an inert lump atop Mr. Dean.

"See, my dear," Mr. Dean said as he lay pinned under the outlaw, a self-satisfied smile on his face, "I told you we could capture these ruffians."

* * *

"I don't deny these men stopped by my chuck wagon," Bill Mason told the sheriff. "We give hospitality to any wandering cowhand. But I never hired them to kill Peter Warren."

The hearing had been scheduled for the sheriff's office, but so many people had showed up that the sheriff moved it to one of the larger saloons. Anne was certain every person in town was in the room. It was so crowded, she couldn't see the faces of half the spectators, but she hadn't failed to notice her uncle and Cyrus McCaine. Apparently they still hoped some twist of fortune would return her to their control.

"Eddie Kessling hired us to kill Peter Warren," the outlaw said. "He's the one who paid us and told us where to hide. That lady told me Mason hired Eddie."

The outlaw pointed at Anne. She cringed inwardly, but she didn't avert her gaze. When it came her turn to speak, she'd tell them what she'd done and why. She hoped it would be enough to convince the sheriff, but things hadn't been going well so far. With Eddie dead, there was no way to connect Mason to the men who killed Peter. Neither was there any proof Mason was behind the deaths of Belser and Eddie. Anne couldn't even prove Mason's men had rustled the Tumbling T steers. Mason's lawyer had been very successful at making sure what little evidence there was pointed in Pete's direction.

Anne's only consolation was they had no proof against Pete, either. If Pete could only convince the sheriff he didn't want the ranch, then maybe the sheriff would agree he had no motive to murder Peter or anybody else. The money and the saddlebags supported Pete's story, but it still didn't look as though anybody believed he meant to walk away from ownership of the biggest ranch in Wyoming.

"I don't believe Anne would have said any such thing," Mason said.

Mason had been careful to act the role of the perfect law-abiding citizen—calm, considerate, concerned for the welfare of the community. Not once had he shown even a trace of his murderous temper. It made Anne sick to see the way he played to the townspeople, the way they accepted everything he said.

"I love Anne," Mason announced, sounding more a model of moral rectitude than the minister of the church. "We're going to be married as soon as—"

"No! It's a lie!"

Every head in the room jerked around at the sound of a woman's voice. Anne turned to see Judy, the saleswoman from The Emporium, fighting her way through the crush of spectators at the back of the room.

"You love me!" she cried. "Only me."

The sheriff tried to restore order, but Judy wouldn't be quiet. She fought her way forward until she reached Bill Mason. Her face was red with anger. His face was white from shock.

"I don't want to know anything about your personal goings-on," the sheriff said to Judy. "We're here to decide who murdered Belser and Eddie."

Judy ignored the sheriff. "Tell her you lied," she pleaded with Mason. "Tell everybody it was just a trick. You love me, not her."

The outburst had shocked Anne as much as it had apparently shocked everyone else. At first she'd been embarrassed. Then she realized Bill Mason had been jolted out of his pious attitude. His face was almost purple with fury. People had been whispering about Mason having a woman somewhere. It was clear now that Judy was that woman. By announcing that he loved Anne and meant to marry her—Mason must have thought that would somehow help his case—he'd broken some promise he'd made to Judy, and she was upset and angry. Maybe she knew something. If Anne could make her angry enough, she might tell it.

"Of course he doesn't love you," Anne said in the most condescending and insulting tone of voice she could produce. "Why should he? You're nothing but a shopkeeper's assistant."

Judy spun to face Anne. "And you're nothing but a redskin," she shouted. "No decent man could love you."

"I'm young and pretty," Anne purred. "And I'm very rich."

"Tell her!" Judy screamed at Mason, who was being restrained in his chair by his lawyer. "Tell her it was all a trick."

"He's told everybody he wants to marry me," Anne said in a loud voice. "He loves me so much, he asked Mrs. Dean to take me into her home so she could launch me into society."

Mrs. Dean, who seemed to be as acute at some times as she was obtuse at others, spoke up immediately. "I've already arranged one party. Bill was so pleased he asked me to arrange the wedding."

"Tell them, Bill," Judy screamed at Mason. "Tell them, or I will."

"Calm down," Mason said, finally finding his

tongue. "There's nothing for you to worry about." He looked ready to kill her. "Sit back down. We'll talk later."

Judy turned and stormed across the room to where Anne sat. "It was nothing but a trick," she snarled. "Once he had your ranch, you'd disappear and we could be married."

"Shut up, Judy! Don't listen to her," Mason shouted. "She's crazy."

"But it's not my ranch," Anne said, determined Judy should tell everything she knew. "It belongs to my husband."

"Your husband's dead. Bill had those men kill him in Montana." She pointed to the outlaw. She didn't notice when Mason started up from his chair. "Then he had Eddie kill Belser so the sheriff could hang that man you've been living with. You thought you'd steal the ranch, the two of you, but Bill is smarter than either one of you."

A shot rang out. Several men wrestled Bill Mason to the ground.

Judy clutched her chest, then looked surprised when she drew her hand away covered with blood. "No redskin is going to steal him from me," Judy said, still looking at her blood-covered hand. "He's mine. He'll always be mine."

She closed her eyes and fell down dead.

Chapter Twenty-one

Anne felt her heart skip a beat when the Tumbling T ranch house came into view. In just a little while she'd see Pete for the first time since the hearing. Seeing Judy killed right before her eyes had sent her into a state of shock. Mrs. Dean had taken her back to her home and refused to allow anyone to see her for three days. Now that she was well enough to return home, Mrs. Dean accompanied her. She insisted Anne have a chaperone until Pete either married her or left for points south.

Anne was returning as the sole owner of the largest and richest cattle ranch in the Wyoming Territory. A copy of the certificate of her marriage to Peter Warren had finally arrived, but it didn't make her happy. She didn't want a ranch. She wanted Pete. Mrs. Dean had sent him back to the ranch with orders to wait until she was well again. Anne was petrified he would believe all the terrible things she'd said to him after he told her about Peter's death. Mrs. Dean had given Pete his money. It had been the only reason he'd come to the ranch in the first place. Anne had nightmares about him leaving before she got back.

Before they reached the house, she realized that someone was standing out front with Pete.

"Did the cowhands come back?" she asked Ray.

"No. You'll have to hire a whole new crew next spring."

"Then who's at the ranch?"

"Some man named Monty Randolph. He showed up the day we got back."

Uncle Carl had said Monty Randolph was one of the most important cattlemen in the Territory. Anne remembered that the letter Pete had written in the lawyer's office had been addressed to him. What could have brought him all the way from Cheyenne?

But she forgot to worry about Monty Randolph when she looked at Pete. Her heart started beating so fast it hurt. He looked just as handsome as she remembered. Not even a big, blond man who was taller, bigger, and even more handsome could draw her attention from the man she'd thought about constantly for three days. She was halfway out of the buckboard when she felt Mrs. Dean's hand on her arm restraining her.

"You will not throw yourself at him," the dowager commanded. "You will wait until the buckboard stops and he helps you down."

Anne wanted to throw off Mrs. Dean's restraint, to throw herself into Pete's arms. But when the buckboard finally stopped and she got a good look at Pete's sober, unsmiling expression, her heart sank. She waited for him to help her down.

"How are you feeling?" he asked.

Concern was evident, but the restraint was still there.

"Fine. I could hardly wait to get back." Before she could say any of the things she'd been wanting to say for days, Mrs. Dean demanded that Pete help her down. By that time, the tall stranger had come down the steps.

"This is Monty Randolph," Pete said, introducing the man to Anne. "Jake used to send his cows to market with the Randolph herds. They even let me go along a couple of times."

She didn't want to talk to Monty Randolph, and she didn't want to talk about cows. She just wanted to find out why Pete was looking so sober, why he greeted her like a family friend rather than the love of her life.

"It was kind of you to come all this way to help Pete," she said to Mr. Randolph, "but he was cleared of all charges."

"That's not why I'm here," Mr. Randolph said. "Pete wrote me about the rustling. We can't have that. If you let it start in one place, it'll spread to the rest of the Territory."

A woman came out of the house. She held a small child in her arms and a little boy by the hand. A thousand ideas occurred to Anne at once, all of them involving this woman taking her place in Pete's heart.

"That's the other reason I came," Monty said.

"Who is she?" Anne asked.

"Gary Warren's widow."

There had to be some mistake. "I didn't know Gary was married."

"Myrtle is his common-law wife," Monty said. "She's been on our ranch for nearly a year. She never told us about Gary until she heard me talking to Iris about Pete's letter."

"I'm not asking anything for myself," Myrtle said, coming toward Anne, "just for my children."

"I should be very careful, my dear," Mrs. Dean whispered rather too loudly. "You don't know this young woman is who she says she is."

Anne thought that if anyone else was accused of being an imposter, she'd scream.

"Come inside," Pete said. "I think it's best you hear her story from the beginning."

Anne didn't want to go inside; she didn't want to talk to this woman. She just wanted to talk to Pete, but he was acting so different. Surely he couldn't believe she'd meant any of those things she'd said to Judy. He had to know she was just trying to provoke her, to get her so upset she'd forget caution and tell everything she knew. Judy's disclosures had cleared Pete of suspicion in any of the deaths. But it was clear Anne wasn't going to get a chance to talk to Pete until this thing about Gary's common-law wife was cleared up.

They were soon settled inside. Dolores provided coffee while Myrtle told her story.

It turned out Gary Warren was just like his father. He ran away when things got difficult. He left Myrtle pregnant with a small child and got himself killed in a blizzard. Myrtle had gotten herself to safety at the

Randolph ranch, where she stayed until she had her baby and got well.

"Gary promised to marry me as soon as we got to Cheyenne," Myrtle said.

"I'm sure he would have," Anne said.

"But the fact remains he didn't," Mrs. Dean said. "You have no legal claim on Anne's ranch."

"I don't want her ranch—really I don't," Myrtle said. "I was hoping to find Gary's brother. As the children's uncle, surely he would . . ."

Anne had had doubts about Myrtle's story at first. But Gary had lived at the ranch until four years ago. She remembered him well. The little boy looked too much like him not to be his son. Peter would have taken them in without question.

"Peter wouldn't have hesitated to invite you to make the Tumbling T your home," Anne said. "I'm happy to do the same."

"I'll work for our keep," Myrtle said. "So will the boys when they get big enough. We didn't come here asking for a handout."

Mrs. Dean interrupted to ask several questions that Myrtle answered willingly.

Anne wasn't interested in the questions or the answers, only in Pete. He seemed to be withdrawing, moving further and further away from her. Maybe he thought that now that she was rich, she didn't want him any longer, didn't need a husband. Maybe he thought that after all the lies he'd told, she would never trust him again.

She wanted to tell him he was wrong, that nothing was more important to her than being his wife, but she wasn't sure he'd believe her. They'd said so many foolish things to each other it would be hard to see the truth.

Then, quite suddenly, Anne knew what she wanted to do. It was so simple, she wondered why she hadn't thought of it earlier.

"You'll have to work all right," Anne said, breaking in on Mrs. Dean's interrogation. "Running a ranch isn't easy. We don't have a foreman."

"That needn't be a problem," Mr. Randolph said. "I'll be happy to help you find an experienced man for the job."

"See, it's getting easier already. I'd offer you Ray and Dolores, but I hope they'll to Texas with me."

"You couldn't keep me here," Dolores said.

"Me neither," Ray added.

"If Mr. Randolph will agree to look in on you from time to time, I'm sure everything will be fine."

"What are you talking about?" Mrs. Dean asked. "This is your ranch. You'll naturally do the hiring."

Anne didn't answer Mrs. Dean. She had turned to face Pete, was watching his expression change from a motionless mask to the impulsive expression of his inner feelings. She saw surprise, doubt, hope, fear, and hope once again.

"Anne, you can't—" Pete started.

"Of course I can. It's my ranch. I can do anything I want."

"I don't understand," Myrtle said.

"I'm giving you the ranch," Anne said. "Uncle Carl wanted it to go to blood kin. Otherwise it would have gone to Belser. I'm sure he would want it to go to Gary's children rather than to me."

"Anne, this is preposterous," Mrs. Dean said. "No one in her right mind gives away a whole ranch."

"But I don't want it," Anne said. "And I can't run it from Texas."

"I couldn't do that," Myrtle said. "Maybe we could own it together."

"Anne, I refuse to allow you to do anything so absurd!" Mrs. Dean declared.

But Anne wasn't paying attention to Myrtle or Mrs. Dean. She had no thoughts for anyone except Pete, who was smiling for the first time in what seemed like forever.

"Do you mean what you said?" he asked.

"Of course I do."

"But you said—"

"I said a lot of things that weren't true. So did you. We had good reasons then, but we don't need to lie or pretend anymore. We just need to be ourselves."

"I'm just a cowboy."

"I'm just a breed."

"You are not," Mrs. Dean declared. "I refuse to allow you to refer to yourself in that manner."

"Are you sure?" Pete asked.

"Positive."

Pete stood and held out his arms. Anne jumped up and threw herself into his embrace. Nothing in her whole life had felt so wonderful. She had no regrets about leaving the ranch. All that mattered was being with Pete.

"If this very foolish conversation means what I think it means," Mrs. Dean said, "let me tell you I'm not allowing Anne to go one step from this house until she's married."

"I think we can take care of that," Pete said, without taking his gaze off Anne.

"And don't get any ideas about beginning your conjugal relations immediately," Mrs. Dean said. "I'm not leaving Anne's side until the vows are spoken."

"I'll agree to sleep in the bunkhouse tonight," Pete said. "But if you can't get that preacher out here by tomorrow, I'm kidnaping Anne. I know of a snug little pine bower that's unoccupied at the moment."

Epilogue

"Don't let him bully you," Isabelle said to Anne as they walked from the corral back to the house. "You don't have to learn to ride a horse if you don't want to."

"But I do want to learn," Anne said. "I want to ride with Pete when he goes out to look after the herd."

Pete had bought his ranch next to Sean's. There had been enough money left over to stock it with the blooded Hereford cows Chet had purchased for them. Using her share of the income from the Tumbling T, Anne had built a house just as big as Uncle Carl's. And an indoor bathroom with running water.

"You won't want to for long," Isabelle said. "Cows are useful enough when it comes to making a living, but there's more than enough work at home to keep you busy. There'll be twice as much after your baby's born."

Isabelle had started coming over regularly to "help out" ever since Anne announced she was pregnant.

"Stop sowing seeds of rebellion," Pete said. "I want a quiet, obedient wife who will take every word I say as law."

"Pete Jernigan, if I didn't know you were teasing, I'd hit you upside the head with the first log I could get my hands on."

Anne went off into a fit of giggles. "She said it," she gasped, when she managed to get control of herself. "I never believed you, but she actually said it."

Pete looked at her doubled up with laughter and started laughing, too.

"I said what?" Isabelle asked. "What are you laughing at?"

Anne couldn't help it. She laughed harder. The harder she laughed, the harder Pete laughed.

"Okay," Isabelle said, "before I lose my temper, somebody had better tell me what's going on."

"Are you bullying them already?" Jake asked. He came out of the house, slipped his arms around his wife, and kissed her on the back of the neck.

"How can I be bullying them when they're laughing themselves silly?"

But she was obviously more interested in what her husband was doing to the back of her neck than in finding out the source of Anne and Pete's amusement. They sneaked away while they had the chance.

"She's going to remember," Pete warned Anne. "She will find out."

"I don't mind. I think she's wonderful."

"No more wonderful than you." Pete kissed Anne on the cheek.

"Will you kiss me on the back of my neck?" she asked.

"Why?"

"Isabelle seemed to like it. I do, too."

She liked it very much. She thought it was absolutely wonderful to be able to sit outside in March and kiss under a big oak tree. It was just one more reason to like being in Texas. Of course, Pete was the best reason of all. If he weren't making her crazy with all the things he was doing to her neck, she'd list a dozen reasons why she was the most fortunate woman in the world, not the least of which was her new house, her new baby, and the enormous family that surrounded her.

But topping the list, filling at least the first dozen places, was her new husband. As long as she was in his arms, nothing else mattered.

LEIGH GREENWOOD

The Reluctant Bride

Colorado Territory, 1872: A rough-and-tumble place and time almost as dangerous as the men who left civilization behind, driven by a desire for a new life. In a false-fronted town where the only way to find a decent woman is to send away for her, Tanzy first catches sight of the man she came west to marry galloping after a gang of bandits. Russ Tibbolt is a far cry from the husband she expected when she agreed to become a mail-order bride. He is much too compelling for any woman's peace of mind. With his cobalt-blue eyes and his body's magic, how can she hope to win the battle of wills between them?

The Cowboys

LEIGH GREENWOOD

SEAN

In the West there are only two kinds of women—the wives and mothers and daughters, and the good-time girls. It is said that Pearl Belladonna shows a man the best time ever, but Sean O'Ryan has not come to the gold fields looking for a floozy. He wants gold to buy a ranch, and a virtuous woman to make a wife. The sensual barroom singer might tempt his body with her lush curves, and tease his mind with her bright wit, but she isn't for him. From her red curls to her assumed name, nothing about her seems real until a glimpse into her heart convinces Sean that the lady is, indeed, a pearl beyond price.

___4490-0 $6.99 US/$8.99 CAN

The Cowboys
CHET
LEIGH GREENWOOD

When Chet Attmore rides into the Spring Water Ranch, he is only a dusty drifter, and then the lovely new owner of the ranch offers him a job as a cowboy. But Melody is also looking for another offer, of the marriage kind, and when Chet holds her soft, sweet body against his, he is tempted to be the one who makes it.

___4425-0 $6.99 US/$8.99 CAN

LEIGH GREENWOOD

The Cowboys BUCK

Golden-haired and blue-eyed, Hannah is lovely enough to make any man forget the past. Any man except Buck Hogan. For though she has more than fulfilled the promise of beauty in the fourteen-year-old girl he once knew, Buck will always remember that back then he was her father's whipping boy. Now he will have his revenge by taking the old man's ranch and making it his own. But he is falling in love with Hannah, whose gentle sweetness can heal his battered heart if he will only let her.

___4360-2 $6.99 US/$8.99 CAN